Originally from the Midlands, DAVID HINGLEY worked in the civil service for eleven years before moving to New York with his husband, where he passed his days in Manhattan fulfilling his long-term ambition to write and penned his debut novel, *Birthright*. He has since returned to the UK and is working on his next novel.

davidhingley.com
@dhingley_author

By David Hingley

Birthright
Puritan

Birthright

DAVID HINGLEY

Allison & Busby Limited
12 Fitzroy Mews
London W1T 6DW
allisonandbusby.com

First published in Great Britain by Allison & Busby in 2016.
This paperback edition published by Allison & Busby in 2017.

A CIP catalogue record for this book is available from
the British Library.

10 9 8 7 6 5 4 3 2 1

ISBN 978-0-7490-2042-2

Typeset in 10.5/15.5 pt Adobe Garamond Pro by
Allison & Busby Ltd.

The paper used for this Allison & Busby publication
has been produced from trees that have been legally sourced
from well-managed and credibly certified forests.

Printed and bound by
CPI Group (UK) Ltd, Croydon, CR0 4YY

For Matthew,
with whom I travel the world

Part One

Chapter One

Two hundred. Drip. *Two hundred and one.* Drip. *Two hundred and two.*

It had been an uncomfortable night, trapped in the close confines of her cramped Newgate cell. No sleep, of course. Not that Mercia cared for sleep, as she sat eyes closed on the sparsely strewn straw, the ever-falling droplet invading her troubled mind. Still, better to be caught in a counting loop than dwell on why she was in this stifling hole. *Two hundred and nine.* She wiped the sweat from her brow. *Two hundred and ten.*

Abruptly the dripping ceased, vanquished by the mad woman's fists in the next cell along, her surely bloody knuckles beating a discordant rhythm on their shared stone wall. The noise in the prison was infernal. Mercia had expected the stench, the darkness, but it was the sound that overwhelmed her the most. Her melancholy diffused through the putrid air. She waited, unmoving, struggling to comprehend what had befallen her.

The banging ceased, the unexpected silence forcing open her eyes. She returned to thinking through how she might be released, but then the drip renewed its attack and a piercing scream rang out, the mad woman striking at the wall once more. Mercia shuffled to the other side of her filthy cell, mumbling curses.

The little light that came through the bars of her door flickered. She looked up to see a silhouetted guard passing in front.

'Be quiet,' he shouted into the adjacent cell. 'By God's truth, there are enough crazed devils here to send a man insane.'

The mad woman growled. Moments later she spat.

'Right.' The guard unlocked the woman's door, crashing it hard against the wall. Mercia heard him stride in, his heavy boots pounding the floor. There was a small chink in the stonework she could have looked through to see what was happening, but she did not. Yet there was no avoiding the harsh sound of a fist striking ragged flesh, a thud against the wall signalling the woman's collapse.

The door slammed shut. The light through Mercia's bars wavered again as the guard walked back, except now it disappeared, blocked by his substantial bulk. He inserted a key into the lock and she looked up, fearful, remembering a moment from long ago. But he merely swung open the door.

'Up you get.' He motioned to her with a jerk of his head. 'Warder says you can go.'

'What?' She stared at the shadowed guard in disbelief, her melancholy morphing into sudden anger. She staggered to her feet, but the feeling had gone from her legs and she had to rub at them for a while before she could hobble towards him. 'I have been kept here in squalor since last night. And now I am just released?'

The guard shrugged, looking her up and down in the light of his near-spent torch. 'Stay as you like. The lads could do with a bit of . . . company.'

Anger gave way to hope. Was there time? She had been here all night, certainly, but how many hours? She limped from the cell, stretching in the corridor, clammy and dark. More screaming sounded out from deeper inside the jail. She glanced at the mad woman's door.

'It was unjust, to strike her as you did.'

The guard stared. 'From what the lads say you're as handy with your fist as I am. Smacked old Dicken right in the mouth, teeth everywhere, that's what I hear.'

She straightened up, pulling straw from the ringlets of her hair. 'There was a disagreement. But teeth – you exaggerate.'

'Imagine.' The guard shook his head. 'A woman striking a Tower guard as bold as that. Now, are you coming?'

He set off down the corridor, Mercia following as quickly as she could. As they turned a corner she looked back, struck by an unexpected sympathy.

'What will happen to her? To that woman?'

'Our Margie?' The guard seemed surprised to be asked. 'She's been here near twenty years. She don't even know the old King is killed, or that Cromwell has been and gone.' He laughed. 'I think she'll be here for ever.'

They arrived at a large wooden gate. Three more guards perching around an oval table broke off their dice game to stare as she passed, but she ignored the leers. Emerging into chill dawn the heavy gate clanged shut behind her, releasing her into the dank London air. Despite the subdued light she screwed up her eyes, squinting. Her brown skirt was crumpled, the damp straw of the prison floor obscuring its criss-crossed pattern. Bending down to brush it off, a hand on her shoulder made her jump.

'I am sorry.' A tall man in a wide-brimmed hat stood before her, his dark eyes radiating concern. He held out a woollen cloak and wrapped her in its warmth before pulling his own firmly around him, covering the scar that protruded from under the simple neck frills of his shirt.

'Are you unharmed?' he asked. The furrows of his lightly stubbled face betrayed his worry. 'I went to your uncle at once, but they refused to do anything until morning.'

She grabbed his arm. 'Nathan, is there time?' She looked at the sky, assessing the amount of light. 'I think there must be. Please tell me there is.'

'There is. But we must go now.'

She felt her heart beat faster. 'Then come. I need to see him before he dies.'

The carriage trundled slowly down the London streets. Impatient, she craned her head through the window, silently cursing every lumbering cart, every rambling pedlar, every early-to-rise housewife who got in their way. She realised she was gripping the edge of her seat, and as she pulled her hands away she noticed a stained news pamphlet on the floor, discarded by a previous passenger. A grisly image of a man carrying his own severed head was emblazoned on one side. She snatched it up to read a sort of verse on the rear.

Good Sir Rowland Goodridge knew
Where his deeds 'gainst the King would lead him
Now his head will be docked for a Stew
And they'll send it to Charles, to please him

She tore up the paper and threw it onto the street.

'Why didn't they let me see him, Nat? I lost my temper, I know, but they would have prevented it anyway.' She ran her hand over her face; remembering where she had spent the night, she sat up straight.

'God's truth, how do I look? 'Tis a blessing this cloak covers me well.'

'You look fine.' Nathan's lips curled into a tentative smile. 'Curls, topknot, all still in place.'

'No straw anywhere? Dirt?'

'Your hair is as brown as mine.' He licked his finger, rubbing a couple of specks from her cheek. 'All gone.'

They lapsed into silence as the carriage jolted down the cobbled streets. Soon the shaking stopped and she looked out the window to see a row of similar carriages stuck one behind the other, not moving.

'Shall I drop you here by the Dolphin?' the driver shouted back. 'I don't think I can get any closer. Too many people up the Hill. Wish I could go myself, but the horses, you know.'

Covering her head with her hood, Mercia flung open the door and jumped out, oblivious to the rowdy group of blue-aproned apprentices who were forced to duck aside. The teenagers swore at her but she took no notice. On the roadside Nathan slapped a silver shilling into the driver's outstretched hand and the carriage rumbled off into a side street, steering a path through the boisterous crowd that was making its slow way down Tower Street. All these people, thought Mercia, come to watch a man die. She fought back her tears as she allowed herself to be swept along with the mob, not wanting to show her despair.

A church steeple rose up from the crowd as they approached Tower Hill. She stopped, unheeding the grumbling melee around her. 'All Hallows,' she mumbled. 'Where they will put him afterwards.' The tears began to well, but still she fought them down.

Nathan reached out his arm. 'Think of it as a place of tranquillity where he will find peace.'

'He will not be at peace until he is brought back to Halescott.' She looked up at the steeple, her hand clutching her neck. 'All his life

13

in the service of his country, ending like this. He was safe, by Jesus. There was no reason for the King to remove him. So why now?' She rubbed at her forehead. 'Damn them all. And damn myself. Useless, useless again.'

'You are not useless.' Nathan turned her to face him. 'You are the bravest woman I know.'

She forced a weak smile. 'You are a true friend, Nat. Thank you for coming with me to this . . . this place.'

'Of course I have come. We have been through a lot, these past years. I will always be here, you know that.'

She looked back at the deepening crowd. 'Well, then. Let us be brave.'

The noise on Tower Hill was incredible. It seemed as though all of London had turned out, more and more people gathering into ever smaller spaces. The wounds of the civil war that had set King against Parliament were fresh and unhealed. For some, what happened today was vindication. For others, it was a tragedy.

'There.' Mercia followed Nathan as he carved a path through the tumult. 'The family platform.' She swallowed. 'Near the front.'

He turned his head. 'Keep your voice down. You don't want people to know who you are.'

'He is my father. I will not hide that.'

He pressed on, using his broad shoulders to intimidate less determined bystanders into giving way. But it took several minutes to reach the family platform, squeezing past the whole variety of London life – well-dressed men in fine wigs leaning on sticks, gangs of predatory pickpockets, hemp-clad women cradling dirty babies in their arms. At the platform steps Nathan kicked off two young girls whose poorly applied face patches were already slipping on their whitened cheeks. They fled, screaming unheard curses.

The roughly hewn steps wobbled as Mercia ascended to the fair-sized platform. Feeling ever more nauseous, she nodded to the three of her father's old colleagues who had dared attend, amongst them Nathan's neighbour, Sir Jeremy Princeton, whose lands he helped manage alongside his own farm. He doffed his hat to her in sympathy.

'Is my uncle not here?' she said, looking around. 'I suppose I should not have expected it.' She paused as her eyes fell on a portly woman standing under armed guard. 'And yet Lady Markstone has come.'

'She has not had far to travel,' said Nathan.

'Don't jest.' Mercia walked to the elderly woman at the back of the platform. Her covered head was thrust back, her fine silk dress of a purple so dark it was almost black. Seeing Mercia approach, she gave her a subdued smile.

'Mercia,' she said. 'I am so pleased to see you, sad day though it is. I hope you do not mind my being here.'

'It is a surprise today, Lady Markstone. I did not think it would be allowed.'

'They let me out my prison to be here. I wanted Rowland to see he had at least some friends left.' She leant in closer. 'The guards say there was an incident yesterday.'

Mercia glanced at the soldier beside them. 'You are right. They would not let me see him.'

Lady Markstone nodded. 'They can be cruel, these Tower warders. They like to pretend they have power. But return soon to visit me. I will make sure they let you pass.' She hesitated. 'How is your mother?'

'As you would expect.' Mercia looked away. 'She does not know what happens here today. 'Tis her melancholy. Her mind will not accept it. But please, I should return to Nathan.'

Not wanting to talk further, Mercia pulled her hood tighter and moved to the front of the platform, standing beside Nathan who was speaking with Sir Jeremy. The crowd below now seemed an impenetrable horde. Many of them were staring up at her, wondering who she was. 'Must be his daughter,' someone guessed. 'Still pretty, though.'

She looked over the crowd at the castle beyond, desperate to avoid anyone's gaze. The Tower of London glared impassively back, its massive walls dismissing her silent entreaties for mercy as irrelevant. Spurned, her eyes rested on an empty platform between herself and the fortress: empty, save for the dented wooden block. She grabbed the rail in front of her. Small splinters of wood drove through her thin gloves into her palm, making her wince.

Nathan broke from his conversation. 'Do you want to leave? We can go whenever you want.'

She shook her head. 'I need to see him. I need him to see me. I am just glad I will not have to see him – afterwards.' She looked up at Sir Jeremy. 'Thank you for taking care of . . . that.'

Sir Jeremy nodded, uttering words she did not really hear. She dared a look back at the crowd, here to witness a bloody blow of the axe, a head severed, a man destroyed. She glanced again at the block, fighting her rising nausea. How would it feel, to be beheaded? They said it was quick, but sometimes the axe stuck. She fixed her gaze on a knot in the wooden rail, breathing in and out, steady and sure, as her husband had taught her before he died. Striving to ignore the scene around her, she listened in to Nathan's resumed conversation.

'Some of my merchant friend's wine barrels were swept away,' he was saying. 'By the time he found them lower down the Thames they were being pilfered.'

'That flood was the worst I can remember,' said Sir Jeremy, grabbing his hat at a gust of wind. 'Water came into the palace itself. The corridors were full of dead rats.'

'Peter says a whole horse washed up in Greenwich. Bits of people too. That superstitious lot down Lambeth Marsh found a finger rotted right to the bone, thought it was sent by the Devil, the mad fools. And what of that jilt on Broken Wharf who brought in a skull? Peter reckons it was a client who refused to pay, and she took her revenge by cutting off—'

He held the finger he was running across his throat dead still. 'By the Lord, Mercia, I am sorry. I did not think.' He looked at Sir Jeremy, mortified, and both fell silent. But Mercia patted his forearm, and they waited.

Not for long. The great din of the crowd ceased as movement was spotted at the Tower's base. An unnatural quiet briefly descended, to be replaced by an ever-growing murmuring as a figure cloaked in a black hood approached, carrying a huge axe in his enormous hands. Gasps of horror and awe intermingled as the man who would deliver the fatal blow came ever closer. Who was he? Some said a pardoned criminal, others a sadistic nobleman, but nobody really knew.

Rejecting the need for steps, the axeman leapt onto the executioner's platform. With one gloved hand he slowly stroked the block. He waited a few seconds, the tension ever rising, before he advanced to face the crowd, and with a triumphant roar he thrust his axe to the sky for all the mob to see. Groans, gasps, cheers, all resounded round the crowd, the people's bloodlust dominant.

A drum began to beat atop the Tower. The axeman backed towards the block, his eyes invisible behind his black hood, his deliberate footsteps in time with the drum's monotonous thud. Then a door opened in the Tower wall and more drummers emerged, adding their rhythm to the other. The crowd hushed, straining to see as the Tower disgorged a man dressed all in white, his grey hair loose around his face, a guard of soldiers behind. As he approached, a shout went up – *Sir Rowland comes, the traitor is here!* – before the mob let loose a baying, illiterate, cacophonous roar in anticipation of the spectacle to come.

Sir Rowland was pushed up the steps to the axeman's platform. He stumbled against the block, but immediately straightened himself. His face and clothes were clean, his beard trimmed. He did not shake. He walked forward to the edge of the dais, surveying the people around, then opened his mouth to begin his last speech.

Chapter Two

A jackdaw called out nearby. Silence now reigned in the crowd.

'I come here,' Sir Rowland began, 'not in misery, nor in anger, but in satisfaction that what I have done in the course of my life has been just, and necessary, to safeguard our country from tyranny.'

The silence evaporated. A deep-voiced man in the crowd called out, 'Shut him up for good and all!' while others clapped a chorus, singing, 'We want his head!' Mercia looked around, disgusted, a nauseous feeling swimming in her heart. But others turned on those who had shouted out, crying *Shame!* and threatening retribution.

Sir Rowland ignored the crowd's taunts. He was scanning the mob, searching for someone, and Mercia knew it was she that he sought. His eyes roved left, and as his gaze fell on the family platform, she leant forward on the barrier until they locked with her own. For a moment the crowd did not exist as father and daughter looked into each other's souls. Then he turned away, the crowd returned, and he continued in a stronger, prouder voice:

'We have witnessed much hardship these past years. It has been our fortune to live in times of great change, to be given the opportunity to forge our own fate; but it has been our misfortune too, that so much blood was shed to secure this inheritance for our children.'

His eyes flicked back to Mercia. But then trumpets blared from underneath his platform, a small band of heralds interrupting his words.

'They are trying to drown out his speech,' said Mercia. 'The bastards. Can they not give him even this last honour?' Nathan squeezed her hand. Behind her, she could hear Lady Markstone murmuring a quiet prayer.

Undaunted, Sir Rowland shouted as loud as he was able, so that despite the trumpets those near the front could still hear.

'And yet now I am glad to die, in the assurance that never again in the history of our people will power be vested so cruelly against them. That is the legacy of Parliament, that our rights and laws are respected by all, and that men are judged by the virtue of their deeds. And if it is an irony that I am condemned to die in the same manner as the King whose claims to autocratic rule created such conflict, then I am content nonetheless. I never approved of that murder, but I hold firm my principles as old King Charles was brave to die for his.'

Those who could hear turned their heads at the mention of the executed King, creating a rippling effect in the crowd, until everyone was looking at his younger son, the Duke of York, who was standing on a high platform to their left. But he merely folded his arms. As she looked at the platform over the heads of the crowd, Mercia saw next to the Duke Sir Bernard Dittering, the man who had overseen her father's trial, and beside him another grandly dressed man she did not recognise but who was looking straight at her. Behind those two stood her uncle. So that was where he was.

The trumpets ceased, but Sir Rowland did not lower his voice.

'I hope that in a hundred years this great nation of ours will remain steadfast in embracing the freedoms of men, so that all may live together in a just society in which hard work leads to a common happiness. To my family, whom I pray God save in their grief, before I pass to eternal life in heaven I want to say: forgive me. If I have brought you pain, I am sorry for it.'

He paused, looking at Mercia once more. There was something in his expression, a deep worry for her, something beyond pain for his imminent death. It was as if he – yes, as if he feared for her. Her heartbeat quickened.

'To my daughter, my own dear fairy queen, I say this –'

His fairy queen? He had not called her that since she was a girl, when he would read to her in his study. *The Faerie Queene* had been her favourite story. It still was.

'– I hope you can understand my reasons, as I taught you to love reason itself.'

He had always told her, as a child, to love reason, to learn. It had never mattered to him that she was a girl, although he was frowned upon for it. Now she leant forward as he clasped his hands together, in that exact way he always did when he wanted to teach her something important. She listened intently.

'For I promised I would make a lady of you, and I did, and behind that promise, I have left you a legacy to explore.'

Mercia stared at him, and there was the gentle nod he always gave when he was satisfied she had understood. He was telling her something, she was sure of it.

Make a lady of you . . . a legacy to explore . . .

But what did it mean? There was no time to think. Her father was finishing his speech.

'I go to my rest, satisfied I have carried out my role in our nation's journey in the honest belief I was doing right. I forgive all my detractors, and those who have brought me to this place. I pray God that the King be a man of charity and honour, that he respect the will of his Parliament, and that the men and women of this blessed England be protected in his care. Please God take me to His immortal attention, where I will rejoice in seeing my departed compatriots again, and hope to see my beloved wife, daughter, and innocent grandson when they join me at their correct time.'

He looked at Mercia once more, his eyes sad but resolute, and he said goodbye in a brief smile. With a flick of his head he signalled that she should leave. She held his gaze for one final moment, then with tears burning the backs of her eyes she put away his words and got down from her viewing point. She had wanted to see him, but it would be barbaric to witness the end.

And then she left, allowing Nathan to forge a way for them through the crowd, the people oblivious to their retreat as they watched the doomed man being led to the axeman's block. As Sir Rowland knelt, now out of her sight, faster and faster Mercia pushed Nathan through the crowd that parted and re-formed around them, until they made their way back onto Tower Street. She looked at him, her face quivering with suppressed anguish, before the horror of the situation finally grabbed her, and she abandoned the mocking scene for the dirty London streets. In her agony, she scarcely noticed the crowd's exultant roar rising up behind her as she fled.

It was nearly nightfall when she descended from the carriage she had hired to take her back to the coaching inn. She paid the driver and he whipped his horses, driving off into the gloomy streets. The sign of the Saracen's Head swung lightly in the gentle breeze, knocking against the darkening wall with a soft thud.

She found Nathan inside, gripping a mug of ale. As soon as she entered he dropped the chipped tankard and came over.

'I walked,' she explained simply. 'I wanted to be on my own.'

He nodded. 'I know.' He looked into her eyes; the familiar brown was somehow comforting, even in her intense grief. 'I searched for you, but you had vanished.'

'I sat by the river for a time, behind a warehouse.' She tried a smile, but none came. 'One of the dock hands brought me a glass of beer.' She sighed. 'I will survive, Nathan. I have done so before.' Her illusive mood faded as an unwelcome memory resurfaced, but she pushed the thoughts away.

Nathan bit his lip. 'Perhaps, but I am worried about you. So is your uncle, it seems. He came here not one hour ago asking for you.'

She paused from untying the lace on her hood. 'My uncle, in a coaching inn? I cannot believe it.'

'I am afraid he wants to see you tomorrow. At the palace.'

'Does he?' She clawed at the lace. 'I suppose he thinks with father dead—'

Of a sudden she found herself gasping for breath, unable to continue; Nathan steered her to an empty table, facing her away from the room. He called to the innkeeper to bring over an ale. She sipped at the brown liquid, calming herself.

'I suppose he thinks he is in charge now,' she said finally. 'Well, he can try.'

'And you will not let him.' Nathan reached out a hand across the table, but checked himself. 'Still, he was adamant he wished to see you. He must know we are leaving by the late morning coach. He is sending a carriage at seven o'clock.'

The sound of horses being saddled in the courtyard below woke Mercia early, a pit of sadness in her stomach reminding her where she was. She lay in bed awhile, unwilling to get up, until the church bells of St Sepulchre's opposite chimed out six o'clock. Reluctantly she rose, pulling a black woollen gown from her battered trunk. She entwined her arms in its darkness for a time before forcing it on over a similarly black petticoat.

She came downstairs as her uncle's grand carriage swept into the courtyard, pulled by four massive horses. But she was hungry, and she made the immaculately dressed footmen wait while she finished a plate of eggs.

Despite the early hour, the streets were flowing with people. The painted carriage trundled along the old city wall, turning right opposite the Ludgate and over the River Fleet, forcing everything in its path to one side. Down Fleet Street they passed seamlessly onto the Strand, easing left at Charing Cross to ride towards the Banqueting House where the first King Charles had faced his execution fifteen years before. Immediately before the columned edifice they pulled into the courtyard of the vast Whitehall Palace where his namesake son now reigned.

The footmen handed her to a waiting palace servant with dark patches under his eyes, evidence of drunken revelry the previous night, perhaps. She did not want to think in celebration of what. Still he led her without pause through the labyrinth of corridors, leaving her in a small, green-walled chamber, fine upholstered chairs set around a welcome fire within.

She was staring blandly at a walnut cabinet, not really noticing its ostentatious splendour, when a slight quivering of the flames heralded a new arrival to the room. Shivering, Mercia rubbed her hands over her arms and looked up. Shaded in the doorway stood a well-dressed gentleman: her mother's brother, Sir Francis Simmonds.

'Uncle,' she acknowledged.

He rested against the doorframe, clutching a parchment. 'Mercia. Such a sorry few days. I know you must be upset.' He walked to the fireplace, setting the parchment on the mantelpiece while studying his reflection in the mirror above. 'Although a night in Newgate is hardly decent.' He brushed a gloved hand over his greying hair, teasing loose strands back into place, not yet taken to wearing a wig like some men of the court.

'I am grateful you secured my release.' She folded her arms. 'But my coach leaves soon for Oxford. You wished to see me?'

Sir Francis turned and smiled, the right side of his face arching higher than the left in that particular way of his that made her wonder about his real thoughts. He was dressed in dark brown, doubtless his concession to mourning in a court hostile to the deceased man. But in contrast to Mercia's subdued clothing he wore a fancily patterned doublet, unbuttoned to show off a snug waistcoat beneath, his well-fitted silk breeches pleated at the knee.

He pulled off his gloves, resting them on an adjacent table: their perfumed scent drifted across the room. 'I thought I would wish you well before you return home. 'Tis a terrible thing to lose a father.' He looked at her. 'Traitor though yours was.'

'My father—' She stopped. He was goading her.

'Your father chose his side.' Sir Francis sighed, but she could tell it was fake. 'And so your care passes to me.'

She let out a bitter laugh. 'Really, Uncle. I can care for myself.'

'Can you?' He sniffed, toying with his fingertips. 'If you refuse to marry again, you can hardly expect me to stand aside.'

She looked through the window beside her. The River Thames flowed below in its steady course to the sea; dotted with boats it still seemed grey, bleak. 'I have managed these past few years,' she said. 'I will manage now.'

'On your widow's jointure? I think not. Rowland cannot add to it any more.'

She frowned. Something was not right. Her uncle's tone was almost – what? Triumphant? She turned her gaze on him. 'I can manage, because I will have care of the lands Daniel is inheriting from his grandfather.'

Sir Francis picked at a thread on his doublet. 'Well, that is the point. Your son has fewer lands than we both supposed.'

She blinked. 'What do you mean?'

His right cheek arched upwards. 'I mean that the manor house and its lands are to pass to me.' He clasped his hands together. 'And Daniel – he gets nothing.'

'What?' A coldness formed in her stomach. 'That cannot be. Daniel is my father's heir. The will is clear.'

'Have you seen this will?'

'No, but Father discussed it with me. My mother receives her jointure from their marriage settlement, and Daniel gets the manor house and lands. Quite naturally I am to be his guardian until he comes of age.'

Sir Francis tapped on the mantelpiece. 'Did you know Rowland appointed me his executor? I reviewed the papers with him last week. It is quite clear in that same marriage settlement you speak of that the manor and all its contents should pass to a son.'

Her face set. 'You know there is no son. I am the only living child.'

'So you cannot inherit.'

'I do not claim that. As his grandson, my son is to inherit. The will makes it plain.'

He held up his hands, his face perfectly composed. 'But there you see the problem. The terms of the settlement must take precedence over the will. Study it if you like.' He nodded at the paper on the mantelpiece. 'In the absence of sons, the estate goes to brothers. Not

26

daughters. Not grandsons through daughters. And as Sir Rowland's brothers are both dead, that means to me, his brother through marriage. I am surprised he never mentioned it.'

Mercia walked over and snatched up the parchment. Pre-marriage settlements were common enough in families of wealth, to ensure property descended down the male line. But she had never heard of it leaping across to the wife's family. She read quickly.

'This says nothing of brothers-in-law, only brothers.' She looked up. 'It is irrelevant.'

Sir Francis folded his arms. 'Mercia, what know you of the law? I have discussed this with Sir Bernard Dittering and he agrees with my assessment.'

She let the paper drop to the floor. 'An assessment which favours you immensely. Validated by the man who orchestrated my father's so-called trial.' Her breathing quickened. 'I will not allow this to happen. You will not disinherit my son.'

He pursed his thin lips. 'You have your own house, do you not, that charming cottage Rowland provided with your dowry?'

'That is beside the point. Halescott Manor belongs to my family. To my son.' She bored into her uncle's eyes. 'I will fight this. Your claim is spurious.'

'Then you will lose. You are a woman, the child of a traitor. I have many friends at court, Mercia. I asked you here to explain the situation. Now accept it.'

The coldness inside her intensified. 'And my mother? The manor house is her home.'

Sir Francis stooped to pick up the settlement. 'Your mother is in my care now. I have sent riders to take her to someone who can look after her properly. The servants will be informed. And I have arranged for a tenant for the house. He will receive the authorisation today.'

Mercia stared at him, pure fury in her heart, her breaths quick and shallow. 'You have no right to do this.'

For an instant his eyes darted away, but then he returned her fierce gaze. 'You are too proud, child. I have every right. I am your uncle, your protector. When you return to Halescott, I expect you to live in your cottage and behave as I say.'

She said nothing. The anger was too acute.

'However, I do have an alternative for you. One that will allow you to keep living in the way that you wish.' He picked up his gloves and strode to the door. 'Follow me. There is someone who wishes to meet you.'

She remained where she was.

'Now, Mercia.' He clicked his fingers. 'This is not a request.'

The whole affair was a set-up. The pain was physical, as though she had been stabbed.

She allowed her uncle to lead her through the huge palace, following in a daze. The magnitude of what he had told her refused to sink in. Instead of inheriting the manor house and its profitable lands, she and her son would be left with nothing but a small amount of money. Her mind flew back to her father's speech, to the message she was certain was hidden within. Had he known this was going to happen?

A chill wind interrupted her thoughts. They had come out onto a paved terrace overlooking the Thames. A light drizzle was falling, irregular gusts propelling stray flower stalks and embroidery threads across the damp stone. Sir Francis stopped, pointing to a man in a thick, fur-rimmed cloak who was standing with his back to them, looking out onto the river.

'Do you see that man?' His tone was curt. 'Do you know who he is?' He grabbed her chin and forced her to look. 'Well?'

She wrenched her head from his grasp. 'No. No, I do not.'

He scoffed. 'That, child, is Sir William Calde. He is one of the Duke of York's most trusted advisors. A man of high influence.' He paused. 'And a man with a fancy for you.'

A burst of cold air swept over her face. 'My father died yesterday.' She felt her jaw clenching. 'And today you want to take my house, whore me out to your friends?'

'Do not be absurd. You should be honoured at his interest.' He sighed. 'Listen to me, Mercia. Sir William is wealthy. He has made a fortune these past several years. You want to live in grand houses, have pretty trinkets? Well.' He waved a hand towards Sir William. 'That is how.'

She looked her uncle in the eye. 'And his wife?'

He shrugged. 'Wife, mistress, 'tis all the same. You will do well by him, as will our family.'

She began to retort but he had already moved away, beckoning her to follow. Unsure how to react, she complied. As he neared his quarry, Sir William turned, the edges of his grand cloak brushing the dusty ground.

'Sir William.' Sir Francis inclined his head. 'Not such a pleasant day, this morning.'

'Not yet.' Sir William looked at Mercia and smiled. 'But I hope it will improve.'

'This is my niece.' Sir Francis laughed. 'But then you know that.'

Sir William beamed at her, his ample cheeks red, before commanding Sir Francis to leave with a barely perceptible jerk of his head. With a penetrating glance at Mercia, Sir Francis bowed and retreated. She watched him leave, a sudden rage flaring within, but Sir William's words snapped her back into the reality of the cruel terrace.

'Will you walk with me?' he asked. 'I know you are to return home on the morning coach, but we have a little time.'

She acquiesced, keen to get away as quickly as she could. As they strolled along the terrace she looked sideways at him. He was about twenty years older than she, just in his fifties perhaps, but his face was pleasant, the ends of his hair still a deep brown, his large hat trimmed with fashionable ostrich feathers. But she had no desire to be his mistress, or anyone's.

'I hope you do not think it unfeeling that I asked to see you today,' he said. 'But I am leaving for Hampton Court shortly, on business with the King, and I do not know when you might be back in the city.' He renewed his smile. 'I am pleased you have come. Your beauty enhances this otherwise forlorn day.'

She hid her impatience at his ridiculous flattery, keeping her expression neutral. Looking at him full on, she realised she had seen him before.

'You were standing with my uncle yesterday.' She spoke without emotion. 'At my father's execution.'

Her brashness discomfited him. He swallowed, looking out to the river. 'Yes, with the Duke of York. I saw you too, near Millicent Markstone. You carried yourself with dignity.' He looked at her as though awaiting a response, but when she stayed silent he continued. 'I hoped, perhaps, to cheer your spirits. I have a gift for you.'

He paused, reaching inside his cloak to retrieve a magnificent necklace composed of three rows of pearls of an intensely white hue. Mercia took an involuntary sharp breath. She thought of her own necklace in her jewellery box at home: it only had one row, but had cost her husband a fortune to acquire.

The breeze teased at her hair. 'You are most generous, Sir William. But I cannot – it is far too grand.'

'Please. I want you to have it.' He stepped behind her to place the pearls around her neck, bringing his face so close she could smell the faint odour of nutmeg on his breath, feel the individual hairs on his chin where he had not been properly shaved. He came round to smile at her. 'There, you look beautiful. It sets off the blueness of your eyes.'

She looked at the busy river, its countless wherries carrying a multitude of people, but on that terrace she felt alone. She bowed her head.

Sir William laughed. 'There is no need to be coy. Let us talk from time to time and see what comes to pass. But now I fear I must go.' He grimaced as if in apology. 'The King awaits.'

He traced an ungloved finger across her cold cheek. She raised her eyes to his, but it was not kindness she saw in them, merely lust.

Chapter Three

It was a two-day journey back to Oxfordshire. The coach was overbooked, so Mercia had to squeeze up tighter than she liked against an excitable woman who would not stay silent, prattling about every piece of scenery they passed. But it stopped her from brooding on all that had happened, and at least she had an inside seat, while Nathan had to sit outside in the pouring rain. By the time they arrived at their overnight halt in Stoaken Church his shirt was more or less part of his skin, the rain having penetrated deep beneath his cloak. While he went to change, Mercia, exhausted, retired to her own room and fell asleep to the sound of yet more pattering on the window. When she awoke it was dark, and she was ready to talk.

She was hungry, having avoided food since her scant breakfast, so when Nathan suggested they eat, she readily agreed. They sat at a candlelit table at the back of the busy dining area, away from the fire where there was most space. Although it was Lent and the King had once more prohibited meat, the innkeeper was not the most scrupulous sort. A calf's head looked up from a silver platter set between them.

Nathan stared back at it. 'Do you remember when my father served one of these at that birthday feast?'

'He objected to the colour of Jane's dress, as I recall.' Mercia looked at him. 'She was beautiful that day. You have mentioned her less of late.'

'It has been some time now.' He lowered his eyes for a second. 'But we are avoiding what matters today. You have said hardly a word since we left London.'

'I am sorry. I am struggling to contend with what has happened.' Taking a deep breath, she told him about her conversations at the palace. As she spoke, his jaw began to clench, and when she had finished, his right hand was balled into a fist.

'I am truly sorry.' He punched his right hand into his left. 'How can he do this to you? To Daniel?'

Mercia scoffed. 'Daniel is nothing to him. As for me, I am just someone he thinks he can use. But Mother, my poor mother. She has lived in that house for thirty years.'

Nathan hesitated. 'And Sir William? Will you . . . see him?'

'I will not.' She lowered her voice. 'He thinks he has me with that damn necklace, but I will not be purchased like the King bought that harlot Castlemaine.' She sighed. 'I should be able to challenge my uncle. His argument is weak. But to fight him and his like? How does a woman do that?'

'With her friends.' Nathan reached for her hand. 'I will help you however I can.'

She smiled. 'Thank you, Nat. I would be lost without you now.'

'You are too strong for that.' Releasing her hand he pushed the platter towards her. 'Now please, eat something. It will make you feel better.'

'So now it is you telling me to eat.' She carved at the head. 'Yet there is one small piece of hope.'

'There is always hope.'

She lifted a morsel of meat onto her plate. 'I mean those strange words in my father's speech.'

He frowned. 'Strange words?'

'He called me his fairy queen, like the book.'

'*The Fairie Queene*.' Nathan shook his head. 'How many times have you read that?'

'Many.' She looked up. 'You know the lady knight Britomart?'

'Ah yes. Your favourite.'

'He used to read those parts to me over and again. I dreamt of being her, of going on adventures as she did. I remember it now.' She smiled, thinking of a happy time. 'He would look at me from his chair, he would waggle his finger and he would say, "Look, Mercia, here is a woman who is strong, as you can be. Whatever you want to do, I will support it." He scared my mother witless. She thought I should concentrate on needlework and dance.'

'You dance well. But you were talking about your father's speech.'

She nodded, recalling the words precisely. 'There was one thing in particular. He said, "I promised I would make a lady of you, and I did." And then: "Behind that promise, I have left you a legacy to explore." I think it was a message.'

'How so?'

She leant in closer. 'When I was eight he commissioned a portrait of me. I was being peevish, refusing to accept I was not a Lady even though he was a knight.'

'No child would be. His title is not hereditary.'

'Yes, but when I was little I did not know that. I acted like a spoilt fool, all upset. He said he would make a lady of me anyway, dressed me up in finery and had a portrait done. So – he promised he would make a lady of me, and he did.'

Nathan raised an eyebrow. 'You think he was talking about that portrait?'

'Yes. And that behind his promise, in other words behind the portrait, he has left me something to explore, to use.' She blew out her cheeks. 'I think he knew what my uncle was planning. It is my one hope.'

His knife wavered above his plate. 'Where is the portrait now?'

She hesitated. 'In the manor house.'

'So go there.'

'Oh, I will. It is my house. I will not let anyone stop me, my damned uncle least of all.'

His eyes gleamed in the candlelight. 'You taught me once there was always hope, even when I did not want to believe it. You were right then and you are right now. Never give up, remember.'

She speared her meat. 'Never give up.'

Late next evening the coach rumbled into Oxford under a cloudless sky. Entrusting their luggage to a carter for delivery the next day, Nathan picked up his horse for the remaining few miles to Halescott, Mercia riding behind him. From experience he knew the roads well enough to manage the nocturnal ride, but even under bright moonlight it was still a harrowing journey, and they were ever vigilant for anyone who might be lying in wait along the muddy tracks. Once a rustling in the undergrowth up ahead caused him to spur on his horse, but it was only a nervous doe running out of their path.

Still, Mercia was relieved when the succession of large oak trees that signalled the boundary of Halescott village came into view. Before long they were passing the high walls of the manor house, an owl hooting in the impenetrable blackness beyond. Outside the iron gates they paused on seeing a tiny light in one of the windows, her uncle's tenant perhaps already in residence. A quick anger shot through her. This should be Daniel's, she thought. Mine until he comes of age. And it will be.

Resisting the urge to go through the gates tonight, she signalled to Nathan to ride on. They came into a wide street lined with stone cottages, but nobody was abroad at this late hour. Trotting quietly along the deserted road they crossed the green at the other side of the village to reach a larger cottage set apart from the rest, although small in comparison to the manor house. Mercia's father had included it in her dowry; now she was widowed it belonged to her. As they approached, a shooting star flashed overhead. A sign of luck indeed – but would it be good or bad?

Dropping her at the cottage Nathan bade her a reluctant farewell, checking several times whether she would be all right before taking his leave. She watched him ride away, staring into the darkness until the sound of his horse's hooves faded. It was still a long way to his farmland, but he was strong enough, and sharp, should he need his muscles or his wits.

Overcoming a momentary feeling of solitude she pushed open the cottage's wooden door, wincing at the creak it made lest it wake her son. Shutting it with care, she tiptoed over the large hall flagstones and came into the sitting room, warm from the still-burning fire. Her maidservant Bethany was waiting in a chair, her baggy folds of skin sinking low into her face. As soon as Mercia entered she dragged herself up, setting down the pair of small breeches she was darning and disappearing to the kitchen, insisting Mercia take her seat. She returned with a plate of thick chicken stew, a homely smell of thyme filling the room.

Mercia pointed at the breeches. 'That hole is new. Has Daniel behaved?'

'Oh yes,' said Bethany, setting the stew on a side table. Her eyes darted round the room. 'But mistress, you need to know.' Her voice shook. 'Something has happened.'

'Yes.' Mercia sighed. 'The manor house. My uncle . . . informed me.' She stared listlessly at her prized globe of the Earth that filled a whole corner of the room. 'Do you know what happened to my mother?'

A great sorrow accentuated the lines on Bethany's aged face. 'There was a commotion in the village. Horses came, riding this way and that. I went to the house to speak with Agnes. She said her mistress was to be taken to Warwick and that she was to go with her.'

'Near family, then. At least he had that decency.' She paused. 'But who has he put in the house?'

Bethany's eyes widened. 'You don't know?'

'No.' Mercia frowned. 'And you look petrified. Come, Bethany. Speak.'

Bethany's face trembled. ''Tis – Mr and Mrs Blakewood. Your husband's parents.'

Mercia sat up in her chair, stunned. 'Anthony and Isabel? You are sure?'

'Yes, mistress. I saw them there myself when I talked with Agnes.'

'But that means they are complicit in disinheriting their own grandson!' She felt sick. 'Why would they do that?'

'I am so sorry, mistress. What will you do?'

Mercia gripped the arms of her chair, talking more to herself than to her maid. 'Whatever I must. I will not stand by and let this happen. I will retrieve what my father has left me, and then—' She threw back her head. 'Then I will fight back.'

Sunlight awoke her, a pleasant sight. She lay in bed for a few seconds, enjoying the way the oak of her bedside cabinet seemed to absorb the light. Then memories of the last few days surfaced. The injustice of the execution, the sorrow at the death. A great ache within her soul.

But no tears. She pulled herself from bed and went to the window, taking in her favourite view as she removed the curl-papers from her hair. The first tiny buds were coming through on the trees, but the village green was still just visible through the gaps in the branches. Daffodils were starting to unfurl their golden promise of warmer weather underneath.

She splashed her face in the pitcher of water that had appeared at the foot of her bed before dressing in her mourning clothes and descending the stairs. Daniel was in the kitchen, stuffing a piece of bread into his mouth. She reached down to kiss his cheek.

He looked up and smiled. 'Mamma! Are you not eating?'

'Not yet. I will have something later.'

He mumbled through his bread. 'Can we go sledging today?'

'Danny, you need snow for sledging. The snow has gone.'

'When then?'

She stroked his hair. 'Soon, Danny, soon.'

'Why are you in black?'

Her heart burst, right there in the kitchen. She hadn't yet mustered the courage to tell him about his grandfather. She turned away, not knowing what to say.

'Listen, Danny. I have to go out again, but I will be back soon.' Mastering herself, she bent down to hug him close. 'I need to talk to you about . . . something.' He squirmed and she released him, managing a smile. 'Behave for Bethany?'

He nodded, returning to his food. Mercia went into the hall, rubbing at her temples, instinctively stepping around the large green vase she had decided would fit well in the narrow space. Somehow Bethany was there with her cloak and hood. As she walked outside she looked back at the cottage, eyes roving over the warm orange stone all the village buildings enjoyed. It had been a comfortable home for her and Daniel. But it wasn't the manor house, and it wasn't where she needed to be.

A swift walk later, she was standing outside Halescott Manor, a chill air drying her lips. Before her the long wall that encircled the grounds ended in two tall columns of stone, framing the iron entrance gates familiar to her from clambering atop the sturdy metalwork during the more mischievous days of her childhood. A stray pigeon, presumably from the dovecote around the back, was roosting up there today.

She pushed open the gates, the left one sticking halfway with its usual loud clang, scaring the pigeon into hurried flight. As she strode towards the towering house, its symmetrically gabled facade beckoning her on, the crunching of her feet on the pebbled drive released a sorry memory, and she saw herself as a girl, playing with her doll on this drive, shouting with infant joy the day her father came home unexpectedly, but he, ignoring her, rushing past, crunching the pebbles as she did today; and she remembered the door wide open, a scream from upstairs – her mother! – and a maid running out, steering her away, but Mercia, unknowing, asking if the baby is born, she wants to show off her doll, but the maid, tears falling, shaking her head, shaking her head.

At the front door she paused. There were no other children to fight this battle. She inhaled deeply, taking in a strong scent of honeysuckle and lavender. Very well, she thought, be brave. She pulled the doorbell rope, sounding a confident ring within the house. Moments later a tall, formal-looking servant opened the door, his suspicious eyes questioning her presence.

'You know who I am,' she sighed, recognising one of her father-in-law's men. 'I would speak with your master.'

The servant hesitated a moment before standing aside to let her enter. He led her through the great hall – her hall – its wainscoted walls intensifying the grandeur of the imposing space. Passing the foot of the mahogany east staircase he left her in a large library covered in panels of lighter oak.

As she waited she roved her eyes across all her father's books, and there, in the corner where it should be, was a copy of *The Fairie Queene*. She hoped to God her parents-in-law would value these books and keep them in place. She could not bear the thought of them being dispersed, or worse, destroyed.

She took another of her favourites from one of the shelves, a well-worn volume bound in musty leather, a history of the kings and queens of the old Anglo-Saxon kingdoms. It fell open on the most perused section, the chapter on the kingdom of Mercia, and she smiled sadly, recalling her childhood fantasies that the kingdom was named for her and not the other way around, when she had played at being the Queen of all the Mercians. She slipped the book into the pocket under her dress, intending to retain the memento as a symbol of her temporary eviction.

She had just straightened her dress when her father-in-law appeared, his expression defiant, and yet with a trace of anxiety in his eyes. Anthony Blakewood was a skinny gentleman in his late fifties, plenty of grey dominating the same jet-black hair Mercia had so loved in his son. The plush green robe he was wearing taunted her, a deliberate statement that he was already comfortably at home.

'Mercia,' he said, 'I am sorry for your father,' and she thought yes, so sorry you moved into his house no sooner than he died. He rested his hands on his hips, the loose sleeves of his robe billowing. 'But you are aware, I think, that your uncle has leased the manor to us?'

She pursed her lips. 'He has no right to do so.'

'That is not what Sir Francis says.' He bit his fingernails. 'You have seen the settlement?'

'I do not recognise his interpretation of it. You realise, of course, he is using you?'

Before he could reply, his wife Isabel strode into the room, her overlong skirt brushing the black and white tiles in her haste, her pointed bodice not quite properly fastened around her waist. Silk too, Mercia noticed. Had Isabel seen her on the driveway and changed to intimidate? As was the fashion, her skirt was open at the front to allow her petticoat to show; it was adorned with a fine gold braid.

'Why are you here?' Isabel seethed, talking over her husband. 'Did you lose your way in the village, or is your mind deserting you already, like your mother's?'

Mercia narrowed her eyes. 'It is I who should question your motive. This house should be Daniel's. Would you see him lose his inheritance?'

'Our reasons for being here are our own.' Isabel folded her arms; the bodice slipped slightly and she tugged it back into place. 'Return to your cottage. Your father is no longer here to protect you.'

Mercia breathed in deeply, composing herself. Even from these people, she had not expected such recalcitrance.

'Be under no illusion,' she said. 'This house belongs in my care and I will not easily give it up.' She held her mother-in-law's gaze. 'I will leave for today, but I would retrieve an item of mine from upstairs.' She forced a difficult smile. 'If you will let me.'

Anthony shook his head. 'The house and its contents belong to Sir Francis. He wants everything to stay where it is.'

'Come now, just one small thing.' She thought how she might best appeal to them. ''Tis for Daniel. For your grandson, if he still means anything to you.'

'Our grandson!' Isabel paced the room like a spinning top. 'Our grandson, who is being raised by the offspring of a traitor! God's death, my girl, if we had known what your family was we would never have allowed you to marry William.'

Mercia's restraint vanished. 'My father was no traitor.' She glowered at Isabel. 'We used to talk, you and I. We were both so excited when Daniel was born. Do you even remember? But now you blame me for everything, for the lost esteem you hoped to gain from marrying your son to my family, to me. I am surprised you even want to live in this house. But I suppose the temptation of occupying the grandest manor in the district was too strong for you, Isabel, all the same?'

Isabel came right up to her. 'You have no place in my family. None. And one day soon I will see my grandson taken from your care and placed into mine.'

Mercia went cold. 'What do you mean?'

'Get out of this house.'

'What do you mean about Daniel?'

'You will find out soon enough.'

Mercia looked at Anthony, but he was staring at the floor. She opened her mouth to retaliate but there was nothing more to gain. Instead she walked from the room, from the house, did not stop walking until she passed the iron gates and re-emerged onto the road. She looked back at her old home, fury and sadness competing in her mind. Damn Isabel, she thought. Damn her stubbornness. I will get what I want in any case. But she was troubled by her threats about Daniel.

An hour later she was on her horse, her mourning gown reluctantly discarded for her more practical loose riding dress, but she knew her father would not mind. His silent blessing urged her on as she sped past the battlefield at Edgehill, foregoing her usual pause to pray for the cousins she had lost in that fight, the very first of the civil war.

She galloped across Nathan's farmland, finding him outside a hay barn giving orders to his men. The violent thumping of the approaching horse made him look up. Seeing her determined face, he signalled to his labourers to move away.

'Nathan,' she cried, leaping to the ground. 'You have to help me break into Halescott Manor.'

Chapter Four

The silver clock on the sitting-room mantelpiece showed five minutes to nine as she left her cottage that evening. A moisture in the air clung to her cheek as she moved quietly down the lane, a dog barking across a field to her left. A full moon illuminated her path, but no one would have recognised her in her thick hood, let alone in the rest of her dark outfit.

At the arranged meeting place she saw Nathan leaning against the solitary elm tree on the edge of the village green, but as she drew near he darted behind its broad trunk. She looked around, but nobody was nearby.

'Why are you hiding?' she asked as she reached the elm. ''Tis only me.'

Nathan emerged from behind the trunk, dressed completely in black. 'By God's truth, Mercia, I thought you were a man.' He looked her up and down. 'What are you wearing?'

'Will's clothes. I never threw them all away.' She folded her arms, causing the musty shirt she was wearing under her cloak to rise up around her chest. 'Come now. I thought they would be better for this sort of thing than a heavy mourning dress.'

Nathan stared, before stifling a laugh. 'You are an amazing woman.' He shook his head. 'And somehow, I should not say this, but you look comely in those breeches.'

She hid her smile. 'Be serious. I want to do this as quickly as we can.'

They stole through damp beech woods to the back of the manor grounds, mud squelching underfoot as they made their way to where she knew the surrounding stone wall was lowest. But it was still six feet high, and failed girlhood attempts had taught her it was not simple to climb. So it proved. At the first attempt she slid back down the wall, the uneven stone grazing her palm, and at the second she fell, but Nathan caught her, holding her for a second before he released her to try again. This time she managed to cling onto enough footholds to ease herself over the top, but her anxious grip pulled a loose stone away on the descent, and she lost her footing, tumbling painfully into the garden.

Nathan jumped down as she was wiping the damp grass from her cloak, his hood fallen back over his shoulders. 'Are you hurt?' he asked.

'No,' she answered, although her right hip was aching. 'But these breeches will stain. And I have lost a button from the shirt.'

'Never mind that. Come on.'

They pressed onwards through the long grass, creeping alongside a twiggy hedge that led into a more formal part of the gardens. Passing through a leafy archway, they stole round a lily-covered pool flanked by statues of the Greek goddesses Athena and Artemis, their divine arms outstretched to each other on either side of the still water. Nearer the house they paused behind a large urn, observing through the wide crack running down its centre.

'There is a light in one of the upstairs windows,' said Nathan, gripping the pedestal of the urn. 'But the back parlour seems dark.' He looked at her. 'Your plan might work.'

'Of course it will. As long as they still have no dogs.'

'And the servants?'

'Hopefully abed. They should be on my side in any case. Most of them have been here since I was a child.' She paused. 'I do hope they will be treated well. Anthony has already brought in one of his own men.'

After a moment of reflection she stooped down, motioning for Nathan to follow, but he held out a restraining arm and moved in front. Mildly irritated, she lost her calm focus; a bird screeching in the woods behind made her whirl around, only to be confronted by a man looming out of the darkness. She began to back off until she noticed his body was made of leaves, merely a well-cut topiary bush. Thankful Nathan had not noticed her foolishness, she turned to follow him.

They reached the house. Mercia held her hand against the rough stone, taking strength from its keen familiarity, but she did not linger, keeping close against the wall until they arrived outside the parlour. She pointed out the window she knew was loose and Nathan rattled it, pulling it open with a sharp tug. He squeezed through the gap, manipulating his broad torso to fit. When he was on the other side Mercia pulled up her legs to follow, glad she was not wearing a dress.

No candle was shining in the parlour, but her eyes, already accustomed to darkness, easily made out the black oblong of her parents' fine dining table running the length of the room. Chests and cupboards surrounded it, full of decorative porcelain and plate. Mercia felt her anger rising again, anger that these things her family had earned were stolen from her, but she mastered herself, striding calmly from the room towards her goal, towards her hope.

They were heading for the Long Gallery on the top floor of the house. Through a small square hall they turned left past the bureau where she had written her very first letter under the proud eye of her father. She knew this house intimately. On their way up the grand mahogany staircase, she knew exactly which steps to jump to avoid creaks.

At the top of the first flight of stairs they passed by a landing which gave onto a suite of bedrooms, but the doors were shut and if anyone was within, nobody heard them. She ran her hand over the warmth of the balustrade as she ascended the second flight, feeling the pulse of her house, before passing through an undecorated room full of clutter and so into a huge vaulted space that stretched the whole breadth of the manor. Moonlight shone through three massive iron-framed windows onto the opposite wall.

Nathan whispered in her ear. 'Where now?'

'It should be towards the end.' She crept down the wainscoted gallery past a succession of portraits, but halfway down she stopped. 'Some of these portraits have come down. There are gaps.' She looked into the darkness. 'Where are they?'

'They must be somewhere. You said your uncle wanted everything to stay in the house.'

She nodded. 'Why don't you stand by the door in case anyone comes up?'

He moved off and she continued down the gallery. At the end of the long space she breathed out in relief as she saw a small picture still in the spot where her portrait was meant to be hanging. Encouraged, she removed it from the wall to examine it at the nearest window. Then she gasped. Expecting to see her childhood self on a white horse, she found herself looking on the image of her dead husband instead. Her parents-in-law must already have replaced her picture with one of their son.

Looking at the portrait of William, Mercia felt a moment of sadness and regret. He was depicted in his soldier's uniform, his horse to one

47

side, the fields of Oxfordshire stretching out behind him. His long black hair trailed across his forehead, his keen eyes looking directly outward at her. It was the painting Isabel had commissioned before he went on campaign – the year Mercia lost him. A similar picture hung in the bedroom of her cottage. But there was no time for sentimentality tonight. She put the portrait back and moved on, studying the other paintings nearby in case hers had merely been moved.

She was peering through the darkness at a fading representation of a youthful Lady Markstone when her husband's portrait fell to the oak-panelled floor with a crash. Cursing herself, she replaced the poorly rehung picture on the wall and stood still, listening. For a few seconds there was silence. But then a door creaking open downstairs resounded loud around the gallery. Her heart beat faster. Moments later, another creak, this time deeper, like a groan. Someone was coming up the stairs.

Nathan appeared beside her, making her jump.

'We have to get out,' he whispered. 'That picture made quite a noise.'

'We can't,' she hissed. 'I haven't found the portrait yet. It has been moved.'

A footstep echoed outside the gallery, a faint candlelight spilling through the open doorway, but no person as yet appeared, clearly deciding what to do. Thinking quickly, Mercia crept to William's portrait, removing it from the wall and setting it on the floor. She tapped Nathan's shoulder, motioning to him to back with her into a small storage room just behind them.

'Hopefully they will think it fell down by itself,' she whispered, daring a glimpse back from the store. A silhouetted figure had now entered the gallery, his teenage face just discernible in the weak light of his candle. 'It is Edward. My, he becomes more like William each year.'

Nathan put his finger over her lips. She frowned but kept silent, continuing to look out as Edward inched down the gallery until he paused beside the fallen portrait. He knelt to pick it up, but instead of repositioning it he slowly stroked his brother's face, his sad expression deepened by the inconsistent candlelight. Involuntarily Mercia cupped her hand to her mouth, sharing his pain. But the action caused her to stumble backwards and she scraped a boot against the smooth floor. Edward jerked his head in the direction of the noise. He set down the painting and approached.

There was no exit from the store other than the door they had entered by. Mercia crouched behind a wooden box to hide herself, but Nathan moved to the side of the door, pulling his hood over his head. As Edward entered, Nathan grabbed him across the chest with his right arm, clamping his other hand over the surprised boy's mouth. He dragged him into the middle of the room, kicking the dropped candle out with one swift movement.

'Quiet lad, or I'll break your neck. It wouldn't be the first time I've done it.' Nathan spoke in a gruff drawl, disguising his voice. Mercia was surprised: he must have learnt the accent during his army days.

Edward began to struggle, but Nathan moved his arm upwards towards the boy's throat and he became still.

'Good.' Nathan kept his voice low. 'I don't want to hurt you. Do you know who I am?'

Edward made a slight shake of his head.

'Better. Now I'm going to move my hand from your mouth. But if you cry out I can put just the right pressure on your throat to stop you for good and all.' He edged his other arm closer to Edward's neck. 'Do you understand?' Edward nodded and Nathan removed his hand.

'There is no one else here,' Edward stammered. 'No one to call to.'

'I know that's not true, boy, so don't lie again.' Nathan squeezed Edward's chest more tightly. 'But you needn't worry for your family. I just want something of value to sell. You'll have lots in this fine house.' He paused. 'I thought, perhaps, the picture of that young man I saw you fondling just now.'

Mercia could feel Edward's despair. 'No,' he said. 'Not that. It is precious to my mother and me.' His voice shook. 'Please. Nobody else could want it.'

'Very well.' Nathan relaxed his grip slightly. 'But listen. I've been in this house before, back in the war. There were some different pictures on the walls then. Where are they now?' Even through the darkness, Mercia could swear she saw him wink at her.

'In the room opposite this,' managed Edward. 'Mother removed what she did not like. Yes, take one of those.'

Hood up to hide her face, Mercia leapt from behind the box. Nathan replaced his hand around Edward's mouth before he could cry out. She dashed across the gallery into the opposite room, a void space that led to the western staircase, with a small window onto the gardens below. It took a few moments of feeling around before she found the missing pictures stacked haphazardly in a corner. Stifling the urge to clap, she flicked through them – her father in his military breastplate; her grandfather, standing in front of the manor house he himself had built; another of her father, this one with Lord Protector Cromwell and a group of unsmiling men; herself, the child Mercia, dressed as a lady.

Her heart pounding, she turned over the small picture but there was nothing on the back. She felt along the edges for any trace of a lump or imperfection, stopping when she came to a slight distinction in the texture of the canvas, a rough tear at its base. Was this it, what her father wanted her to find?

She was about to see if she could prise open the tear when she heard footsteps running down the gallery. Uncertain what was happening, she hurried back to the long room with the painting, meeting Nathan as he emerged from the store.

'I'm sorry,' he said, wincing as he rubbed at his stomach. 'My attention slipped. He will come back with help.' He lowered his hand and pointed at the painting. 'Is that it?'

'Yes.' She opened the adjacent window. 'But we had best leave before we investigate.'

'Mercia, we cannot jump from here. 'Tis three storeys high!'

She looked at him, then threw the painting from the window. It made no sound as it landed on the rose bush she knew was directly below.

'In case we are caught. Now this way.' She ran through the room where she had found the painting, ducking beneath a low-hanging beam to access the plain west staircase. They hurtled down to the first floor, swerving right into a bedroom she knew was unlikely to be in use – her own before she married – feeling past the bed for the hidden door the maidservants used to access the private chambers from their part of the house.

'Quickly,' she said, thrusting open the door to pass into an undecorated corridor beyond. She led Nathan along the narrow space to a workaday staircase, jumping two steps at a time to reach a dark passageway that came out into an exposed inner courtyard. Skidding across smooth stone slabs she tumbled into a damp cellar where she pushed off the thick columns that supported the ceiling to race through an open doorway and out of the house.

She emerged into fresh air, nobody in pursuit, hurrying to the rose bush where her portrait lay thankfully unpierced atop its bed of thorns. Then she and Nathan were gone, running round the pond, past Artemis and Athena, along the twiggy hedge, almost hurdling the stone wall in their eagerness to escape. Through the woods, past the elm, across the green, they didn't stop until they reached her cottage, throwing themselves against the garden wall, hands on their thighs, struggling to recover their breath.

Mercia gazed on her childhood image, a splendidly dressed girl riding a white unicorn through a sun-dappled forest glade, her bangle-covered wrists golden against the bustling sleeves of a flowing green cloak.

'No wonder Isabel took it down,' joked Nathan, warming himself at the sitting room fire. 'She would not want to look at that every time she walked past.'

'My father made it to look like a Saxon princess.' She smiled. 'He was obsessed with the Saxons. You know I am named Mercia after the old Saxon kingdom.' She paused, lost in thought. 'He said it was too beautiful a word to be a place alone.'

She fell silent, taking in the portrait of her infant self, the orange glow of the fire casting shadows over its bucolic scene. Rousing herself, she turned the painting over to show Nathan the imperfection in its back.

'I think there are two canvasses here,' he said, taking it. 'See? The actual painting at the front, and a blank one inserted at the back. And there, at that tear, is a gap.' He squeezed a finger inside it. 'Mercia, there's something inside.'

Holding her breath she leant closer, watching him reach into the tear to pull the back canvas away.

A hidden piece of paper slipped out, drifting straight for the blazing fire.

Chapter Five

For an instant Mercia stood paralysed as she watched her hopes fluttering towards the flames. Then both she and Nathan grasped for the wayward paper, knocking their forearms together but missing it entirely. She swooped again and this time the air was disturbed, altering the paper's descent. It came to rest just in front of the hearth.

'God's truth! We nearly lost it.' She picked up the paper, unfolding it against the light of a candle. Nathan cleared his throat and she stepped back from the flame.

''Tis a sort of letter,' she said. 'Written in Father's hand.' As she progressed through the contents the initial saddened creases of her face changed to an incredulous frown. When she had finished she fell into a chair, staring at the note.

'What is it?' Nathan looked at her but she stayed silent. 'Come, what?'

She looked up. 'What do you know of the King's art collection? The late King, I mean.'

Nathan shrugged. 'He bought a great number of paintings over the years, spending a lot of money in the process. Then after he was . . .' he hesitated.

'After he was executed. You can say it.'

'Well, after then, Cromwell sold them off to finance his own regime. Now the new King is restored he is trying to recover his father's collection.'

'The paintings went all over the country,' said Mercia. 'All over Europe, in fact. Even the King's old servants were given some in place of unpaid salary. It always amused me to think that a fine painting of the King could be hanging in someone's privy.'

'King Charles resplendent on his mighty throne. So what is in the note?'

She sucked in her lips. 'Do you recall the stories about the Oxford Section?'

'Of course. Everyone round here does.' He lapsed into a monotone, revisiting a well-known tale. 'When London declared for Parliament at the start of the war, the King moved his capital to Oxford. He brought his favourite paintings with him. They became known as the Oxford Section. After the war, Cromwell ordered the Section back to London to be sold with the rest. But they were burnt in a failed robbery on the way. Hell, Mercia, is this what the note is about?'

She nodded slowly. 'Father writes the Oxford Section may still exist.'

Nathan stared. 'How? Your father was in charge of investigating the robbery himself. I thought they found fragments of the paintings in the remains?'

'What we have been told is rather different to what father writes here.' She looked down at the note and read out loud.

January 1664

My dearest daughter,
I write this letter with a sad heart while you are absent with your cousin, uncertain if we will meet again. If you ever read it, I am

sorry for anything that has happened since that has caused you pain. Your happiness was ever foremost in my heart.

But time is short. I am informed by a knowledgeable friend that on a whim the King wishes me away to the Tower on charge of high treason. Why this sudden reversal of my fortune afflicts me now I cannot explain. It appears the King's amnesty has been stolen from me by my enemies, diverting me from the hope I had nurtured of restoring my standing through the use of some ancient knowledge of mine. In the event I am now unable to act on this opportunity, I shall hide this note so you may find it and act yourself.

The Oxford Section of the late King's great collection of art was not lost as all believe. It is said that when the soldiers escorting the Section to London to join in the Great Sale of Goods passed through our Shire, they were attacked by Villains, and in the fight that followed, the soldiers in their negligence did set the Section ablaze with their own unhappy muskets. This is not the truth, so I swear by Almighty God. The real misfortune was that one of those guards turned on his fellow men and slaughtered them as they marched, robbing the Section himself, and fleeing into the Greenwood with his gains.

As you know, Sir Edward Markstone and I were appointed to examine the tragic event, but finding no trace of the Villain nor any word of the Section itself, Cromwell ordered that the Incident be forgotten, indeed that a lie of highway robbery be devised, not wanting a Disastrous abuse by one of his own soldiers to come to light with our great victory at Worcester so near in memory. We never heard of the Section again, save a faraway rumour when Cromwell died, but we had no occasion to investigate. The King was returning.

Knowing the Section had not been destroyed, but instead hidden or treacherously sold to Buyers without scruple, I decided to discover it myself if I could, having recently come into some information relating to the theft these many years since it occurred. I cannot say what information this is, as should anyone else discover this note, it may be dangerous to the source of it. I also could not count on Edward Markstone to assist: as you know, he is recently dead, poisoned they say by his wife, although I am doubtful of that. There were difficulties. But I deviate from my purpose.

I made brief enquiries in London before receiving the unwelcome news of my arrest. I am hopeful I can convince them I am not their enemy, but if this ends badly, I know full well what your uncle is capable of. News of the Section may be a road to the King's favour. You will think I have left you scant information, and you will be right, but your mind is sharp and your spirit is tenacious. Discover what you can, but have a care. Life is precious, and you most precious of all.

'God's death,' said Nathan. 'If those paintings do exist, think what it would mean.' He began to pace the room. 'We should tell Sir Jeremy.'

'No,' said Mercia. 'Don't you see? This could be the key to winning the King's support against my uncle.' She rose from her chair, a steadfast resolve animating her face. 'Father knew all this would happen. I am going to find those paintings myself.'

Drizzle spattered Mercia's black hat as she rode her horse Maggie to Warwick the next morning, intending to visit her mother. The rain suited her low mood, all the enthusiasm of last night washed away as she was forced to confront reality. Her father's death had left a gap inside her that she knew would take time to close. But as the grey horse trotted north, the steady clopping of its hooves drilled into her a keener determination to take up her father's mission, not only for Daniel and herself, but for her mother too, unjustly evicted from her home.

As she rode past Banbury Cross, Isabel's words came through the chill air with a vindictive spirit. In truth her mother-in-law had frightened her. She had many friends in the county, and she was a practiced manipulator. She could mount a powerful case to gain custody of Daniel if she wished. Mercia briefly thought how easily she could secure a protective influence by becoming mistress to Sir William Calde, but she dismissed the notion immediately. While there was another option, however uncertain, she would take that chance.

Pushing Maggie hard, she arrived in Warwick just as the two churches of St Mary and St Nicholas were competing to ring out their bells for noon. Crossing the River Avon she turned right into Mill Street, heading for the only place she thought her mother could be, her dead spinster aunt's town house on the south side of town, also part of Sir Francis's estate since he had acquired it two years before. Mercia had always believed the inheritance was legitimate. Now, who could be sure?

When she knocked on the door of the black and white timber-framed house she was relieved to find she was right. After a brief word with Agnes, her mother's maidservant, she climbed the stairs to find Lady Goodridge in a small second-floor bedroom. She was staring out onto the courtyard garden, the turrets of the famous castle where her distant Beauchamp forebears had helped shape the long-gone age of the Plantagenet kings visible on the hill beyond. Today, weak rays of sunlight splashed through the patterned window of this modest home, disappearing into the faded brown dress that wrapped her gaunt physique.

'Hello, Mother.' Mercia entered the bedroom not knowing how much Lady Goodridge would recall of recent events. She had suffered in the civil wars, more than most, retreating when all was done into a life of delusions. When Sir Rowland had been taken away two months before she had simply refused to believe it. Mercia worried that the loss of the manor house would be the final assault her affected mind could withstand.

Lady Goodridge turned on hearing her daughter come in. 'Mercia!' Her dull eyes brightened. 'Wait, let me find Elizabeth for you.'

'You need not look for my doll, Mother. She is safe in her house.' Mercia sat on the small bed, patting the bright embroidered cover to signal her mother to join her. When she did she took her hand. 'Mother. Do you know what has happened?'

Lady Goodridge looked away. 'He will come back. I know what you said before, but he will.'

'I am sorry, Mother. But he will not.' Mercia looked at her mother's sunken cheek, stroking her hand, not knowing what to say for the best.

'Agnes says he is coming to see me,' said Lady Goodridge, after a pause.

'She said Francis is coming to see you. Your brother. He has taken Halescott for himself. He expects you to live here now.' She spoke slowly, as though to a child, hating herself for it. 'Do you understand?'

Lady Goodridge looked back at her, a faint smile deepening the creases of her face. 'Yes. Francis is coming soon.'

Mercia closed her eyes. Why could her mother not see what was happening? For that instant she felt crushed, as if the whole world were against her. But then she opened her eyes and saw her mother looking at her with a deep concern. She forced herself to focus.

'Mother, you are right. Sir Francis is coming here.' She gripped her hands. 'He will say you are to stay in this house now, but I am going to fight it.'

Fear briefly dilated Lady Goodridge's eyes. 'Don't fight, Mercia, don't fight.' She shook her head vigorously, loose white strands of hair falling from under her cap.

'I am sorry.' Mercia bit her lip, scared at her mother's reaction. She changed the subject, wondering if her mother would know anything about the contents of her father's letter. 'Mother, do you recall the Oxford Section? When the King's paintings were thought burnt in the wood?'

Lady Goodridge frowned. 'Which King? There have been so many.'

'Charles, Mother. The first. The one who raised his standard at Nottingham when I was little, with the Catholic wife nobody liked.'

'But he was killed, Mercia. Do you not remember when your father came to tell us the news? We were feeding those birds.'

'Yes I do.' She smiled in reassurance. 'But the Oxford Section – did father ever say anything to you about that? Did Sir Edward Markstone?'

'Edward Markstone was—but never mind that.'

She raised an eyebrow. 'Mind what?'

'Oh, he was brutal.' She pursed her lips. 'They say he beat his wife. But then she could be a sly creature. He was never other than a gentleman with me.'

Mercia sighed. 'Mother, please try to remember.'

Lady Goodridge thought awhile. 'Those paintings that were burnt, you say? Your father said Cromwell was livid. Why don't you ask him?'

Mercia hung her head, loosening her grip on her mother's hands.

'Perhaps this is hopeless,' she muttered. 'Perhaps I should just settle for what life has given me.'

'No!' Lady Goodridge looked sharply at her daughter, speaking with a sudden lucidity Mercia had not heard for months. 'Child, you are in your own hand. Your father and I, we disagreed about your books, but he was right. You are a beautiful woman, you have a mind the equal of any of those Oxford scholars. Do not give in, not like I did. I have always been proud of you. Always.'

The unexpected praise penetrated to Mercia's soul. She forgot about the Oxford Section, seizing the chance to talk about all those things her mother never seemed to remember, about her achievements, her disappointments, about Daniel's schooling, about how she had helped Nathan through his time of grief. But when she ventured again to talk of her father, Lady Goodridge's eyes dulled, and when Mercia spoke of her feelings, she did not reply, instead walking to the window to look out on the garden, choosing to forget Mercia was there.

From long experience Mercia knew the sign, that there was nothing more she could say. For a moment she sat on the bed, alone. But she too had a choice, and it was to fight, whatever her mother said, lest the sadness overwhelm her. Kissing her mother farewell she walked from the room, vowing she would see her back in Halescott where she belonged.

Dark clouds were obscuring the setting sun when she arrived back at the cottage. She was unsurprised to see Nathan's blood bay horse tied up outside, its nose in a bag of oats. In the sitting room Nathan himself was flicking through the Anglo-Saxon history she had taken from the manor house, waiting for her return. She told him what she had decided to do, how seeing her mother had convinced her. Now she had a favour to ask. He questioned. She explained. He argued. He agreed.

In the street she found Daniel playing at ball with one of the village boys. She called him over and slowly stroked his hair.

'I shall have to go to London again, Danny, just for a few days.' She knelt down to look at him. 'Would you like to stay on Nathan's farm while I am away? He asked if you could help him with the cows and the sheep, you were so good and strong at it the last time.'

Daniel's face shone with excitement. 'When?'

'That depends on the coach. And – once I am ready.' She stood, letting her hand run across his shoulders. 'Go and play now. But not too long, it will be dark soon.'

He ran back to his game. Mercia watched him, and she could tell he was thinking of all the things he would do on the farm. She smiled inwardly that he was so keen to leave the cottage to stay with Nathan, but she remembered how much she had loved staying away from home with her cousins, before the war.

Nathan came out to join her. 'What did he say?'

'He is looking forward to it.'

'Good.' He sighed. 'But I still say I could be of help to you in London. How your father described it, looking for those paintings could be dangerous. Especially you being a—'

'A woman?' Mercia laughed. 'I should think that gives me perfect licence to meddle in others' affairs, is that not how some of your kind view our weaker sex?' She softened her tone. 'Do not worry, Nat. Bethany will come with me. And I need someone here who can stand up to Anthony and Isabel if they come looking. You know they will accuse me of neglecting Daniel, even though he wants to spend his time with you.'

'I fear that may be part of their problem.' He ran a hand through his long hair. 'But very well. And good luck.'

Three days later she buried her father. She did not see the body; she did not want to look on the headless corpse. He was buried in a simple tomb alongside his father and grandfather in the village churchyard. Sir Jeremy and three other of Sir Rowland's friends carried his black oak coffin through the ivy-covered lychgate, the smaller, head-sized casket on top joining his bodily remains in their eternal rest.

Mercia stood with Daniel by the grave, a steady rain falling on them as relentless as his tears when she had finally told him his grandfather was gone, but he did not cry today. Nathan stood behind at a distance, head bowed in prayer. Lady Goodridge was still in Warwick, her fragile mind unable to attend.

When the mourners had gone, and Daniel was back with Bethany in the warmth, Mercia knelt alone at her father's grave.

'I promise you, Father. I will put all this right. I will make you proud of me. I swear it.'

And then she left him in the ground, though she carried his soul forever in her heart.

Part Two

Chapter Six

Songbirds chirruped a welcoming greeting as Mercia's coach juddered into London under glorious evening sunshine. The packed coach halted at the now familiar terminus of the Saracen's Head, but this time she was not staying at the inn. A few days after the funeral she had ridden to thank Sir Jeremy for his efforts in bringing her father home, and over a cordial glass of wine he had offered her his London town house for the upcoming days, although he had known nothing useful about the Oxford Section when she had asked. Alighting from the coach in the shadows of the inn's stable yard, she paid a boy a silver penny to find her a hackney carriage for the final leg of the journey, and a penny more for the feat of carrying her heavy luggage from coach to carriage under such a sparse physique.

Bethany had never visited the capital before, and the amazement on her face as she leant through the carriage window to take in the dirt and the noise added to the infectious energy Mercia herself was absorbing from the vast numbers of people in the streets. The new Holborn roadworks were aggravating the usual London traffic jams, but the driver pulled out past the queue of drays ahead of them to cut into Drury Lane across an oncoming cart, bringing them to the

Queen Street town house before sunset. Bethany went straight to the kitchen, professing an affinity with the pans and the pots.

For her part, Mercia slouched in a comfortable leather-padded armchair in the first-floor parlour room, thinking through her next steps. Although he had renewed his enquires into the Oxford Section before his arrest, her father had left her with scant helpful information, presumably in deference to his mysterious source. But his letter had mentioned one person by name: Sir Edward Markstone, his fellow investigator from the time of the Section's loss.

The slight problem of Sir Edward's death did not deter her. She reasoned he might have revealed something to his wife, or perhaps her own father had, the Markstones being friends of the family. She remembered visiting their grand house when she was a girl, peeking out from behind her father just as the Markstones' elder son Robert was descending their mahogany staircase, his jawline firm, his hair an intense black, his fashionable clothes tight on his slender frame. Open-mouthed, she had fallen in love, no matter that he was seventeen and she was eleven, she could wait. Except he died the year after, fighting for the King at the battle of Marston Moor. Amongst the thousands of massacred troops, his parents never found his body.

Lady Markstone was a prisoner in the Tower of London, and so there was no escaping a return to that terrible place. Despite recent memories, Mercia forced herself to the castle gates the next morning to enquire after an audience. She walked swiftly over Tower Hill, her face veiled by her loose hood of mourning black, the cloth billowing in the gusting wind. At the site of her father's execution she offered up a silent prayer, the sorrowful locale now bereft of voyeurs. No one was to be sacrificed at that vengeful altar today.

When she pulled the hood from her face at the Tower entrance the guard smirked.

'Good morning, Mrs Blakewood. Come to strike Dicken again, have you?'

Recognising him from her previous attempt to gain entry – the day she had finished in a cell – she kept her composure. 'I was hoping to see Lady Markstone,' she said, holding the guard's gaze. 'It would be some comfort to me, as I was denied a meeting with my father.'

His cockiness faltered. 'I'll see if I can . . . I'll have to ask the Lieutenant.' He bit his lip. 'Can you come back tomorrow to get his answer?'

'I can.' She was about to leave when a thought struck her. 'Has anyone else been allowed to see her of late? Anyone close to the family?'

The guard's smirk returned. 'She poisoned her husband, Mrs Blakewood. There's not many want to visit, though folk come and go. Some folk lower than others, if you take my meaning.'

She waited for him to continue. 'Such as?'

The guard laughed. 'The only fellow who's wanted to see her this week was some princock claiming she owed him wages. I soon kicked him out on his arse.'

She frowned. 'So he worked for her?'

'For her husband, I believe.' The guard grinned, tossing his spear-like partisan from side to side. 'I don't know, and I don't much care. All I know is he said he'd see me in the Anchor any afternoon I wanted.' He drew himself up. 'I said there was no problem with that.'

'I see.' Ignoring his swagger, she passed the guard a sixpence and walked away, thinking.

By afternoon she had made up her mind. Whispering an apology to her father she changed from her mourning dress into a less noticeable grey jacket and skirt. She felt guilty, but her black petticoat was still visible through the skirt's front slit, and she was wearing the mourning ring she had first put on at the funeral, made of black enamel wending through gold. The inscription on the inside was simple but heartfelt: *RG – 1664 – Always with me in Hope.*

It was time to look forward. Pulling shut the town house door she went into the street, waiting only a few moments before a hackney carriage came into view around the corner. She called out to the driver and he swerved across the cobbles to pull up beside her. Peering down from his perch, his hair fell so low over his eyes she was surprised he knew where to steer the horses.

'Where to?' he mumbled, brushing the mop aside.

'The Anchor, please.'

'Which one love?' He stared at her smart outfit. 'There's two in town, neither of them much welcoming. You sure you got it right?'

She decided it would be more polite to lie than to tell him to mind his own. 'I am to meet my brother outside a tavern with that name. Only, he did not tell me where it was.'

The driver scoffed. 'I'd leave him there. Bunch of drunken sailors in those hives, whichever it is.'

'Still, I need to go. Try whichever is closer to the Tower of London.'

He looked at her and sniffed. 'The Anchor then, my lady. But you'll pay me in advance.'

Fifteen minutes later she was standing in a dingy street set back from Pudding Lane: more like an alleyway, the bulging roofs of the surrounding buildings cut out most of the light. Directly opposite, she could just make out a faded anchor on a lopsided sign that hung above what passed for the Anchor tavern door, its lintel half-caved in.

Further down the sorry row, a mangy crowd of cats was screeching over a trapped discovery, pawing at a pile of rotting wood.

And yet Mercia did not hesitate as she pushed open the collapsing door. Inside, the light was dim, but as her eyes adjusted to the gloom she was surprised to see the decoration was not as dilapidated as the exterior would suggest. The tables and chairs appeared new, the walls recently painted. The clientele were a different matter. Despite the afternoon hour several unshaven men were already indulging in drink, smoking tobacco or gambling at dice. The place reeked of stale beer, her boots sticking to the floor as she walked towards the serving hatch. She was the only woman, aside from the two shifting their weight between the laps of leering men, and they were not here for the ale.

The door banged shut behind her. Of a sudden the entire room was silent, some of the men roving her body with lascivious eyes. The two whores jumped from their prey, ready to evict this interloper from their personal domain. Mercia held her nerve, but she felt increasingly uncomfortable the further she came from the door. Out of the corner of her eye she noticed a pair of men nod at each other and stand. She glanced around, looking for another exit should the need arise, but there was none save the door she had entered by.

'Strange place to see a lady,' said the innkeeper from behind the hatch. He leant over to one of the two customers sitting in front of him, not taking his tiny eyes from her. 'I wonder, John, if she ain't wandered' – he chuckled at his pun – 'into the wrong establishment?'

'Seems that way.' The man called John looked her up and down. 'What's your business, love? Not often we get such a rum mort here.' When she looked blank he sniggered. 'A pretty lady, love.'

Mercia ignored him, addressing the innkeeper. 'I am looking for a man.'

He laughed. 'There'll be plenty here looking for you.'

'A particular man, then.'

'What's his name?'

'I don't know.'

'Well then, what's he look like?'

She felt herself reddening. 'I don't know.'

The innkeeper glanced at John. 'By the Lord, what *do* you know?'

'Only that he is owed money by Lady Millicent Markstone.'

'Hangs around with high-born folk, does he?' The innkeeper leant in closer. 'Who would you be to want to find him?'

'A friend, I hope.'

He began to reply, but his eyes flicked over her shoulder and he turned away, busying himself with wiping an already clean tankard. She looked round to see the two men who had risen from their seats standing directly behind her. The larger of the two rested his hand on her shoulder, caressing it with his tobacco-stained fingertips.

'Now then, my pretty ladybird,' he said, 'how 'bout we go round the alley? You can help me and my mate out.' He smiled, toying with a ringlet of her hair.

Her back to them, Mercia stood completely still. 'I am not such a woman.'

The stocky man laughed, the smell of stale smoke reeking through the gaps in his teeth. 'Well this is far from home, love, and what I say to you is what you does.' He pressed himself against her and groaned, running the tip of his tongue over her ear. 'Christ, I need this.'

She closed her eyes, determining her response. She felt an iciness inside, a rising fear, but she had reason to hate men such as these, and in no way would she be cowed by them. Bringing her right hand to her mouth she let out a faint whimper, feigning timidity. Then she slammed her elbow backwards into the man's stomach, shocking him into a quite different groan. She tensed, sliding away while the man's angered friend leapt round and pulled back his fist to strike.

He did not get the chance. As he was about to swing, the second customer at the hatch jumped from his stool, sending it tumbling to the floor. He grabbed the man's forearm with his left hand, bringing his right up in a fist to connect with the man's cheek. Blood sprang from the wounded man's mouth as he screamed in pain, a loose tooth clattering to the dusty inn floor, and he staggered backwards, giving Mercia's defender time to pick up the stool and swing it. One hard thrust into the larger man's stomach was enough. The two fled from the tavern in shame, crying retribution.

Breathing hard with excitement, the man who had come to her aid thumped down his stool. He was fairly young, messy blonde hair running across his brow. When he turned to look at her, the intensity of his green eyes was startling.

'That was a smart trick.' He pointed at her elbow. 'How did a woman learn to do that?'

She held his gaze. 'I know a few things.'

'I'm sure.' He ran a rough hand over his hair. 'Now why don't you tell me what you want with me?'

'What I want with—? Ah.' The edges of her mouth creased into a constrained smile. 'You are the man who wished to see Lady Markstone.'

'The same.' He glanced around. 'But before we talk, let's get out of here. Not everyone will appreciate my fighting skills.'

She hesitated, uncertain whether to trust him. The pause was long enough for one of the whores to snatch up a tankard of beer and throw it in her direction. The glass was full but the aim was poor, and in mid flight the beer spilt over a group of hooded men playing at dice. As one they leapt up and drew knives. It was all the convincing Mercia needed. She followed the young man into the street.

A grey patchwork of clouds had gathered in the sky, rendering the street still more depressing than earlier, but at least the mewling cats had moved on. Mercia's companion led her to the main road, away from the tavern and anyone who might run after them. Her would-be assailants were nowhere in sight.

'Thank you for your assistance,' she said as they walked. 'I am grateful.'

'Don't thank me. I helped because you said you were looking for me, something about Markstone.' He looked wistfully back down the crowded street, his fingers thrust into the loose belt that encircled his knee-length coat. 'That was one of my favourite drinking dens. Thanks to you, I don't think I'll be welcome there again.'

She felt a twinge of guilt. 'I am sorry.'

He stared at her from under his close-fitting hat. 'You clearly had no idea what a place like that is like. I mean, look at you. I bet you even have money hidden in that fine dress.'

She did, in her pockets. She stepped away, almost tripping over a young fruit seller passing by with her basket.

'By the Lord!' He shook his head. 'Don't worry, I'm not about to rob a defenceless woman.' He raised an eyebrow. 'Although not so defenceless. That elbow must have hurt. Come, how do you know such a move?'

She looked away down the street; a soot-covered sweep had stopped the fruit seller and was examining her produce. 'Because once I was powerless,' she said at last. 'And I promised myself I would never be so again.'

His brash demeanour softened. 'Let's keep moving. We don't

want anyone coming after us. Then you can tell me your business.'

'Agreed, if you tell me your name.'

He held open his arms in a gesture of introduction. 'Nicholas Wildmoor, friend to the crazed. Now come, before you cause even more havoc.'

Mercia watched as her new acquaintance devoured a huge plate of pork chops and peas. Her smaller dish of boiled carp was already just bones, and she found his appetite fascinating. The remnants of the oysters they had already eaten – Mercia's three and Nicholas's seven – lay discarded at their side. Finally, Nicholas wiped his chin and looked up.

'Cannot keep your eyes off me, eh?' He reached for his tankard. 'And plying me with drink. I doubt your motives, my lady.'

She smiled. 'I am a widow, Mr Wildmoor. My motives are straightforward. I merely want to ask some questions.'

He looked around at their comfortable surroundings: several tables, mostly empty, were laid out in the white-walled room, the dim light of dusk coming through the simple window beside them. 'Is this a regular place for you?' he asked. ''Tis a step up from the Anchor.' He held up a two-pronged utensil. 'They even have forks here. Where I eat, we only get a knife.'

She shuffled in her chair. 'Do you live in the city?'

He nodded. 'Just outside the wall. To the north, round Cow Cross. I don't recommend you go there.' He looked her up and down, sucking the last morsel of meat from his fork. 'Well then. You seem to know the Markstones owe me money. Will answering these questions help me get it?'

She hesitated. 'I'll see if I can talk to Lady Markstone on your behalf. She is a friend of my family.'

He set down his fork. 'Then ask away.'

'Let's start with how you know Lady Markstone.'

He shrugged. 'I don't particularly. I did farrier work for her husband, the man everyone is saying she did in. I didn't get paid before he died.'

'I see.' She arched an eyebrow. 'So you tried to get to his widow instead. Given her situation, that seems a little unfair.'

He looked at her askance. 'She owes me. Maybe you don't need money, but I have rent to pay.'

She glanced down, embarrassed at her thoughtlessness. 'I'm sorry, I should not have—'

'Don't worry. Please – carry on.'

She smiled at him, grateful. 'How long did you work for Sir Edward?'

'Depends how you look at it.' He blew out his cheeks. 'I first knew him on the ships, when I looked after the horses we took on board. I used to be a sailor, you see, back when Cromwell was in charge. Sir Edward was captain of the *Hero*, the same ship I served on.'

She studied his face. 'You must have been young.'

'Old enough. Then, like most of the lads, I didn't get what was due me after we were let go. Story of my life, it seems.'

Feeling sorry for him, Mercia gestured to the serving girl to bring more ale. The girl ignored her, persisting in her conversation at another table, until Nicholas whistled across and smiled, at which she sped into swift service and brought over the drinks.

'Thanks.' Nicholas took a sip, returning to his story. 'Start of last year I ran into a soldier friend from the *Hero*. He said he'd done some work on Markstone's estate himself, that the noble sir was a charitable fellow, and why didn't I see if he had a job for me? So I approached him, cap in hand. He said he'd be pleased to help an English sailor. Not that he remembered me from before, of course. He never dirtied himself much with us tars.'

'Tars?'

'Sailors. Short for tarpaulin, the clothes we wore.' He took a glug of the deep-brown ale. 'But you didn't come to hear about me.'

'No, but 'tis an interesting story.' She sipped her own drink, setting it down on the rickety table. 'So,' she said, trying to sound nonchalant, 'when you worked for Sir Edward, did he ever talk about his past?'

He peered at her over the rim of his tankard. 'What part of his past?'

She thought back to her father's letter. 'Around the time of the battle at Worcester. That would be thirteen years ago – 1651.'

He considered. 'Well, I know he fought for Parliament in the war. Course, when I was his farrier he was all for the return of the new King, raving about how wonderful he is.'

'A lot of people who fought for Cromwell changed their minds.' She smiled. 'Whether they are truly converts to the cause, or just because of convenience, 'tis not always easy to tell.'

Nicholas laughed, chinking his tankard against hers. 'True. But really, I had little to do with him or his wife. They owned horses but didn't ride out much.' He looked at her. 'Why is '51 so special?'

She hesitated, unsure how much she should reveal to a man she had only just met. But the drink had loosened her tongue enough that she was happy to talk.

'In 1651 your former master helped to investigate a robbery. Some paintings were stolen. I am trying to discover what happened.'

He pushed aside his ale. 'What paintings?'

'King Charles. Charles the first. He owned a huge art collection.'

'Everyone knows that.'

'Well then, the Oxford Section.'

'The Oxford what?'

'Come, you must have heard of it. The King's favourite paintings that he kept at Oxford. They were supposedly burnt on their way to be sold.'

He shook his head.

'What?' She stared at him. 'It was famous. The most cherished paintings in the whole collection.'

'1651, you say.' She nodded. 'In 1651 I was thirteen years old, living in no more than a pit. I didn't have much interest in paintings. I was more interested in staying alive. Look, what is this about?'

Mercia tapped at the tabletop. What had she to lose by telling him what she knew? In truth it was hardly anything, and the thought of confiding in this rough-edged man was somehow – enticing. She rested her elbows on the table and leant forward. 'Your old master was part of a cover up. Everyone was told the Oxford Section was burnt, but it wasn't. It was stolen by one of the soldiers who was meant to be guarding it.'

'Devious!' Nicholas leant in nearer. 'But I still don't see what this has to do with me.'

'Maybe nothing.' She could see right into his eyes; realising how close their faces were, she sat hastily back. 'I know 'tis unlikely, but did you ever come across anything relevant when you worked for Sir Edward? Anything about paintings, or a theft perhaps?'

He tilted his head. 'If you're a friend of the family as you claim, why all these questions now?'

She began to regret her candidness. 'I only found out about it recently. My father investigated the robbery with Sir Edward at the time, but nothing was discovered.'

He frowned. 'So why not ask your father?'

She looked away, any cheerfulness she had felt evaporating. 'I cannot.'

'Why not? Who is he? And while I'm the one asking questions, who are you for all that?'

She looked through the window. 'It does not matter.'

'It does if you want me to help. You know who I am. Fair is fair.'

She watched as a silhouetted bird flew past, alighting on a nearby rooftop. 'I am Mercia Blakewood, if that means anything.'

'No, but 'tis a pretty name. And your father?'

She was going to refuse to answer when she felt a surge of filial pride. Why should she keep silent? Turning from the window she looked directly at him. 'My father is dead. He was Sir Rowland Goodridge.'

Nicholas banged both fists on the table and pushed back his chair in surprise. 'What, the fellow who just had his head—on Tower Hill? You're his daughter?' His eyes flitted to her clothing. 'But you're in grey.'

'I am not in mourning because I do not want attention.' She looked around the room. 'Please, be quiet.'

'But I was there!' he continued. 'And not three weeks later here you are looking into some supposed crime from the past.' He shook his head, but his lips were smiling. 'You have some nerve.'

Her face set. 'So now you know, will you answer my question? Did you ever hear anything about the Oxford Section?'

He paused for a moment, thinking. Then his smile broadened to a grin. 'Mercia Blakewood. My new friend.'

She frowned. 'Well?'

'Being honest, I would have to say that the answer to your question—'

77

'Speak, man!'

'The answer to your question is no.'

She threw herself back in her chair. 'Wonderful.'

He chuckled. 'But I can still help you, I think.'

'How?'

'Well, if I was looking into this mystery – me, a lowly farrier, and not a noble lady such as yourself – I'd go back to the robbery itself. Do you know who the thief was?'

'Unfortunately not.'

'I'd say that was a good place to start.'

She narrowed her eyes. 'And how would you, a lowly farrier, propose to go about starting it?'

'It was an army escort, right?' He raised a playful eyebrow. 'So ask another soldier. There are plenty of them about.'

Chapter Seven

'Where are you taking me?'

Mercia was struggling to keep up as she followed Nicholas the long length of Thames Street. She was wearing pattens underfoot, their chunky iron bars raising her boots above the mud of the road, but she was unaccustomed to using them over such distances, and the going was tiresome. Fortunately, Nicholas was a master, forcing people aside so she could walk under the overhangs of the houses and shops, helping her avoid the sewerage that periodically rained down from above.

'Not far now,' he called as he turned into Benet's Hill, passing St Benet's church where Inigo Jones, the great architect, had been buried twelve years before. Soon after, the great bulk of the massive St Paul's Cathedral that Jones had helped maintain came into view and they emerged onto the surrounding square.

Despite Jones's efforts, the huge church was in a sorrowful condition, sadly neglected in recent years. What should have been the city's foremost place of worship instead hulked over its flock, forlorn. Nicholas weaved his way through the shouting crowds to the cathedral's west side. Here, on the steps of Jones's new portico, several beggars sat huddled around the towering columns, calling for alms from worshippers entering the church.

'Time to bring out your money,' he said.

She stepped back. 'Why?'

'One of these poor lads served in the army. What he doesn't know about soldiers . . . let's just say he knows a lot.'

They approached a grimy, cross-legged man with very short ginger hair. Wearing a faded jerkin that seemed more holes than cloth, he was beckoning to passers-by with his one remaining arm to add to the scarce coin in the cap on the step beside him.

'Amputated in the war,' said Nicholas. 'That was fifteen years ago and he's still on the streets. Such folk fight readily for their masters, then when all's done they're cast adrift. London is full of old soldiers like him.'

Mercia looked on the beggar with compassion. 'You think he can help?'

'If you help him, yes.' Nicholas crouched down to the piteous figure. 'Hello, Michael. How've you been?'

'Nick, you old rogue.' The beggar looked pleased to see him. 'Not seen you for a while.'

Nicholas shrugged. 'I got a job.'

'Good for you.' Michael glanced between him and Mercia. 'Got any grigs?'

'Don't make me laugh. Who has farthings these days?'

'Any tokens, then?'

Nicholas pointed up at Mercia. 'This lady wants to ask a question. She'll pay you for it.'

'Oh yes?'

Feeling sorry for the amputee, Mercia passed him a silver shilling, worth a whole twelve pence. It was so old Elizabeth I's face adorned the front, but now the King had recalled all the coins hammered during Cromwell's regime, money was becoming scarce, particularly the smallest denominations such as halfpence and farthings. Enterprising merchants were producing tokens of their own for housewives to use in their daily shop.

'That's generous.' Michael's voice was croaky, hoarse from years of calling out. 'What do you want to know, love?'

She sat on the step beside him. An unpleasant odour rose from his jerkin, but she shuffled closer all the same. 'Hello, Michael. Nicholas says you served in the war.'

'That's right.' Michael nodded. 'Lot of good it did.'

'Do you remember around the time of the Worcester Fight?'

'I was down here by then.' He coughed into a tattered piece of cloth that was lying on the step. 'Got my arm blown away at Dunbar the year before. Cromwell's great victory over the Scots.' He scratched at his stump. 'Changed my life, sure enough. But ask your question. I had mates at Worcester.'

'I'm sorry.' Her father had been with Cromwell on the Dunbar campaign. For all she knew this man could have been under his command. 'There was an incident around then. A coach caught on fire. It was carrying the King's paintings.'

He set down the cloth; it was as black as soot. 'You don't mean the Oxford Section? That robbery gone wrong?'

She looked at Nicholas. 'See, it was famous.' He pulled a face and she turned back to Michael. 'Do you recall anything about it? About the men who guarded the coach, maybe? They would have been soldiers, perhaps fought alongside your friends.'

He rocked back and forth. 'I know quite a few things, me.'

A twinge of excitement stirred. 'Could you tell me?'

'Perhaps.' He looked at the coins in his cap.

'Now, Michael.' Nicholas stood up. 'She gave you a shilling. That'll get you a good dinner and you know it.'

'Bah.' The beggar shuffled on the step. 'I don't know much myself, is what I mean to say.' He coughed again. 'But the man who was in charge of the escort, him I do know. We all do, us old lot. He's a gunsmith now. Colonel Stephen Fell.'

Nicholas grinned. 'Fell off what?'

'Fell's his name, you little arsworm.'

'You make it sound like he's still alive,' said Mercia, ignoring the joke. 'I thought all the guards were dead.'

'Of course he's alive.' Michael shook his head. 'Those highwaymen killed the rest, didn't they? But the lucky bastard lived, even if he couldn't fight any more. He came to London too, and doing much better than me.' He sniggered. 'He sells arms, and here's me begging for alms with one arm.' He looked at Mercia. 'Why do you want to know?'

'It doesn't matter,' said Nicholas. 'You have your shilling. But thanks.'

The veteran shrugged, turning his attention to other passers-by. Thanking him herself, Mercia followed Nicholas round the side of the dilapidated cathedral, dodging the cheese merchants who were busy distracting their customers' attention to slip semi-green slices in their unsuspecting baskets.

'That was very helpful,' she said. 'Thank you.'

'It was, wasn't it?' Nicholas smiled. 'You still don't know who the thief was, mind.'

'But this Fell should, if it was a solider under his command. Do you—no, thank you.' She waved away a smartly dressed man who was patting her sleeve, trying to sell her a trinket box. 'Do you know where the gunsmith quarter is?'

'Just outside Aldgate,' said Nicholas. 'I'll take you there.'

'There is no need. You have been kind enough already.' She sighed, wrenching her arm from the persistent hawker. 'Will you stop that?'

'She said no.' Nicholas grabbed the peddler by the shoulders and pushed him away; almost stumbling, the man shook his fist and swore, but Nicholas lunged forward and he scurried on his way. 'See,' he said, brushing at his hands, 'London is dangerous. It would be on my conscience to let a woman wander the rough streets alone.'

She scoffed. 'You sound like my friend Nathan.'

'He seems a sensible fellow.'

'And you have no other motive?'

He grimaced. 'Well, I might want to make sure you don't forget your promise about Lady Markstone. To be blunt, I've been let down by the high and mighty before.'

'Please, I am not high and mighty. And I keep my promises.' She walked towards the street. 'But if you wish to come' – he bounded after her, enthusiastic – 'then find us a carriage to take us.'

She smiled as he stalked away to do as she asked.

Stephen Fell's workshop occupied the ground floor of a large timber-framed building in a dusty alley between the Minories and Goodman's Fields to the east of the city. A freshly painted sign of a pistol and musket hung still in the absence of wind: the alleyway was close, stifling even in mid April.

A blue-clothed apprentice of about sixteen glanced up from polishing a musket as they entered. His bored gaze rested on Mercia for an instant before he went back to the weapon, one of a range of firearms displayed around the shop, no doubt to impress potential clients. The sound of metal on metal rang out from a separate room behind.

Nicholas picked up a doglock pistol. 'Impressive. Mercia, these are good quality.'

'Can I help?' asked the boy, not looking up.

Mercia approached him. 'Is your master at home?'

'If you want to see the colonel, you'll have to make an appointment. He's not available.'

''Tis important,' she persisted.

'Of course it is,' yawned the boy. 'But—'

'My mistress would like to buy a gift for her betrothed,' interrupted Nicholas. 'But she will only speak with the master, not some novice whelp.'

The boy stopped his work, narrowing his eyes. 'As I said, the master is out.'

'Do not lie, whelp. We can all hear he is working in the back.' Nicholas fingered the smooth edges of a decorative crossbow casually displayed amongst the firearms. He pulled back the shaft, playing with the taut string. The boy stayed put until Nicholas drifted the crossbow's aim in his direction and stroked the trigger mechanism. Swallowing, the boy disappeared into the back.

Mercia swivelled round. 'Put that away. You could have killed him.'

'No I couldn't, there's no bolt in here. And you get to see Fell now – look.'

A gigantic man was entering the room, his stocky frame bursting from under his filthy work apron. Black grime was caked across his sweating forehead, or rather his sweating head, for the man was completely bald.

'Colonel Fell?' said Mercia, feigning indifference at his bulk.

'I am Fell,' he said. 'Jeremiah says you want to see me about a gift? What is this, a gentleman's toy house?' He laughed, contorting his abused face into a kaleidoscope of lines and dimples. Several small scars lined his cheeks, while his nose was pushed to one side, evidence perhaps of a poorly healed injury.

'I am sorry to distract you from your work,' said Mercia, 'but in truth I do not want a gift.'

'Damned fool always gets things wrong.' Fell rubbed his sweating head with a cloth. 'Jeremiah! Get out here!'

'No,' she said hastily. 'I am here about a different matter.'

Fell sniffed, wiping his nose on his apron. 'And what would that be?'

She looked at him. 'The Oxford Section.'

Even through the dirt she could see Fell's face pale. He stared at her, as if trying to determine her intent. Then the apprentice reappeared, looking sullen.

'I—'

'Go fetch a pie.' Fell kept his eyes on Mercia. ''Tis time you ate.'

'But—'

'Go!'

The boy blew out his cheeks and shuffled off, helped into the street by Nicholas's heavy boot. Fell glanced at him.

'Where did you find him, the bear pits?'

'In a tavern brawl, rather.'

'You should have left him there.' He began to circle her, round and round, an intense heat seeming to radiate from his body. 'You want to talk about the Oxford Section, do you?' He stopped. 'Why?'

She put on a warm smile. 'I am interested to know what happened, Colonel.'

Fell scratched at his injured nose. 'It burnt, love. Burnt to nothing in the embers of a highway robbery gone wrong.'

'I know that is a pretence of Cromwell's. Please. I merely want the truth.'

Fell came closer, staring at her nose, her brow, her cheeks. She could feel Nicholas tensing behind her. Then Fell recoiled, reaching behind him; of a sudden she was staring into the barrel of the musket the apprentice had left on the counter.

'Put that down,' said Nicholas.

'Or what?'

He scoffed. 'You aren't going to shoot.'

'Aren't I? I suggest you both leave.'

Mercia stood her ground, guessing the gun was unlikely to be loaded if the apprentice had been cleaning it. 'I need a name, Colonel. Then we will leave you in peace.'

Fell snorted. 'Why in heaven's name should I help the daughter of Rowland Goodridge?'

She raised an eyebrow. 'You know me?'

'You must be his child. You may be out of mourning but you look exactly like him. The same pompous nose, the condescending eyes.'

'Hey,' snarled Nicholas. 'You treat her with some respect.'

'Her precious father never showed me any.'

Mercia clenched her jaw. 'I assume you knew each other in the army.'

'You could say that. I'll never forget his face, at least. Not even now 'tis clean off his neck.' He sucked in his cheek, calculating. 'Very well, my girl,' he said at last. 'As you're here I'll play. Whose name do you want?'

She held his gaze. 'The villain who turned on you as you marched. I know the Section was stolen, not burnt.'

'Oh yes? That sort of knowledge could be dangerous.'

Nicholas edged closer. 'Are you threatening her?'

'What do you think this is?' Fell waggled the musket. 'It was made clear to me at the time that I should forget the whole thing, and I have done.' He narrowed his eyes. 'But you want to know, I'll tell you.' He dropped the musket on the countertop. Nicholas darted to Mercia's side, but she stayed him from approaching Fell with a finger, suspicious as to why he would suddenly be willing to talk.

'There were four of us in the escort, the paintings stacked in a cart.' Fell stared over their heads into the past. 'Not an hour out of Oxford I heard a gunshot. Fairchild behind me cried out, goes down. I look to the forest, thinking to see a highwayman, but then another gunshot, and now Allinson falls. I look all around, but nobody's there. "North," I call. "North, draw arms!" Then a noise behind me, the cocking of a gun. I turn and I ask, "Where is he?" and North answers, "He is here, you fucking fool." And he smiles, child of Satan. He shoots. I fall, red playing on my chest, black spinning before my eyes.'

'But you survived,' said Mercia after a pause.

'As you see.'

'This North is the thief?'

Fell nodded. 'James North. Nobody has seen him since, not that I know of.'

'Does anyone else know what happened?'

His face clouded. 'Not from me, save my wife. And then she gossiped she knew something others did not, so they sent a brute to beat me to keep her quiet.' He pointed at his misshapen nose. 'They made her watch. She barely spoke to anyone ever again, she was so scared.'

Mercia winced. 'Cromwell was an unfeeling creature to set such a punishment on you.'

'Oh, it wasn't Cromwell.' Fell laughed, a deep malice in his eyes. 'The man who ordered me beaten was your father.' He wrung his large hands. 'Why do you think I'm telling you this? Rowland Goodridge destroyed my wife. Perhaps this knowledge will destroy his daughter too.'

'You bas—' Nicholas bent back his arm, but Mercia grabbed it before he could strike.

'No. Let us leave this sad man to his toys.'

Troubled by her encounter, Mercia sped from the alley into the street, knocking into an old man collecting money for the city poor; his wooden box slipped from his shaking hands onto the sewage-strewn road. It was one little thing on top of everything else, and she hurried on, upset. Behind her, Nicholas handed the box back to the trembling man.

Catching her up, he dared a hand on her shoulder. 'Don't mind what Fell said.'

She shook it off. 'Please, there is no need to talk of it.'

'He accused your father of ordering those injuries on his face. I think perhaps you do want to talk of it.'

She whirled around, scaring three scavenging pigeons into flight. 'Mr Wildmoor, I do not know you. I am not obliged to discuss anything with you. I thank you again for your help today, and I will return the favour by speaking with Lady Markstone for you. That is all.' She stormed away, leaving him standing beneath the Aldgate.

In truth, she was desperate to talk. Her exhilaration at roaming the big city in the search for answers with a strange, alluring man had dissipated into the hazy air. She realised how much she wanted Nathan to be with her, rather than this unknown man she had met following an inn fight. In that instant the city was disappeared to her, and she was completely alone, sensing nothing of the life going on around her.

Yet as she continued to walk, and a soft rain began to fall, she stopped dwelling on what her father might have done. No doubt Cromwell was involved, whatever Fell said, and those were brutal times, by God she knew that. She glanced over her shoulder to see

Nicholas following at a tactful distance. She halted beside a thin jet of water that was shooting from a hole in the ground, of the sort enterprising householders created by boring into the underground elm pipes to save themselves a long walk to the public conduit for their water. Pretending she wanted to freshen her face, she stooped towards the spray to give him chance to draw level.

'So,' she said, beads of water dripping from her ringlets, 'I will visit the Tower tomorrow to deliver your petition. Will you meet me later on so I can give you the answer?'

'Of course.' He paused. 'Though that's Saturday, and I said I'd shoe the horses at the local inn over the weekend. They don't pay much but it's something.' He considered. 'How about Sunday evening? Or will you be resting?'

'No. Come to my lodgings at seven. I will order food.' She surprised herself at her boldness, but Bethany would be in the house, and right now she was too tired to think of an alternative. Nicholas just raised an eyebrow.

She gave him the address as he walked her to a hackney, then he left, back to odd jobs so he said, but when she looked from the carriage window he was disappearing towards the wherry stand from where gambling men took a boat to Southwark for the prize fights. She was surprised to realise she didn't care, that she just liked the man. But as the horses set off, a caution developed within, a more sensible voice reminding her he was a stranger, an inappropriate companion for this personal search. But she had promised she would help him, and she would.

Chapter Eight

Thankfully, the Lieutenant of the Tower had agreed to Mercia's request to visit Lady Markstone. Once more back at the gates, she nodded to the familiar guard on duty and passed within the cloud-framed Lion Tower that formed the barbican entrance of the ancient fortress. A strange feeling came over her as she realised she was walking into the place where her father had lived his final weeks. Whatever he had done to Stephen Fell, he was still her father. The injustice he had suffered seemed to ooze from the very air.

The tension dissipated in an instant as a sound akin to a muffled trumpet tore her from her sorry reflections. Staring through a window slot she was amazed to see a huge grey beast with a ridiculously elongated nose, two massive tooth-like rods protruding from its wrinkled cheeks. This must be one of the wondrous creatures the King kept at the entrance to his London fortress, but seeing the elephant up close startled her. What else must exist in the lands beyond our island, she thought.

She knew there would be lions, of course. Her father had brought her to see them when she was a girl. She remembered the largest cat she had ever seen, a magnificent golden animal with a tangled mane that was nothing like the thin beasts adorning the royal coat of arms. It had looked at her and she had run behind her father, peering out from behind his legs. Today a pang of nostalgia struck her as she continued across the viewing platforms, wondering if the same lion she had been scared of then was still here. Crowly, was that his name? Probably dead by now.

Exiting the Lion Tower, she traversed a drawbridge to meet two velvet-uniformed guards manning the twin-towered gatehouse to the main complex beyond. They stepped aside to let her pass, banging their fearsome partisans on the ground in a posturing attempt to impress. She passed through the gatehouse and across the water-filled moat to reach the Byward Tower, taking in its raised portcullises and numerous defensive slits before she emerged into the Outer Ward, a wide, open walkway that snaked around the entire inner fortress.

Directly opposite rose the imposing Bell Tower, where a century before the great Elizabeth had been imprisoned by her own sister before becoming queen. Normally, Mercia would have been fascinated by the history, but today she was more concerned with the squat-faced guard waiting for her at the tower's base, a light bruise fading from his cheek. She cursed, for this was Dicken, the same warder she had struck when she had been denied access to her father. No doubt he had contrived to be on escort duty today.

She pulled her black hood over her face. 'Good morning,' she said. 'I am here to see Lady Markstone.'

Dicken folded his arms. 'No use trying to hide your face, my lady. Although not such a lady, the way you acted, screaming as you were pulled away.'

'I wanted to see my father.' She pulled back her hood in defiance. 'To prevent it was cruel.'

He shrugged. 'I do what the chief yeoman tells me, my lady.'

Riled, she held his fierce gaze. 'Presumably he would now say take Mrs Blakewood to Lady Markstone.'

'Don't you want to make up for last time first?' He leered. 'We could have an hour in the guardroom. The lads'll clear out.'

She narrowed her eyes. 'You could last an hour? I would have thought minutes.'

Dicken clenched his right fist. She could tell he would like nothing better than to lash out with it. She stood her ground, waiting.

'Come then,' he growled, brushing past. 'The lady poisoner's in Beauchamp, quite cosy. But you better have something for me.'

She followed him down the cobbled walkway, still slippery from yesterday's rain, the sun casting faint shadows across the ground. After a few yards they turned through a gate under the Bloody Tower and came into the Inner Ward. A stone wall muffled the clanging of workmen constructing the King's new weapons store to their right, but Dicken led her left towards a striking crenelated tower in the middle of the surrounding wall: the Beauchamp Tower, ironically named after one of her own mother's ancestors from centuries before.

Storming past a bemused guard, Dicken clunked up a circular staircase to the tower's middle floor, where a hefty wooden door confronted them. He took two large keys from a chain around his belt and waited. Despite her acrimony, Mercia passed him a newly minted half-crown, the King's silver face shining on the front.

Dicken looked at it. 'These coins are much better without Cromwell's ugly head.' He gave her a malicious smile. 'But then I can see his rotting face at Westminster whenever I like. Do you know it took eight blows of the axe to cut that bastard's head from his body when they dug it up?'

She knew. Her father had told her how the crowds had rejoiced when the corpse of the King's arch enemy Cromwell had been dragged through the streets to be decapitated in death. She looked at Dicken in revulsion, but he merely smirked and turned the weighty keys in the door, holding it open for her to enter. Once she was through he locked it behind her, his footsteps disappearing back down the stairs.

She found herself in a spacious room full of elaborate furniture, sunlight falling through a large window onto a red-carpeted floor, the orange glow of a homely fire burning in the stone grate. It could have been the parlour of a happy country house, but the imposing view of the White Tower at the heart of the fortress belied that untruth in an instant.

Lady Markstone had been writing at a desk under the window, but when Mercia came in she set down her quill pen and stood. Like Mercia, she was wearing a simple black dress, an undecorated black petticoat showing through the fashionable front slit.

'Mercia,' she smiled. 'It is wonderful to see you. Please forgive my surroundings. 'Tis not how I would like to receive guests but I am kept comfortable enough. Life leads us to strange destinations, does it not?' She pointed to an oaken table. 'At least I can offer you wine and some fruit.'

'Thank you.' Mercia filled a goblet and took a sip, accepting her host's invitation to sit in an upholstered green chair by the table. Realising she was hungry she took a small bite of an apple from the platter Lady Markstone pushed across.

'I am indebted to you for coming.' Lady Markstone brushed down her dress as she sat. 'I am kept here all the hours of the day, with none but my Bible for succour. Which is good company, and sustains me in my grief, but I do miss the pleasure of female companionship.'

Mercia nodded, understanding. She couldn't remember when she had last spent significant time with female friends herself, other than the cousin she visited once a year around her birthday. Somehow her old friends had all drifted away, whether to husbands and children, or like Nathan's wife Jane, to death.

'This is a fine chamber,' she said, recalling her foul Newgate cell. The difference between the rooms could not have been more pronounced.

'But still a prison. Nor am I the first.' Lady Markstone indicated the stony walls with a gloved hand. 'The one over the fireplace is my favourite.'

Mercia peered at the walls. A multitude of names and messages were scratched all over the stone, hewn out to surprising depths by previous occupants. She read above the fireplace:

quanto plus afflictionis pro Christo in hoc saeculo
tanto plus gloriae cum Christo in futuro

'Something about glory in Christ?' she guessed. 'I'm afraid the pleasures of Latin were denied me.'

'It means, the more suffering for Christ in this world, the more glory with Christ in the next. I think that must be true. By God this life has brought me suffering enough.' Lady Markstone sighed. 'But enough selfish indulgence. You are no doubt wondering whether the accusations against me are true. The lady poisoner, I know that is what they call me. Did she kill her husband, or not?'

Mercia was curious, but she was not about to admit it. 'Please, there is no need to speak of it.' She looked up. 'Unless it will help you in your need.'

Lady Markstone stood, gazing through the window. 'They say Anne Boleyn was beheaded down there, and Catherine Howard, for daring to be themselves in the face of a powerful man. I cannot claim such elevation, but the principle is the same.' She rolled up her sleeve, revealing a badly healed scar. 'Look.'

Mercia stared at the wound, appalled. 'How did it happen?'

''Tis a lasting reminder of my husband's power. He was a great man, oh yes, a strong fighter and a patriot, and I respected him for it.

But his temper – it became too much to bear, however I prayed God to allow me to suffer it.'

'Sir Edward beat you?' Her mother had suggested as such in Warwick, but the news was still a shock.

'Nothing so brutal. It was always a subtle trick he played, with his mind as well as his fist. Although this was a dinner knife, one evening when wine inflamed him.'

Her eyes remained fixed on the wound. 'Did my father know?'

'Sometimes others noticed things were amiss, but I never let on. Somehow I still loved him.' She shook her head. 'Then one day the Devil came, told me Edward was old enough to die without suspicion. I acquired the means to hasten his end.' She scoffed. 'A poison, can you believe? But the Lord works His will in ways we do not understand. I overcame my brief weakness and repented my sinful thoughts, but He allowed Edward to die nonetheless, struck down by an affliction of the body. The arsenic was discovered, and I was blamed.'

'But if you did not kill him?'

'It matters not. Either I killed him or I intended to, and I am judged the same, a murderer in deed or in thought. I have enemies at court. You know how it works.' She rolled her sleeve back down and sat. ''Tis treason for a woman to kill her husband. They say 'tis against the order of nature.' She took a slow breath. 'But I do have a plan to save my head. I will ask for exile to America.'

The idea seemed fantastic. 'Is that possible?'

'I can enjoy some freedom across the ocean. I have acquaintances in New England who will help me procure land and build a house. I am told the King is receptive to the proposal. And the alternative is not attractive.' She smiled weakly, drawing a line across her neck. 'You understand this, Mercia. We may be women, but we are as clever as any man if we have the liberty to act.'

Mercia reached out her hand; the older woman took it in a firm grip.

'I shall miss my son, of course.' She sighed. 'But Leonard no longer needs me, and I will not disabuse him of his love for his father by telling him the truth about his ways. But enough of me. You have your own troubles. I am told Sir Francis has claimed Halescott.'

The change of topic briefly took her aback; she realised for a short moment she had forgotten her own plight. 'He purports to,' she said, recovering her wits. 'But his claim is dubious. I will get the manor back.'

Lady Markstone lightly stroked her hand. 'Sir Francis grows in influence. He will be a difficult opponent.'

'Unless I can secure the help of someone more influential still.' She paused. 'Indeed, I wanted to ask you a question that may help. But it is – sensitive. It concerns your husband.'

'How so?'

She lowered her voice. 'Before his death my father wrote me a message. It was about the Oxford Section.'

Lady Markstone's hand twitched. 'Go on.'

'He said the paintings were not burnt, but stolen. I am hoping Sir Edward told you the same.'

Lady Markstone slowly nodded. 'If your father told you the story, you know everyone was ordered to keep the truth quiet for the sake of stability. To save Cromwell's face, more like.' She roved her old eyes across Mercia's face. 'What do you intend?'

'I hope to discover the truth, then use it to earn the King's favour.' Withdrawing her hand, Mercia sat back in her seat. 'Does the name James North mean anything to you?'

Lady Markstone frowned. 'North was the thief, a vicious and dangerous man. Neither my husband nor your father could find him.'

'But how did he just vanish? It makes no sense.'

She shook her head. 'Cromwell came to see Edward not long

after Worcester. I heard the shouting from two floors up. But Edward never spoke of it with me.'

'Not once?'

'Not really.' Shuffling in her chair, she straightened out her dress. 'The only thing I know is that North was suspected of fleeing abroad. But surely the paintings were disposed of, into some private collection perhaps?' She sucked in her lips. 'Mercia, take an old woman's advice. Do not resurrect past dangers. Think of your son.'

Mercia lowered her gaze. 'I appreciate what you say, but I am lost just now. Those paintings could be the very means I need to help Daniel. With the King's patronage I might be able to right some of the tragedies that have afflicted us.'

Lady Markstone leant forward, setting her hand on Mercia's knee. 'Yes child. It is unfair what befalls us women betimes, but we must be strong for those who depend on us.' She looked at Mercia through searching hazel eyes. 'There are other ways to look after yourself and your son. Ways you may not like, but which might provide more comfort. William Calde, for example.' She smiled. 'No, I am not devoid of courtly gossip in here.'

'I do not wish—'

'I know. But consider the alternatives, and choose what is surest and best. You have no master to guide you now, save yourself.' She reached for a flask of wine. 'Now let us discuss more pleasant matters.'

'That would be welcome. And – oh.' She paused, recalling her promise. 'Before I forget, you had a farrier in your employ, a man named Wildmoor. It seems a minor thing with all else, but for him 'tis a lot.'

'Wildmoor?' She laughed as she poured out two goblets. 'An unusual acquaintance for you, Mercia. How have you met him?'

She waved an embarrassed hand. 'We crossed paths after I came to arrange a visit with you. He had come about – well . . .'

'He has not been paid, is that it?'

'Yes. And he suffers for want of money, I think, although he is too proud to say. He was not paid when he left the ships.'

'That is not my concern. But as to what Edward owes him, tell him to petition my son.' She sipped at her wine, looking at Mercia over the rim. 'I seem to recall my husband was very pleased with Wildmoor, thought him trustworthy. If you are considering him yourself, I believe he would be of good service.'

Mercia smiled. 'Thank you. But a farrier would be an excess right now.'

For the next half-hour they lapsed into more cheerful conversation of a sort Mercia could never share with her mother, chatting of women they both knew and discussing current events. Then all too soon Dicken's gruff voice barked from behind the door that it was time to leave. Lady Markstone took Mercia in her arms, looking wistfully into her eyes.

'How I wished for a girl. Had my Robert been a daughter, he would not have marched to his death in our ridiculous wars.' She let her go. 'But that is the past and we must take care of our futures. I wish you luck, my child, in your life. Marry again. That is the solution for you, I think.'

The keys turned and the door swung inwards, Dicken's pudgy face protruding round the side. With a final farewell, Mercia followed the warder down the stairs. As she crossed the courtyard outside, once more in the rain, she looked up to see Lady Markstone standing at her window. It could have been the raindrops on the glass, but she seemed to have tears rolling down her face.

Chapter Nine

Mercia was perusing a volume of George Herbert's poetry the next evening when Bethany knocked on the parlour door to show Nicholas in. He was wearing smarter clothes than on Friday, a clean white shirt hooked into the top of close-fitting breeches beneath a brown waistcoat, and she could see his hair had been trimmed as he removed his hat. It made her feel guilty for what she was about to say, even more so when he presented her with a small bunch of yellow primroses, which Bethany arranged in a vase she found tucked away in the top shelf of a fine court cupboard. He was neither pleased nor disappointed with the news she brought about petitioning Lady Markstone's son, merely grunting a resigned acknowledgment.

'In truth 'tis what I expected,' he said. 'But I've spoken with him already. A lovely fellow. Threw a few coins at my feet, told me to seek the rest from his mother, whom he clearly loathes, by the way, by how he spoke.' He sighed. 'So now I'll never be paid. Perhaps I'll take to sea again. They say a Dutch war is coming soon.'

'I have heard talk of a war,' she muttered.

He grew animated. 'The Intelligencer is full of bile against the Dutch. Seems the Navigation Acts are working and now the King wants to take things further, or his brother does, at least.'

Mercia looked at the primroses and felt a sharp pang of pity for this man who had come into her life only two days before. But the decision she had come to that afternoon arose from such sentiment, and she put the feeling away.

'I didn't know you had spoken with Leonard – the Markstones' son. My friend Nathan knows him slightly. I could ask him to intercede, if you like.'

'Thank you, but I'll manage. I'm a big boy.' He raised an eyebrow, frowning when she didn't laugh. 'What's the matter? Have the victuallers let us down with the food?' He turned towards the door. 'I can fetch something.'

She closed her eyes. Over the past two days, the excitement she had felt at inviting him to her lodgings had turned to nervousness at her boldness. Now it was time to speak sense.

'Nicholas, it has been a pleasure to meet you. I wish you luck and hope you find work soon.'

'Want to be rid of me, eh?' he joked.

'I do appreciate the help you have given me, but this is my concern. I cannot presume further on your time.' She walked to the parlour door, pulling it open. 'There is no food because I have not ordered any. I think it is for the best.'

She did not realise a smile could vanish so quickly. 'Oh.' He played with his hat. 'I had hoped we could talk some more.'

'We barely know each other.' She tried to inject a touch of warmth in her voice. 'Please, I will be quite safe. And I have fulfilled our agreement.'

He cast down his gaze, shuffling his boots. Once more she felt the pang of sympathy; once more she pushed it away.

'Nicholas, I cannot keep you from your work. Besides, I am a lone widow. People would think it strange for me to associate with a man without company.'

He scoffed. 'With a man of my standing, you mean.'

''Tis naught to do with that. But I think it best we part.'

'So I am dismissed once more.' Again the pang. Again pushed away. Nicholas came to the door, pausing beside her, a flash of anger in his eyes. 'I thought perhaps you were different. But I see you are high and mighty after all.' She opened her mouth to respond, but he quietened her with a wave of his hand. ''Tis well. Goodbye, Mrs Blakewood. I hope you find the paintings.'

He descended the stairs with a heavy tread. From across the small landing Bethany peered from the dining-room door, looking on her mistress with concern. Mercia just nodded to reassure her. She waited until she heard the sound of the front door shutting before she withdrew inside the parlour, feeling a solitary guilt.

From the window she watched Nicholas disappear in the direction of Lincoln's Inn. A bobbing light floated near him, coalescing into a small boy bearing a lamp at the end of a wooden stick. It was a linkboy, one of the many who wandered night-time London offering their light for a price. Tonight the moon was new, the sky dark, and Nicholas gestured for the boy to walk in front. Mercia watched them go until she could see them no more.

She was taken by a strange desire to run after him, to apologise for asking him to leave. He had intrigued her and, not that she would ever admit it, she had found him appealing. Nicholas was an attractive man, despite his coarse edges, or maybe because of them. But she dismissed such thoughts as a ridiculous fantasy she knew would very quickly pass. Still, he had been kind, and she hoped his life would turn out well.

* * *

She was in her bedroom pulling her nightshirt over her topknot when she heard a faint mumbling outside her door. Letting the nightshirt fall into place, she strained to make out the muffled noise. For a moment there was silence, but when the mumbling resumed she picked up a candle and opened the door. The flickering light sent an otherworldly glow over Bethany, casting an oversized shadow on the opposite wall.

'What—?' she began, but Bethany placed an urgent finger over her lips. Removing it, she came in closer to Mercia's ear.

'There's someone in the house,' she whispered.

A shiver ran through her. 'Are you sure?'

Bethany nodded, her eyes wide. 'In the parlour.'

Motioning to Bethany to stay put, Mercia crept onto the second-floor landing and tiptoed down the top set of stairs. Halfway down she paused, listening. A cold feeling stole up her back as she stood in silence, wondering what to do. Then the floor behind the parlour door creaked. She blew out her candle and pressed against the wall, the smell of snuffed wick permeating the air.

The door pulled slowly open, stopping halfway. A figure squeezed through the gap, but it was too dark to make out any features. Barely daring to breathe, she thought she could discern a man's gait, but whoever it was, the figure did not stop. It crept down the lower flight of stairs until it merged into the enveloping blackness. A fluttering of crisp air raced into the house as the front door scraped open and was eased back shut.

For a moment Mercia felt stuck to the wall behind her, but she heard nothing to suggest anyone else was in the house. Looking up towards Bethany, she pulled her arm forward to point first to herself and then towards the parlour. Gripping the blown-out candle, she descended to the first-floor landing to push open the parlour door.

Nobody was in the room, but the darkness was near absolute. Returning to the landing she nearly cried out when she saw a light bobbing down the stairs, but it was only Bethany come to bring her a lit taper. She returned to the parlour to light the wall sconces, but looking around it seemed nothing had been taken. Puzzled, she toured the house checking windows and doors, but there was no sign of a break-in, and she was sure Bethany had locked the front door before they had retired. Locking it again she sent Bethany to bed, reassuring her all was secure. For herself, she was too agitated to go back upstairs.

She sat in the leather armchair, looking at Nicholas's primroses. With a start she realised that between his leaving the house and Bethany locking the front door a period of around thirty minutes must have elapsed. The intruder could have entered in that time and hidden until free to move about. But to what end?

She was dismissing the thought it was Nicholas himself, too embarrassed to admit he had left something behind, when she noticed the piece of paper on the mantelpiece. One word was emblazoned in large letters on the front: her name. It had not been there when she went to bed.

A prickling sensation shot through her body. Fingertips tingling, she rose from her chair, eyes fixed on the paper. She snatched up the white card, turning it over to reveal a short message scribbled in very poor handwriting:

I know what you're doing. Desist if you value your life. JN

She clapped the note to her chest. JN. James North. Here in London, in her lodgings. By God's truth, was he the man she had just seen? Her heart pounding, she searched the house again in irrational fear he had returned, but besides Bethany she was alone. She stood in the kitchen with a carving knife, breathing in and out to calm herself. Snuffing out the candles she took the knife to bed, but her agitation made it hard to sleep. Two questions kept tormenting her mind: how could North know she was pursuing him, and how could he know where she lodged?

It was nearly dawn before she fell asleep and so she was still abed, tired, when the front door slammed in the morning. Instinctively she leapt up, opening the bedroom door just enough to peer through. At the bottom of the two staircases, a well-dressed gentleman was handing Bethany his familiar black gloves. She cursed, ducking back as Bethany climbed the stairs to announce Sir Francis.

She took a deliberately long time to get dressed, stopping by the kitchen for her usual cup of minted whey before forcing herself to the parlour. Her uncle was waiting at the window, looking out.

'You are late to rise,' he said. 'If I had known you would keep me, I would have sent my man.'

She was in no mood to be civil. 'Why are you here?'

Sir Francis glared at her. 'I have warned you before about your tone. And the question is more why you are here, in London.'

'My private business is my own affair. How did you know where to find me?'

'I was in Oxfordshire last week. I went to the manor house to check on my new property.' He sniffed. 'I was perturbed to hear there had been a robbery.'

'At the manor?' She clutched her neck, feigning shock. 'If anything of mine was taken—'

'Nothing of value, apparently.' He looked at her keenly but she kept her expression constant. 'In fact nothing at all. Then I discovered you were not at your cottage. I went to see that man friend of yours.'

'Uncle, you imply an impropriety where none exists. Nathan was my husband's best friend, and a great comfort to me now.'

'No doubt.' The two words oozed with disapproval. 'He was reluctant, but he told me you were here, something to do with your father. I swear, Mercia, if you are trying to cross me, I will not hold back.'

'And I told you before, I will not abandon my son.'

'Then perhaps you should return home and stay with him, as I ordered.'

She folded her arms. 'How I care for my child is up to me.'

He scoffed. 'Have you any idea what your mother-in-law is plotting? Keyte tried to hide him from me, but I know full well Daniel is with him. If Isabel finds out, she will take advantage of the fact.' He flicked a mote of dust from his shirt frill. 'She will not act yet, but when she has assembled her case she intends to petition for custody.'

'What?' Mercia went cold. 'Then . . . then she will lose. She knows I will never allow it.' She overcame her momentary shock. 'I will do anything I must.'

'I see.' He smiled, the right side of his face arching higher. 'So when I take you to see Sir William this afternoon you will not protest?'

'By our Lord!' She stared at him, aghast. 'So that is your intent. You think to frighten me into obeying you by stirring Anthony and Isabel against me. You seek to encourage their repugnant custody threats through the lease of my own manor house.' She paced the room, furious. 'But I am my own self, Uncle. I will not comply.'

Sir Francis's face darkened, his jaw clenched tight. He strode across and grabbed her by the shoulders, twisting her to face him with a painful wrench.

'If you were not my niece I would strike you for your insolence.' His narrow eyes drilled into her soul. 'I did not want to be so blunt. But if you do not do as I say, I will make sure Isabel's petition is heard and I promise you will lose your son for ever.'

He let go, her shoulders smarting from his grip. The anger inside was so intense she wanted to break the heavy vase beside her over his scheming head. She would have had the strength; somehow she stayed herself.

He straightened his doublet. 'I will return at two. Spend the morning preening yourself, or whatever you women do.' His eyes flicked over her mourning dress. 'And if you must wear black, try to make it look inviting.'

They travelled through London in silence, the carriage's leather blinds blocking out all light. The rattling of the coach jarred her mind to a madness of competing thoughts. Part of her was desperate to rush back to Halescott to scoop Daniel up in her arms, but then her rational mind asserted itself, insisting Nathan was the best protection he could have. Why was she in London anyway? Tracing North and the Oxford Section was not a whim. It was to gain the protection of the King, to save Daniel's future. If she gave that up at the first difficulty, she may profit for now but end up losing for ever. As for North, her new fury had blown away any fear. He had miscalculated with his threatening note. There was no way she was going to give in.

The horses juddered to a halt. She opened the carriage door, thinking they had arrived, but a flailing fist slammed it back shut. 'War!' shouted a zealous voice, banging on the carriage side. 'Expel the Dutch!' She released the blind to see a jeering crowd obstructing their progress down Whitehall, about thirty men and women screaming their bile. But the carriage forced a way through, entering the palace grounds unscathed.

She descended from the carriage, feeling inside her pocket for Sir William's necklace. It was stuffed carelessly between her coin purse and the malicious note; having brought it to London, she intended to use this forced opportunity to return it. Around the arch they had passed beneath, a throng of palace servants was milling about, gawping at the protestors in the street.

'You!' Sir Francis crunched the dirt as he marched towards a liveried page. 'What is going on outside?'

''Tis this Dutch business, sir. It is getting out of hand.' The page jerked his thumb at the heckling protestors. 'Some lad was sodomised walking home last night. They blame Dutch sailors, though none were about. They want the King to expel all Dutchmen from the city.'

Sir Francis shook his head. 'Nonsense and scandal. See to your duties.'

Mercia was surprised, for his tone was not unkind. He beckoned her follow him inside the palace. As they walked, she could see the walls were scattered with a number of paintings and portraits, the old King's grand collection returning piece by piece.

'Sir William will be finishing a meeting with the King's privy council,' he said as they approached a grandiose staircase. 'Before you see him, I want to be informed of what was discussed. You saw the crowd. The city is crazed for a Dutch war.'

She looked askance at him. 'Were you not invited to the meeting, Uncle?'

Letting out a long sigh, he stopped at the foot of the stairs. 'I have worked hard, Mercia, to regain the credibility this family has lost through your father. It has taken a huge effort, but I am now in favour with the King and his brother the Duke. Yet I can only climb so high. Maybe my grandchildren will be able to attend meetings of state with the King's son, should His Majesty ever produce an heir. Maybe your son too, if you play your part.'

She scoffed. 'He may find it difficult without his inheritance.'

'There are other houses.' Irritated, Sir Francis continued on, leading her up the wide marble staircase. His shoes echoed across the open space.

'How is the Queen?' asked Mercia as they reached the top, her desire to know outweighing her wish to avoid conversation. ''Tis difficult enough to bear a child without the constant attentions of the entire court. Doubtless she misses Portugal.'

'Indeed she is pregnant again.' Sir Francis halted beside a colourful tapestry that lined the whole height of the wall beside them. 'Pray God she is delivered of a healthy infant this time. The court already begins to fear for the succession, with the Duke so close to the—' He stopped himself.

She smiled. 'To the Catholics?'

Sir Francis stared, his eyes questioning how she could know such things, never considering she might read the news pamphlets. Before he could reply, a door at the far end of the landing opened, a procession of straight-backed clerks filing out.

'Right on time,' he said. 'The meeting is over. We should wait here.'

A group of five grandly dressed men exited the room, stopping on the landing to continue their discussion. At their centre was the Duke of York, stressing his points with firm gestures; the other four surrounded him, nodding as one.

She heard her uncle tut. 'Those three are always together.'

'Which three?'

He jerked his head in the direction of the group. 'Sir Peter, Sir William and Sir Bernard.'

She narrowed her eyes, craning her neck to look behind the Duke, where Sir Bernard Dittering, the man they said was responsible for her father's trial, was laughing with his master. She would have loved to challenge him here in the corridors of power, but even she baulked at doing so in front of the King's brother. Next to Sir Bernard a grey-wigged man was smiling at the Duke's every word, his pompous expression marking him for Sir Peter Shaw, and beside him, talking animatedly, Sir William Calde. Noticing her watching, he gave her the swiftest of waves. Sir Bernard followed his gaze until his eyes met the hatred in hers, forcing him to look away.

The final member of the group excused himself from his colleagues and marched along the landing, his fine doublet slashed to reveal the silk shirt beneath. Seeing Mercia and her uncle, he paused.

'Sir Francis,' he acknowledged.

'Colonel Nicolls. I trust you had a profitable meeting?'

Nicolls nodded. 'We may be getting somewhere with this Dutch business at last. The Duke is pushing for a more direct intervention in Guinea, Sir Bernard now, too. The King is still uncertain but I think we will convince him.'

'And Sir William?'

'He is with Bernard, as he often is. 'Tis only surprising he demurred so long. I think they had a long talk while at the Tower the other day.' He looked at Mercia. 'Is this—?'

'Yes. My niece.'

Nicolls bowed to her. 'Then I am sorry to have mentioned that place. Your father was a principled man. He handled himself well at the end.' Nodding a curt farewell he disappeared down the staircase.

'Who was he?' asked Mercia, intrigued.

Sir Francis dropped his shoulders, visibly relaxing. 'That was the Duke's groom of the bedchamber. They say he is in line for advancement, like many of the Duke's favourites. 'Tis the Duke who will lead this war, should it come.'

She could not resist a retort. 'Well, yes. He is Lord High Admiral.'

Sir Francis frowned. 'And despises the Dutch. If I can just – by the Lord, they are walking off. Wait here.' Outside the council chamber, the Duke's group was disbanding in the opposite direction. Sir Francis hurried to follow them, leaving Mercia alone.

Abandoned, she dropped herself into a lavish yellow-backed chair, her mind flitting back to the note James North had left. Then an irritated shout from the meeting room startled her from her thoughts. She looked up to see another man emerging, waving away a clerk with an impatient flick of his white ruffled wrist. It was his height that gave it away, his confident bearing, that and the rich black wig that cascaded over his broad shoulders. Mercia widened her eyes as the King stormed in her direction, muttering under his breath. Hastily she stood up and curtsied as he passed. He glanced at her and managed a smile before turning out of sight.

A bold idea surfaced. But could she be that audacious? She did not take long to decide. Life was full of unexpected chances and this was one she had to dare take.

Chapter Ten

She followed the King through the labyrinthine palace, pausing behind columns, darting around corners, watching everyone from privy councillor to maidservant bow or curtsey as he passed. She knew she should despise him for his part in agreeing to her father's execution, but as she looked on the King, the man, seeing the smiles he received, the excited looks, she found it hard to feel the deep bitterness she had thought to bear on him if ever they met. Besides, she needed his support, and was it not her father himself who had suggested she seek it?

After a hasty conversation with a liveried servant, the King finally turned left from a ground-floor corridor to pass through a covered jetty that jutted into the Thames, ascending a gangplank that took him to his private yacht. She held herself straight as she pursued him, nodding to the guard at the gangplank's base as though she had every right. She expected to be challenged, but she was not: perhaps the guard was accustomed to strange ladies going aboard.

Inside the boat the King bent his head to vanish through a narrow door. Mercia glanced through the gap between door and frame to make sure he was alone; he was, but she covered her eyes as he removed his wig to scratch at his real, greying hair. Overcoming her embarrassment, she took a deep breath and knocked.

'What now?' shouted the King. 'Can I not have peace even on my yacht?' A rustling suggested the wig was being replaced. 'Come in if you must!'

'Your Majesty.' Setting aside her personal feelings she entered the cabin and curtsied, keeping her eyes on the floor.

'My lady.' She could hear the surprise in his voice. 'I was not expecting such enticing company. Please, stand.'

'Thank you, Your Majesty.' She raised her eyes.

'But you are in mourning. My condolences.' He frowned. 'Did I not just pass you in the palace?'

'Yes, Your Majesty.'

'So you followed me here?'

'I wished to speak with Your Majesty, if you will allow it.'

His keen gaze flitted across her face. 'I will if the interview is short. I have promised Barbara – that is, Lady Castlemaine – an afternoon in Hyde Park.'

A pair of liveried groomsmen entered. Charles waved them away, but the interruption was long enough for Mercia's attention to be captured by a series of charts rolled out on a table beside her. She quickly looked back at the King, but he had noticed.

'You are interested in such things?' he asked.

'Oh yes.' She glanced at the topmost chart, a map of the west coast of Africa. 'The Guinea coast?'

He widened his eyes. 'You are a knowledgeable woman.'

'These places marked here are Dutch outposts?'

'The same my council would have me raid.' He sighed. 'But you are not here to talk of war. My lady, I would know your business and your name.'

'Forgive me.' She bowed. 'My name is Mercia Blakewood. I wish to present a petition.'

'There are more proper avenues, Mrs Blakewood, but as you are here, ask.' Charles indicated a plush, red-velvet chair and sat across from her, his simple white stockings tightening against his legs as he lowered himself into his seat. In contrast to the stockings, his black breeches were finely embroidered; his unbuttoned red doublet revealed a magnificent gold-laced waistcoat beneath.

'Your Majesty should know,' she said as she sat, 'that my father was Sir Rowland Goodridge.'

'Ah.' The King sucked in his cheek. She looked at him, worried he would now merely dismiss her, but his next words surprised her. 'Then I am sorry for what you have suffered.' He looked across at her. 'Whatever his acts, his daughter should not be judged the same. Deliver your petition.'

'Thank you.' She swallowed. 'Indeed it concerns my father's estate.' She hesitated, suddenly struck by whom she was addressing, but she cleared her throat and made herself speak. 'When he died, it should have passed to my son, in accordance with my father's will. But my uncle, Sir Francis Simmonds, claims my parents' marriage settlement makes him the heir. It is not true.'

The King nodded, surprising her once more. 'In fact I know something of the case. Given your father's . . . situation – it was discussed briefly at council. As I understand it, the matter has been settled.'

'Could it not be examined again?' she pursued, a boldness stirring within. 'Regardless of my father's fate, the law of England must still apply.'

Charles raised an eyebrow. 'You are a brave one. Was it not Good Queen Bess herself who said must was not a word to be uttered to princes?' He waved a hand as her face fell. 'I am teasing. As for what you ask, you can petition the courts if you wish, although I am not sure it would achieve much.'

'If Your Majesty were to intervene—'

'Mrs Blakewood, I could only do so in extraordinary circumstances.'

She swooped on his words. 'Then I will have to see what I can do. Thank you for hearing my petition, Your Majesty.' She smiled, deftly turning the subject to the extraordinary circumstances she hoped to provide. 'It was pleasing to have the opportunity to walk through the palace today. I see that much of the royal collection has been restored.'

Charles nodded. 'You appreciate fine art as well as fine maps, Mrs Blakewood. My father's collection was his life.'

'I remember when the paintings His Majesty kept at Oxford were being taken to London.' She ran an innocent hand through her hair. 'It was a tragedy when they were lost.'

'A tragedy indeed. Ten of the best paintings in the entire collection, my father's favourites.' The King sighed. 'I have sent my agents across the country. They have regained much of what was lost. But not the Oxford Section. I had hoped the stories about their burning were false, and yet no trace has been found.'

She kept her expression neutral. 'You have been generous to those who have helped you.'

'Deservedly so.' He shook his head, a wistful look on his face. 'To see those pictures again, hanging where they should, I would pay dearly for that. But there is no sense in dwelling on the impossible.' He rose. 'And now, Mrs Blakewood, I fear I must ask you to take your leave.' He smiled. 'We cannot keep Barbara waiting.'

Mercia stood and curtsied, aware the interview was at an end. She retreated backwards from the King's presence: a difficult manoeuvre, but she managed not to trip. Once outside the cabin she pulled herself upright, ignoring the twinge in her knee as, encouraged by the King's words, she span lightly on her feet. But her cautious good humour soon dissipated. At the end of the covered jetty her uncle stepped into her path, Sir William at his side.

'What in heaven's name have you been doing on the *Folly*?' hissed Sir Francis. Despite his godly reference, his forehead bubbled as though a demon were about to stab through with its hellish pitchfork.

Mercia shrugged, thinking to disconcert him. 'I was talking with the King.'

'Whatever for?' Sir Francis frowned. 'He will be most displeased you have disturbed his rest.'

'He was not displeased.' Turning away from him she addressed Sir William, knowing her uncle would restrain his temper in the presence of a man he sought to impress. 'Sir William, I have kept you waiting.'

Sir William pulled his grand coat around him. 'Well, of course, if you were with the King, I cannot be offended.' He smiled, but his worried gaze flicked towards the yacht. The action made her uncle's face twitch, and he looked down the jetty, his darting eyes clearly assessing the possibilities. Her irritation increased.

'Shall we go?' she asked Sir William. 'The Privy Garden perhaps?' She led him away, leaving her uncle to contemplate and plot.

The Privy Garden, a series of grassy squares intersected by a number of straight gravel paths, brought greenery to the southern side of the palace. Confident new statues graced the middle of each square, but the centrepiece was a hulking stone sundial, its numerous discs displaying time in a perplexing variety of ways. Unlike the surrounding statues it was in poor condition, but Mercia had little doubt that the King, with his love of science, would soon restore or else replace it.

'The gnomon is casting a shadow,' she mused, looking at the nearest disc. 'Spring must finally be here.'

'The gno – what?' said Sir William beside her.

'The shaft on the sundial that creates the shadow. See, it is long because the afternoon is late.'

'Hmm.' He grunted, guiding her away along one of the criss-crossing paths. Stopping beside a statue of a proud and naked Venus, he reached out a hand to stroke her hair.

'Have you considered what I said when last we met?'

'I have.' She took a small step back. 'And I fear I must return your generous gift.' She felt inside her pocket, holding out the three-layered necklace for him to take.

He smiled. 'Stay. I know how this game works, how you women like to pretend. The necklace is yours.'

She sighed. 'Sir William, what of your wife?'

The great man flushed, the furs of his coat heaving like a trapped animal. 'Do not concern yourself with Harriet.' He closed her fingers around the necklace. 'I have many more gifts for you, many . . . pleasures.'

'Sir William, I—'

'I understand. You are in mourning still for your father. Perhaps you feel aggrieved his house was denied you.' He stroked her cheek with the back of a finger. ''Tis no shame to think so. How could you know anything of the law? But you must not worry. I will set you up inside the palace itself. You will have your own apartment full of fashionable hangings, beautiful trinkets and clothes.' He looked at her. 'You know I can do it.'

'Sir William, I insist—'

'You are right,' he interrupted once more. 'I have been unfeeling. Visiting the palace can be tiring for a lady.' He nodded as if agreeing with himself. 'I will leave you now, but let us meet next in my own apartment. I am sure you would admire my . . . tapestries.'

'Please, I—'

He rested a finger on her lips. 'There is no need to talk.' He glanced at the pale statue. 'Even Venus cannot best your beauty.'

He kissed her hand and walked away, turning once to look back, his eyes lingering longest on her chest.

She stood in the shadow of the greatest palace in Europe, life throbbing through its hundreds of rooms, the cacophony of London rising up beyond its walls. As if in contrast, a tiny sparrow landed on Venus's outstretched finger, whistling its carefree tune. Yet all that passed scarcely noticed to Mercia, alone in the garden, the obscene jewellery somehow still dangling from her thumb.

As she replaced Sir William's necklace in her pocket, her fingers brushed against James North's note. She knew most women would think her absurd to renounce Sir William, the powerful man with the ear of the King, the man who was promising her luxuries, in favour of hunting down this dangerous other, this violent soldier she was desperate to unmask. But powerful as he was, Sir William could not give her what she truly desired. Finding the Oxford Section would put the King himself in her debt. And yet her task was not simple: she was thinking of pursuing a man who had killed to accomplish his goals. Standing there alone, the freshly cut grass of the Privy Garden diffusing its scent of happy evenings past, she yearned for a friend to confide in, wishing Nathan was with her, not to hold her hand, but to talk, to assist.

A gull called its screeching cry high above. She looked up to see the great white bird fly out towards the river, towards the sea. Into her mind floated an image of the enticing young sailor she had so harshly dismissed, the rough-edged farrier who had brought her primroses to brighten her evening. Whether she had been afraid, or worse contemptuous, she could not say. She felt an ungrateful fool. He had helped her and received nothing in return.

Damn convention. Nathan was not there, but maybe she could have a friend, of sorts.

She was mad, she knew it, to go in search of a man she hardly knew. Her mind spent half the night debating it, awake and asleep, when she wasn't straining to hear if anyone was roaming the house. But only one answer seemed right. After a comforting breakfast of cold meats and eggs she put on the least assuming outfit she had brought, a plain brown skirt and woollen jacket over an equally basic bodice, all under a light-grey cloak. Aside from her mourning ring she took off all her jewellery and pinned a loose hood to her hair. The hackney driver looked at her strangely when she asked for Cow Cross, but he shrugged his shoulders and kept quiet, dropping her on the corner of St John's Street.

She set off down the dirty road. Two apprentices in their blue aprons stared at her from the doorstep of a tanner's shop. One whispered in the other's ear, making his mate laugh. Stepping out from the doorway they began to follow, calling out obscenities across the street. She put her head down and walked faster. Concerned with eluding them, she turned left, right, left again, not paying attention to her route. When she came into a wider road, and after a few seconds looked back, they were nowhere to be seen.

Heart racing, she penetrated further into the grimy area.

Despite the intense blue sky, the sun seemed to be absent here, the tightly packed houses leaning over each other as though sharing their ill-gained intelligence. A woman called out shrilly from above. Mercia jumped aside as a torrent of foul sewage rained down, the splattered mess just missing her leg.

A man ran from an alley, nearly colliding with her before careening on past into the maze of streets. She dared a glimpse down the passageway, but it was dark, the devilish shadows tempting the unwise to explore. She thought she could discern a figure lying prostrate on the ground, but whether human or animal she could not tell, and she was not going to look.

A sharp anxiety settled over her as she realised she had no idea where she was. Eyes darting left and right for danger, she turned another decaying corner. The same apprentices were directly in front, blocking her way. One blew a lewd kiss, the other laughed, casually untying the lace of his breeches and slipping his hand underneath, feeling himself in front of her. Alarmed, she turned around, walking quickly back the way she had come, aware of the apprentices' pursuit. Then a severe female voice rang out behind her. She turned to see an elderly woman in a hole-ridden hemp smock dragging the vulgar apprentice by the arm, his accomplice walking meekly alongside. They were never any real threat. It would have been comical, but Mercia did not feel like laughing.

More footsteps ground the dirt behind her. She was now paranoid, uncertain whether people were following her or just walking behind. She crossed an unkempt square and hurried down two more streets before she dared pause, stumbling into a narrow alley full of shops, their various faded signs competing for attention. She scurried to the nearest open hatch, a rickety grocers' stand, hoping for information.

'What'll it be?' asked the shopkeeper, eyeing her clothes. She pointed at the first thing she saw, a bunch of yellow carrots. She handed over the coins, taking care to hide the other money she had in her pocket.

'I'm looking for a farrier,' she said. Try as she might, she could not disguise the richness of her accent. The grocer looked at her intently, as though determining who she was, where she was from, what she had to offer, all in one glance. 'His name is Nicholas Wildmoor. He lives in these parts.'

The grocer smirked. 'Farrier, that all he is to you?' He laughed, revealing a rotting set of teeth stained with all the colours of his produce. 'I never heard of him.'

She moved on. As she left she heard the shopkeeper making coarse jokes about her to someone behind him. She would have to do better to blend in, but she was terrible at it. Even her least attractive dress stood out here.

Throwing the carrots into the dirt she came into a second square, the putrefying stench of overflowing waste abusing the air. A crowd of boys sat along the right-hand side. Sensing the presence of prey, they rose without looking, in a routine perfected through countless attacks. As one organism they drifted over, joining together as a terrifying mob, jostling her, their fingers everywhere, searching for a pocket, a locket, anything to steal. She shouted at them to stop, but as one they laughed, telling her not to come to their streets, if she didn't want to share her goods.

Frightened, she struck out, hitting one of the dirt-ridden boys. He could only have been eight or nine, not much older than Daniel. The boy fell, his mouth bleeding, sending the others wild, their nimble fingers morphing into aggressive claws. She lashed out, kicked in every direction, but the mob's integrity held. She was in danger.

A man shouted across the square, his words vulgar and sharp. He ran at the boys, waving a plank of wood, a dog leaping from his heels. They released their appalling grip and scattered. Breathing hard, Mercia looked over to thank him, but he merely swore at her, his dog growling through bloody jaws. Head down, she carried on.

She was dispirited and scared, but she would not give in. Another corner turned and straight in front rose a wonderful sight, a church steeple thrusting out of the poverty, pointing to the saints in heaven. Relief powered through her as she pushed open the wooden door, but inside all was dark, and what passed for pews smelt rank, the promise of salvation broken. She did not even stay to pray for help. God seemed to have abandoned this building years ago.

She left the forsaken church, replacing her hopes of divine deliverance with her own, more fallible thoughts. Be calm and think. Where to find a farrier – at a stables, maybe an inn? An inn . . . hadn't Nicholas told her that was where he sometimes worked? Which way? Try left, it looks a little cleaner.

She followed the street into a broader road, pressing onwards until she saw a sign swinging in the distance. It looked like – yes, an image of the Green Man, an inn. Faster she strode, gaining confidence at every step, when an arm curled round her waist. She was dragged into an alley, slammed face forward against a damp wall, her hood wrenched painfully back on its pin. A mouth pressed against her neck, riding upwards until she felt the moisture of wet lips at her ear. She elbowed backwards, striking nothing. A hand felt under her cloak, round to her breast. An intense fear burst out. She struggled, but she stayed entrapped.

'Desist.' A deep voice. 'Or this won't be the worst that happens.' A painful squeeze, a groan in her ear. 'Desist.'

Then the hand was gone, the menace lifted. She pushed back off the wall. A cat was screeching, kicked by her fleeing assailant, but no person was now there.

She was shaking, but she was close to the inn. She replaced her hood and walked from the alley, her body begging all the while to run, but her mind won out. She would not let this defeat her, not let men overcome her, no more, not after the heartache of her past.

At the inn she found more boys running about, leading miserable horses here and there, but it was better in this stable yard, less filth. She asked if any of them knew Nicholas Wildmoor. Yes, said one, keep going to Turnmill Street, at the sign of the Horse and Star. He is working there today.

She walked fast, turning her head at each sound, at each alley, but she arrived at the inn without trouble. She walked into the courtyard and there he was, Nicholas, the man who had been kind, the man she had only briefly met, but in that instant the most welcome man alive.

He looked up from the horse he was tending. What must he have seen? A wild-eyed woman crossing the yard, her arms outstretched, her cloak and jacket loose. He stood up straight, sweat dripping from matted hair across his stubbled cheek. His mouth opened in surprise, and he quickly grabbed a shirt from the ground, trying to cover his bare chest.

'I am sorry,' she managed, 'that I was rude to you before. I have come to beg your pardon.' He began to speak but she shook her head, resting her hand on his warm shoulder, oblivious to the naked flesh. 'But first, I need a drink.'

Chapter Eleven

Nicholas sipped the last dregs of his ale. 'I'm glad you came to find me.'

It was later that same day. They were in the Boiled Mutton on Holborn, well clear of the Cow Cross slums. After returning to her lodgings to clean up, worrying Bethany senseless in the process, Mercia felt considerably better. She had spent the last half-hour telling Nicholas what had happened in the past two days; talking had been a relief.

'I was too hasty the other day.' She tugged at a loose curl in her hair. 'I suppose I was nervous of confiding in you. But you seem a decent man.' Nicholas swallowed, casting down his eyes. 'Come,' she said, 'there's no need to be embarrassed.'

'I'm not. I suppose I'm not used to people like you showing an interest.'

'Besides, I never thanked you for the flowers.'

He smiled. 'I did notice that.'

'Well, they are lovely.' She paused. 'You still look embarrassed.'

'Honestly, I'm not. But I do have a confession.' He ruffled the front of his hair. 'Truth be told, I was going to come to your lodgings tonight, to find you.'

She sat back in surprise. 'After I dismissed you so rudely?'

He nodded, swigging from his empty glass; he set it down on the square table and pushed it to one side. 'What happened with Fell, the inn fight, even Michael – it was exciting. It was different. Even when you . . . threw me out, I couldn't get it out of my mind. Then it came to me. Obvious, really.'

Mercia leant forward. 'What was obvious?'

He craned his neck to look over her. 'Where is that lad?'

'Nicholas – what?'

He put on a sigh. 'That damn boy.'

Impatient, she looked behind her, clicking her fingers at the boy who was serving them. He folded his arms but came over anyway to take their order of more ale.

'Now.' Mercia turned back to Nicholas. 'What was obvious?'

He grinned. 'Remind me never to give you slow service.'

She laughed, heartened by his returning humour. 'I am not usually so – but come, speak!'

'Very well.' He leant back in his chair, stretching out his booted legs. 'I realised I could ask Pikey what he knew.'

'Let me guess. Pikey was a pikeman?'

'How did you know?' His grin broadened. 'We were mates on the *Hero* when we ferried the troops about, used to drink the other lads' rum when they were sleeping, things like that. He was the one who suggested I see if the Markstones had any work.'

'Ah, I see.' She felt a prickle of excitement, interrupted by the serving boy banging down her tankard of ale, the frothy head spilling over the rim. Nicholas slapped his hands on the table, making to get up; the boy jumped and hurried away.

'Bloody kids.' He took up his own beer. 'Pikey's older than me. He'd served with Markstone before, at the end of the war.' His green eyes danced. 'He fought at Worcester.'

She sat upright. 'About the time the Oxford Section was stolen. Don't tell me your Pikey knows something?'

'Oh, maybe.' He raised an eyebrow. 'He certainly had something to say about James North.'

The excitement returned. 'What?'

Nicholas took a gulp of his ale. 'Like many a soldier then, North was meant to be at Worcester as well. But there was an incident while the troops were camped at Warwick waiting for the order to march. Pikey remembers it because he and the rest of Markstone's lot were camped very close to North's troop.'

She widened her eyes. 'Did they meet?'

'Afraid not, but 'tis an interesting tale.' He shuffled in his chair. 'The story goes that while they were bored, North's group raided a supply of ale they found lying about. One of the kid soldiers got bowsy on it, and as a dare he pulled off North's left glove.'

'That doesn't sound like much of a dare.'

'No, but apparently North was famous for never removing this glove. Everyone wanted to know why. When the kid pulled it off, he revealed a brand on North's thumb. A letter T.'

Mercia sucked in air between her teeth. 'Well, well. The mark of a thief.'

Nicholas nodded. 'Then North went mad, nearly crashed him.'

She held up a hand. 'He did what?'

'He nearly beat the boy to death.'

'And got off without punishment, I suppose.'

'Not exactly.' His eyes darted away. 'North's commander . . . ordered a finger chopped off.'

'How pleasant.' She screwed up her face. 'So how did North end up escorting the Oxford Section?'

'His commander gave him the job. Pikey reckons it was to get him away from the troop for a while. But then he disappeared. Everyone was told he'd deserted because he was angry at his punishment, but we know better.'

'He stole the paintings and ran off.' She nodded, thinking. 'I wonder if it was some sort of revenge?'

''Tis possible.'

She drummed her fingers on the table. 'Did Pikey say who North's commander was? If he is still alive, he might be helpful.'

Nicholas hesitated. 'I'm afraid he's not.'

'Damn. Still, who was he?'

He shook his head. 'It doesn't matter.'

'Nicholas?'

'Mercia, you don't want to know.'

'Why?' She frowned. 'Just tell me.'

He bit his lip and sighed. 'It was Sir Rowland Goodridge.'

'My father was James North's commander?' She sat open-mouthed. 'But this is unbelievable. First he orders Fell beaten, now he maims North.'

'Mercia, everyone knows those were savage times. North could have been shot for attacking a fellow soldier. He got off lightly.'

'If you say so.' She looked into her ale. 'Really you're saying my father was slightly less sadistic than the rest of them. All North lost was a finger.'

'I'm not saying that at all. Think about it. By assigning him to the escort, your father gave North another chance. Apparently, when word got to Worcester on the eve of the battle that the paintings were lost, Sir Edward was furious, shouting at the top of his voice how North had let your father down.'

She looked up at him. 'For having given him that chance.'

'Yes. Not that Pikey knows that. They all thought it was because he'd deserted and so left the Section more open to attack.'

'You're right. I am sorry. Maybe Father should have had him shot after all.' She drummed again at the table. 'You know, I am certain I heard something about a finger recently. But I cannot remember where.' She rubbed her forehead. 'Very well. So the Section was stolen just before the battle?'

'It seems so.'

'And then Cromwell appointed my father to investigate as he was the one who misjudged North in the first place.' She looked out a nearby window. 'North steals the paintings and eludes the search. Then what?' She let out a frustrated groan. 'Lady Markstone suggested he fled abroad, although he seems to be back now. I wonder if the same thing happened with the paintings? If they were in England, surely Hawley would have found them when he was ransacking everything he could a couple of years ago.'

Nicholas held up his hands. 'Who?'

'Colonel Hawley.' She scowled, recalling the zealous inspection he had bestowed on Halescott. 'The King had him searching the length and breadth of the country to try to recover his father's collection. But as for North, if he did leave, why has he returned now? And how the hell does he know I'm after—my God!' She gasped. 'I bet North was the man who attacked me this morning!'

Nicholas frowned. 'Do you think so? It was probably just some common cloyer, there's enough about.'

'Common what?'

'Thief.'

She shook her head. 'No, he told me to desist, twice, the same word North used in his note. And his hand.' She looked down, embarrassed. 'It didn't feel right. As if there were something missing.'

'You don't mean – like a finger?'

'Perhaps.' She sighed. 'This would have been so much easier if Father had told me about North in his note. I wonder why he did not.'

A sudden worry crossed his face. 'Mercia, if it truly was North who attacked you, then you must be very careful. Maybe . . . think if you want to continue with this. He may not be so easy on you next time.'

She leant forward, gripping the edge of the table. 'I will not let a man like North scare me away. Such men have destroyed my hopes before, and I will be damned in hell before I allow this one to succeed!'

Nicholas sat back, driven into his chair by the force of her words. 'You are very determined.' He hesitated. 'What happened to you in the past?'

Her cheeks flushed red. 'I do not like to talk of it.'

He looked down. 'I . . . understand.'

His voice betrayed his disappointment. She looked at him, feeling guilty at her lack of trust. Once again he was trying to help with his new information, and all she could do was hide behind her usual defensive walls. After the way she had treated him, didn't he deserve to know something of who she was, why she could be so hard?

'Very well,' she said after a pause. 'I will tell you.' A hazy film of water formed in her eyes. 'I was only fourteen. Too young.'

She wiped her eyes, and she began.

She is a girl, though growing fast. She likes boys now, more than her dolls. She is clever, like many of the girls she knows, but she is encouraged in it, unlike any of them. Her father has seen to that. So she is different, suspected, always slightly apart.

She is in the manor house at Halescott. She loves it here. The space, the freedom, the open air of the beautiful gardens. Her father is away, fighting against the King in the war. Mercia adores him. He is a brave soldier, a commander of men, forging victories at Cromwell's right hand. She knows little of politics. But she knows her daddy is a hero and she loves him.

She is reading in her bedchamber alone. Her mother is in the room next door, worrying, no doubt, that Mercia likes to read so. Think of marriage, she continually says, not this unneeded knowledge. Concentrate on your needlework and dance. Lately she speaks of William Blakewood, how he seems tolerant, but Mercia only cares that his face is pleasant. Although she is not supposed to think of that.

So Mercia reads while her mother frets. She is trapped in the words. The door to the bedroom opens, but she does not hear. A figure enters the room, but she does not see. The figure approaches, but she does not notice. Only when the light changes minutely on her book does she finally look up, startled. The figure is close. She drops the book into her lap.

But it is only her brother, Lawrence, come to tease. He should not, he is sixteen now, growing to be a man. But he does, out of habit, out of a peculiar love. She ignores him. He laughs, asks when she will come out of her lair to act as a real woman should. He wants his breeches sewn. She knows he is teasing, but she is annoyed. She folds her arms and asks him to leave. He takes up the book, mocks a yawn. She demands it back. He laughs again and throws it at her, but not hard, so she can catch it. He says he will see her when they eat, and he leaves. She goes back to her book.

Some minutes pass. She becomes aware of a steady sound,

getting louder. It is — yes, horses approaching the house. She looks up, confused. Is it her father? He is not due home today. He is busy, commanding men, being a hero. She looks out the window. Four horses are racing up the driveway. Their riders rein in just in front of the house, dismount, remove their helmets. They are wearing the plumes of the Royalists. Mercia grows worried. These are the men her father is fighting, although her uncle is on their side. Perhaps they are sent from him.

The men are harassed. They are dirty. They file into the house. Mercia thinks, why are they here? Moments later, a scream from downstairs. One of the kitchen maids. Not her favourite? Not kind Bethany? Another scream, and onto the driveway, Mercia sees servants running, shouting out.

The dull thud of many boots pounding up the staircase. Mercia's stomach freezes inside her, a glacial cold that arrives all at once. She hears doors being thrown back, plates smashed, furniture scraping. Oh God, this is the moment she has overheard her parents speaking of, hoping it would never happen. Desperate soldiers from the war, arrived at Halescott.

The door to the next room is slammed open. Mercia holds her hand to her quivering mouth. Her mother is there, her mother, please Lord, protect my mother! She begins to cry, silently so the soldiers will not hear, her mouth gagging, she cannot breathe. Her mother screams. Mercia is afraid, she does not know what to do. So she hides under a table. She is only fourteen.

A thunderous crash in the room next door. Her mother cries out, groaning, keening, a wretched sound. The men laugh nervously, urge each other on. Mercia cannot make out the words, but she does not want to. She knows what is happening. She knows enough of the world, of this war, to know that. She covers her ears. She is scared. So bitterly scared. She knows too, she will be next.

A loud cry. A powerful, masculine scream of rage. Her brother has run in to the room next door. Mercia uncovers her ears. The sound of metal on metal. Her panic subsides, just a little. Lawrence, her older brother, he has come to beat them off. He is strong, he is handsome, he is clever. He will win.

Another cry. A shocked yell of surprise and fear. Her brother. Then a different sound, an inhuman sound, a long, hideous, terrible wail. This time her mother. Why is she crying so? Mercia is petrified, she feels as though she is no longer alive.

The sound of hurried boots on the stairs again. Shouting in the courtyard outside, panicking, frantic shouts, while the wail from next door continues, never-ending. Horses galloping madly away. The wail, the wail still there.

Mercia crawls from under the table. She is shaking, but she can move. She stands up, walks to the door. She goes onto the landing. The next door along is open, flung back on its hinges. She looks in. She sees her mother on the floor, her bodice torn away, her breasts exposed. She sees her brother, immobile and bloody, lying in his mother's embrace, calm as a suckling babe.

Except he is dead. His blood stains the floor. His mother wails. And his sister is useless.

'So you see,' said Mercia, Nicholas listening on silently, 'I made myself a promise. I would never be useless again. Not ever.' Nicholas held out his hand, and she took it with one of hers, brushing away with the other the solitary tear that was drying on her right cheek. She smiled to reassure him. 'Do not worry. I am fine. But now you understand.'

'Thank you,' he said.

'For what?'

'For sharing that with me. It was not easy.'

'No. But it is the truth. It is why I am who I am. And why I will follow that bastard North to the ends of this Earth if I must, before I will give him up.'

Nicholas turned the conversation to trivial matters. The changing weather. Last week's bear fights. The latest rumours about the King's French brother-in-law, who was spending too much time with his companions, and not enough time with his wife. Mercia found herself returning to good spirits.

'So what next?' he asked.

'You still wish to help?'

'Very much.'

'I am glad.' She smiled. 'Then I see two courses of action. One – we find North. We are certain he is around London. Two – we find the paintings regardless of him. The sale of the King's art was a huge affair in the fifties. We ask about dealers. We seek out rumours. If the Section was smuggled out of the country, we find out how and to where.'

Nicholas scratched his stubble. 'I might be able to help with that.'

She inclined her head. 'Oh yes?'

'Let's just say that when you're on the ships, you never assume you'll get paid by legitimate means.'

'You have dubious connections, you mean.' Mercia looked intently at him, then laughed a loud, mirthful laugh that made Nicholas smile too.

'If I didn't, I would have starved long ago. I'll ask around.'

'And I will try to trace North.' She rolled her eyes. 'Do not pull that face, I will not pursue him alone, merely make some enquiries of my own. Try to find out where he may have been hiding these past several years, for one. Then let's meet again. Is the day after tomorrow sufficient time?'

'Yes. I can speak to some people tonight, tomorrow at the latest.'

'Excellent.' She was animated again, back to her enthusiastic self. It was time to accelerate this investigation into the next phase.

Chapter Twelve

The sailing ship drifted past, one of several magnificent vessels plying the river, obscuring Mercia's view to the houses and wharfs of the Southwark side. Shouts of the men on board brought a discordance of gruff slang to the riverbank. Just down from London Bridge, this was as far as such ships could travel before their passengers were forced to disembark or transfer their cargo onto smaller barges to be sent upriver.

She had spent the morning at her father's Lombard Street goldsmiths, discussing the safekeeping of her small inheritance of gold with Mr Backwell himself. Now outside the London customs house, she was hoping an assiduous clerk could help her track James North's movements, if he had ever left England for abroad.

Her luck started well. The clerks were being especially diligent at present, the King desperate for any fresh news of the men who had authorised his father's execution. Many of the so-called regicides had already been hanged, drawn and quartered in that cruellest of deaths her father had been spared, but others had fled overseas, surely, she thought, never to return. Their portraits were pinned on the office wall, their names scribbled beneath – Edward Whalley and William

Goffe, John Dixwell and John Lisle. England's most wanted.

'So what is it you are looking for?' asked a periwigged, middle-aged clerk, eager to help. Wobbling in a rickety chair he had pulled up for her, Mercia was turning on all her charm to elicit fast results.

'I am seeking information on a man who left the country around the time of the battle at Worcester. Not long after, perhaps.' She smiled, employing a lie she had devised. 'He is my cousin. Our grandmother has left him money in her testament, in the hope he can be found to claim it. I appreciate this may be a fruitless request, but I wonder if there is any record of his departure?'

'Worcester was – what? Twelve, thirteen years ago?' The clerk wrung his hands as though washing them, a habitual gesture Mercia was trying to ignore. 'But fortunately we do keep records. Are you certain he would have left from London?'

'No, but I think 'tis likely, given where he was last known to be.'

'I will look. But I pray you are not too disappointed if I fail to discover anything of use. What was your cousin's name?'

She straightened the sleeves of her dress. 'James North.'

The clerk sat sharply forward. 'Not a tall fellow, black hair? A bit . . . aggressive, if I may say so?'

She stared at him, holding her breath. She could not be this fortunate. 'You recall him?'

'Indeed I do, but not from thirteen years ago. James North is the name of a fellow who arrived through this port but five, maybe six months since.'

'Five months!'

The clerk scratched his forehead. 'But if this is the same man, why has he not thought to contact you?' He frowned. 'I thought he was family?'

She coughed, recovering herself. 'He might not want to. There

135

were . . . words said. He will not know about the bequest.'

'It could be a different North, of course.' He wrung his hands. 'Perhaps if you could describe him?'

It was clearly a test. Fortunately Mercia had a star piece of information. 'He was certainly tall,' she agreed to convince him. 'And if you met him you must have noticed – such a source of shame for us – the brand on his thumb?'

The clerk rippled his nose. 'I remember it vividly. That and the gruesome finger.'

A shiver went through her. This had to be him. 'Yes, I think it was cut off at some time, the poor man.'

He shook his head. 'I don't mean the stump. I mean the bones round his neck.'

'I do not understand.'

'Didn't you know?' The clerk jutted out his chin. 'He kept the finger after his accident, attached the bones to a cord as some kind of odd memento. Or so he claimed. We saw no reason to confiscate it so we let it pass.'

She pulled herself closer, the leg of her chair screeching as it scraped on the hard floor. 'Forgive me – are you saying he wore his finger bones around his neck?'

'Ha! You should see what else we get, Mrs Blakewood. People who travel abroad can be very strange.' He glanced at a walnut cabinet in the corner. 'Just last week, someone returned from the Indies with a foul thing, a shrunken head.'

'But my cousin?' she urged, cutting through his prattle. 'If he is back, did he leave any address?'

'He mentioned something about Buckinghamshire, I think, but nothing precise.' He clapped his hands on his knees. 'Now, do you still want me to check the records for '51?'

'If possible. We never knew where he went, you see, and I suppose he may return there.'

The clerk rose from his chair. 'I probably should not, but for you I will. Though I can tell you now that last year he arrived from Amsterdam.'

While she waited she looked around the vaulted office, the steady drone of chattering clerks helping to distract her thoughts from North and his macabre necklace. Then the walnut cabinet caught her eye, and she turned to imagining what its closed doors might be hiding. Perhaps if she opened them, the shrunken head would gawp out at her, thousands of miles from home.

'Mrs Blakewood.'

The clerk had returned, a peculiar expression on his face. 'I do not recall your cousin's accent,' he said, 'and 'tis evident you are not yourself, but he wasn't Scottish, was he?'

In truth she did not know, but being with Cromwell's army it was unlikely. At Worcester most Scots had fought with the Royalists. 'No. Why do you ask?'

He lowered himself into his seat. 'I can find no reference to a James North leaving the country when you say. But there is a record of a ship called the *John and Sara* that sailed from here two months after Worcester. It transported some of the captured Scottish prisoners to a life of indentured servitude in New England.'

She inclined her head. 'What does this have to do with my cousin?'

The clerk smirked, wearing the excited expression of someone with a secret they cannot help but tell. 'There is no James North in the list of prisoners. But there is a Jamie Thorn.'

'What of it?'

'Ah, Mrs Blakewood.' He smiled. 'Criminals often change their identity on starting a new life. Well, Jamie is James, anyone can deduce that. But 'tis fortunate I have such a trained eye for detail.' A self-satisfied look burst across his face. 'Thorn, do you see? 'Tis an anagram of North.'

That night she dreamt of James North, filling in the scarce description she knew of him with ever-changing imaginations. At first his face was scarred, lined with age, but later it was fresh and young, his eyes a deep red, his hair black. Once he was dressed in rags, leering against a dirty inn, and once standing on the terrace at Whitehall, resplendent in furs, offering her a necklace of bone. She protested, fighting him, and jumping over the parapet she flew low across the river, landing in the garden at Halescott Manor. Nicholas led Daniel and Nathan on her horse Maggie from a ship moored in the grounds, while Lady Markstone looked down on them from a rain-lashed window, although the sky was blue. Then North emerged from his hiding place in the branches of an oak tree, bearing her uncle's face in place of his mysterious own, before he morphed into a snarling creature with twenty bony fingers writhing along its back. The black beast charged towards her but she was unable to move, four Royalist soldiers laughing at her feet.

Her eyes flicked open. It took a moment to remember she was in London, alive, no trace of fantastic creatures in sight. When her breathing calmed she realised sunlight was flooding into the room. She had slept for hours.

Stretching her arms she got out of bed, pulling on a robe and looking through the window at the rooftops opposite. Soon Bethany would be leaving to visit her niece who worked in service in town, and she would have the house to herself until she went to meet Nicholas. She was looking forward to the time alone, hoping to think through the questions that were absorbing her. Where was James North now? Were he and Jamie Thorn one and the same? It was an intriguing possibility that would fit her theory that North had left the country all those years ago, but it was just supposition, and it raised the further question of why he had done so in amongst a shipload of Scottish prisoners of war. But if that was conjecture, one thing was undeniable: for North to have returned, he must previously have left.

A small movement across the cobbles below drew her attention, another rat sniffing its way along the road. Queen Street lay in one of London's more upmarket areas, but rats thrived throughout the city. She screwed up her face, wishing someone would empty their foul buckets into the gutter and wash the long-tailed pest away.

And then, like the rat scurrying through the dirt, a memory shifted deep within her mind, stirred by the vivid interconnections of her dream. She thrust out her hand on the window pane in shocked recollection, the stinging of her palm the final jolt she needed to remember. A whisper in the midst of her acute grief, a tale of rats washed up in a terrible flood. And something else too, much more interesting than vermin.

'It was Nathan,' she said as a nauseating stench hurried them past the bear pits on the south bank of the Thames. 'At the – execution. He was speaking to Sir Jeremy Princeton about last December's flood.'

'That was a ferocious storm.' Nicholas barged through a row of muttering touts, all boasting they could find them the best spots to watch that afternoon's fight. 'People are still talking of it, that's certain. In some parts things are only just back to normal.'

Mercia nodded. 'When I saw that rat this morning it made me think of what Nathan said. Rats being swept up, a horse too I think.' She glanced at him. 'And a finger bone on Lambeth Marsh.'

'By God's truth!' He came to a halt. 'So that's why you've got us marching down here. You don't think it was North's?'

A group of laughing boys ran past, swiftly pursued by an angry tout. 'Think about it. Finger bones are made up of three small parts. For anyone to have recognised it as a finger bone after such a violent flood, the individual pieces must have been connected somehow.' She looked at him. 'Like on a cord, perhaps?'

He grinned. 'Oh, very good.'

She set off again. ''Tis April now. According to the customs clerk, North arrived in London five or six months ago, which means he was here before that storm. And Lambeth Marsh is just the sort of place a criminal would hide away. The people there have a reputation.'

'That's one way of looking at it.'

'I think North lost his morbid necklace to the flood, then when the waters receded somebody else found it not knowing it was his. 'Tis just a guess, but it fits what we know.'

Nicholas quickened his pace. 'We have to get to Lambeth now.'

Her experience around Cow Cross had persuaded her of the need to blend in better to the London streets. She had spent her supposedly quiet morning at one of the less disreputable pawnbrokers, handing over good money for a coarse woollen dress that made her itch. Nicholas had laughed at the pitiful garment when they had met, making her turn away in embarrassment before succumbing to the comedy and laughing herself.

She walked him westwards as they talked, past the tenements on the site of the black and white Globe playhouse that had briefly delighted audiences before its demolition twenty years earlier. Along Banks Side the number of dwellings gradually diminished until they passed onto the thoroughfare of Upper Ground. The dusty road stretched its long reach ever further from the city, the clanging and sawing of timber yards replacing the houses and inns, until under a slowly turning windmill the road petered out into open fields on the northern tip of Lambeth Marsh.

On the spur of land where the river bent south, a small collection of makeshift huts for the timber workers and their families sat raised above the dangerous marsh amidst specially dug furrows. Much of the land round about belonged to the Archbishop of Canterbury, his grand Lambeth Palace being very close, but the workers here, locals from Southwark or the Lambeth Marsh hamlet to the south, were not a godly sort. Straight across the river sprawled Whitehall Palace. Whores and thieves of a different type lived there.

Nicholas walked ahead, pointing out the muddiest patches for Mercia to avoid. As they came in amongst the huts the wind rose up, whipping across the marshes and chilling her face even under her hood. She pushed stray locks out of her eyes, straining to hear him speak through the biting wind.

'What do we do now?' he was shouting. 'I don't think we should just ask for him.'

'No.' She pulled the hood closer round her face, the fresh scent of newly sawn wood floating over on the wind. 'If he is here, I don't want him to run away, or for anyone to tell him later we were looking.'

'That won't be easy.' He nodded at a hut doorway where a man and woman were standing watching them. 'I don't think they get many visitors round here, other than men looking for something cheap and discreet.'

They made a quick tour of the improvised settlement, but not many people were about, most of the men presumably at work. Outside one of the small huts, two young girls were jumping over barely intelligible numbers etched into the dirt. The wind was calmer here, making it easier to talk.

'Playing at scotch-hoppers?' Nicholas asked, but the girls just stared. Two dogs ran barking from the hut, a squat teenage boy emerging close behind.

'Get away from them,' he growled.

'We're no harm,' said Nicholas.

'That's what everyone says.' He picked up a long plank of wood. 'Get out of here.'

From the corner of her eye, Mercia saw the couple who had been watching walking over, the woman carrying a tiny child swaddled in a dirty blanket, the man, much older than his companion, dwarfed in an oversized, hole-ridden coat.

'Off to work, Luke,' said the woman, her eyes on Nicholas.

'But—'

'Get on.'

'For fuck's sake.' Luke threw down the plank but did as he was bade. He stormed off, kicking the dogs back into the hut. The girls returned to their game.

'Now.' The man folded his arms, looking between the newcomers. His face was riddled with creases, the wrinkles around his eyes eating into his skin. 'What's your business?'

Mercia pushed back the front of her hood. 'We are interested in finds from December's flood,' she improvised, hoping news of the finger would lead her to North. She could see Nicholas frowning, but she carried on. 'We heard a bone came up here, on the marsh. We would like to speak with whoever found it.'

The couple looked at each other, clearly uneasy. The man moved his hands to his sides, fingering a small knife that was tucked into his belt.

Nicholas stepped forward. 'There's no need for that.'

The man ignored him. 'Lad gave that bone up last winter. Harmans weren't interested then, so why are you here now?' He drew his knife, waving it at Mercia. 'Constables, love. And you're not one, that's certain.'

'Will this help?' She felt inside her pockets for a shilling, holding it up in her fingertips.

The man stared at the coin, sucking in his cheeks.

'You just want to ask a question?' He glanced at his companion, but she shook her head. 'Emma,' he pleaded. 'We could use that.' But the woman just closed her eyes.

'Wait.' Mercia swapped the shilling for a silver half-crown, worth two and a half times as much. The man bit his fingernails and looked again at the woman; this time she nodded, her eyes flicking to the baby. Replacing his knife, the man grabbed the coin and walked off.

'He's half-seas over on sack,' whispered Nicholas. 'I could smell it on his breath. You think that coin will go on the baby?'

Mercia watched Emma gently rocking her child. 'Some of it, I hope.'

They waited in silence, a cold marsh breeze caressing their cheeks. Soon the man returned, dragging a protesting boy by the arm. His grip was tight: the boy was going nowhere.

'This is the arsworm found the bone.' He smirked. 'Give me another coin and you can do as you want.'

Mercia folded her arms. 'You have enough.'

The man grumbled but he kept his word, shoving the boy towards Nicholas who caught him by the wrist before he could flee. He was around twelve years old, his pale face red and wet as though it had just been scrubbed. Timber dust still speckled his unkempt hair.

Nicholas marched the boy along a walkway towards the windy marsh, out of earshot of the watching couple. He stopped at a small leat that ran parallel to the Thames. As Mercia caught up, he bent to stare into the boy's face, still holding his wrist.

'What's your name, lad?' The boy remained silent. 'Mine's Nicholas. Nicholas Wildmoor. Now you say.'

The boy shrugged. 'Tom Finch.'

Nicholas released his grip. 'Very good, Tom. Was that man your father?'

'That's Ben Willis.' Tom gave Nicholas a defiant stare. 'I don't have a father.'

'Well, Tom. You made a grim find here last winter?'

Tom nodded, making the sign of the cross over his chest. A Catholic, Mercia supposed. She wondered what Tom's neighbour, the new Archbishop of Canterbury, would make of that. Gilbert Sheldon had been installed a few months before, but just last year his predecessor had renovated Lambeth Palace in a traditional style, a striking snub to the Puritans who had ransacked it during the war. Was this the latest direction in which the religious winds were blowing, that had buffeted these islands so ferociously over the past century and before?

'Mercia, pay attention,' said Nicholas. 'Tom's going to take us to where he found the finger.'

'Thank you, Tom.' She smiled to reassure him, for she could see in his young face that his defiance had turned to fear, although he was trying not to let it show. He led the way further into the marsh, away from the settlement.

'Careful,' he said. 'This ground's nasty. It floods and becomes very muddy. See!' Mercia had slipped off the path, trapping her foot in the grasping mire. Nicholas pulled hard on her leg to release it, but it took a sharp tug before it squelched out, her foot inside the boot now wet.

Further along Tom pointed to the top of a ditch. 'That bone was here on the reeds.' He looked up at them. 'I thought it was just a necklace, I did, until I picked it up.'

'Looking for booty from the flood, eh?' said Nicholas.

Tom shook his head, but his eyes darted downwards. 'When I got back they tried to take it, but then Emma said it was touched by the Devil.' He crossed himself again. 'I don't scare, but that ain't natural. I ran to Southwark to give it the priest.'

'Who must have handed it to the constable,' mused Mercia. 'Who did nothing, as usual.'

Nicholas scratched his head. 'Stay here with the boy while I search around.'

'What for?'

'If the bone was lost here, maybe our man lost other things too. I can at least look.' He eased himself into the ditch, keeping hold of the slippery sides.

Tom cupped his hands together. 'You'll get sucked down!'

Mercia peered over the edge. Nicholas was testing the ground with each step, but his boot was sinking further each time. 'I think you'd better come out,' she said.

'In a bit. Why don't you ask Tom about . . . you know who? I don't see how it can hurt.' Nicholas moved back up the sides of the ditch where the ground was firmer, holding onto reeds and marsh grass for support. He inched along until he turned a corner into another channel and passed out of sight.

Mercia looked down at Tom, who was staring in the direction Nicholas had taken, biting his lip. 'He shouldn't do that,' he said. 'He don't know the paths.'

Mercia shared his anxiety, but she beat it down. 'Do you live round here too, Tom?'

He was still looking towards the marsh. 'I come up from home, help out. I'm going to be a carpenter.'

'It must be interesting work.'

He shrugged. 'Sometimes.'

She couldn't think how to be anything other than direct. 'Tom, do you know a man called James North?'

Tom hissed. 'That piece of shit?'

She blinked. 'You do?'

'I'd say so.' He unhooked his shirt from the top of his breeches, showing his waist. 'You can't see now, but this was bruised not long back. By him.'

'Tom, I'm sorry.'

'Why?' He snorted. 'You don't care.'

'Tom, I do. Where is North now?'

He reattached his shirt. 'Gone.'

'Are you sure?'

'Course. He was here a month for the work. Got it together with that Kate bitch. Then he hid that finger in the marsh and went. Took some money, Ben says.'

She closed her eyes, the elation she had felt just seconds before evaporating into the soggy air. Tom had confirmed North had been in the area and dashed her hopes of finding him in one short conversation. They were wasting their time out here. But something did not make sense.

'Why would he hide the finger, Tom?'

He frowned at her as though she were stupid. 'As a curse!'

She looked out to the marsh. A heron took flight a small distance away. Supposing Nicholas had disturbed it, she ventured further along the narrow path, arriving at a low wall near the river itself, presumably a flood defence, if one of little use against the force of the December storm. As she walked, Nicholas came back into view, pulling his way in her direction. Then his head jerked down and he stopped. Testing the strength of the reeds around him, he dropped back into the marsh.

146

Several seconds passed. She covered her nose against the peaty stench of the bog, waiting. Insects played their steady tune in the undergrowth. Still more seconds. Now there was no sound but the wind blowing through the reeds. She could understand why Inigo Jones, the architect, had buried his money here during the war. She felt totally isolated. An apprehensive feeling grew in her stomach, moving up towards her chest. Suddenly she heard Nicholas cry out. In the distance, Tom crossed himself once more.

Worrying Nicholas was trapped, she decided she had to go into the mire herself. She moved off down the path, straining to see any sign. But as she was nearing the spot where she last saw him, his head reappeared beneath her, followed by his hands, then his chest. Slowly he pulled himself from the ditch, his clothes splattered in mud.

She knew something was wrong when he didn't joke about his appearance. Instead he rested his fists on his thighs, lightly panting. Then he held up his right hand and flung away a clump of mud, scattering dirt onto the bottom of her dress.

'Well.' He looked up. 'I don't know where North has been all these years, but I know where he is now.'

She waited.

'He is lying dead here in this God forsaken swamp.'

Mercia made the sign of the cross herself.

Chapter Thirteen

'You found a body.'

He nodded. 'Hidden under mud and reeds.'

She held her hand against her chest. Her heart was beating wildly. 'An accident?'

'No. The skull is smashed. There is a bullet hole in his head.'

'Could he have killed himself?'

He looked at her. 'Why would he?'

'Murder, then.' She felt nauseous. 'How do you know it is North?'

'The body is vile, rotted. It must have been here some months. But the mud has saved it somewhat.' He retched involuntarily. 'By God's teeth, 'tis disgusting. The priest needs to be called to bury it.'

'How do you know 'tis him?' she repeated.

He waved his hand, looking out towards the Thames. 'There is some hair left, very thin now, but the black is just visible. And the left hand is missing a finger. My guess is he was killed before the storm and left in the marsh, then the flood snapped the chain from his neck and washed it to where the boy found it.'

'Was the storm powerful enough to do that?'

'Oh yes.'

Then there was little doubt. James North had ended his days here in this marsh, murdered. Mercia closed her eyes. The breeze lapped against her face.

'What do we do now?' asked Nicholas.

She opened her eyes. 'We report it to the constable.'

'Won't they ask why we're here? I thought you wanted to keep what you're doing quiet?'

'We cannot hide this body. But we do not have to mention his connection to the paintings.' She thought a moment. 'We will say we came for a stroll to see the palace from this side of the river. You went into the mire, not knowing its dangers, and in your struggle to get out you saw the body.'

He frowned. 'Will they believe that? 'Tis not what you told Ben Willis.'

'Hell.' She shook her head. 'I do not know. I do not think they will investigate at all. But Nicholas . . .'

'Yes?'

'If North has been dead some time – who left me that threatening note?'

Running on ahead to call the constable, Tom had spread the news of their grim discovery by the time they returned to the huts. A sweating collection of workers was milling around, their work forgotten, a ragged assortment of women chattering amongst them. One of the youngest stared at Mercia, her face ashen.

'Bastards!' she cried, running towards the marsh.

'She knew James.' The woman Emma came up, her indifference lost with the shock. 'He didn't live here long, but it was enough for them to become close. She thought he'd run away, fearing she was with child.' Her eyes narrowed. 'Why have you come here? A coin won't make me believe what you say.'

149

Mercia sighed. North was dead. She had nothing to gain by staying silent. 'Can we go inside? It will be easier to talk.'

Emma assessed her with suspicious eyes, then nodded. 'You might wash first,' she said, indicating an improvised well.

The hut was tiny, merely one large room, the floor bare earth. A pile of straw that served as a resting place filled one corner; a few rickety stools were tossed against the thin walls. A cold draught circulated, causing the limp fire in the middle to roar periodically. They were offered water, but neither accepted it. Water from the Thames was dangerous enough without worrying over any effect the marshland would add.

'So talk,' said Emma as she sat.

Mercia leant forward on the stool she had dragged across. Its legs sunk into the moist ground.

'There was an incident some years ago,' she said. 'North was involved.'

'If you came here looking for hearsay, I won't help you. Even if James is dead.' Emma lowered her baby onto the floor. It began crawling around, stuffing dirt into its mouth.

'No,' said Mercia. 'But I would like to learn what he knew.'

Emma pursed her lips. 'What's it about?'

'There was a robbery. People were hurt.'

She sighed. 'He said he'd run into trouble overseas. Is this to do with that?'

Before Mercia could respond, the young woman who had sworn at them ran into the hut, her dress caked in mud.

'You have done this!' she screamed. 'You have taken him from me!'

Emma leapt up to grab the shaking woman, holding her in a powerful grip. The baby chortled, bemused by the commotion. 'Murderer!' the woman howled, deranged.

'Come now, Kate.' Emma turned her by the shoulders. 'How could they? They've just got here.'

'They want to take his body, then.' Kate glared over Emma's head. 'I won't let them.'

Emma shook her. 'Think, girl. That don't make sense.'

Kate's face began to tremble. She looked at Emma, her fury turning to pain, before collapsing into her arms. Softly, Emma stroked her hair. ''Tis most likely he wandered into the marsh and got sucked down,' she said. 'Like happened to poor Sarah's girl two summers back.'

'But you looked for him,' said Kate, her voice muffled by Emma's shoulder. 'You didn't find anything.'

For an instant Emma's hand stopped. But it was clear Kate trusted her, for gradually she calmed herself, her breathing becoming steadier. Wiping her eyes, she pushed back from her friend and looked at Nicholas.

'Did you know James?' she asked. Nicholas smiled and shook his head. 'You're not from New Amsterdam too?'

Mercia looked up. 'You don't mean Amsterdam?' she said, recalling her conversation with the clerk.

'No.' Kate's tone was scornful. 'New Amsterdam, in America. Don't you think I know where he lived?' Her eyes shone with renewed tears. 'He was going to take me there when he went back.'

Nicholas glanced at Mercia. 'New Amsterdam?'

''Tis a Dutch outpost,' she said. 'Near New England.' And so, she thought, near where Jamie Thorn was sent. She turned back to Kate, her mind churning. 'What was James doing there?'

'He was a carpenter. That's why he came to Lambeth, to find work at the timber yards.'

'But why come back to England at all?'

A tear ran down Kate's cheek. 'I thought he'd left me. But now

I know the truth, I don't know what's worse.' She scratched at the teardrop, her anger flaring once more. 'Why are you asking all these questions? Who are you?' Agitated, she ran from the hut. Moments later a door slammed further up the makeshift street.

'She's upset,' said Emma, bending down to remove a slab of mud from her baby's hands. 'And I still don't understand what you wanted with James. When you came here, you told my husband you were interested in what young Tom found.'

'Well, what I don't understand,' said Nicholas, folding his arms, 'is if that girl was close with North, she must have seen what he wore round his neck. I'm guessing you would have known too.' He jerked his head towards the door. 'That search you made when he disappeared. Very thorough, was it?'

Emma stood up. 'I think you should leave.'

'And when Tom found the bone – North's, as you must have known – did you search again? The storm had disturbed the body by then. I found it quite easily.'

Mercia realised what he was implying. 'What are you hiding from us, Emma?' No reply. 'Would you prefer to tell the constable?'

'Jesus.' Emma paced the hut. 'We didn't kill him, if that's what you're thinking. He did disappear and we did search.' She stared at Nicholas, defiant. 'But yes, we found his body. And we left it there. Covered it with reeds to keep it hidden.' She rubbed at her arm. 'James was a nasty piece of shit. He wore that finger bone like a talisman, intimidating anyone he could with it.' She scoffed. 'If someone killed him, what of it? We left the bastard to rot, fooled Kate into thinking he'd run away. She's better off. Stupid girl thought he cared for her. Obvious what he really wanted.'

'But then the flood came,' said Mercia.

'God sent that flood, made that damn bone float off.' She sighed.

'When Tom found it we said James had left it behind, that he'd got the Devil to curse it to bring the workers bad luck. But the fool panicked, took it to the bloody priest. The constable came, but we sorted him out.' She glared. 'We will again.'

'And Kate?' said Nicholas.

Emma shrugged. 'We made sure she never knew it had been found.'

Mercia rested her chin on her clasped hands. 'I still don't see,' she mused, 'why North came back.'

'I don't know much.' Emma stooped to pick up the baby. 'But Kate said one night, when she was done with business' – she shot Mercia a look – 'that James was after someone at the palace who'd give him money. A nobleman. That if this noble sir refused, there was some threat he would use against him, something from his past.' She looked up, her expression sharp. 'He tried, didn't he, and was murdered for it.' She crossed herself. 'This is truly the Devil's work. Now please go. I need to feed my baby.'

Aware Emma's mood was darkening, Mercia nodded and rose, beckoning Nicholas to follow her out. They stepped into the cold air just as Tom was coming up from Southwark with a constable. Without warning, Nicholas yanked her behind the hut, motioning for her to keep silent.

'What was that for?' she said, once the constable had passed.

'Just – I don't think we need speak with the constable any more. Now that Emma's talked, we know for certain the body is North and why he was here. We'll gain no more from confessing our part.'

'But he will want to speak with the people who found the body!'

Nicholas laughed. 'He'll be glad not to have to. You know yourself they're paid so little they don't care. And don't forget – what are you going to say about why we're out here? Nobody knows where we live. We can just go.'

She hesitated. Then she nodded. They walked quickly away from the huts, just as Ben Willis was draping his arm around the constable's shoulder, a smile of prepared deceit broadening his face.

Troubled by their discoveries, Mercia barely noticed the severed heads that were rotting atop London Bridge's southern archway; the traitors' quartered body parts would be decorating the various city gates. The King could have ordered her father's head so displayed if he had wished it, but in an act of clemency he had returned it to be buried with the rest of his remains.

Through the archway they came onto London Bridge proper, still the only road across the river since the first bridge had been erected on the site in Roman times. The mass of people was so intense it was a wonder anyone was able to jostle past the teeming shopfronts. Even their muddy clothes failed to persuade people to move aside, although they suffered many stares and shouts, especially Nicholas, who was dripping foul ooze onto the pavement.

After twenty minutes they were still only halfway across. Two drays, the sideless wagons that delivered heavy goods throughout the city, were facing each other in the middle of the narrow roadway. The bridge overflowed with buildings, many jutting six feet over the water, but shopfronts still spilt into the road and the drays were unable to pass. The drivers were currently fighting over who should reverse, their horses adding to the bridge's filth as cursing pedestrians tussled to heave them aside.

'What are you thinking about?' asked Nicholas, looking askance at Mercia as they waited to file into the small gap beside the drays.

She sighed. 'How this has just become more complicated.'

He lowered his voice, indicating with outstretched palm that she do the same. 'Because North is dead?'

'Because of this nobleman. He has a secret to hide, and he is scared enough of being discovered that he will kill to protect it.' She looked at him. 'Could North have been hired to steal those paintings? A nobleman would have had the means to pay him to do it.'

'Perhaps. But you are assuming this nobleman was the one who killed North.'

'Ordered him killed, at least. Who else could it have been?'

He thought a moment. 'Anyone North had a rivalry with. An argument gone bad.'

'I doubt it. I think North returned to England to demand more money from his paymaster and was killed for his trouble. And you forget, somebody out there is anxious to scare me from my purpose, and 'tis not North. That cannot be a mere criminal, surely? But a nobleman – if the King were to find out he stole from his father, he would lose his position, perhaps even his head.'

He blew out his cheeks. 'You may be right.'

'But I wonder. Would this nobleman have kept the paintings for himself, or sold them on for profit? If they are not abroad they are very well hidden. Oh!'

As if it were the contents of a shaken beer bottle, the crowd shot forward towards the drays. The force pushed one of the wagons aside, jarring its cargo of barrels to the ground. The wider space formed was immediately filled with barging pedestrians, but they managed to squeeze themselves through without injury, at last coming off the bridge onto Fish Street Hill.

'Remind me to take a wherry in future.' She shook her head as a fight broke out on the bridge behind them. 'Talking of selling the paintings, did you have any luck with your . . . connections?'

'Mmm.' He nodded. 'I've arranged a meeting for two days' time. I didn't want to mention it in all the commotion before.' He looked sideways at her. 'I don't know these people myself, you understand.'

She raised an eyebrow. 'Naturally.'

'A mate of mine is arranging it. He says if you wanted – special things – smuggled in the fifties, you went to One-Eye Wilkins. Anybody else tried to get in on the act, One Eye cut them down.'

'A monopoly?' She laughed. 'And . . . One Eye?'

He grinned. 'That's what I was told. Still, names are just names.'

'Oh, I think they can be more than that.' She rubbed her tired eyes, spreading mud across her lashes. 'But this is no good. I have to go home to wash.'

'Then I'll come with you. With all this going on I want to be sure you get there safe.'

Mercia kept the hackney driver talking when he pulled up, allowing Nicholas, caked in mud, to dash into the carriage unseen. Back in Queen Street, he was not so nimble. The driver swore profusely when he saw him get out, but Mercia left a hefty tip.

'You give money away easily,' said Nicholas. 'How rich are you?'

'Not very. I should be earning income from the estate my uncle has seized, but—Nicholas!' She stopped as she tried the front-door latch. 'The door is unlocked.'

'Perhaps your maidservant has been careless.'

'She has gone out for the day. She would never forget to lock the door.'

He surveyed the facade. 'Then our friend may have returned. Christ, what if he's still here?'

Biting her lip, she eased the door open halfway, entering first despite Nicholas's protestations. The old wood of the hall floor creaked slightly, making her wince. As her eyes adjusted to the semi-light, she heard muffled voices talking in the parlour above.

Hearing them too, Nicholas pushed in front. She mouthed her

irritation but he shook his head, signalling her to stay put. He began to climb the stairs, as quietly as he could; when she followed he waved her back, but she slapped away his hand. She was not going to be cowed, not in her own lodgings.

At the top, the final step croaked a deep groan. Nicholas swore under his breath. No longer able to be stealthy, he skidded across the small landing, throwing open the parlour door. A man within shouted in surprise. Nicholas rushed through, and there was a loud crash as he grappled with the intruder, knocking him to the floor.

By now Mercia had reached the landing. She snatched up a brass candle holder, but then someone fled from the room: a tiny figure, no taller than a child, grabbing at her muddy dress.

'Mamma!' the boy cried. 'Help!'

She opened her mouth in disbelief. Looking down she saw her own son's beseeching face staring up at her. In one swift movement she picked him up and pivoted towards the parlour, peering inside. Nicholas was astride a man on the floor; the stranger was flailing his arms, trying to reach for an object to use as a weapon. Of a sudden Mercia realised who he was.

'Nicholas!' she cried. 'Get off him!' She put Daniel down and dashed over, pulling at the arm Nicholas had drawn back to strike at the struggling man. 'Get up!' she insisted. 'Now!'

Frowning, Nicholas clambered off the prostrate figure, his fists still clenched. His adversary was sprawled in an awkward position, caught off guard by the unexpected attack. Mercia bent down to look at him.

'Hello, Nathan,' she said.

'Mercia.' Nathan pulled himself up. ''Tis good to see you.' His eyes raked over Nicholas. 'But who is this oaf?'

Chapter Fourteen

It took Mercia well over an hour to clean off the mud, even with Bethany's help after she returned from her day out. Heaven knew how long it would take Nicholas, who had eventually calmed down and left, promising to tell her the arrangements for their meeting with the smugglers as soon as he knew himself. A great melancholy came over her as she washed, a morbidity at having found James North dead, but Bethany spoke with such pride of her visit to her niece that the monologue distracted her, and by the time she returned to the parlour she felt refreshed, as though removing the dirt had also cleansed her spirit.

'Mamma!' Daniel ran to her as she entered the room, hugging her through her mourning dress. She looked down at him and felt a surge of maternal pride. What she did here – all the threats, all the setbacks – she could face them all, in the knowledge she was doing it for her family, for her son.

She looked over at a chessboard Nathan had found. 'Is Uncle Nathan teaching you to play?'

Daniel nodded. 'I like the horses best, and the prawns.'

'Very good.' She stifled a smile and bent down to him. 'Bethany has some food for you in the kitchen.'

'I'm not hungry.'

'Go downstairs. You can finish your game later.'

He scowled. 'I don't want to eat.'

'Daniel, go. Bethany is waiting.' She steered him from the room then turned to Nathan with a questioning look. 'Prawns?'

Nathan shrugged. ''Tis a hard game to master.' He stood up from where he had been sitting cross-legged on the floor, his doublet in a heap beside him. Stretching his limbs he joined Mercia on the more comfortable low-backed couch.

'I'm sorry I caused you a fright,' he said. 'Sir Jeremy's servant let me in. He keeps a key at his rooms in the palace.' He tugged on his shirtsleeves. 'I did not realise you would have company.'

'We had a tough time on the marsh. I am afraid Nicholas got carried away.'

He looked at her. 'I think you had best tell me who he is.'

She patted at her topknot; it still felt loose, even after Bethany's administrations. 'A friend, I hope. When I arrived I was desperate to find anyone who might know something. Nicholas used to work for Sir Edward Markstone. He has been of great help.'

Nathan nodded slowly. 'Can you trust him?'

'I admit he is not a usual acquaintance, but these are hardly usual times.'

'I suppose not.' He smiled. 'Well, I am here now.'

'I am glad.' She paused. 'But – why are you here?'

His face set. 'There is trouble at home. Isabel.'

A coldness flared up in her stomach. 'What trouble?'

He bit his lip. 'She discovered you were in London, that Daniel was staying with me. Anthony sent men to the farm threatening to take him by force.' He sighed. 'I am not his father, however much I care for him. 'Tis difficult for me to refuse his grandparents. But

159

I sent the men away and prepared Daniel to travel here. I did not know what else I could do.'

Mercia stared at him, horrified. 'By God's truth! I have been chasing after dead men while my son has been threatened!' Her voice shook. 'What kind of mother would do that?'

'Dead men?' He shook his head. 'No, tell me later. Mercia, you are an excellent mother. You have raised that child on your own since William threw away his life. And you are doing this for him, are you not?'

'I am. And I will carry on doing it. But I had not anticipated how wrathful Isabel would be.' She wrung her hands. 'She must truly hate me. I think she blames me for William's death, that I took him away from her and allowed him to die.'

He sucked in his cheek. 'That is madness.'

'Maybe so, but a mother's love is a powerful force, Nathan, never forget that.'

'So is a father's,' he said, a sadness in his eyes.

'I know.' A moment passed. 'What will Isabel do now?'

'She will discover I have taken Daniel, and she will react.'

'Then she may come to London. We must make sure he is protected at all times.'

'We will. Now tell me what has happened this past week.'

The morning sunlight shone through the study window as Nathan fixed a blank parchment to the cucumber-green wall; made of pine rather than oak, the panelling still looked expensive.

Mercia winced. 'Won't that damage it?'

'Nobody will notice.' He unfolded an oval table and set a quill and ink stand on its smooth walnut surface. 'When we talked last night you were despondent. I know you are upset at finding North dead, but I hope this will show you that you know more than you think.' Dipping the feathered quill into the ink, he turned to the parchment. 'Tell me what you have learnt.'

'Very well.' She leant forward in her chair. As she made her points, Nathan wrote them down. 'One. North is dead. Two. He was murdered. Three. He came back to England around October or November last year, having previously lived in New Amsterdam. Four. He might have been transported to New England after Worcester, but that is supposition.'

'Excellent. What else?'

'Five. North wanted to extort money from someone at the palace. One conclusion is this person hired him to steal the paintings, or at least bought them from him, although again, that is not definite. Except – six – someone who clearly is not North is trying to scare me off.' She smiled. 'Do not look so worried. We talked about that last night.'

'I know. But you cannot blame me.'

'Seven,' she resumed. 'We know the paintings are still missing, or the King would not be so eager to get them back. Given Colonel Hawley could never find them, there is a good chance they were smuggled abroad. That would, of course, suggest the nobleman sold the paintings on.'

'That could make sense.' Nathan chewed at the end of the quill. 'Do you remember the Spanish ambassador at the time, how many of the King's paintings he bought from Cromwell in the Great Sale? There were plenty of foreign buyers, and those were the less interesting works. The Oxford Section would have been quite a prize, no matter how it was acquired.'

She leant back, studying Nathan's scribbles. 'So we still have two approaches. Either we learn ourselves where the paintings have gone, or we uncover this mysterious nobleman and hope he tells us.' She stood up, warming to the discussion. 'Nicholas aims to help with the first approach.'

Nathan scoffed. 'With his dubious associates, according to you.'

She tutted. 'Let's focus on the nobleman. Who could it have been?'

He sighed, but didn't press the point. 'If the nobleman did hire North, he could not have done so much in advance. He would have to have known that North was being assigned to the escort, and you say that only happened after his trouble at Warwick.'

'But there was time?'

He ran his tongue round his teeth, thinking. 'Yes. North would have been seething with rage. It might not have taken long to persuade him with the promise of money and a new life. But if so, it would narrow it down to anyone who had access to him at Warwick, or else at Oxford while he was waiting to leave with the escort.'

'That is still a lot of people. All the commanders on Cromwell's side, and any nobleman who happened to be in the area who knew the Section was about to leave.'

Nathan blew out his cheeks. 'I suppose it could even have been a Royalist who was at Worcester with Charles.'

She frowned. 'How?'

'There would have been spies everywhere, Mercia. As I understand it, Cromwell chose to move the Section then in case the Royalists pushed him back and swept straight round to Oxford. News of the impending escort could easily have reached their camp.' He paced the room. 'Think about it. We know how their mood was bleak. One of their commanders could have devised the plan in desperation, thinking to sell the paintings against any loss he feared a victorious Cromwell might impose to his estate. He could have ridden hard to

Oxford, if he found some excuse. Or used an accomplice, perhaps.'

She smiled at his imagination. 'I am pleased you are here, Nat. I have missed you.'

He laughed. 'Come, I think we have had enough of this. We were going to take Daniel out.' He unpinned the parchment, peeling it from the wall. 'Hell!'

Mercia put her hand to her mouth, stifling a gasp. The ink had run through onto Sir Jeremy's stylish panelling beneath.

In spite of the uncertain conclusions, the discussion had stimulated Mercia's mind, and as Nathan had hoped she felt much better than the night before. He, conversely, was in a melancholy mood following their excursion with Daniel to the physic garden in St James's Park. Mercia had spent much of the afternoon praising how helpful Nicholas had been.

'Are you jealous?' she teased as they meandered their way home.

He grunted, walking ahead down King's Street, emerging into the lively square of Covent Garden. The piazza was relatively new, built thirty years before as an upmarket residential area, and as such the north side was lined with grand, terraced town houses. Unfortunately for the incoming families of quality, the south side had quickly been taken over by noisy market stalls and coffee houses. Salespeople of all types were pushing barrows and heaving baskets, peddling coal, selling water, demonstrating mops. In the midst of all, a boy was standing on a crate shouting out news: 'Coronation Day tomorrow. Long live the King.' And then, just as cheerfully: 'Dutch raid our African forts. War expected soon.'

'They say John Dryden drinks there.' Nathan pointed out a coffee house in the corner of the square, the sign outside advertising 'a most Invigorating drink from Java'. 'I wonder what they make of the prospect of war. Perhaps I will call in sometime, join the conversation.'

'Now you are being petulant.' Mercia shook her head, keeping a close hold on Daniel as they pushed through the crowds.

Nathan laughed. 'You wouldn't want to go in, anyway. Save to cause indignation at men raging at a woman daring to join them.'

'I have better things to do than talk with fawning poets.' She stopped to buy cherries from a woman balancing a precarious basket of the tiny fruit on her head. 'Danny, have one of these.' She pushed a cherry in his mouth, holding out her hand for him to spit out the stone.

Gradually they made their way towards the middle of the square. The boy on the crate was still shouting his news. 'Guinea outposts raided. Commons wants action. Famous gunsmith shot. Colonel Stephen Fell killed in tragic accident.'

Mercia stopped dead, causing Nathan to stumble behind her. Still holding Daniel's hand, she pushed a red-jerkined juggler aside in her haste to reach the newsboy. The entertainer's crowd jeered as he dropped his colourful sticks, but Mercia was too preoccupied to notice.

'What do you mean, Stephen Fell is dead?' she demanded. 'What news?'

The boy broke off his chant. 'Don't know, missis. I just tell what's happened, then people buy me dad's pamphlets. This one's brand new, printed an hour back. Look.'

He held out a single sheet. Mercia gave him a penny, scouring the contents until she found the paragraph about Fell. It was badly worded, but the story was clear enough.

Renowned Colonel Stephen Fell Master Gunsmith was Yesterday found shot in his own shop by apprentice Jeremiah Frome. Constables suspect an Accident, Fell being killed by a Flintlock

gun he was mending and so shot himself. The Affair was yesterday
evening, when the Apprentice drinking with friends in his room
above heard a gun and found his Master dead, who was clutching
the terrible Weapon in his mortal hand.

'My God,' she said. 'Fell is dead.'

They walked back to Queen Street in a more sombre mood, although
Daniel was still happy, his lips progressively reddening from all the
cherries.

'Fell knew everything about guns,' whispered Mercia. 'To kill
himself like that, 'tis preposterous.'

'So what are you saying?' said Nathan.

'I do not know.' She sighed. 'I only spoke with him last Friday.'

He hesitated. 'I don't think you should presume anything. It
probably was an accident. These things happen.'

'I'm sure you are right.' Agitated, she nearly stepped into the
Drury Lane roadway as a swerving hackney hurtled past; Nathan put
his hand across her waist just in time.

'Careful,' he said. 'You nearly had an accident of your own.'

'Thank you.' She looked around her. 'Where is—Daniel, stop
right there!' Daniel skidded to a halt on the other side of the street.
Annoyed, she ran over to him, this time checking for traffic. 'I told
you before, do not run off. And now look, all that cherry juice down
your new doublet.'

'I am sorry, Mamma.' He looked innocently at Nathan, who
failed to be stern back, his attention focused on Mercia.

'We just passed the new playhouse,' he said. 'You need a
distraction. How about going to see the King's Company tomorrow?
It must be years since you've been.'

He was right: it had been a long time. Parliament had banned the theatre at the start of the war, and even though the drama-loving King had now reinstated it, Mercia hadn't seen a play for over twenty years, not since she was ten years old. The thought made her nostalgic.

'What is on?' she wondered.

He ran to look. 'Something called *The Carnival*, by Thomas Porter.'

'I have heard of him,' she said, continuing to walk. 'Yes, why not? Maybe not tomorrow – it is Coronation Day – but perhaps next week, if we get the chance.'

They turned into Queen Street. Outside the town house, a ragged boy was tracing pictures in the road with a twig, the few loose cobblestones scattered about him pulled up to expose the earth below as his improvised canvas. Bethany was staring down from the top-floor window, visibly aggrieved.

'Hey!' Nathan folded his arms. 'What are you doing here?'

'Waiting,' said the boy, not looking up from his drawing. The crude picture was of a cockfight: quite good, thought Mercia, although the birds were larger than the pit.

'Waiting for what?'

'For the lady, all right?'

'Which lady?'

'Merce.'

'What do you want with her?'

The boy looked up. 'Who are you, her husband? Eve told me she weren't married. I've to speak to Merce.'

Her hand on Daniel's shoulder, Mercia cleared her throat. 'My name is Mercia. Are you looking for me?'

The boy jumped up, throwing his twig to the floor. 'I'm to give you a message,' he said, rubbing his hands on his threadbare trousers.

She frowned. 'Who sent you?'

'Eve Standish. I'm to say her brother's hiding from the constables at her place.'

'I do not know an Eve.'

'Well, you know her brother. Nick Wildmoor. He'll meet you tomorrow night at Lion Quay, eight o'clock, but don't try to find him 'til then. They want to arrest him.' He held out his hand.

'Arrest him?' Nathan looked at Mercia. 'By the Lord, I knew he was trouble.'

She was still staring at the boy, confused. 'Why do they want to arrest him?'

He stayed silent, keeping his hand outstretched. She let out an exasperated sigh and rummaged in her pocket. 'Here is a penny. Now answer.'

The boy shrugged, kicking at his drawing with his bare feet. 'Killing a man. Or something. Ask him.'

He snatched the penny and ran.

Chapter Fifteen

Had Nicholas really killed a man? Mercia spent an agonising day fretting over what her new acquaintance might have done. Her anxious thoughts led her mind onto Fell's death, questioning whether the hulking gunsmith had met his end by fouler means than a mere accident, or whether her new-found paranoia was besting her natural judgement.

As the sun set and London vanished into dusk, she left Daniel with Bethany to ride with Nathan to Lion Quay. His protective attitude galled her as he insisted she wait in the carriage while he jumped out and scanned the area. At length he strode towards the corner of a darkened warehouse; she leant out the carriage window to see Nicholas skulking behind a battered post. The two men began to argue, the occasional unintelligible shout drifting over with the wind.

'Damn this,' she muttered. Asking the driver to wait, she got down from the coach and marched towards them.

'I haven't.' Nicholas was seething. 'She's in no danger.'

Nathan threw back his head. 'You want me to let her go with you now?'

'What's going on?' she said, storming in.

'I told you to wait,' said Nathan.

She glared at him. 'Nicholas, what's happened?'

'The constables are looking for him because he fled from a crime,' answered Nathan. 'With you.'

'Lord above, Lambeth Marsh!' She rounded on Nicholas. 'I told you we should have spoken with the constable!'

'Don't worry,' said Nicholas. 'They don't know who you are.'

'Well how do they know who—Christ! You told that boy Tom your name.'

Nicholas gritted his teeth. 'I know.'

'And for once the constables have done something about it,' said Nathan. 'They want to accuse him of the murder, it seems. Which is what that boy meant about killing a man. He had it confused.'

'But North's body was months old!'

'You know how it works. They just want someone to accuse and be done with it. And apparently our boy here is not the most law-abiding of folk, which is why he wanted to avoid the constable at Lambeth.' He scoffed. 'Even though he doesn't live there, it seems the Southwark constables know of him. Gambling, illicit trading, that sort of thing.'

She looked at Nicholas. 'I knew none of that.'

'Come, you're not naïve. And now he wants to take you to see more of his freebooting crew?'

'And what?' Nicholas thrust his face into Nathan's, his eyes quivering with suppressed rage. 'Look at you, your trim clothes, your pretty hat.' Nathan narrowed his eyes. 'Some of us don't have such an easy life. Some of us have to fight to make what money we can, and if that sometimes means dodging the laws your sort make to keep people like me down, what of it?'

'My sort?' Nathan was angrier than Mercia had seen him for a long time. 'What the hell do you know? You think because I talk differently to you, because I wear slightly finer clothes that I have things easy? I've fought battles, seen friends die. Good friends. I've seen my own wife and daughter die! If it wasn't for Mercia I'd probably be dead myself.'

Nicholas stepped back. 'You had a daughter?'

'Yes. What of it?'

'Nothing. Just . . . that I'm sorry.'

'It happens,' said Nathan, his expression neutral. 'Children die.'

'You don't mean that,' said Mercia. She knew the extent of his grief. She had held him all those days he had raved and cried.

'No.' Nathan sighed. 'No, of course I don't.' He sucked in his cheek. 'Mercia, I don't think you should go tonight. You are dealing with people you cannot trust.'

'She can trust me,' muttered Nicholas.

Nathan ignored him. 'He says I cannot go with you, that these – smugglers – are only expecting the two of you.'

''Tis understandable,' she said. 'And we already agreed you would go back to Daniel. I do not like him being alone here with only Bethany at night.' She touched his forearm, the unexpected gesture making him look down in surprise. 'Nat, you know I have to try. I need to find those paintings. And if that means meeting people who do not much respect the law, so be it. Please, go home to Daniel. Nicholas will look after me. I am sure of it.'

'I will.' Nicholas glanced at the river. 'But we really must go. The boatmen will be waiting.'

Nathan glowered. 'Very well,' he conceded. He jabbed a fingertip into Nicholas's chest. 'But see you bring her back safe, or I will hold you to account.'

* * *

The sound of gentle water lapping against the flanks of the small boat soothed her uneasy spirit. A brackish seaweed scent, disturbed by the smooth oars, released a salty tang onto her tongue. At the riverside, candle lights flickered in unseen houses and taverns where people were eating an evening supper, or else preparing for a welcome bed.

Mercia was surprised. She had expected to hate this journey, but other than the discomfort of sitting on a hard bench in a dress not designed for boating, all was calm. She closed her eyes and tried to enjoy the sensations from voyaging down the river at night. Her heightened senses picked up a bird trilling its call from a riverside tree, searching for a partner to share the lonely night.

''Tis peaceful, is it not?' whispered Nicholas. 'A different world.' It was like this sometimes on the ships, sailing across the waters. Of course, other times it was the opposite, waves rising, wind roaring. But not here.'

'A good thing we are not on a ship, then,' she said, her voice laced with annoyance. 'Although I must admit to feeling a little . . . uneasy.'

'Don't worry. All will be well.' He paused. 'I am sorry. About . . . you know.'

She sighed. 'It should be I who is sorry. 'Tis my fault you were on the marsh.'

One of the hitherto silent oarsmen hushed them quiet. Mercia went back to staring across the black water. The night flowed by as surely as the river itself.

An hour or so later, the boatmen brought them to a rocky landing place tucked away in the mudflats some short distance past the great docks at Blackwall Yard. The City of London was now far behind them, back beyond the Isle of Dogs where the eighth Henry was fabled to have reared his hunting hounds. They came ashore near the mouth of the River Lea. There was no one and nothing about.

'I thought you said we were to meet in a tavern?' said Mercia.

'I did.' Nicholas turned to the nearer boatman. 'Why are we here?'

'This is where you'll met One Eye,' he shrugged.

'On the beach?'

He pointed into the darkness, his arm just visible against the cloudy night. 'Over there.'

'But 'tis dark. We can't see a thing.'

He set down his oar. 'We've rowed you here. You're not going back 'til you've seen One Eye.'

Mercia looked at Nicholas. They were trapped out here. But her determination stayed any fear, and she motioned to him to climb from the boat. They were still some way out; cold water penetrated her skirts, seeping up against her shins as she splashed to a pebble-strewn shore.

'I don't like this,' said Nicholas when they were out of earshot.

'There is nothing we can do about it. We are caught in a situation of our own making.'

She heard him exhale deeply. 'I've brought you here,' he said. 'I'm sorry, for this and for—' He stopped. A tiny light had appeared to their left, not far off, moving from side to side.

They made their way towards it, stumbling over the shingle until a narrow path appeared in a grassy knoll behind the beach. As they followed the path, an orange glow that seemed to emanate from the ground itself gradually intensified until the tip of a quivering fire came into view within a concealed hollow. A dark figure at the top of the recess blew out the candle that had summoned them and motioned for them to descend from the rim. Nicholas held Mercia's arm as they slipped down together, sliding on the flat-leaved plants that clung to the hollow's edge.

Two black silhouettes were sitting astride barrels set back from the fire. Their accomplice skidded down to join them, the firelight picking out the folds of his long coat, but it was insufficient to illuminate the others. As Mercia craned forward to make them out, the closer of the two leapt from his barrel and landed on the earth with a soft thud, sending embers flying skyward.

'What business have you here?' he said, his tone gruff.

'Martin Oakes has arranged for us to meet One-Eye Wilkins,' said Nicholas. 'But it was to be in a tavern. Why have you changed the arrangement?'

'We have agreed to meet. Does it matter where?'

'No,' said Mercia. 'As long as we can speak with One Eye. Our business is with him.'

He laughed. 'Then go ahead.' He indicated the third figure, who was still cloaked in night.

Mercia drew her mantle around her as she approached. 'You are One-Eye Wilkins?'

There was a pause, then out of the darkness a woman's voice spoke. 'I am. I understand you have questions for me.'

Nicholas let out a startled laugh. One Eye jumped from her barrel and walked into the light. She was a woman of some years, the creases and lines of an outdoor life marking her tanned face. It was not so much that she was a woman that surprised Mercia, but that One Eye unmistakably had two glinting eyes reflecting in the firelight.

'So,' said One Eye. 'Mercia Blakewood, daughter of the late Sir Rowland Goodridge.' She took off her broad-brimmed hat, revealing a clutch of short white hair. 'Oh yes, I know who you are. 'Tis only because I am intrigued why you would want business with me that I agreed to meet.' She tossed her hat to one of her men and inclined her head in greeting.

'I thank you for it,' said Mercia. 'In spite of the altered surroundings. But I am curious how you know me.'

'I had to give Martin your name,' admitted Nicholas. 'Although he told me nothing of – her.'

Mercia threw him an accusing look. The smuggler merely laughed.

'Allow me to introduce my associates.' She indicated the two men, who doffed their hats. Then she made a fast sweeping motion with her hands. Her men leapt forward, the one grabbing Mercia's arms painfully behind her back, the other punching Nicholas on the jaw, momentarily stunning him. The smugglers dragged them to the now vacant barrels and threw them to the ground. Recovering, Nicholas crouched to jump up, but One Eye had a pistol on him.

'I think not,' she said. 'Boys, tie him.'

Furious, Mercia watched as the men roped Nicholas to a barrel, looping a thick cable three times around his chest. Nicholas sat subdued, his narrowed eyes like soulless slits.

'I should have known,' he said. 'Smugglers can't be trusted.'

One Eye laughed once more, the firelight casting deep shadows across her furrowed face. 'And you can, Nicholas Wildmoor?' She turned to Mercia. 'Now, what business do you have? Speak quickly, or I'll let them at him.' She nodded at her men; the taller kicked Nicholas in the stomach, making him cry out.

Mercia dragged herself up, rubbing at her aching shoulder. 'You need not tie him. Even if your word means little, mine does not. Nothing you tell me will be reported to the constables.'

'You can say what you like to the constables. I am known by the one eye I always keep on them.' She smiled. 'But of course, you thought I was called that for a different reason. My dear, it is never wise to assume anything with me. Now speak.'

Mercia glanced at Nicholas shifting in his bonds, trying to get free. Years of copying her brother as he amused himself tying and loosening all kinds of knots had made her just as competent as he had been, and she remembered the techniques still. But that knowledge meant nothing while One Eye's men were watching. Instead she thought how best to phrase her questions, hoping Nicholas would be freed once their business was concluded.

'I am searching for some objects stolen many years ago,' she began. 'A collection of paintings acquired for a man of high standing. They may have been shipped abroad. I understand you would have taken care of such matters at the time.'

One Eye remained impassive. 'And what time would that be?'

'Sometime in the fifties. Not before the end of '51.'

One Eye came up to her, staring unblinking into her eyes. 'Why do you want to know?'

She did not flinch. 'I want to retrieve them.'

'Were they yours?'

'No.'

'Then why should I help?'

'I am prepared to pay a reasonable sum for your . . . kindness.'

One Eye jeered. 'I don't want payment. I've earned enough, and these boys take care of things now.' She lunged at her men. 'When they're not gambling and whoring, that is.'

'So what do you want?'

One Eye began to circle Nicholas, fingering her pistol. 'The satisfaction of my curiosity? I want to know if this concerns what I think it might.'

'How does she know what you think, old woman?' growled Nicholas. The men clenched their fists, but One Eye held up a staying hand, continuing to circle:

'Bold cove, isn't he?' She looked at Mercia. 'Your night-time amusement?'

Mercia held her gaze. One Eye's prior words had opened a chink of hope, but she kept her face straight. 'Why?' she jested. 'Do you want him?'

One Eye cackled. 'And you're a bold woman.' The first drops of a light rain began to fall. 'Tell me more about these paintings. You ask what I want? I merely want the truth.'

Mercia nodded. 'I think we understand each other. We are both the inquisitive sort.'

'I am waiting.'

She summarised her deductions, hoping she was right. 'They were paintings from the King's own collection, stolen at gunpoint, delivered to a man of the court, and sold on for profit.'

'How beautifully treacherous. You think I got them out?'

'The seller would have wanted the best,' bluffed Mercia. 'That had to mean you.'

The smuggler continued to pace, oblivious to the strengthening rain. Finally she stopped. 'There was an unusual cargo around that time. A consignment of paintings, as you say. Nine, maybe ten, spread over a couple of years. Around . . . 1653, I'd say. I didn't ask questions. The payment was extremely enticing for me to keep my mouth shut.' She scoffed. 'I knew the stories, of course. Those paintings that were supposedly burnt. I'd heard too many rumours about them, too many tales of an unknown gentleman with something secretive to sell. I was sure it was them.'

Mercia's heart raced. 'How did you smuggle them?'

'I prefer to say "liberate", my dear, from the bonds of tariff and trade.' One Eye laughed. 'The seller had an agent, always the same. He brought the paintings rolled up in tubes, tied with string and waxed shut. The buyer's men at the other end had orders to report back if I broke the seal, so I left all as it was. But I always suspected they were the King's. Bloody thieving hypocrite, I was glad to get one over on him, headless though he was by then.'

Mercia ignored her politics. 'Where did they go?'

One Eye tutted. 'You haven't said yet why you want them.'

She thought how to phrase it in a way One Eye would approve. 'Someone at the King's court has stolen my life from me. I want to use the paintings to get it back.'

One Eye smiled, revealing a row of yellow-black teeth. 'You are a bold one, aren't you? I like that.' She sniffed, dropping her pistol on the empty barrel. 'Well, it doesn't matter to me what you do. But you be careful. Such men as these don't want to be found out.'

'So where did you take them, old woman?' said Nicholas, his hair dampening over his forehead.

One Eye glanced at him. 'Hoorn, young man.' She returned to Mercia. 'Or else Amsterdam, but always a Dutch port. They went to a rich client with a connection to the WIC.' She sneered. 'At least that's what the agent said once, when he was being less discreet than he should.'

Mercia frowned. 'The WIC?'

'The *Geoctroyeerde West-Indische Compagnie*.' One Eye pronounced the words in perfect Dutch. 'Oh yes, I'm not stupid, even if I am a smuggler.' Mercia looked blank. 'The Dutch West India Company, sweetheart. Did Papa never teach you languages?'

'One or two.' She tilted her head, taking a deliberate pause. 'Who was the seller?'

One Eye barked out a laugh. 'You expect me to tell you that? But it doesn't matter. I'm afraid he preferred his anonymity. Truthfully, I don't know.'

Mercia nodded, disappointed but not surprised. 'Then perhaps you can tell me about his agent.'

One Eye looked into the darkness, wisps of smoke rising from the fire beside her as the rain fell on the firewood. 'Reckon that would be worth something to you, that information. You trace the agent, you trace the paintings.'

Mercia smiled. 'And you said you did not want payment.'

'Not right now.' One Eye swivelled to face her, widening her eyes; the wavering firelight gave them a demonic air. 'I'll make you a bargain, my girl. I'll tell you his name, and if I ever need something, I might come to you.' She scraped a boot on the ground. 'Just once, in payment of this debt.'

'Don't,' warned Nicholas.

Mercia hesitated. 'This agent. Is he still alive?'

'As far as I know.' One Eye waited. After a few seconds she sighed, pointing at Nicholas. 'Jink – your knife.'

Her taller associate bent down, resting his knife on Nicholas's left cheek. He nicked the skin and a drop of blood fell.

'Sly bitch!' Nicholas struggled against the ropes. 'Mercia, don't trust her!'

'Have you decided?' said One Eye. 'No? Jink, go deeper.'

Jink pierced Nicholas's skin with the tip of his blade. 'Shall I twist it?' he leered. He tightened his grip on the handle.

'As you like.'

'Wait!' Mercia closed her eyes. 'I agree.'

'Very wise.' One Eye smirked at Nicholas. 'See, your mistress is kind to save your handsome face.' Nicholas spat at her feet, but One Eye just laughed.

Mercia rubbed at her temples. 'Did I have a choice?'

'There is always a choice, as there are always consequences.' One

Eye wiped the rain from her eyes. 'The agent's name was Pietersen. Joost Pietersen. Such a pretty name for such a pretty man.'

'Where is he now?'

'How should I know? When we did business he was a WIC negotiator up in London. But I haven't seen him in a long while.'

'And the paintings? After you delivered them, where did they go?'

'They could have gone to hell for all I cared. I had my money.' One Eye stooped to pick up her hat. 'But I'll tell you this. I saw young Joost a few years later about something he wanted for himself. We talked a bit of old times, as you do. I made a joke about the salons of Amsterdam being adorned with the King's art, to test my suspicions. The bastard laughed, said they'd travelled a lot further than that.' She pulled on her hat, tipping it to one side. 'An ocean away, was how he put it. But now I think our business is concluded. Leave, Mrs Blakewood, and don't come back.'

As if responding to an unspoken order, Jink's unnamed mate punched hard into Nicholas's stomach, making him groan in pain. Then the smuggler-queen walked away, vanishing into the night.

By the time the boat cast off to row them back, the rain had turned into a torrent. Thunder split the skies, lightning flashing at steady intervals across the stars. Mercia huddled under a tarpaulin with Nicholas while he rubbed at his arms, stiff from being tied.

Another Dutch connection had emerged tonight, the English enemy, the King's pet hate. But Mercia was only thinking about one Dutch man. Joost Pietersen, she thought. The pretty boy. I lost James North. I will not lose you.

Chapter Sixteen

Mercia returned to her lodgings completely wet, but she did not much notice the rain. After the discovery of North's body she had faltered, but once again she felt there might be hope, that if she could find Joost Pietersen she would uncover the truth about the paintings. And if he did not want to talk, well. She would find a way to make him.

As she entered the parlour Nathan looked up. The relief on his face at seeing her return was evident. 'How did it go?' he said. 'You look wet through.'

'I am.' She pointed to the book he was reading. 'Shelton's translation of *Don Quixote*. Which bit are you at?'

'He has just promised Sancho lordship of an island.' Nathan held the novel up, looking at its creased spine. 'I have been reading this since I put Daniel to bed and I am barely on from the beginning.'

'How is he?'

'Who, Don Quixote?' He smiled. 'No, Daniel loves being here. But you did not answer my question.'

'I got what I wanted.' She took off her mantle, dripping water on the floor. 'Nicholas was right about One Eye being the smuggler of choice. It seems she did spirit our paintings away.'

Nathan leant forward. 'She?'

'That is not what's important here.' Sitting down, she recapped her evening, omitting her agreement with One Eye, knowing it would worry him. 'So now I need to find this agent,' she concluded. 'If he still works for the WIC, let's hope he is not too far away.'

Nathan came over and knelt at her side. 'Mercia, do you think perhaps you should reconsider this? James North is dead, and Stephen Fell too, maybe in an accident, maybe not. What if they come for you?'

'They have come, and they did not harm me.' She took his hand. 'Nat, why should Daniel suffer because my uncle plays games and my father was unjustly condemned? I have to follow this through. You know why.'

He sighed. 'I know. And I will be here to protect you.'

'You are too good to me.'

'You deserve it.' He looked into her eyes a moment longer, then stood. 'You said the paintings were bought by someone connected to the Dutch West India Company, correct? And this agent, Pietersen. He worked for them too?'

'Yes, to both questions.'

He stroked his chin. 'Well, tomorrow is Sunday, but on Monday I know where we should go.'

'Where?'

He affected a dramatic tone. 'The very heart of world trade.'

'Of course.' She smiled. 'The Royal Exchange.'

Come Monday, Nathan spent his morning in the nerve centre of British commerce, where orotund men argued over prices and shook hands on profitable deals. Mercia spent it shopping, in the adjacent arcade. She said she wanted to fit Daniel for a new outfit, but really she wanted to browse for gloves for herself. By the time Nathan found her, Daniel had conquered his boredom by forcing his mother to a shop full of wooden toys.

'Make any good deals?' she asked, shaking her head at Daniel who was holding up a pair of shaved-off stilts.

'Mmm. I bought ten bushels of Kentish wool.'

'Doing your own business, eh?' It was a gentle rib.

'No, yours. I asked the WIC men if they knew of anyone back in Holland who might have bought paintings in the fifties, but they wouldn't talk to me.'

'I am surprised they are still in London with all this talk of a war. And Pietersen?'

'Now there I did have luck.' He picked up a spinning top and twirled it round on the counter. 'This Kentish wool merchant, for instance. Once I agreed to buy his wool, he introduced me to a friendlier Dutchman trying to make deals despite the Navigation Acts.' He arched an eyebrow. 'He sells tea.'

'I hear the Queen likes it.' She looked over his shoulder. 'Daniel, I said no.'

Nathan craned his neck. 'He would have fun with those.'

'Don't start. What did you find out?'

He groaned. 'A lot about tea. It comes from the East. I pretended I was a potential buyer and the Dutchman talked. And talked. How anyone can be so interested in a drink made from tiny leaves, I do not know.'

'Nathan. What about Pietersen?'

'I'm sorry. The tea merchant works for the VOC, the Dutch East India Company, which operates in Java. And he does know your man. According to him, Pietersen is famous.'

An excitement stirred. 'Famous how?'

'It seems Pietersen is ambitious – the sort of person who treads over everyone else to get to the top. He is notorious for it, amongst his colleagues – and amongst his enemies. So when I asked, this merchant was more than happy to talk.'

She frowned, for despite his words his expression was bleak. 'So why the glum face?'

He leant on the countertop. 'Well, Pietersen does still work for the West India Company, doing very well for himself.'

'West, east, they go all over the world, these Dutch.' She mouthed at Daniel to put down the stilts. 'Is he in Amsterdam? Is that why you seem worried? I confess, I do not relish the prospect of travelling there, but needs must. We are not at war yet.'

Nathan bit his lip. ''Tis not that. Pietersen works for the WIC, but not in Amsterdam or London or anywhere near.'

'Where then? If not Amsterdam then—' She closed her eyes. 'Oh no.'

He nodded. 'He lives in one of their colonies, Mercia. In New Amsterdam, in America.'

She buried her face in her hands. 'Why is life never easy? But – wait a minute.' She jerked her head back up. 'North lived in New Amsterdam too.'

'Indeed.' He looked at her. 'And there is something else.'

'What do you mean?'

'After confiding in me what a bastard Pietersen was, and how I shouldn't trust him if I ever had to do business with him, the merchant told me that when Pietersen left for America a few years ago, it was all very strange.'

'How so?'

'It seems he returned to Holland just a few months later, as if he could have spent no more than two or three weeks in the colony.

Then almost immediately he went back to America.' He shrugged. 'Well, 'tis a long way to come just for a forgotten coat.'

'You think he was up to something else?'

'He had to be. Now this is the best bit.' He leant in closer. 'One of the WIC agents stationed in New Amsterdam brought back an odd story about Pietersen's second arrival there. Apparently he took ashore a large chest with a great number of locks on it, but when he opened it, it was totally empty. He claimed it had been full of a personal supply of food and ale that he had hidden from the rest of the passengers. Like everyone else, the merchant believes that must be true, because – how did he put it? – it was the damn sort of bastard selfish thing that miserable shit would do.' He raised an eyebrow. 'But what if the chest had something else inside? Something valuable, that actually merited such a protected casket?'

Mercia gasped, realising the implications. 'Then why was the chest empty?'

'Obvious. Before he left the ship, he smuggled the real contents into the colony somehow.'

'Hell's teeth, Nathan. What you are saying—'

He nodded. ''Tis not just Pietersen who went to New Amsterdam. I think the Oxford Section may be there too.'

'So what happens next?' said Nicholas, strolling with the other two through the Moor Fields under a warm afternoon sun. It had been his suggestion to meet in the mostly open space, presumably, as Nathan had teased Mercia, so he could easily spot any constables who might be lurking about. Still he did seem anxious, his eyes frequently darting around. Daniel was back with Bethany, practising on the stilts he had finally harassed his mother into buying.

'I am not sure,' said Mercia. 'It seems everything has to do with

New Amsterdam.' She counted out points on her fingers. 'Whoever acquired the paintings from North, he sold them on. Pietersen was his agent, and Pietersen lives in New Amsterdam. When Pietersen moved there he took a well-protected chest with him, which may have held the Section – remember what One Eye said, Nicholas, about the paintings being an ocean away? And the buyer is connected to the West India Company, which owns the colony. Well, 'tis possible he moved there himself. A rich man could retire there, or seek to make yet more profit.'

'Not forgetting that North lived there too,' added Nathan. 'A coincidence?'

'So what are we saying?' said Mercia. 'That I have to board the next ship out there? Aside from the distance, by the time I arrive we may be at war.'

Nicholas stopped, bringing them all to a halt. 'I've never known anyone so determined as you are about finding these paintings. You say they may be in New Amsterdam, that this Pietersen is your best link to them? Then that's where you need to be too.'

'I hate to agree,' said Nathan, 'but if you want to pursue this, he might be right. Pietersen is the only one who knows where the Section is and who stole it. Else we stay here and uncover the nobleman, but I cannot think how we do that.'

She looked at him, surprised. 'I thought you would not want me to go?'

'I would be concerned. Travelling the ocean is not an everyday venture. And there is no guarantee the King will be as generous as you hope.'

'No. But he is desperate for those paintings.'

In the distance, she saw a small girl being carried on a man's back, presumably her father, laughing and screaming. It sent an image flying into her mind, a memory of her own father, his study, *The Fairie Queene*, the tales of Britomart, the desire awakening in her childhood self to be like her heroine, to see the world. Had she forgotten those dreams?

She resumed their stroll. 'And I wonder. Perhaps there is a way of using this to scare the nobleman into the open. If he learns I am going for Pietersen, he will have to intervene or risk exposure. By heaven, I would love to unmask that fiend.'

Nathan blew out his cheeks. 'Mercia, that sounds dangerous.'

'Life is dangerous.' She paused, thinking. 'I would have to take Daniel with me. 'Tis not safe for him here with Isabel on the hunt. But still, 'tis an incredible notion.' She looked at the fields of London around her. 'Too incredible, perhaps. But my house. Danny's house. I cannot give up on it.'

They fell silent for a moment. 'If you did go,' said Nathan eventually, 'I could not let you go alone. I would come too.'

The kindness of his gesture overcame her. 'You would do that?'

'For you, I would do anything.' He spoke with friendly humour, and yet she thought she could hear something more in his words. Over his shoulder, Nicholas raised an inquisitive eyebrow.

'Nat,' she said, 'I could not make you go all that way. What of your farm? Your obligations?'

'Sir Jeremy did say he would do anything to help you. Besides, my brother can take care of the farmland, 'tis about time he—'

He did not get to finish his sentence. A loud zing flew past Mercia's head, a nearby birch tree vibrating with a low thud. They all looked round at the shaking trunk.

'Is that – an arrow?' said Nathan, squinting to focus.

A second zing tore past.

'Lord above! Some rogue is shooting at us!' He scanned the area behind them, his soldier's training coming into immediate use. 'There he is. Come on!' He signalled to Nicholas and began to run.

Staring after them Mercia saw a dark-clothed figure dart from behind a tree, holding some sort of large object. 'My God,' she exclaimed, realising it was a crossbow. Not pausing to think, she set off herself.

The assailant was a fair distance ahead, but Nathan was sprinting and gaining fast. Aware of the chase, the bowman dodged right, barging into two finely attired women who were taking a walk on the fields. One of them tripped, stumbling to the dirty ground; Nathan had to slow down to run round her, causing him precious seconds delay.

Checking the land ahead, Mercia shouted to Nicholas to run right, while she went left in a sort of flanking action to try to keep the bowman in Nathan's path. It was open fields here, and the grass was long, hindering her in her bulky dress. But she was indignant. Someone had shot at her and she wanted to know who.

Encumbered by his weapon the bowman began to slow. Mercia cried out, calling at him to stop. Still running, he turned his head towards her; she caught a glimpse of a tanned face and thick black eyebrows, his hair equally bushy. Seeing her attempting to cut him off on the left, he swerved to the right, straight into the path of Nicholas. But he was a way in front and so had a chance to run left again, although by now Nathan was nearly at his back.

They were running at him from the north, forcing him towards the lower part of the fields, close to the city wall. There were more people down here, and they were beginning to take notice of a man wielding a dangerous weapon running crazed in their midst. Nathan was now nearly on him, but the bowman reached in his pocket to pull out a crossbow bolt, throwing it blindly at Nathan's feet. Nathan jumped aside, causing him to drop back. The bowman took advantage to run towards the Moor Gate, pushing his way through the startled crowd. Now level with Nathan, Nicholas rushed on in pursuit, but he slipped where the grass gave way to gravel, and by the time he reached the wall the bowman had fled through the gate, vanishing into the streets. A swerving cart was the only indication of the route he had taken to escape. Nicholas swore a loud oath as Nathan reached him, skidding to a reluctant halt.

Breathing heavily, they returned to where Mercia had stopped just near the Moor Gate, surrounded by a crowd of curious spectators all sharing different versions of the chase. Doubtless the story would be further embellished by the time it was repeated in the taverns that night.

'Did you see who it was?' she asked.

Nathan shook his head. 'He was too fast. All I could see was a man with black hair.' He looked at Nicholas. 'Did you see anything?'

'No. I nearly had him. Damn it!' He punched one hand into the other in rage.

A woman in the crowd spoke up. 'At the last, when he barged through, he shouted at us in a foreign tongue.'

'Spanish, I think,' added another.

'No,' said a man. 'Portuguese. I have been in Brazil, I know their speech. *Saiam do meu caminho*, he said. Get out of my way.'

'Portuguese?' said Mercia. 'Why would he be Portuguese?'

Nathan shepherded her away from the crowd, lowering his voice. 'Whatever his origin, this was aimed to scare you. He shot two precise bolts, one past your head, one straight between us. If he wanted to hit us, he could have done. Someone clearly wants to worry you, but they do not want to kill.'

'That is scant relief. But it shows we must be on the right track.

Evidently somebody is very bothered by what I am doing. And still following me.'

He shook his head. 'That bowman was lying in wait. He knew exactly where you would be this afternoon.' He looked at Nicholas, who was pacing round and round. 'Mercia, it was Nicholas who asked us to meet here. And he was in your lodgings just before that intruder got in.'

She scowled, waving a dismissive arm. 'I do not think so. What would be the point? I met him by chance, Nathan, and he has helped so much. I hardly think . . . besides, there is no connection between him and North.'

'Yes there is. Sir Edward Markstone.'

She sighed. 'How is that relevant? North was a crooked soldier Sir Edward was investigating, Nicholas a farrier in his employ. Now leave it. He is coming.'

'I'm sorry I couldn't catch him,' said Nicholas, joining them. 'I'm furious.'

'You did the best you could,' she said. 'Better than me.' She held up her skirts. 'This rather held me back.'

Nathan folded his arms. 'We were wondering how that bowman knew where we would be.'

'You think it was arranged?' Nicholas cupped his chin. 'Perhaps someone overheard something.'

'Or someone said something.'

'Nathan,' warned Mercia.

'Well I didn't – hey!' Nicholas took a step forward. 'You'd better not be suggesting I had anything to do with this.'

'No he is not,' said Mercia, her eyes on Nathan. 'Are you?'

'No,' said Nathan. 'Very well, no!' Next to him, Nicholas stood frowning. 'But maybe, Mercia, this should make you think twice about trying to entrap that nobleman. Whoever is behind this, next time he may use more deadly force.'

'I will not let him beat me, Nat. I cannot. But I do not know what to do for the best.' She sighed in exasperation, looking to the clear blue sky. 'Father, what should I do?'

A commotion in the crowd caused her to look towards the wall. Someone was trying to push a way towards them through the protesting onlookers. Nathan and Nicholas both tensed. But the elderly woman who emerged was very familiar.

'What is Bethany—?' Mercia clapped her hand to her mouth as she saw the dark bruise that was forming on her maidservant's cheek. Her white cap was askew, and she looked more agitated than Mercia had ever known. And then she noticed the empty space at Bethany's side where Daniel should have been.

'Mistress,' cried Bethany, her voice shrill and shaking. 'I couldn't stop them. They've taken him, mistress. Lord forgive me, they've taken Daniel!'

Chapter Seventeen

'What do you mean they've taken him?' said Nathan. 'Who has?'

'Some men came after you left.' Bethany's old face began to quiver. 'He was playing on his little stilts. I chided him for it, he was damaging the floor.'

'Bethany, tell us!' Mercia was fighting every urge not to run straight back to the house.

'There was a knock on the door. I thought it was you, but it was them. One searched the house, the other held me against the wall. I struggled, mistress, really I did, but he struck me.' She felt her bruised cheek. 'It dazed me, made me confused. When I came round I was sitting on the floor.' She began to cry. 'Daniel was gone.'

'Nathan, what do we do?' Mercia was frantic. Nicholas grabbed her as she made to run off. She pushed him away. 'I have to do something!'

Nathan took Bethany gently by the shoulders. 'Did these men say who they were?'

'They didn't say much. But I know who they were.' Her face set. 'It was those Pelton brothers.'

'The Pelton boys?' said Mercia. 'Those ruffians from back home?'

'Jesus,' said Nathan. 'They followed me down.'

Mercia snapped her gaze on him. 'Isabel.'

'They must have found out I left not long after I came down.' Nathan helped Mercia from the hackney they had taken with Nicholas from the Moor Gate. 'They would only have been a day or two behind. Enough time since to discover your lodgings.'

'Then wait for me to leave and strike. My God, Nathan. I never should have left him alone.'

'You left him with Bethany. You could hardly have foreseen this would happen so soon.'

'Couldn't I?' She stopped under the sign of the Saracen's Head, the faded Turkish visage mocking their approach. 'What matters now is that we find him. But they will never be here. Even the Peltons know it is the first place I would look. 'Tis too obvious, even for them.'

While Nicholas scoured the courtyard, Mercia entered the inn where she had stayed on the night of her father's execution. It would have brought back bad memories, but today she had a singular purpose. The innkeeper was standing by his bar, talking with customers. The Pelton brothers were not amongst them. She did not expect them to be. The Saracen's Head was the main coaching inn for Oxford; with no public coach scheduled until tomorrow, it would be a poor hiding place, and one the Peltons would know she would check.

Recognising her, the innkeeper broke off his conversation and came over. 'Do you need a room, Mrs Blakewood? Going back on tomorrow's coach?' He took in her worried appearance. 'Is everything well?'

She took him to one side. 'Do you know the Pelton brothers? From up in Oxfordshire?'

He scratched at his beard. 'They've stayed here once or twice. They like their ale, that's certain.'

'They aren't staying here now?'

He shook his head. 'You have business with them?'

'You could say that.' Across the room, Nathan was beckoning her over; she signalled to him to wait. 'Have they ever mentioned anywhere else in London they might go?'

'I don't generally ask what folk get up to, Mrs Blakewood. What's this about?'

'Never mind.' She excused herself and crossed the room to Nathan. A long-haired man beside him was turning a silver coin between his callused fingers.

'Tell her what you told me,' said Nathan.

'I met them in an inn on my way down,' the man said. 'I was on the coach but they were riding by themselves. I lost out when the bastards cheated me at dice. Your man says you're looking for them.'

'That's right.'

'Bet I know where they are.'

'Where?'

He grinned. 'Also bet you want them badly enough to pay for that.'

Mercia sighed, reaching into her pockets, but Nathan kicked out the man's legs from under him and pinioned him on a table, sending a tankard shooting to the floor. He rested his forearm on the man's throat.

'I already gave you a sixpence. You said you wanted to get back at them, well here is your chance. Where are they?'

'I don't know,' gasped the man, his hair fanned out across the sticky table. Nathan pressed harder. An entering customer took one look and walked straight back out. 'I think they're in Uxbridge. At the George.'

'Why?' Nathan lightened his grip.

The man clutched his throat. 'They were talking with some fellow in the King's Arms where we stayed. They wanted a safe house for a night, a flexible arrangement for whenever they needed it. They arranged it for the George. They thought I was passed out on the bench, but I heard every word.'

Nathan looked up at Mercia. 'See,' he said. 'It was worth coming here after all.'

They needed horses, and fast: Nicholas took them to the aptly named Horse and Star, the same inn where she had found him at work just a few days before.

'A safe house makes sense,' she said as she waited in the yard with Nathan. 'The Peltons could hardly take him up in public, certainly not on the coach. He would be kicking and screaming. Anthony will have given orders not to harm him. We can expect that much, at least.'

Nathan nodded. 'You think they're making their way back on their own, bit by bit?'

'Yes. They'll have made a similar arrangement further up, High Wickham perhaps. Fortunately Uxbridge is not too far from here.'

'Horses,' said Nicholas, leading three out. 'But I need to pay something for them.'

'Give the landlord this.' Mercia handed him a golden guinea. 'Is it enough to borrow them for the night?'

Nicholas stared at the golden coin: dated the year before, it was one of the first batch of guineas issued. 'I should say so.'

'Good. Then shoe them and let's go.'

While he was readying the horses Nathan paced the yard. 'It will be dark soon,' he said, 'and there are highwaymen about. We need to get started.'

She called across to Nicholas. 'Can we get a gun?'

'For a price.' Nicholas set down the hoof he was holding. 'I'll ask Welshie.'

Finishing with the horse he took a half-crown from Nathan, returning five minutes later with a pistol and shot. 'Good job that lot don't ask questions.'

Mercia held out her hand. 'Give it to me.' Nicholas laughed nervously. 'I mean it. This is my son we are chasing. I cannot expect you to shoot anyone for him, so I will take it.' She took the gun from his hands. 'Is this loaded?'

'Yes,' he said, a respect on his face she had not seen before. 'You know how to use it?'

She looked him in the eye and set the pistol to a half-cocked position. But she had to pass Nathan the gun to mount her horse, and in spite of her protests, he kept it for himself.

They powered out of the city, forcing their way through the Holborn crowds. Once they had left the London traffic behind, they rode quickly. Mercia spurred her horse as fast as she could.

''Tis near twenty miles to Uxbridge,' shouted Nathan, drawing alongside her. 'The horses will tire at this pace.'

She kicked her horse still faster. 'They will cope.'

They galloped through a series of villages – Kensington, Shepherd's Bush, Acton – startling all they passed into turning their heads and following them with wondering eyes. Further into the countryside the woods came in close, but they never once met a highwayman, not even after the sun had set and the waxing moon had risen. By then they were passing Hillingdon and were almost at their goal. Coming into Uxbridge they flew past the vast Place House, where nineteen years earlier, in the midst of civil war, envoys sent by King and Parliament had faced each other across a table of futile truce. Their failure to reach an unwanted accord had prolonged the bloody war, sad news for those like Lawrence Goodridge who had paid the sorry price.

Tonight his sister, grown up, rode into the large courtyard of the George Inn where the parliamentary commissioners had made their base. The rambling tavern surrounded the yard, its gabled roofs and leaning walls seeming to beckon the traveller in to be swallowed whole, never to emerge. It was a wickedly suitable hiding place.

Dismounting to the muddy earth, Mercia left her panting horse with a stable boy, forcing herself to wait while Nathan and Nicholas did the same. After what seemed an age they joined her, but as she stepped on the stairs that led up to the entrance, Nathan drew her back.

'Wait,' he said. 'If they are in there and they see us, they may scare. Who knows what will happen then.'

She paused with her right boot hovering over the middle step. 'You are right. What shall we do?'

Behind them Nicholas cleared his throat. 'What do these Peltons look like?' he asked. They turned round and he shrugged. 'Well they don't know who I am, do they?'

Ten minutes later he was back outside.

'They're in there all right. Ugly bastards, singing to some arsworm of a fiddler and playing at dice. But there's no sign of the boy.'

'There must be rooms here,' said Mercia, looking up at the inn's top floor. 'We need to find which is theirs.'

'I asked one of the serving maids. She won't say.'

'Can't you turn on the charm?' said Nathan.

'I did.' Nicholas smirked at him. 'Why don't you try?'

Mercia cut off his response. 'I have a better idea. Nicholas, you play at dice, do you not?'

'Yes, but—'

'Then here.' She threw him a few pennies. 'Go and play. Find which is their room. And win us back the cost of hiring that pistol while you are at it.'

She sat under cover of her thick mantle, Nathan facing away from the Peltons at her side. The inn was busy, but they managed to squeeze onto a rickety bench, pretending to enjoy their ales. The smell of burning logs mixed with the malt and hops, the heady mixture teasing her nose, making her want to sneeze.

She watched from under her hood as Nicholas wormed his way into the Peltons' game. For the next few minutes he rolled the dice, making bets, dragging his arm across the table to collect his frequent winnings, until the Peltons' drunken mood turned sour. One of the brothers produced a knife; Mercia nudged Nathan to ready the pistol, but it turned out to be a challenge, double or nothing, for Nicholas to lay out his hand and play the game of stabbing the knife back and forth between his outstretched fingers. She tensed when he took up the knife, but he made easy work of it, from endless practice while cooped up on the ships, she supposed. The younger Pelton stood up, outraged, but his bald elder brother pulled him back down.

'We don't have the money with us,' he spat, loud enough for his drunken voice to carry over the crackling fire. 'You'll have to take what you've got.'

Nicholas sliced a corner of wood from the table. 'I don't think so. I'm guessing you have what you owe in your room.'

The bald Pelton growled. 'You're not going up there.'

'Why not?' Nicholas leant on the table, pushing himself half up. 'Got something precious hidden away?'

Bald glanced at his brother, almost imperceptibly, but Mercia saw the signal for what it was. 'Come, then,' he snarled, leading Nicholas through a lopsided wooden archway into the back room. After a few seconds his brother followed. Setting down their ales, Mercia and Nathan followed him in turn.

The sparsely furnished back room was cold, even through her mantle: the warmth of the drinking area seemed unable to pass the archway. Crossing the slippery flagstone floor, they climbed up the wide staircase that led to the lodgings above. At the top was a galleried landing; halfway down the narrow space, the two Peltons had Nicholas hemmed in.

'Thought you could beat us, did you?' The elder brother's shaven head was pockmarked and squashed, his nose askew, broken from one of his many fights. 'We'll teach you southern princock some manners.'

'Good luck,' called Nathan, cocking the loaded pistol. He strode down the landing, pointing the barrel at the younger brother's head.

'What's this?' said Bald, staring at the gun. Nicholas drew back his fist, but Nathan shook his head.

'I believe you owe this man money,' he said. 'So take us to your room.'

The elder Pelton spat on the floor, defiant. 'You pussies want my brother's arse for the night, that it?' He looked at Nathan. 'Wait a moment. I know you.'

'Now can I punch him?' said Nicholas. Nathan gave a curt nod and Nicholas jabbed at Bald's face, cracking his head against the wall. He groaned but remained conscious.

'Which room?' barked Nathan. The younger brother stared, but then his gaze flicked briefly to the last door down. Mercia pushed past and tried the handle. It was locked.

She lowered her hood. 'Open it.'

'Shit,' said the younger Pelton.

'Good. You know who I am. So you will understand I am quite prepared to get him to shoot you if you do not open this door, right now.'

'No one's in there,' mumbled Bald, rubbing the back of his head.

She looked at Nathan and shrugged. 'Shoot him.'

Slowly, Nathan brought the gun to point directly at the younger Pelton's forehead. His forefinger teased the trigger.

'Wait!' cried Bald. 'Wait.' He stumbled along the landing to join Mercia by the door. Nathan followed him with the pistol, Nicholas holding the knife he had pocketed downstairs at his younger brother's throat.

As Bald unlocked the door, another swung open adjacent. A young woman emerged, tying up her front-closing bodice. She glanced at the scene before her and retreated back inside, calmly, as though she were used to such events. But the distraction gave Bald his chance. He pushed his door open just wide enough to slip through; once in he slammed back on it hard, but Nathan thrust out his arm and the fragile door rebounded. Through the gap, Mercia caught sight of Daniel tied to a chair. Seeing his mother he began to scream.

'The bastards,' she cried. She pushed against the door with a superhuman strength, Bald fighting her on the other side, but then Nathan was pushing too, and Nicholas, and together they flung the door back, sending Bald flying to the ground. An old woman lying on the bed leapt up to run past, but Nathan threw out his foot and she tumbled to the floor, joining Bald with a crash. As he covered them both with his gun, Mercia made short work of the poorly tied knots holding Daniel.

'What happened to the other one?' Nathan asked Nicholas.

'I got fed up waiting. He's out cold.'

Nathan smiled, clapping Nicholas on the shoulder with his free hand, his gaze remaining firmly on Bald. Now free, Daniel grabbed his mother close. She stroked his hair and kissed his forehead, asking if he had been hurt. He shook his head, but it was clear he was upset.

Mercia rounded on his abductors. 'You take this message back to Anthony and Isabel. You tell them not to play their games with my son. You tell them I will never give him up.'

'They want him,' said the old woman. She seemed unbothered by the pistol. 'They will come for him again.'

'They will never get the chance.'

She picked up the key where Pelton had dropped it, passing it to Nicholas as she backed Daniel onto the landing. Nathan kept his pistol aimed into the room until Nicholas shut the door after them and locked it. Then they walked down the landing, stepping over the prone body of the younger Pelton, and back through the still-crowded inn to fetch their horses from the stable yard. Only when they had ridden back to Hillingdon, to take rooms at the inn there, away from the Peltons, did they pause.

'So what now?' said Nathan.

Mercia scooped her son up in her arms. 'Now, I will take him a long way away. I will keep him safe. I will get back the manor house. I will do whatever I must.' She looked Nathan in the eye. 'I have made up my mind. I will go to America.'

Chapter Eighteen

The grey light of dawn was only just breaking through when she made them all leave Hillingdon, eager to return to London for the encounter she had lain awake all night planning. Arriving back in Queen Street while it was still early, she forewent breakfast – she was in no way hungry – and after washing her face in the bowl by her bed, she splashed rosewater under her arms and changed into her tidiest black dress, the one she had kept aside in case it was needed at short notice. Bethany helped her into her equally black bodice, tying the back loops tight, leaving just enough room to thrust her fiercest rod of whalebone down the front. She applied a tiny amount of Spanish cochineal to her cheeks, a sliver of red paint to her lips. Bethany brought out the severest of combs to fix her hair into a perfect topknot and send her ringlets cascading down her chest.

By mid morning, the air still crisp, she was in position beside the glittering canal that cut through the newly restored St James's Park. A group of finely dressed men were playing the popular mallet and hoop game of Pell Mell on a white alley away to her left, but she barely noticed them from behind her tree as she searched for her quarry. Soon enough, the tall figure she was hoping to meet – or rather, accost – came into view, striding briskly through the park as he always did at this hour. He seemed in good humour, greeting the people he passed with a lively nod, his slashed doublet festooned with cheerful ribbons – the King himself, taking his renowned daily walk.

As he came level with her tree, she stepped out beside him and curtsied low. The whalebone beneath her bodice dug into her skin, but she bore the pain.

'Good morning, Your Majesty.'

He turned to look, not slowing his pace. 'Mrs Blakewood! The park is delightful this morning, and even more so now.'

She flashed him a demure smile. 'May I walk with you awhile?'

'Please do. Although I hope you walk quickly. My courtiers are in pursuit.' Mercia turned to see a group of men following some distance behind. 'They wish to discuss many things, all of which can wait, but to them they are the most important concerns in the land.'

'Then I must apologise,' she said, 'for I have come hoping to discuss a matter of some delicacy with you, but it is an urgent one, and I hope you will not be displeased to hear of it.'

He glanced at her. 'Then let us discuss it – after I finish my walk. Keep up, if you can.'

He strode off along the canal, his long legs in his loose-fitting breeches causing her some difficulty in keeping pace, but she shuffled along quickly enough. They passed through the physic garden with its orange bushes and exotic herbs, before he headed back towards Whitehall on a long pathway on the southern side of the park, the bright sun reflecting off a series of silver cages placed at intervals alongside. A low-pitched squawk greeted them as he stopped beside one of the tallest. Skittering up and down a narrow perch, two large birds resplendent in a cacophony of rainbow hues were opening and closing their pudgy beaks.

'Magnificent fowl, are they not?' he said.

She peered in, fascinated. 'Are they parrots?'

He seemed pleased at her knowledge. 'That is right. Such a bounty of colour. And look at this.' He led her to a larger cage which gave off a musty smell. At first she saw nothing, but then a crest-topped head rose up, rocking left and right atop a long, blue neck.

'Do you like it?' he asked.

'It is magnificent.' Mercia watched the peculiar creature walk its distended black body around the cage. 'What is it?'

'It is a cassowary, from the Indies. It took several men to find it and bring it here.'

'And it is a bird?'

'Hard to believe, but yes. See the beak, and the talons of the feet. Although this bird does not fly. Too fat, I imagine, like many of my courtiers.' He laughed, resuming his walk. 'Well, Mrs Blakewood. You wished to speak with me.'

'Thank you, Your Majesty.' She paused, steeling her courage. 'It is a private matter. It concerns your father as well as mine.'

'My father?' He looked at her askance, his cheerful expression falling away. 'And I was so enjoying our conversation.' He sighed. 'Very well. Follow me to the palace. We can talk there.'

She told him almost everything. About the note from her father, about the paintings that were not destroyed, about the thief who had killed for them, and died for them himself, about the Dutch agent who knew of them, but who lived so far away. As she talked, he listened, appalled when she spoke of the audacity of the theft, captivated when she spoke of the events on Lambeth Marsh. When she had finished, he sat looking out over the Thames, reflecting on unknowable thoughts.

Finally he turned to her, his face grim. 'We spoke of these paintings when we met before. Why did you not mention this then?'

'I did not know the whole story, Your Majesty. I did not want to raise false hopes.'

'But you wanted to see how I would react.' The King was no fool. His eyes roved over her face. 'You are implying that some person of high rank stole these paintings, kept them from me, and still profits from their theft. When the whole country knows I ordered all my father's art returned. You are speaking of treason.'

She did not know if it amounted to that, but as far as the King was concerned the betrayal would be the same. 'Yes, Your Majesty. I wish I were not.'

Charles stood up, pacing the room. It was clear the news had greatly agitated him. 'I do not know if you realise, but the Oxford Section contained some of the most precious pictures in the whole of my father's collection. Paintings by Titian, Rembrandt, others that he just liked and . . . something else. Something unique. It was as though I had been run through when I was told it was burnt. I still think of it to this day.' His all-penetrating stare scoured her soul, but she did not flinch. 'And now you are saying it may still exist, that the answer lies in America?' He paused a moment more, then leapt for the door. 'Wait here. I must consult with my brother.'

The eagle-headed clock on the grand marble table opposite showed minutes were passing, but to Mercia all time had ceased. Had she done the right thing? She had come here in a calculated gamble, hoping she was correct to tell the King what she knew. If she had acted too soon, all would be over. She sat waiting, staring at nothing, while the golden clock ticked on.

* * *

The door opened. Mercia turned to look as the Duke of York strode into the room, the King directly behind. She stood up to curtsey, almost knocking over her chair in her haste. The Duke was shorter than his brother, his paler face radiating with suspicion beneath his deep-brown wig. In contrast to the King's colourful attire, his doublet was sober, its braiding and embroidery as dark as his jet-black shoes. An unseen servant in the corridor pulled the door shut.

'My brother has told me your story,' he said. 'It is an extraordinary tale. Can you prove that you speak the truth?'

'I have no reason to lie, Your Highness.' Mercia kept her eyes focused on the floor. 'I promise that what I have said is true.'

'I have had occasion to speak with Mrs Blakewood recently, James,' said the King. 'In spite of holding back her story until now, she appears an intelligent and honest woman.'

'And yet her father was a traitor,' said the Duke. 'At his execution he made a pretty speech about liberty and justice. Why would his daughter not seek any opportunity to harm you?'

'Because she is a realist, and a woman in need of compassion,' said Mercia, playing to the King's gallantry. 'I have nothing but respect for His Majesty the King.' Now she looked up. 'It is true that my father sided with Parliament in the war, but he did not sign your father's death warrant, indeed he abhorred that tragic event. He did not want the country to descend again into war when Cromwell died, so he did not support the army when they tried to take control. He accepted His Majesty's return, indeed was glad of it in the end.' Her voice became strident, her eyes looking straight into the Duke's. 'He was a noble and an honourable man. I do not pretend to understand why he was condemned, but whatever his actions, he was no danger to this court, and neither am I.'

The Duke stared at her for several moments. Then he glanced at his brother. 'You believe her?'

'I do not see why she would invent such an intricate tale.'

'Very well. Say she is speaking true. You wish to recover these paintings?'

'Of course. I have sought to re-establish our father's collection since before I was restored to the throne.' Charles turned to Mercia. 'You see my brother is naturally mistrustful of those who would injure me. We have heard tall tales before.'

'Mine is no invention,' she said. 'I have the threatening notes, the bruises, the mud-stained dresses to prove it.'

The King smiled. 'The question is why you would go through such trials? Mrs Blakewood, as I told you before, I will only arbitrate in the matter of your father's manor house in extraordinary circumstances. This information is invaluable – but I will not be held to ransom.'

'Your Majesty, all I ask is that you allow me to prove my loyalty. I have not brought the information in expectation that you will intervene. I know you require more. I am asking you to let me continue to prove myself.'

The King lowered himself into a high-backed seat. 'You have my attention.'

She took a deep breath. She was in the presence of the King and the Duke of York, the most powerful men in the land. Normally it would be unthinkable for her to make the proposal she was about to suggest. But Daniel's near abduction had lit a fire in her blood, and she spoke with a persuasive strength.

'Then I request you permit me to travel to America, to secure the truth from the agent Pietersen. I am aware of the mood in the country. Everyone calls for war with the Dutch. It would not be surprising if a royal ship were to harry the Hollanders' American colony, as a show of strength. A rowing boat could slip me to shore, where I could locate him and discover where he sent the paintings before anyone knew it.'

The Duke let out an incredulous laugh. 'My, you are an audacious creature!'

'A bold plot, indeed,' said the King, his eyes roaming her face as if seeking her truth of heart. At his side his brother studied the air, thinking. 'You would be prepared to do this?' Charles said at last.

She bowed her head. 'I would.'

The Duke broke from his contemplations. 'You cannot be thinking of granting her this impertinent request.' He walked to the window, looking out on the cloudy day. 'Although she is right. All the country, all the court is eager for war. That fellow Pepys tells me the Commons has spent weeks hearing from merchants wanting nothing else. Both they and the Lords expect you to act.' His eyes flashed. 'And we are ready. We have our fleet waiting to sail to Africa, to wage further raids on the Dutch in Guinea, as we have discussed in council.'

'Indeed,' said the King. 'But full-out war? The Navigation Acts, brief skirmishes at sea, they are one thing. Escalating matters is another.'

'Yet I think you must act, and soon. And this woman has provided you with a ready excuse for your conscience.'

The King looked at his brother, beckoning him to continue.

'Send the Guinea fleet instead to America. We intend to strike there in any case. This merely hastens events.' He paced the room. 'Just last month you granted me the land above Virginia which the Dutch claim is theirs. Well I say 'tis ours. Let us send the fleet and take it.'

The King stroked his chin. 'We seize New Amsterdam, consolidate our territory, and capture this agent at the same time?'

'Exactly that. And put those conceited New Englanders in their place while we are at it.'

The Duke waited, expressionless, while the eagle-headed clock ticked on. Finally Charles spoke. 'I agree. 'Tis a sensible stratagem.'

The Duke merely nodded, keeping his enthusiasm contained. 'Then I will see to the arrangements. You will need to award a commission. I have some men in mind, if you approve. I recommend my groom Nicolls commands the fleet. When he is victorious, he will rename the territory in your name.'

'No, brother,' said the King. 'I awarded that land to you.'

All this time Mercia had been listening patiently. Now she broke her silence, drawing once more on the arrogant fire coursing through her veins.

'Your Majesty,' she dared. 'If you intend to send a fleet to capture New Amsterdam, then I wish to accompany it.'

The Duke rounded on her. 'Know your place, woman!'

'If I may be so bold,' she persisted.

'There is no fear of you holding your tongue,' he said. The King laughed.

'I appreciate I am just a woman' – she glanced at the Duke – 'but there is an important consideration in all this. The man behind the theft of the paintings is most likely a nobleman, and so privy to affairs of state. It may be possible to use this plan to bring him into the open.'

The King arched an eyebrow. 'How so?'

'The villain knows I am on his trail, and he will know Pietersen is in America. If he discovers I am on my way there too, he is bound to try to stop me. If the paintings are there as we suspect, doubly so.'

'You think if you go, the rogue will follow.'

'Or at the least he will send a man. He has invested some effort into keeping his secret. He will not give up now.' She looked at the King, her eyes gleaming. 'I assume Your Majesty wishes him apprehended?'

'That is obvious,' said Charles. 'But I could as easily appoint a trusted advisor to interrogate this Pietersen to find out the truth.'

She cast down her gaze. 'That depends how secretive you wish this mission to be. So far, not many people know the Oxford Section still exists.'

The King nodded. 'A fair point. It would need to be very secret. I do not want anyone to know of this, especially when one of my own nobles is suspect.'

'Then I offer myself as bait. I will invent a subterfuge so that nobody knows my true purpose. When the villain acts, he will be revealed.'

The King leant back in his seat. 'You are a courageous woman, Mrs Blakewood. I am nothing if not impressed.'

'This is ridiculous,' muttered the Duke. 'My men can take care of this.'

Charles looked at him. 'Who is King here, brother? I shall decide how this proceeds.' He sighed. 'Besides, can we trust any of our advisors with such a delicate task, if one of their very number is the guilty man? Nicolls will need to know, if he is to command, but he will have no time for this.' He shrugged. 'And if the task is fruitless, well – nobody will be any the wiser.'

None of the noblemen you depend on for your throne's stability will have cause to think you untrusting, you mean, thought Mercia. But if she was using the King to get what she wanted, he could certainly use her.

'Your Majesty, I want to catch this man,' she pressed. 'There is not one of your subjects with my determination, my zeal.' She knelt before him. 'I will not deny that I wish to earn Your Majesty's support in regaining my house. To say otherwise would be to lie.' She looked up. 'But I ask you – let me do this. Let me prove my family is loyal.'

'Mrs Blakewood, your strength of heart is extraordinary.' The King smiled. 'I will not appoint you to this venture under any obligation on my part. But if you can bring me those paintings, I would gladly volunteer to assist you.'

She kept her expression constant. 'Your Majesty, I can ask no more.'

'Very well,' said Charles. 'If you are truly prepared, then you have our permission to join the fleet.' He held up a hand as his brother made to protest. 'But I will not allow you to travel on a ship full of sailors alone. You will need female companionship, a chaperone of some kind. I will think on it. There is time enough to prepare.'

'Several weeks.' The Duke turned to her, a quiet mischief in his gaze. 'You realise we will appoint a number of men to this invasion? Aside from leading the soldiers, we will need to survey the land, seek out the most profitable avenues for trade. Your noble criminal might not be so easy to spot in the crowd.' He smiled slyly. 'What do you think, brother? Perhaps I should appoint Sir William Calde to the fleet?'

It was obvious the Duke knew of Sir William's interest in her, but she hid her displeasure. 'His Highness is quite naturally correct. But whether the man we seek is chosen for this expedition, or volunteers himself, it matters not. I will be ready. I have a good friend, a trained soldier, who is willing to accompany me, and I intend to take a manservant, if the man I have in mind agrees. We will be vigilant together. This noble will come, and he will not escape.'

'Mrs Blakewood, we are convinced.' The King gestured for her to stand. 'Rise, and not a word to anyone, save those who will attend you. You will be advised when to join the fleet.'

'Thank you, Your Majesty. I will be waiting.' She backed from the room, bowing low.

A little way down the corridor she let out an excited shout. Her tactic had worked. She had the King's blessing. She was going to America, across the ocean, all that way.

She grabbed a nearby table corner as she realised what that meant. But she set premature seasickness aside. She could travel the waters, voyage so far, because of her hope. Hope the long journey could bring her home, back to Halescott.

Part Three

Chapter Nineteen

The last faint speck of white foam crashing on tiny black rocks disappeared from view. Now all Mercia could see was the majesty of the ocean and the ship on which she stood, minuscule by comparison and unutterably fragile as the waves permitted it to travel a path across their gentle peaks.

She closed her eyes, resting her palms against the late spring warmth of the wooden rail of the stern, feeling the passage of the ship through the waters. A breeze whipped around her face on its way into the vast sails, giving the ship an invisible forward motion towards the west, towards the complete unknown. It was a new sensation for her, this feeling of being isolated from the land, a minute dot on an incomprehensible ocean vastness, and yet part of a floating community that represented the order and industry of where she had embarked.

Several seconds went by when all that existed was her, the ship and the ocean. Then she opened her eyes, running her hands over the rough rail, hearing the creaking of the mast and yardarms above. Quietly, Nathan came up from behind, resting his hand next to hers, sharing the experience in silence. After a few moments,

Mercia turned her head to look at him, her faithful friend who was journeying across the world to protect her.

'So that is it,' she said. 'Ireland behind us, and two months on the *Redemption* until we reach America.'

''Tis hard to conceive we can sail so far in such a short time,' said Nathan. 'And yet 'tis still two months. We must keep occupied.'

'I think I will have my hands full with Daniel. He loves it on this ship, running around here and there. He has no fear of it.'

'Your chaperone, now that is a different matter.'

She sighed. 'Yes, it appears Lady Markstone was not born to travel the seas.'

Nathan nodded, a grave expression on his face, but the corners of his mouth were twitching. 'The side of the ship is well lashed. She has washed all the barnacles from the hull.'

'Nat.' She turned around, resting her back against the wood. 'Personally, I feel unburdened of the cares of England already. I must remember we are here to complete a mission.' She looked sideways at him. 'Did you learn anything from the captain? I have been told nothing, even though I am on business for the King himself.'

'That may be, but I do not think the Duke cares for his men to be distracted.' He steadied himself on the rail as the ship bounced on a rogue wave. 'The captain told me names, at least. Colonel Nicolls is on the *Guinea*, in overall charge as we know. Colonel Cartwright is with him, and Captain Hyde.'

'The Duke's brother-in-law. And on the *Elias*?'

'William Hill as captain, Sir Robert Carr in charge of the soldiery. Sir Bernard Dittering is on board too, something to do with trade.'

Mercia scoffed. 'Lucky for him he is not here with us. I don't think I could stop myself from challenging him about my father's trial.' She stared up at the straining sails. 'What of my other favourite?'

'Commanding the soldiers on the *Martin*.' He looked at her. 'Have you done as I suggested with that necklace?'

She waved an impatient hand. 'It is locked away in my coin box.'

'And the key?'

'Yes, yes. Hidden in the hole you carved for it. I am not a fool, you know.'

'Good. I am still not sure you should have brought it.'

Her eyes gleamed with mischief in the sunlight rebounding from the sails. 'I told you, we might be able to use the pearls as trade. We don't know what will happen, and I doubt the native people will accept shillings.' She blew out her cheeks. 'I just wish the Duke hadn't been so malicious as to go through with his threat to appoint him.'

Nathan leant in. 'I don't know as he did. Captain Morley thinks Sir William asked to join the invasion force.'

She widened an eye. 'Does he really?'

He smiled. 'I know what you are thinking. But 'tis all moot for now. We are stuck on the *Redemption* with the other hangers-on, no suspicious noblemen to keep watch of yet.' He paused. 'How are you faring with Sir William's wife?'

'Oh, that . . . woman.' She shook her head. 'Quite why she has to be here, I do not know. She does not like me one bit.'

'You know why. The King wanted a second chaperone for you.'

'Yes, but she doesn't know that, does she? She thinks she is here for Lady Markstone. She has no intention of being pleasant to me.' She sniffed. 'Lady Markstone at least is decent company, even if she is an old busybody, advising me with this and that. I would miss having a woman to talk to otherwise, with Bethany looking after the cottage.'

Nathan looked out to sea. 'A busybody and as good as a murderess.'

'She was abused, Nathan. I will not condemn her for what she did not do, even if the rest of society does.' She turned back to the waters, changing the subject. 'Will we find the paintings, do you think?'

He brushed his arm against hers. 'Whatever happens, this will be an adventure. And it keeps the hounds at bay.'

'Maybe. If this does not work they will keep pursuing.'

'Then let us make sure it does.'

She squeezed his hand. 'I am glad you are here, Nat. Sir Jeremy is generous to allow you to travel with me all this time, is he not?'

Nathan nodded as he looked out to sea, his unkempt brown hair shimmering in the salty breeze.

Even with the Duke of York's eagerness for action, it had taken a month for the small fleet and its many missions, of varying degrees of secrecy, to be prepared. To the world, the fleet's commander Richard Nicolls was ferrying a team of the King's commissioners to New England to consolidate royal authority over the faraway colonies. But the private mission was for him first to conquer New Netherland through its prime trading post New Amsterdam, the King going so far as to write to the Dutch government to deceive them of the fleet's purpose. The very private mission, Mercia's mission, none but her close companions and Nicolls were supposed to know.

As Lady Markstone had hoped, the King had been persuaded to commute her sentence to exile; both she and Mercia had leapt on the opportunity to request that they voyage to America together. Keen Mercia should have her chaperone, the King had seen the logic, on one condition: that she have a second companion untainted by the stench of the Tower. The Queen made subtle enquiries amongst her ladies; only Lady Calde volunteered, and that because her husband was with the fleet, or maybe despite it. But like the rest she was deceived as to Mercia's true purpose, told they were travelling to provide comfort to Lady Markstone on her journey to her new life. Sir Francis had been furious to learn of Mercia's intentions, Anthony and Isabel apoplectic. But in the face of the King's will there was nothing they could do to prevent her taking Daniel away.

Accordingly, towards the end of May, Mercia arrived at Portsmouth harbour with Nathan and Daniel, the three of them laden down with as many items they thought they could take – mostly clothes and shoes, and things to pass the time, toys for Daniel, even for Mercia some embroidery unfinished from last winter, as well as a description of the paintings in the Oxford Section that the King had quietly compiled. Most dear of all, she had packed a number of books, her history of the Anglo-Saxon kingdoms of course, works of poetry by Mary Wroth and John Donne, while Nathan hoped to finish the *Don Quixote* he had started in Queen Street.

Wanting as much help as she could get, she had raided her scant inheritance to offer Nicholas a position as their manservant. She knew Nathan didn't like it, but it wasn't his money. She had wondered whether the prospect of a long ocean voyage would hold sufficient appeal, but Nicholas had been eager to accept, for as he said himself, the discovery of North's body had affected him, and he wanted to finish what he had begun. Still, part of her had expected he would not show up, despite his good advance. She need not have worried. By the time they arrived he had already spent a week reliving his naval past in the taverns that littered the Portsmouth docks. In the end, she had easily persuaded the constables of his innocence on Lambeth Marsh – although the letter she had obtained from the Lord Chancellor's office might have helped.

Colonel Nicolls was terse before they embarked, no time for being sidetracked by discussions of paintings and lost art. But he welcomed them civilly enough, assigning them quarters on the merchant ship *Redemption*, an adapted Dutch *fluyt* that was ironically to be used as transport in the subjugation of New Netherland once the surrender of New Amsterdam was complete. The invasion force of several hundred was packed into the three other ships, much larger and more imposing, but despite its fewer passengers, conditions on the *Redemption* were still cramped. On the King's special orders, the crew had built three small cabins on the quarterdeck towards the back of the ship for the women, screening off a small section beside the rail for their personal ablutions. Nathan took an existing cabin beside the captain's underneath those, although he was to share with Daniel. Nicholas was given a hammock with the regular sailors, one of many threadbare sheets stretched out amongst the posts and cannon on the stuffy 'tween deck below.

A week passed. The initial excitement was gone, the voyage already proving long and tedious. By now Mercia was accustomed to her tiny quarters, if not to the salted meat, dried peas and biscuit that passed as food on the days when the sailors hadn't slaughtered one of the ship's pigs, or paused their journey to try their luck at catching fish from the longboat. When she wasn't minding Daniel, or trying to freshen whichever mourning dress she wasn't currently wearing, she spent the time reading, or struggling with her needlework, or engrossed in her most regular pastime, indulging her fantasies of what she would do when she found Joost Pietersen. Her favourite scenario involved chasing him into the heart of the unexplored continent, where she would chance upon hidden cities of gold like the old Spanish conquistadors, battling whatever unhuman monsters lay in wait. Occasionally these fantasies ended with her not finding Pietersen at all, but she set those imagined failures aside.

Having conquered the steep ladder to the foredeck, she was observing Daniel on the main deck below her, showing off his toy lion to a group of patient sailors. Of them all he was the most confident on board, not worrying when a large wave struck the side, not falling over as the ship rocked in its wake. Lady Calde was the worst for staying upright, but today she was taking the air on the quarterdeck with Lady Markstone, who seemed to have conquered her seasickness. A paranoid element in Mercia feared they were talking about her. Although Lady Markstone had promised not to talk about their conversation in the Tower, who knew what two acquaintances might gossip over when trapped together for weeks at sea.

A young sailor hauling a thick cable of rope across the deck noticed her looking down. He smiled, running a hand under his loose white shirt that was hanging open over his tanned chest. Returning his smile, she glanced up to see Lady Calde scowling in her direction. Mercia rolled her eyes, making the sailor laugh, and he went back to his work.

She had turned to look out to sea when she heard Lady Markstone's voice. She peered over the top of the forecastle to see her chaperone standing just beneath her.

'How you manage those ladders I cannot fathom,' Lady Markstone called up. 'I am grateful the men built proper steps to the quarterdeck or I would never have been able to walk the ship.'

Mercia shinned down the ladder to join her. 'It takes a special skill.' She raised an eyebrow. 'And a willingness to alter a dress.'

Lady Markstone chuckled and took her arm, leading her to the rail. 'Now, Mercia,' she said, 'I am sure you do not need my advice, but it would be wise to avoid too much familiarity with the sailors. Perhaps you had best keep to the quarterdeck, where the men do not usually go. You are the only woman on this ship, save myself and

Lady Calde, and I do not think the rogues will care for what we can offer, at our age.'

Mercia smiled. 'Do not trouble yourself over me, Lady Markstone. I can deal with these men.'

'I am sure. But be careful all the same. I have already overheard some of them calling you – but no. It is too ridiculous.'

'No, tell. Called me what?'

The older woman leant in to her ear. 'A well-rigged frigate.'

Mercia laughed out loud. 'And you, Lady Markstone. You are faring better on the ship now?'

'Yes, thank the Lord. I must confess I was not looking forward to leaving England, but now we are on our way, the thought of a life unburdened by the repercussions of the war and the endless scheming of our menfolk has taken on a great appeal, even to one as old as myself.'

Mercia gave her a wry glance. 'You are not old.'

'You are too kind.' Lady Markstone patted her shoulder. 'I am glad to travel with you, Mercia. Perhaps once your task is over I could convince you to stay with me in Massachusetts Bay. You would thrive there, as would your boy.'

She smiled. 'Yesterday you spoke of Connecticut. The day before, you even told me of Virginia. Where will you ultimately go, I wonder?'

'Ultimately, I will go to heaven. But while I am still on this earth, I intend to profit from the years I have left, now I am able. Whether that is in Massachusetts, Connecticut, or any other place with a strange and beautiful name, I care not, if I can be free.'

That evening, while Nathan was playing with Daniel at the very back of the ship, the young sailor she had smiled at approached her on the main deck as she was leaning against the stowed longboat to watch the spritsail flapping at the bow. The folds it created were fascinating in the absence of little else to do.

'Enjoying the journey?' he asked.

Mercia swivelled to face him. 'To a point. I shall be pleased when we arrive in America.'

He nodded. ''Tis a long while yet. But I love New Amsterdam. Been there before, see.' He traced pictures in the air with his fingers. 'The fort looking over that windmill on the shore. The tall houses, the canal. And the people, course. I could tell you about it, if you like.'

'It sounds exciting,' she said to be pleasant.

'It is. I could tell you a lot more things too.' He smiled, his blue eyes shining in the fading light. 'I was wondering whether you might want a bit of company. It gets lonely at sea.' He fell in on the rail beside her.

She began to feel uncomfortable. She sidled along the rail but he stepped around to block her, resting his hand on her arm. She shook it off, but he drifted it up to caress the back of her neck. She stared him in the eye. 'And there I was thinking you were interested in talking. Lady Markstone was right. Let me go, or I will cut those fingers from my neck.'

The sailor laughed and placed his hands on the rail either side of her, effectively hemming her in. 'Come, 'tis a long voyage.' He moved his body closer, his loose red trousers billowing in the wind. 'Your friends don't need to know.'

Over his shoulder she noticed a group of sailors watching from the forecastle. He looked back at them and grinned. One of the group urged him on, but the others were staring uneasily. Cursing her naivety, she waited for him to relax his grip on the rail so she could bob down and escape, or else push him aside. But then a hand gripped his shoulder and twisted him round. To her surprise he fell to the deck, blood spewing from his nose across the rough wood.

Shocked, she glanced up. Nicholas was standing over the felled sailor, rubbing his fist. He crouched down to the sailor's ear. 'If you or any of your mates behave like this towards her again, I will throw you into the sea.' He stood and kicked him hard in the side. 'Do you understand?'

The sailor turned a look of total malevolence on him, his eyes pulsating with fury. He pushed himself up from the deck and limped away, clutching his wounded side. The watching sailors jeered; humiliated, he hissed at them to be quiet.

Nicholas watched him go. 'Been in this situation before, have we not?'

'The day we met,' said Mercia. 'But this time we cannot just walk away. That kick was somewhat excessive, don't you think?'

He turned to her. 'I take looking out for you to be part of my duties. He won't bother you again.'

She glanced at the red patch seeping into the deck. 'He will be after your own blood now.'

'He doesn't scare me. I don't think he'd have done anything, but sailors get bored, dare each other to do ridiculous things. I should know.'

'I am sure you do.' Her tone was terse, but secretly she was pleased he had come to her rescue. 'But thank you.' Keen to discuss something else, she cleared her throat. 'How are you and Nathan getting along?'

He folded his arms. 'Well, I hope. He spends much of his time with Daniel. He cares for the boy a great deal. I respect that, especially when he's not his own.' He leant back on the rail beside her. 'I was wondering – if I can ask – what happened to his own daughter? I know 'tis not my place, but . . .'

She swallowed. 'It was very sad. But he does not hide from it, not any more. There is no harm in telling you.' A melancholic ache tugged at her words. 'Everyone was in the streets celebrating the King's return, or pretending to, but Jane, Nathan's wife, she went into labour. And she died, giving birth.' The ship blurred as she remembered. 'Nathan called the girl Anne. She was so beautiful, always laughing. She kept him from his grief. And then before she was two her nurse overlaid her.'

'God. I'm so sorry.'

'People can say all they like how common that is, for a nurse to roll onto the baby in her sleep, but it is heart-wrenching to endure. I will never know how he was strong enough to manage. Save I tried to help him through the pain.' She lowered her eyes, saddened as she always was when she thought of that tragedy.

Nicholas hesitated. 'Don't think it untoward of me to say, but he clearly cares for you. He looks at you all the time. You must notice it.'

She waved her hand, embarrassed. 'I could never replace Jane in his heart. And Will still lives in mine.' She looked out across the darkening ocean. 'Although that was a long time ago now.'

'Don't let chances slip away, Mercia, when one comes along.'

She shook her head. 'Do you have nothing useful to do?'

'Yes.' He brought his face round to smile at her. 'I am doing it.'

Chapter Twenty

As Nicholas had foreseen, Mercia was not harassed again, other than the furtive looks that continuously came her way from lonely sailors at sea. The ship made excellent speed, the captain pleased with his vessel and crew. But one morning, a Monday, or a Tuesday perhaps – she found the days were merging into one – she stepped from her cabin to find a thick fog all around, her vision limited to just a few yards. Flames shone through the sticky gloom as the sailors lit torches roundabout, but their light was weak against the depth of the fog. The ship limped on in its course, the sea dead calm, but when the wind picked up to lift the fog the other ships had vanished.

'No worry,' reassured the captain. 'We will come on them again soon enough.'

But for the rest of the crossing they were alone, the bigger ships with their mighty guns and the King's invasion force never again in sight. One afternoon Nicholas descried a ship off the starboard side in the distance, but the captain could not tell its colours, so he gave orders to evade it. They were not at war with the French, or the Spanish, nor yet with the Dutch, but piracy was prevalent, and the warships were gone.

* * *

It was a month into the voyage when the inevitable storm hit. The sailors had been warning of it since they left Portsmouth. 'You do not tempt the limits of Creation without God reminding you of His power,' the captain said, and he spoke well enough, for when the storm arose, it was truly awesome.

Mercia had developed a surprising friendship with Captain Morley. He told her stories about the world outside Europe, some more believable than others, but all of them riveting. He, well she supposed he was pleased by the attentions of a woman, although at first he had been less than welcoming to the three on his ship, muttering under his breath that it would bring bad luck, and what did Nicolls think he was doing. All that prejudice faded as soon as she showed an interest in his tales.

The old man had an erudite air, gesticulating as he spoke.

'We were sailing through the clearest of waters,' he enthused, 'when a huge beast twice the length of London Bridge emerged from the depths. It reared up and we feared it must crash down on the ship, for it would surely have destroyed us if it had. The crew ran for shelter but I stood on deck, captivated by its grandeur.' Mercia laughed. 'But it fell the other way, and with a flourish of its forked tail the beast dived back into the ocean. It was as if Neptune himself had dispatched his surest envoy to spy on us.'

'I have seen such a creature drawn on a chart,' she mused. 'Next to the men with two heads and the dogs with six legs.' She paused. 'But Captain Morley, the ship is rocking somewhat.'

'You are right.' He led her out onto the quarterdeck. In the few minutes she had been in his chart house the sky had turned a deep grey, a fierce wind buffeting the sails. 'As I feared,' he said. 'The skies are likely for a storm. I am afraid, Lady Mercia' – he insisted on calling her 'Lady' – 'you should fetch your lad and seek shelter.'

She took in the captain's concerned gaze and the frenzied shouting of the sailors in an awful instant. She recalled one of his less delicate moments, when he had told her about a storm that had obliterated the sun and cast a deep misery over the ocean. She learnt now he had not embellished that particular tale, for the intensity of the sky above the tiny ship grew darker than a countryside night, the sun cast down by an army of impenetrable clouds formed up tighter than any well-trained phalanx.

By the time she found Daniel running – or rather, falling – round the capstan, the storm had broken. Thinking to make for her cabin she pulled him out on deck, but the ship was already beginning to lurch forward and back. Urgent sailors were hurrying barefoot around and above, attempting to secure the sails to the yards and the masts, but she heard none of their clamour, for the roar of the wind had become all encompassing, taunting their very souls. Its irresistible power swept her and Daniel down the ship, forcing them against the forecastle ladder; with one hand she grabbed the side rail, with the other her son, striving to stay upright in the force of the whirling air.

Nathan fought his way shouting towards her, but she could not look at him, the wind too strong in her face, let alone hear. He grabbed at her, pulling her by inches across the main deck, each of them taking hold of whatever purchase they could reach, a rope, a mast, a sailor, all the time gripping her son, until they staggered to the steps to the quarterdeck. A second's break in the wind allowed her to take shelter behind a thick coil of rope, and she looked up to see faint dots in the rigging, brave sailors, Nicholas amongst them, attempting to furl the sails in the face of the growing tempest. But then the wind rose up again, stronger than before, and Nathan, still exposed, was thrown back to the forecastle, falling away into the false night.

There was no time to panic. The ship continued to pitch to inconceivable angles. Up it went, up a fiery mountain of water, then down, down into the openings of hell itself, the demons of the Beast waiting to receive it, but no, up it went again, seemingly uncontrollable against the magnificent power of the sea. A pain-giving rain was lashing on the deck, stinging her face as it swarmed around her, making it impossible to see the mighty waves.

By now the deck was strewn with seawater, barrels that had been poorly secured rolling dangerously about. Mercia wrenched Daniel, the boy crying with fright, from their haphazard path. A sailor fell from the rigging to crash into the deck, splintering the wood beside her before sliding down the rough planks at the next pitch of the ship. Still she held on, drenched with cold water, her dress whipping around her, waiting for a gap in the storm. Eventually, she knew not how, she clambered to her feet to struggle to the quarterdeck. At the top step a powerful gust threw her against her cabin, the nearest. She reached out an arm to tug at the door, forcing it open as the wind shifted. She pushed Daniel in, but then the wind slammed the door shut before she could follow, and the ship lurched, sending her skidding to the side, teetering against the suddenly inadequate rail.

For an instant she thought she would tip over. Then a hand grabbed her arm, pulling her back towards the cabins at a levelling out of the ship. Together, the two of them battled the wind until the Samaritan yanked open the door to Mercia's cabin and heaved them both through. Inside, they forced the door closed, dragging across the small table to try to secure it.

The storm was hardly more muffled inside the cabin. Mercia turned to thank her saviour and was startled to see Lady Calde, now collapsed on the floor against the bed, her blue dress soaked, offering up prayers to God. Clothes and boxes were strewn everywhere, and a loose wall plank was thumping out its own destruction, splinters of wood flying off in the strength of the outside wind. She joined Lady Calde in her devotions, beseeching God's compassion that her companions would be safe from this mighty demonstration of His power. If they survived, she would know she had passed His test, would have been found worthy of the trust her father had placed in her. But for now, as the storm lashed at the ship in its zephyrous rage, tormenting those who in their arrogance had dared leave the haven of their own land, she held her son, and made sure he felt safe.

She did not know how long the storm persisted. Time ceased in the face of such a mighty foe. Yet when she looked up, the ship was no longer rocking so ferociously, and the roars of the winds had quietened. Gradually the cabin became still. Against the lopsided bed, Lady Calde was sitting ramrod straight, staring at her, unblinking. Her grey-auburn hair had come loose, dripping water down her pale cheeks.

'Thank you,' said Mercia simply.

Lady Calde did not move. 'My door flew open. I put myself at risk to drag you back here. Do not think it means I have forgiven you.'

'Forgiven me?' Mercia frowned. 'For what?'

'I will not let you take my husband.'

'Oh.' She ran a hand over her wet face. 'Lady Calde, I have no interest in Sir William.'

The elder woman's jaw clenched. 'I saw you with him in the Privy Garden at Whitehall. I was watching from a window. I saw him kiss your hand.'

'Lady Calde, there is nothing to—'

She broke off as the door banged open, the fragile table skidding onto its side. A heavily bedraggled Lady Markstone rushed in.

'You are here, praise the Lord,' Lady Markstone cried. 'There was no time to find you when the storm hit. Some of us found refuge in the captain's cabin. Thank God you are safe, and your son.' She smiled benignly on him. At her feet, Lady Calde pulled herself up. 'And you here, Harriet, also.'

'We are safe.' Mercia attempted to stand herself, only now feeling the weight of her soaked dress. 'You seem less wind-whipped than I, at least.' She bit her lip, looking towards the open door. 'But what of Nathan? We were together, then he slipped down the ship.'

'Perhaps your man will know,' said Lady Calde, now in the doorway. Her words were tinged with bitterness. 'He is coming this way.'

Without another glance, she left; Lady Markstone looked questioningly at Mercia, but then a stubbled face painted with wet blonde hair appeared round the door.

'Are you all right?' asked Nicholas. 'I saw you get into your cabin.'

'Yes,' replied Mercia. 'But Nathan? Have you seen him?'

He nodded. 'I am impressed. He helped the crew when he could have taken refuge. He even climbed to the foreyard to help secure the sail, but then—'

She grabbed his arm. 'Then what?'

Nicholas smiled. 'Then he couldn't get down, the storm was so ferocious. He clung to the mast so tightly that when all was over he couldn't move his arms. It took two sailors to prise him off.'

Breathing out in relief she took Daniel's hand and passed into the battered open. The ship was a total mess, baskets and crates everywhere, but the crew were experts and had secured everything they could. Descending to the main deck, she peered around first one sailor, then another, until she saw Nathan coming in her direction. When his eyes met hers he fell to his knees, clasping his hands together in a thankful prayer. Then he ran to hold her and Daniel tight, taking her in a powerful embrace, while she hugged him back, glad everyone was alive, grateful they had passed God's test. As they embraced, Nicholas walked past smiling, and a few moments later Lady Markstone too.

'Everything is fine, Nat,' said Mercia as the two of them walked Daniel back to her cabin. 'Do not fret. It was fierce, but we are through it now.'

He cast down his eyes. 'I should have come straight back to you. I am sorry.'

'No, you did right to help the crew. They will remember that.' She smiled. 'Especially you stuck in the mast.'

She pulled open her loose cabin door; Nathan had to bend his head to fit into the small space. Her possessions lay tossed about, but she shrugged her shoulders. 'What matter. We are unharmed and I can pack this back together. See, my clothes are all here, my coin box, my combs.' She held her hand to her mouth. 'My coin box!'

'What about it?' frowned Nathan.

'It was next to that loose plank when I was in here during the storm.' She pointed to where the panel had now come totally away. 'I remember hoping it would not slip through the gap. So how is it now on the other side of the cabin, against the bed?'

He looked across. 'It probably just slid there.'

'No, it was by the hole when Lady Markstone came in, when the storm was over. It cannot have moved on its own, not with this clutter everywhere.' She reached down for the box and studied the lid. 'My God, Nathan. 'Tis unlocked.'

'Here is the key, Mamma.' Daniel held up a small iron object. 'It was on the floor.'

Righting the fallen table, Nathan inspected another of the wall planks. 'The plug I made to cover the key's hiding place has shaken loose. It won't have stayed put in that storm.'

'So anyone coming in here could have found the key on the floor.'

'In this mess?'

She rummaged inside the box. 'I think the coin is all still here, but—' She took a sharp breath. 'The necklace has gone.'

Nathan stared. 'You are sure?'

'Of course!' She held the box open to show him.

'Perhaps, Mamma,' said Daniel, 'the storm took it. Everything else has been thrown around.'

'No, Danny. There would be coins all over the cabin too, yet they are still in the box.'

He thought a moment then pointed at the floor. 'Maybe it snapped and the pearls fell through these cracks.' He looked anxiously at his mother.

She knelt down to him. 'Do not worry, Danny. I do not resent the loss of that necklace.' She glanced up at Nathan. 'But still, it appears there is a thief on board.'

He paused, thinking. 'Who has been in here?'

'Me. Daniel. Lady Calde, Lady Markstone. Nicholas.'

'Nicholas? Alone?'

'No, Nathan. I did leave him at the cabin door when I came to look for you, but the same is true of Lady Markstone. Besides, any of the sailors could have seen the cabin empty and taken their chance. There are far more of them on the quarterdeck than usual, cleaning up after the storm.'

'I suppose.' He sighed. 'What do you want to do?'

They sifted through her belongings but nothing else was gone, nor could they find the necklace when Captain Morley ordered a search of the ship. Mercia thought Nicholas might well be right when he suggested that a thieving sailor could later have panicked and thrown it over the side. Neither Lady Calde nor Lady Markstone had lost anything. It vexed her she could not discover the truth, but in the absence of evidence she was obliged to forget it. For now, she was content she had lost nothing of real value in the storm, like her son.

Chapter Twenty-One

The ship resumed its westward course, the sailors swiftly patching up whatever damage they could under the experienced eye of the ship's carpenter. But the barber-surgeon could not save the young man who had fallen from the rigging, and to the firing of a sombre gun he was cast into the ocean for his long rest. Nor had any of the pigs survived, or so the crew at first thought, until swabbing the foredeck a boy heard a strange squealing from over the side, and was amazed to find a pig trapped by its legs in the disturbed anchor rope. Three sailors hauled it back on deck; in a panic it charged at the boatswain, making him jump aside just as a loose piece of rigging crashed down where he had been standing. From then on the crew took to calling it their lucky hog, refusing to butcher it for meat. Instead the ship's longboat came into more frequent use, the men endeavouring to trap slow-moving turtles or curious sharks whenever the captain permitted a halt.

The weeks passed by with no real excitement. Four weeks became five, became seven. The men drank and played at dice. Mercia memorised the description of the Oxford Section in private, and learnt how to use a ship's quadrant in front of a bemused public.

Nicholas was a dutiful manservant, although in truth there was little for him to do: a fortunate happenstance the morning after his birthday. Lady Markstone enjoyed her embroidery. Daniel ran about with his lion, getting in everyone's way, but nobody really minded. The necklace stayed missing. Lady Calde wrote her journal when there was anything of note to record, say a passing dolphin. The barber tried his best at cutting the women's hair into a remotely fashionable style. Nathan sat against the mizzenmast, reading *Don Quixote*. Mercia worried he was more distant since their embrace after the storm, and she hoped he wasn't embarrassed. But he regained his old demeanour soon enough, and their friendship went on as before.

Around ten weeks into the voyage, Nicholas approached Nathan as he was standing on the raised poop deck at the stern, a telescope to his eye to look out over the ship to the calm sea in front. Sitting hidden in the shade of the mizzenmast below them, Mercia set down the volume of Donne's poetry she was perusing and listened in. After all, she couldn't help it – so she told herself.

'Anything?' asked Nicholas.

'Not yet,' said Nathan. 'The captain said it would be any day now. By God's truth, I will be pleased to glimpse land.'

'As will I. I've not sailed so far since I first joined the ships, must be eight years ago now.'

A pause. 'I don't think I have ever asked you where you went.'

'No you haven't.' Nicholas laughed. 'Spain. Tenerife.'

'You were at Santa Cruz?' Nathan's tone was impressed.

'First time I saw battle. I'll never forget it – seven huge Spanish galleons completely ablaze, smoke filling the air, cannon fire raining down on us from the fort onshore. Then their flagship exploded, bloody pieces of men flying everywhere. But the thing I remember most was the heat, like the air itself was on fire. That and the screams of the burning men, of course.'

Mercia could feel Nathan nodding. 'They say war is glorious, but I never found it so. Too many innocent people die. Men who should not have been fighting. Women. Children.'

'Yes.' Another pause. 'Mercia told me what happened with her brother.'

'Did she?' Nathan sounded resigned. 'Then she must like you. It is a wound that never really healed, I think.'

'And her husband?' pursued Nicholas, almost a whisper. 'Did he really die in a duel?'

Had she spoken with him of that? She supposed she must have: she couldn't remember. Her breathing quickened as she edged round the rough mast, straining to hear the two men above.

'That is not really your business,' said Nathan. 'But you are right. A band of Royalists attacked him when he was riding home with some of his men after the battle at Dunkirk.'

'In '58?' Nicholas seemed surprised. 'I was at Dunkirk too, on the *Hero*.'

'I didn't know that. Edward Markstone's ship?'

'Yes. I was looking after the horse by then.' A pause. 'What happened?'

Nathan sighed. 'There was a fight. William's men came across this other group. I can only guess there was some slight on his honour, for he insisted on a duel and he was killed. The Lord alone knows how. He was an excellent swordsman. I always think if I had been there, would it have been different? Would I have been able to stop him?' He blew deeply out. 'I don't know. I'd left the army by then, gone back to the land. One of his men came to see me. I had to tell Mercia myself.'

From her hiding place Mercia swallowed, remembering how she had felt when he had brought her the news. Numb. Unbelieving.

Then for weeks – a wreck. But she had survived, as she would survive the trials afflicting her now. She was strong. And not alone.

'Now she has you,' Nicholas was cajoling.

'I try to be a good friend for her.'

A moment of silence. 'Is that all?'

'I don't know what you mean.'

Behind the mast, Mercia was totally still.

'I think you do,' said Nicholas. 'I know you think me a common rogue, but any fool can tell how you feel. Even me.'

Nathan laughed nervously. 'That is definitely none of your business. And I do not think anything will change anytime soon.' He drummed his fingers on the rail. 'Well, I best see to Daniel. Lady Markstone is reading to him, but I do not like him spending too much time with her. She is being exiled, after all, and despite what Mercia says I worry for the boy.'

'Daniel has no need to worry,' said Nicholas, 'with you and Mercia looking after him.'

Nathan clapped him on the shoulder and walked off down the ship, oblivious to Mercia's presence, leaving Nicholas at the stern. She sat for a while under the creaking wood, feeling her heart beat, feeling the warm breeze, thinking about the past, about the future, about Halescott. And she found herself thinking, for the first time in – how long? Surely an age? – about herself, about her own needs, her own wants. But then she thought, such indulgences were not helpful right now. She had a difficult task ahead, and she could not afford distraction.

Two days later an excited voice atop the mainmast shouted down to deck. 'Land ahead! I see land!'

Mercia dropped her mangled embroidery to rush to the starboard rail, accompanied by a tangled mixture of everyone and everything on the ship, all falling over each other as they leant over the side to try to make out land for themselves.

'There,' said Nathan, squinting as he looked over the waves. 'That grey line. Can you see? Land! 'Tis land!'

He seized Mercia's hands and danced her around the deck, before doing the same with a visibly elated Lady Calde. Nicholas clapped his hands and joined Daniel in an impromptu jig, while Lady Markstone just stood, holding her hands to the heavens and giving thanks for their safe passage across the ocean.

'Danny, can you see?' Mercia lifted him up. ''Tis America! A new land!'

'Are we going ashore?' he said, delight in his young voice.

She whirled him round, making him scream with joy. 'I am afraid not yet. We have to sail along the shore until we meet the other ships.'

'Here, let me,' said Nicholas, and he held Daniel up as high as he could. Suddenly Mercia fell to the deck and began to laugh.

'What is wrong?' asked Nathan.

'Nothing.' She shook her head. 'Just I cannot believe that is actually America, that we have come all this way across the sea. 'Tis inconceivable, and yet here we are.'

'Here we are,' he smiled. 'America.'

The ship came closer to shore. Mercia craned her neck, gripping the rail and standing on tiptoe to see what this unknown new world was like. As they sailed closer, the nondescript blur of grey land began to give up its secrets, splitting into tiny beaches, into rocks, into colours, overwhelmingly into trees, a mass of dark green stretching back as far as she could see; and they were good trees, strong trees, promising much to anyone who had dared make the crossing, who had dared pass God's almighty test.

For the next three days she could not keep off deck, fascinated by this new place. The swooping, unfamiliar birds; the sturdy cliffs; the frisky waves against the virgin shore – she was amazed by it all, like a child discovering something new. And she realised, we are all still children, that the sight of a new land, the thrill of a new experience, it can all still excite us, and we should let it. For a few hours on each of those three days, she forgot her cares, and she was glad.

The captain thought they had come to land too far north and turned the ship southwards. And at the end of the third day, the ship rounded a headland to find two others bearing British colours waiting in a bay, two of the three they had lost so many weeks ago in the fog. Sailing joyfully towards them, the *Redemption* came alongside the two ships, the *Elias* and the *Martin*, before the captain ordered the anchor thrown overboard, and the ship, finally, came to a halt.

'Piscataqua,' Captain Morley enunciated, when he came back from meeting Captain Groves and Captain Hill on the *Martin*. 'That is the name of this region, or something like.' He sniggered as Nathan turned the word over between his lips. 'You will have to get accustomed to such words now, my friends. Many place names we take from the Indians.'

'Where is the other ship?' asked Mercia, attempting to bite into a particularly hard biscuit. 'Is it still to come?'

'It made land further south, near Boston. Colonel Nicolls has dispatched a letter to say he is delayed there on the King's business, but 'tis not far. They will not be more than a day or two now, so Groves thinks. We are to await the *Guinea*'s return before the four ships head south again together to New Amsterdam.' He leant in closer to Mercia. 'You never told me you knew someone on the *Martin*.'

She sighed. 'Sir William Calde. How is the charming man?'

The captain looked puzzled. 'I don't mean him.'

'Oh? Then who?'

'I didn't know he was with us. He arrived in Portsmouth after I came aboard the *Redemption*. But surely, Lady Mercia, you must have known?'

'Captain Morley – who?'

'Why, your uncle, of course.'

Biscuit crumbs flew from her mouth. 'What did you say?'

'Sir Francis Simmonds is on the *Martin*. I'm sorry, I thought— He is your uncle?'

'Yes, but—' She wiped the crumbs from her dress. 'You are sure?'

'You didn't know?'

'No.' She looked at Nathan. He shook his head, as mystified as she.

Morley coughed. 'Groves says the Duke appointed him at the last minute to work with Sir Bernard Dittering. But between you and me, he thinks the Duke doesn't trust Sir Bernard and is keen that they . . . have an eye on each other.'

'Appointed him.' Mercia was scathing. 'And I was so enjoying this coast.'

The captain fiddled with the rim of his hat. 'You do not much like him?'

'Not one bit.'

'Then I am sorry.' He shuffled in his seat. 'I have agreed he can come aboard the *Redemption* with Sir William. They want to voyage the last few days with us.'

She stared at him. 'They are coming here? Should they not be preparing the soldiers for the invasion or such like?'

'I think that is the problem, Lady Mercia. After two months at sea with a crowd of boisterous soldiers they are eager for respite.' He smiled as if in apology. 'They promise to transfer additional provisions for the crew.'

She raised an eyebrow at Nathan. 'Those two, here with us.'

The captain swallowed. 'Three. It seems Sir Bernard and Sir Francis had a choleric discussion on the *Elias* yesterday. Now Sir Bernard wants to . . . establish his authority with your uncle before they arrive in New Amsterdam. He is coming also.'

'Sir Bernard too,' she muttered, staring at the floor. Then she looked up. 'So, Nathan. Three noblemen, begging to come on this ship with us.' She pursed her lips, considering. 'Sir William amongst them. Well, I am glad the sailors will get extra, but for once I am more pleased Lady Calde is aboard.'

The captain was a man of the world, both the old and the new. He stroked his chin and said nothing.

While they were waiting for the flagship to return, Nicholas declared he wanted something to do, so he offered to oversee the transfer of the promised provisions from the *Martin*. Mercia's recommendation to the captain secured him the job, and he spent a day rowing with a group of the strongest sailors backwards and forwards between the two ships. The sailor he had punched to the deck at the beginning of their voyage volunteered to go so he could meet with some of his mates on the *Martin*, but Nicholas refused him, a wicked smile on his face.

'You should not tease him so,' said Mercia as Nicholas was taking a quick rest. 'He will certainly be after your blood now.'

Nicholas laughed. 'He can try.'

She looked at the *Martin*, anchored at the other end of the bay where a wide river flowed into the ocean. The *Martin*'s longboat was fetching freshwater enough for all three ships, part of the cargo Nicholas was ferrying back.

'Have you seen my uncle and Sir William?' She drummed her

fingers on the rail. 'Is it not an inconvenience for them to come here?'

'Perhaps,' said Nicholas. 'The *Martin*'s a larger ship than ours, better equipped. But the soldiers are bored. They're itching for a fight. I can see why more refined men would want to leave.'

She scoffed. 'Those are not refined men.'

'Don't worry.' He smiled. ''Tis only a few days to New Amsterdam.'

'I always worry where my uncle is concerned.' She folded her arms. 'I suppose I can try to avoid them, as much as my task will allow.'

'Good luck,' said Nicholas, his eyes roving around the small ship. Mercia laughed, knowing her hope was impossible.

Three days passed before a cannon sounded out to sea announcing the return of the *Guinea*. It was a magnificent sight to see the flagship sail into the American bay, its billowing sails straining in the wind, the brightly painted colours on bow and stern betraying little indication of damage from the crossing. Two rows of cannons gleamed out of portholes the length of the ship, while the crew shouted greetings from their stations in the rigging, the huge masts stretching towards the sky under fluttering pennants of red, white and blue.

Anchors dropped, the four captains were summoned to a council of war on the *Guinea* with the King's commissioners and the Duke's noblemen. When he returned, Captain Morley could not tell all, but he explained that while in Boston, Nicolls had attempted to muster support for the invasion of New Amsterdam from the New Englanders. Some had agreed to help, but the commander had found it difficult encouraging them all to comply. Still, nearly five hundred soldiers already on board the warships would soon put the Dutch to rights, and the pragmatic Governor of Connecticut stood ready to assist, promising to gather a host of armed men at the tip of a place called Long Island. As Morley said, there could be no doubt. Victory was certain.

Thus the captain's confidence. It was contagious, and as they again set sail, all on board the *Redemption* began to think of conquest, of seizing a mighty prize for the King and his brother. In a positive frame of mind, Mercia was even glad the three noblemen had come on board, hoping her entrapment plan was working, although she didn't know if Nathan agreed, banished with the senior officers to hastily panelled-off compartments at the back of the 'tween deck to make room for the high-ranking courtiers. She watched the noblemen from a distance, even her uncle, looking for any sign one of them could be the criminal she sought. It was unfortunate that Lady Calde mistook her interest in Sir William for something more libidinous, but Mercia could live with her glares, even when their regularity began to feel harsher than the piercing sea rain.

They ploughed their way southwards, passing shores beyond which she knew her countrymen and women had already begun to forge a new destiny. Now these same shores were to become part of her own life, this captivating land where she had never expected to be. As the majestic *Guinea* slipped out of sight, the wind in its tremendous sails powering it faster than the rest, the *Redemption* sailed on around the shoals of Cape Cod, speeding Mercia in pursuit of what she hoped would be her happiness.

Chapter Twenty-Two

The late afternoon sun was almost as low as Mercia's mood. Now Sir William had been on board the *Redemption* for a few days, Lady Calde had reverted to a particularly hateful suspicion, and Mercia was in vain trying to persuade her of her disinterest in the non-started affair. She had barely managed to tear the mistrustful woman from her journal, when walking down the deck they broke off their dispute on hearing Nicholas's raised voice.

'I cannot,' he was saying. 'I work for Mrs Blakewood now.'

'He is arguing with my husband,' said Lady Calde. 'What can the rogue be thinking?'

Mercia looked over as Sir William leant towards Nicholas, muttering in his ear before pulling away and wagging his finger right in his face. Nicholas ignored the gesture, causing Sir William to shake his head, clearly exasperated.

'You will do as I say when I ask it!' he shouted, walking away.

'Can you not teach your man respect?' hissed Lady Calde, her fingertips clawing into her book. She looked at Mercia, a simmering resentment in her eyes, and stormed off after her husband.

The force of her words took Mercia aback. But she composed herself and called to Nicholas.

'What was that about?'

'Nothing.' Nicholas folded his arms. 'I can handle him.'

'Be careful. Sir William is a powerful man. You cannot talk to him as you sometimes do Nathan.'

He smiled. 'I like Nathan. Sir William just wanted to make it clear who was in charge.' He made to move off. 'Well, I said I would help with the sails.'

Left alone, Mercia returned to the quarterdeck. The ship had just turned westwards: on the starboard side, a flat-looking island was floating by in the near distance. Fed up with Lady Calde, she slumped her chin on the rail to watch the quickly passing coastline. But not many minutes elapsed before Nicholas reappeared, a resigned smile on his face.

'Mercia, you had better come. I think some of the lads are playing about.'

She swivelled round to face him. 'What is it?'

'Come and see.'

She shrugged and followed him down to the main deck, passing a group of sailors who were half-heartedly swabbing the boards. None of the noblemen were in sight; perhaps Sir Bernard and her uncle were having another heated debate. Then a shout sounded out, or rather a shriek. Ahead of them on deck, Lady Calde was calling out.

'Stop him someone! He will fall!'

Nicholas frowned. Mercia craned her neck around the mainmast to look in the direction of the shouts. She saw Lady Calde panicking near the forecastle door before disappearing down the steps to the 'tween deck below, crying for help. Feeling something was wrong, Mercia hurried to the front of the main deck, where a number of sailors were now spilling out from below. They stared skyward, straining to see, but the white of the mainsail reflected the sunlight painfully into Mercia's eyes and she had to turn away her gaze. A general cry went up, and a series of curses from the sailors.

Nathan appeared next to her, squinting as he looked up at the foremast. 'Hell's teeth,' he swore. 'Mercia, do not look.' He pushed her gently away.

'Look at what?' She turned her face upwards, this time using her arm as a shield from the sun's glare. It was difficult to make anything out, but as she squinted she could see a tiny object with little arms and legs hanging from the yardarm at the very top of the foremast, blowing in the wind. And just beneath, someone making his way up the rigging towards it. Someone small.

Her heart plummeted in her chest. Somehow Daniel was high in the narrow rigging, fifty feet up the mast.

'Lord help him!' she cried. She dashed up the ladder to the foredeck, ignoring the pull of her skirt. Unheeding the difficulties, she grabbed the foremast rigging, intending to pursue Daniel herself. But here her heavy clothing defeated her; she had barely begun when she fell back to the deck, her hands dirtied with the tar the sailors painted onto the rigging to protect it.

'Stay back!' barked a sailor at her side. 'You can do nothing.'

'Are you sure of that?'

While everyone was looking up, she untied the lace on her front-closing bodice and pulled both it and her skirt off faster than she had thought possible, until she was standing on the foredeck in just her petticoat, stays and boots. No thought for anything but Daniel, she jumped at the rigging and began to climb, pursuing two sailors who were already ahead of her. The sailor on the foredeck tried to pull her back down, but she kicked at his hand and he let go with a pained cry. She was dimly aware of Nathan and Nicholas shouting at her from the main deck to stop, but she ignored them, continuing her ascent.

The white of her stays was covered in tar by the time she had climbed not ten feet. Despite the stickiness the rope was hard, digging painfully into her hands. Still she kept going, the wind whipping around her body, her arms aching with each conquered bit of rope.

After a while she looked down. By now four sailors were surrounding Nathan, restraining him from climbing to the foredeck after her, while Nicholas stood next to them, his hand over his mouth, his eyes fixed on Daniel. Behind him Lady Calde emerged back on deck and tapped his shoulder, making him jump. She spoke into his ear, and he looked back at the hatch to the 'tween deck before shaking his head and running to the foredeck ladder himself. But the sailors did to him what they had done to Nathan, trusting in their two mates in the rope work to resolve the situation.

Mercia kept going, dragging herself higher, and higher, closing her eyes to the gusting wind, until summoning all her strength she reached the horizontal foreyard halfway up the mast, the bottom sail billowing beneath it. The rigging was tapering to a point just above her at the foretop, the small round platform from where the crew looked out to sea. Seeing Daniel close above it, she made one final agonising effort and hauled herself, arms burning, inside.

One of the sailors who had climbed before her was standing in the foretop, shouting instructions to his mate above; he turned to look at the person who had climbed in with him and let out an astonished gasp, swearing as he beheld a filthy, ragged woman in her underskirts. It would be a tale to beat all he had accumulated during his life aboard ships.

'What in God's creation?' he said. 'Stay here. You will be in the way.'

Mercia looked up. Against the white topsail she could see the man above her was now on a level with Daniel, her son clinging tight to the narrow rigging, shaking, tar over his little face. Involuntarily she put up her hand to go after him herself but the sailor beside her pulled it away. Unable to speak, she watched as the man above released Daniel's right foot from where it had become trapped, then holding onto the mast with just the strength of his legs, prised Daniel's hands off the tar-covered ropes.

'When I say,' shouted the sailor, 'put your arms around my back and hold tight.' He paused a moment, making sure his grip on the mast was secure. 'Now!'

Later, Mercia would say her heart stopped at the moment when her son grabbed at the sailor's loose shirt. But he managed it, clinging to his back, and the sailor with his human load descended to the foretop. Lowering himself in, he shook Daniel gently off. Oblivious to the tar on her hands, Mercia squeezed her son tightly, her heart resuming a steadier beat.

'Be careful,' said the sailor. 'I haven't risked myself for you to crush him to death.' But his tone was kind.

She looked up. 'Thank you.'

'We're not on deck yet. Give him back and I'll take him down.' He looked at her. 'It was brave, climbing up here. But in future, leave it to us.'

Mercia smiled at Daniel to go with him. He let her go, tears in his eyes. She watched them descend until moments later he was back on the foredeck, safe. Then she realised where she was, perched above the foresail with her clothes far below. It looked a lot higher from here than from the deck. She began to feel nervous. She could see Nathan pushing against the men surrounding him, trying to come to her aid, but the sailors were still preventing it.

'Wait here,' said the sailor beside her. He shinned up the rope above him, hauling himself towards the tiny object that was still hanging from the higher yardarm. She looked up at it and took a small step back as she recognised Daniel's toy lion. She stared at its tufted mane gone rigid in the wind, wondering why it was there.

A shout from below diverted her attention: Nathan, barking at the sailors to help her down. But then she thought, would they be so concerned if I were a man, and in her indignation she forgot her fear. Carefully, she placed one foot out of the foretop, then the other, feeling for a firm hold on the rigging. Loosening her grip on the platform, she began to descend; gradually the voices on deck grew louder until her left foot felt the wood of the forecastle and she stepped off the rigging, collapsing onto the floor. Daniel had been taken to the main deck; she pulled herself up and managed to clamber down the ladder after him.

Released from the sailors' confinement, Nathan ran to her. 'Are you unhurt? You could have fallen!'

She looked around. 'Where is he?'

A blur in the corner of her eye rushed to collide with her, holding on tight. 'Danny, why did you go up there?' she asked. 'Were you after your lion?' Daniel nodded, bursting into tears as the sailor from the foretop jumped down, handing Nathan the toy he had retrieved.

'That was his lion?' Nathan twisted it round. 'What the hell was it doing up there?'

'I don't know. Nicholas might. He said something about the sailors playing games.' She pointed him out with a nod. 'There he is, coming over now.'

'By Jesus, I am so, so sorry.' Nicholas walked up, his fist clenched against his side. 'How is he?'

''Tis not your fault,' said Mercia. 'We cannot watch over him all the time.'

'Someone put this in the rigging.' Nathan thrust the lion at him, furious. 'Do you know who?'

Nicholas looked at the toy. 'It must have been a sailor's dare. I . . . don't think they'd have thought he'd climb for it himself.'

'Nicholas, I don't care. I want to know who did it.'

Nicholas glanced round at the crew, who were gawking at Mercia with eager eyes. 'I know you do, but they won't talk. And there's something else.' He pulled a shining object from his pocket, handing it to her. 'Look what I found.'

'Lord above!' she said. 'The necklace!' Quickly, she wrapped the expensive pearls in a fold of her petticoat. 'Where in the name of heaven was that?'

'Stuffed in one of the sailor's bunks. I just found it.'

'Whose bunk?'

'I have no idea. I'm going to get some answers.'

He walked off, leaving Mercia to look at Nathan open-mouthed. 'How did this turn up now?' she whispered. 'It has been weeks.'

'I don't know,' said Nathan, staring after Nicholas.

'We will find out later. What matters now is that Daniel is safe.' She looked down at herself, caked in sticky tar. 'Nat, could you bring me a cloak? I cannot walk the deck like this, with all these prying eyes.'

'Of course.' He lunged at the sailors standing around them. 'What are you all looking at?'

He disappeared across the main deck towards the cabins, passing Lady Calde who was coming the other way, the three noblemen and Lady Markstone in her wake. The aristocratic quintet stopped as they beheld the surprising scene.

'What is happening here?' said Sir Bernard. Shadowed by the foresail his trim build seemed sparser than usual. 'Harriet says that boy has—Mrs Blakewood!' His grey eyes widened in outrage. 'Put some clothes on now!' He turned to the sailors. 'And you, get back to your work!' The sailors broke up, smirking.

'Mercia.' Lady Markstone clasped her hands together. 'Perhaps you could tell us what happened.'

Mercia pulled Daniel close. 'It seems one of the sailors put Danny's toy in the rigging as some sort of feeble jest. He went after it, and I went after him.' She glared at Sir Bernard, the man who had promoted her father's trial, with loathing. 'There have been enough tragedies in this family of late.'

Sir Bernard scoffed. 'This ship is no place for a boy such as he. You do wrong to bring him. And this . . . indecent state of dress.' He waved his hand at her dismissively. 'Is your family not shamed enough for you to behave like a common harlot?' He turned to Lady Markstone. 'Quite why you want this woman to accompany you into your exile is a mystery to me. One criminal family helping another, I suppose.'

'She is here because she wants to be,' said Lady Markstone, her face set. 'And because she is kind.'

'She is a menace,' rasped Sir Bernard. 'God's death, Mrs Blakewood, your wretched family seems to delight in causing trouble.'

Daniel buried his face in Mercia's petticoat. Indignant, she turned to Sir Francis. 'Uncle? Will you let him slight our family like that?'

Sir Francis stayed silent, his face red with embarrassment. Next to him, she noticed Sir William peering at her from behind Sir Bernard, his eyes darting between her stays and the deck. She began to feel exposed, but then Nathan reappeared with one of the spare cloaks she had packed for winter, uncertain how long she would remain in America.

'About time,' she said, annoyed. She let him place the cloak around her, then with Daniel still sitting she stood to face Sir Bernard. As she did, the necklace she had hidden in her lap clattered to the deck.

Sir William stared at the pearls, biting his lip. He looked involuntarily at his wife.

'Why, that looks like—' Lady Calde stooped to pick up the necklace. Mercia and Nathan looked at each other, eyes wide. 'It is!' Lady Calde rounded on her husband. 'You said you could not find this months ago, when I presumed I had lost it at the Russells' house. Yet here it is on the deck of this ship next to this – this woman!' She nodded, furious. 'I thought I saw her with it in the Privy Garden that once. But I could never believe it!'

'Your necklace?' said Mercia.

Lady Calde ignored her. 'So, William, my fears were correct. You have been betraying me with this' – she looked at Sir Bernard – 'yes, this harlot. That is why she is here. It is nothing to do with Millicent. You intend her to be near you while we are in America.'

'But Harriet, are you sure 'tis not just similar?' Sir William bowed his head. 'The explanation may be—'

'The explanation is obvious. You want a cheap whore and do not even have the grace to buy her new things. My, you are pitiful.' Lady Calde stormed off, her head thrown back, more in triumph, it seemed, than anger. Sir William glanced at Mercia before hurrying in pursuit.

Sir Bernard laughed out loud. 'I warned him not to get close to Goodridge's child. And you, Francis, telling him all would be well, that she would want him.' He shook his head. 'He will pay the price now. You, Millicent, be careful she does not corrupt you too.'

Lady Markstone narrowed her eyes. 'You are not one to talk of corruption, Bernard.'

Sir Bernard opened his mouth to retaliate, but Lady Markstone shook her head, as though daring him to try. Instead he pivoted on his heels and walked back down the deck, busying himself in straightening his doublet. With a wink at Mercia, Lady Markstone did the same, leaving her with Sir Francis.

'Mercia,' he said. 'Why could you not—?' He growled, running his hands along his face. 'By all that is sacred, why could you not be normal? He would make you rich! He still can, if we can arrange things right.'

'I do not—' she began, but he held up his hand.

'No. Not now.' He set off after the others. 'I have to think.'

She watched him go, her breaths fast and hard. 'How can he talk like that to me, as if he owns me? In front of Daniel?' She looked at Nathan, her eyes quivering with rage. 'And as for Sir Bernard, one day I will make that serpent pay for his part in what he did to my father.'

Nathan laid his hand on her shoulder. He too was trembling, clearly angered by what had been said. 'One day we will. But let me take you to your cabin. Let us all calm down.'

'You are right.' She coaxed Daniel to his feet, wrapping her cloak about her body. 'I can wash the tar off my hands and face.'

They made their way to the quarterdeck, nodding at Captain Morley who had been watching from a respectful distance. Mercia disappeared inside her cabin while Nathan went to fetch water. Two minutes later she put her head out the door, clutching a dress across her chest.

'Nathan!' she called.

Nathan was talking with the captain, a wooden pail of water at his side. Seeing her waving, he brought it over. 'I'm sorry. We were speaking about what happened with Daniel.'

She tugged at his arm. 'Quickly, inside.'

He smiled. 'No need to worry, I have your water. The captain had a barrel to hand.' He dragged the pail into the cabin and shut the door. Daniel was lying on the small bed, already fast asleep.

'Forget the water.' She pointed at the table. 'Look!'

'Why, what is—?'

'The cabin has been searched again,' she interrupted. 'There are things moved around. But look there.'

He followed her gaze. 'God's teeth!'

On the table her book of the Anglo-Saxon kingdoms lay open. It was stabbed into the wood by a knife.

'Look closer,' she said.

He peered at the open page. It was the beginning of the section on the kingdom of Mercia, the kingdom her father had named her for. The knife was one of those the sailors used to skin the fish they caught, and a small amount of gore had stained the page. Its point was stabbed through the heart of the large title word – right through *Mercia*.

'And there is this.' She thrust a piece of paper into his hand. Under a crudely drawn stick image of a woman hanging in a noose was a short note.

Return to England on the first ship back, or next time the knife goes through you. JN.

Chapter Twenty-Three

Nathan looked at her. 'My God. JN. James North?'

She nodded. 'My plan is working. Whoever the bastard is, he knows my intent and comes to scare me off. It is precisely as I thought.'

'But this is vicious, Mercia.'

She struck her fist against the cabin wall, making it shake. 'We think 'tis a nobleman. Well then, he must be one of the three who came from the *Martin*. Sir William, Sir Bernard—' She paused. 'Or Sir Francis. Masquerading as James North, reminding us he is dead at his hand.'

'Then he is taking an awful chance. What if you had come to your cabin while he was here?'

She shook her head. 'I have a feeling that diversion with Daniel's lion was not a mere sailor's prank.'

His eyes widened. 'You think it was arranged to distract you? That Daniel was encouraged to climb for it?'

'Maybe so, but even without Daniel I would have been busy making sure the sailors retrieved the toy. You know it was a present from his father.' She swept out her arm. 'It would have been long enough to do this.'

Nathan looked again at the knifed book. 'I do not like this, Mercia. He must be sorely worried. If he feels there is no other way, he may go through with this threat, regardless of who he is.' He paused. 'Who would know the toy was so precious?'

'Everyone. Daniel has been showing it off this whole time.' She looked at her son sleeping on the bed. 'I will not be intimidated like this. We will find this man and unmask him. Even if it is my uncle himself.'

He scratched at his chin. 'Could it be him? We have never much considered it.'

'Why not?' She rubbed her tarred fingertips across her right temple, leaving a thin mark. 'He lives not far from Oxford, so he could have had access to North before the Section left for London. He did well for himself when Cromwell was in power, even though he supported the King. We know he is obsessed with wealth.' She sighed. 'But really, I do not know. It could be him, yes. But it could as easily be either of the other two.'

Nathan hesitated. 'Even Sir William? Does he not . . . have a fancy for you?'

'I wonder.' She bit her dirty nails. 'So far, this man has not made a serious attempt to kill me. He has threatened, tried to scare, but nothing more.'

'Not yet.'

'But could that be why? As for Sir Bernard, he was the most venomous on deck, but that means nothing.' She blew out her cheeks. 'Whoever he is, he has made a mistake with this note. All we need do is find a sample of each of their writing and compare it.'

'If such samples exist. Most of their belongings are still on the other ships. And Mercia, he has been careful with his identity until now. It cannot be so simple.'

257

'Maybe not. But it behoves us to check. My uncle at least likes to note down his thoughts.' She studied the message. 'I do not think this is his hand, but it could be disguised. It does look peculiar, somehow, and neater than the note left in the town house.' She ripped the paper in two, giving Nathan half. 'Here. 'Tis nearly dark, and I want to play a scared mouse tonight, make whoever left this think I am affected by his act. But tomorrow morning we will see what we can discover.' She bent down to the pail. 'Now, I had best get this tar off.'

'Do you need help?' He turned towards the door. 'I can ask Lady Markstone.'

She pointed to the floor. 'Pick up that cloth and help me yourself. Just here on my face where I cannot see. I will do the rest.'

He flushed, wetting the cloth and kneeling beside her. 'This won't take long. 'Tis mostly your hands that are dirty.' He brought his face close to hers, gently rubbing the damp cloth across the patches on her forehead and cheek.

Their lashes nearly touched as she looked into his eyes. 'Can you believe Sir William gave me second-hand jewellery as a gift? Clearly I am not worth much.'

His fingers brushed against her cheek as he rubbed harder at a spot near her lips. 'You are worth ten times Lady Calde. A hundred.'

She smiled. 'Flatterer.'

'What of the necklace, anyway?' He leant still closer: she could fell his breath on her neck. ''Tis strange it was found today.'

'Ask Nicholas, perhaps. I need to sleep. I am too tired tonight to think on that as well.'

'I will.' He shuffled back, studying her face. 'Much better.'

'Thank you. I can manage now. And do not worry about this.' She jerked her head at the mutilated book. 'I will be quite fine.'

'If you are sure. I am not far away if you need me.'

He held her gaze for a second until he flicked down his eyes and pulled himself up, resting his hand on her shoulder for a moment longer than he needed – or was that her imagination? Only when he had gone did she allow herself to stop pretending that the violent warning had not truly scared her. Pleased as she was her plan seemed to be working, in truth she felt troubled at the stark confirmation her enemy could be known to her. But when she pulled the knife from the book – her book – and saw the damage it had caused, her uncertainty turned to conviction. This book was her birthright, and so too, much more so, was her house. Nothing and nobody would deter her from restoring it.

Entrusting Daniel to Lady Markstone, next morning Mercia did what she had thought she would never do: voluntarily seek out her uncle. He was looking out to sea from the quarterdeck, cupping his chin with his gloved hands, his elbows on the rail.

'Uncle,' she called from behind. 'We have not spoken much since you came on board.'

He turned from his contemplation, observing her crossing the deck. 'Ah, my wayward niece. Have you come to apologise?'

She had known it would be like this. 'For what?'

He let out a sharp laugh. 'Oh, for shaming the family, removing your clothing, talking back to Sir Bernard. Shall I continue?'

She clasped her hands in a false gesture of contrition, bowing her head. 'You cannot expect me to do nothing if my son is in danger.' It was a barbed remark, referring to his appropriation of the manor house as much as yesterday's events, but she laced her words with contrived respect. 'As for Sir Bernard, you must surely understand I have no esteem for him.'

'Or for Sir William, it seems.' He shook his head, making his hat bobble in the wind. 'He should be an easy means of providing you with the fortune you so lament. But now I do not know. His wife will make things difficult.'

'How terrible of her.'

'Perhaps there is still hope. I wonder.' He looked away, his eyes roaming the sea. Then he jerked his head back round, the hurried action startling her. 'Why are you on this voyage if not for Sir William? Do not tell me you have come all this way to keep that crazed old woman company.'

The force of the question threw her, but she quickly recovered. 'I wanted to escape for a while,' she essayed. 'Father's death has affected me.'

He pulled on the tip of his glove. 'I suppose it would.'

'Lady Markstone offered me the chance to come a long way away. It seemed reasonable. I have known her all my life.'

He folded his arms. 'And Keyte?'

'Nathan wishes to see something of the world before he spends the rest of his life on his land.' She turned the question back at him. 'Why are you here, Uncle? I was not expecting it.'

He sighed. 'Because, Mercia, I am trying to keep our family strong. There is great opportunity in America. New Amsterdam lies at the very mouth of Hudson's River, a gateway to all those commodities waiting within. Assessing such prospects will be a very lucrative enterprise, one the Duke seemed most keen for me to grasp.' He smiled, the right side of his face arching higher than the left. 'Besides, we both wanted to make sure you were safe.'

She tilted her head. 'Is that so?'

His smug expression darkened. 'You take that tone with me too often, child, so have a care. And listen to me now. Take Sir William as a lover. He will not disappoint either of us.'

He strutted towards the chart house, inserting himself into a discussion the captain was engrossed in with the boatswain. Feigning nonchalance, Mercia sauntered down to the main deck, turning past the capstan and smiling at the pilot at the whipstaff as she strolled into the cabin area where the noblemen were lodged. She could hear movement inside one of the cabins, and what sounded like a woman's measured scolding in another, but she had no inclination to eavesdrop for gossip. Checking nobody was near, she pushed open her uncle's door.

As she expected, the cabin was well ordered, everything in its proper place. It was easy to find the few pages of scribblings she was hoping he would have drafted during the brief journey from Piscataqua. Glancing continually at the closed door, she laid the threatening note alongside them. But when she compared the two, even allowing for attempts at disguise, she was not surprised that they did not in the slightest match.

She had seen Nathan only briefly that morning, just after dawn. He had seemed in a hurry, scarcely pausing to tell her he would try to find some samples of Sir Bernard's and Sir William's writing before disappearing again. Wanting to know whether he had found anything out, she fetched Daniel and set off round the ship.

'Did you behave for Lady Markstone?' she asked.

'She would not let me do anything.' Daniel pulled a face. 'She made me stay in the cabin the whole time, even when she went for a piss.'

'Danny! Where did you learn such a word?'

He shrugged. 'The sailors say it.'

'Hmm.' Mercia frowned. 'Perhaps you should spend less time with the sailors.'

'The sailors are fun.' He twirled round. 'I want to climb the mast again.'

Mercia bent down to him. 'Yesterday you were terrified. You need to learn fear, Danny, or you will get into trouble.' She sighed. 'But no. You do not want to know fear.' She stroked his cheek. 'I want you to promise me you will be careful. We are about to get to a dangerous place. So I need you to be good.'

Daniel nodded. 'When I grow up, I want to be a sailor. It is much more exciting here than being bored in the cottage with Bethany.'

She stood up and ruffled his hair. 'Maybe so, but do not climb the mast again. Do you promise?'

'What if Uncle Nathan comes too?'

'Not even then.' She looked around. 'Uncle Nathan seems to be hiding this morning. Will you help me find him?'

'I can do that!' Excited, he ran off ahead, reluctantly skidding to a halt when Mercia bellowed at him to behave.

They scoured the deck from forecastle to stern but Nathan was nowhere to be found. Nor was he in the cook's room, or in the chart house, and peeping once more into the steerage area the only person there still was the pilot, taking orders from a navigator on the quarterdeck above. He interrupted his tedious task to confirm Nathan had been through earlier, before she had herself, but that he had immediately left. Back out on deck she crossed paths with Sir William, who made a poor feint of pretending not to notice her, probably embarrassed by the previous day's scene.

She realised she had not seen Nicholas either, and thinking Nathan might have gone to his hammock to ask him about the necklace, she decided to venture below. Leaving an annoyed Daniel once more with Lady Markstone, she descended the steps to the 'tween deck, the ship's middle tier where the sailors slept amongst the cannons. It was sunny outside, but much more heat than light penetrated the sweat-filled space. In her heavy dress, Mercia felt immediately uncomfortable. She wondered how Nathan and Daniel, now relegated to a makeshift cubicle down here, were able to sleep.

Knowing Nathan hated his new bunk, it was no surprise to find it empty. Tentatively, she peeked into the area where the sailors' hammocks were stretched out at night, thirty of them nailed into the posts in a ramshackle manner, but they were mostly rolled up now it was morning, and aside from a few men dozing between work duties little was happening. Grime-stained sailors stared at her as she squeezed past the windlass used for raising and lowering the anchor, and then around the lower section of the capstan that hauled goods from the hold, but there was no sign of Nicholas or Nathan.

Had she missed them on the main deck above? She hadn't looked into the rigging, but while Nicholas might well be helping the sailors, there would be no reason for Nathan to assist in this calm weather. The gunroom was empty, so that only left the hold. A slight nervousness fluttered into life inside her belly as she walked towards the larger floor hatch that opened onto the vast dark space below. As she drew near it, the sailor who had made a pass at her all those weeks before scuttled past. For a moment her eyes met his in the semi-darkness. He opened his mouth in surprise before lowering his head and walking on.

The gaping hatch was open. She called into the darkness: 'Nathan, are you there?' A couple of nearby sailors turned to look at her. She called again. 'Nathan, if you are looking for supplies, come out. I want to talk to you.'

There was no reply. Instinct told her something was wrong, or maybe it was the claustrophobia of these darkened conditions.

Whatever the reason, the faint panic in her chest grew stronger. Peering through the hatch, she made out dark shapes of barrels and crates, but the blackness was too dense to see detail. She thought about going to the captain, but she did not want him to think her a fool. The top of a ladder stuck out of the hatch; she put one foot on the highest rung and began to descend.

'Hey! You can't go down there!' One of the sailors shouted at her to stop, but too late – her head was already through the hatch. Each step down drew a darker veil over her eyes, but her feet soon felt the wooden planking that made up the hold floor, carefully laid over the cobblestone ballast that kept the ship stable in the waves.

The irritated sailor called through the hatch. 'What are you looking for? The hold's no place for a lady.'

'Do you have a torch?' she shouted up, gripping a ladder rung with an anxious hand. 'I will not be long. I need to . . . check on my belongings.'

The sailor swore and vanished. Moments later he returned with a flaming torch that he must have lit on the cooking fire. Leaning down, he held it out to her; she reached up and grabbed it.

'Be careful,' he warned, his voice gruff. 'I'll wait here if you need me.'

She turned away from the hatch, making her way deeper into the silence of the unfamiliar hold, her feet squelching through unseen puddles of water that would have leaked inside during the voyage. It was fiendishly hot, the summer humidity amplified in the confined, windowless space. The torchlight flickered off the various cargo, creating devilish shadows that intensified her panic. She felt trapped, as she had felt trapped under the table in Halescott Manor, eighteen years before. She began to have to fight her own fears to press on. Slowly she moved forward, repeating over and over that her anxiety was groundless.

She ran the torchlight over every object she saw, the corners of her eyes making out blurry images that darted swiftly out of sight. They were small shadows, but her imagination turned them into sea demons. She gripped the torch harder but still she continued, sliding past barrels and ropes, boxes and blankets, chairs and chests, telling herself this was most likely a fruitless endeavour, that she had just missed Nathan on deck above.

The hold seemed bigger from the inside than it looked from the face of the ship, but again she told herself this was her fear at work. She took care to stay on the wooden planks, avoiding the wobbling ballast that could make her trip. She was beginning to conquer her disquiet when halfway through the space, behind the wide bottom of the mainmast, a different sort of object loomed into sight, a slumped uneven mass strewn across the floor. Her panic intensified, increasing threefold. Sweating, she swept the torchlight across whatever lay at her feet.

The torch nearly fell from her grasp. She beheld the figure of a man, dark and silent, his back to her, unmoving. Her heartbeat accelerated, pounding out an erratic thump. She stepped over him to look at his face. Then she gasped, and only a quick reaction caught the torch as it did fall. Worried something had happened to Nathan, she was not expecting this. She bent down to check the man was still breathing, and he was, but the tips of his hair were matted with blood. His blonde hair, for the man was Nicholas.

Chapter Twenty-Four

Holding the torch with one hand, Mercia used the other to try to shake Nicholas awake. When he did not stir she felt over his body, but there were no gashes evident in his clothing, no wounds discernible in his skin. It was only his face that showed signs of trauma, a small amount of clotted blood around his cheek. He looked more asleep than anything. Most likely he had been punched and left there.

She gripped the still-burning torch and made for the ladder as fast as she could. 'Quickly!' she shouted to the sailor above. 'There is a man down here! He has been attacked and will not wake.'

'Attacked?' came his voice. 'Who?'

'Nicholas. My manservant.' She began to climb. 'Here, take this torch.'

The sailor reached down to help her up the ladder before running for assistance. Her breaths shallow, Mercia followed him onto the coolness of the open deck above. A strong wind was now blowing, filling the sails, turning the air about her cold.

'Where is the barber-surgeon?' the sailor was calling. 'Nick Wildmoor has been beaten and left for dead.'

As the news spread, a great clamour broke out on the ship. The crew began to congregate on the main deck. Some of the sailors went below with the barber, the ship's doctor, to see what was happening.

Mercia was leaning on her thighs taking in gulps of salty air when the captain appeared at her side. 'They say Wildmoor has been attacked in the hold,' he said, his face hard. 'Is this true?'

'Yes,' she gasped. 'The barber is with him now. Someone has struck him senseless, but there are no serious wounds. I think he will recover.'

'Did anyone see who did it?'

'I don't know. I don't think so.'

'No matter.' Morley looked over at his crew. 'I wager I know who it was.'

She looked up in sudden realisation. 'I did see that sailor he has a rivalry with coming away from the hold.'

'You have it.' He stormed across the deck. 'Jamieson!' he cried. The sailors around him began to fall silent. 'Jamieson! Show yourself!'

As Mercia's breathing settled, the young sailor who had spoken indecently with her at the start of their voyage emerged onto deck. Now she had calmed down it seemed obvious. Nicholas had only recently denied this man the chance to visit his mates on the *Martin*. It was perhaps one insult too many. Maybe he had followed Nicholas to the hold and struck.

She noticed the noblemen coming out on deck from their quarters, Lady Calde with them, doubtless attracted by the noise; soon after, Lady Markstone too appeared, Daniel in tow. Not knowing what might happen, Mercia motioned at her to keep him where he was. She nodded, pulling him towards her. Daniel bounced left and right, eager to see, but Lady Markstone held him close.

Under the mainmast, Jamieson was dragged in front of the captain, more of insolence than of panic in his eyes. He stood in the middle of the deck, obstinate in the glare of his captain's gaze.

Morley called for silence. 'Nicholas Wildmoor has been found beaten in the hold. You were seen coming from there and are known to be his enemy. What say you?'

Jamieson shrugged. 'I say nothing. I've not done it. Though if he's been beat I wish I had.' He spat on the deck, defiant. 'That shit deserves it.'

The captain folded his arms, waiting. Finally Jamieson cracked. 'Fine, I was in the hold. I found him there and left him. But I didn't strike him. I'm innocent.'

Morley narrowed his eyes, roving them over his crew, assessing the mood. The sailors were all grinning and shaking their heads, clearly as sceptical of Jamieson's denial as he was.

'Innocent,' repeated Jamieson slowly, as if to a dull beast, accentuating each syllable, but the captain was in no mood to listen. An infraction had been committed on his ship and he needed to assert his authority. Mercia noticed Sir Bernard nodding approvingly on the quarterdeck. Swift justice, she thought, that is what Sir Bernard is about. Swift justice, even when the evidence does not exist.

She began to feel uneasy. There was no actual proof of this fellow's guilt. Uncertain, she considered what to do. She did not want an innocent man punished, but neither did she want to tell the captain of the other suspicion that was forming in her mind, that Nicholas had been attacked by her enemy, in a further attempt to scare her off. If she said anything now in front of the sailors, in front of the noblemen, her secret could spread all over the ship.

So she said nothing, hating herself for it. And where was Nathan? In vain, she looked through the crowd of people to see where he could be.

The captain nodded to one of the mates, who beckoned over two sailors.

'No,' said Jamieson, taking a step back. 'Keep away. I've done nothing.'

Unheeding his plea, the two sailors walked across the deck towards him. He shook them off as they took hold of his arms, but at a nod from the mate they grabbed him more firmly and dragged him to the mainmast. Stripping him to the waist, they turned him about and tied him securely to the thick pole. He rested his head on the wood, closing his eyes, now resigned to the inevitability of punishment.

The mate strode through the crowd into the captain's quarters, re-emerging moments later with a sadistic device from which every sailor on the ship involuntarily recoiled, a long wooden stick capped by a series of leather straps. Alarmed that Daniel might see, Mercia looked over at Lady Markstone, but she was already escorting him away. Relieved, she turned back to Jamieson, and then away again as the mate pulled back his right arm to administer the first stroke. She winced as she heard the sharp sound of the lash fall. Jamieson cried out in agony; she peered through her fingertips to see his flesh cut in six bleeding diagonal lines across his back. The next time she forced herself to watch, holding her entwined hands over her mouth as the mate whipped Jamieson's tortured back with a powerful strike.

Captivated by the scene on deck, nobody noticed the lone individual climbing down the rigging from the foretop. But feeling sick at the sight of Jamieson's bloody back, and sicker still at her self-interested silence, Mercia looked up towards the foredeck and was startled to see Nathan descending the last few lines of the rigging. He dropped down the ladder to the main deck to join her, his hair tangled and unkempt.

'What were you doing up there?' she asked.

'Nothing, I—what is happening?'

'Nicholas has been attacked. This man is being punished for it.' The third lash fell, Jamieson's cry blunter this time. She lowered her voice. 'But I am not sure he is culpable.'

269

'Nicholas?' Nathan looked at Jamieson tied to the mast, then back at Mercia. 'Was he – found in the hold?'

Mercia nodded, her eyes fixated on Jamieson's back, now become a bloody mass of welts. And then she jumped as right beside her Nathan cried out: 'Stop!'

She wrenched her head to look at him. He chewed his lip, his eyes sorrowful. Composing himself, he strode forward into the midst of all. 'Captain Morley,' he said. 'You must release this man at once. He did not attack Nicholas. I did.'

Uproar broke out. The sailors shouted and screamed, punching their fists into their palms. The noblemen looked at each other, mouths half-open, craning their necks forward in surprise. Lady Calde stood impassive, her arms folded. But Mercia barely took in the scene as she registered what Nathan had said.

'You attacked Nicholas?' the captain asked, incredulous. Nathan simply nodded. Staring at him, the captain clicked his fingers and ordered Jamieson's release. The lashed sailor collapsed against the mast, sliding to the deck, before he picked himself up and stumbled to the hatch that led below.

The crew began to beat out a violent rhythm with their feet. Fired up, they clamoured for Nathan to receive the punishment instead. 'Lash,' they repeated, 'lash, lash,' over and over. Mercia looked at Nathan, mouthing a simple 'why?', but he turned his face away. She entreated the captain, but he was adamant. Such a grievous incident as the beating of a fellow on ship could not pass unpunished, not with the crew in such a fury as they were.

'I am happy to accept the penalty,' said Nathan. Although he spoke with dignity, there was fear in his eyes as he looked at the lash. 'I lost control of my actions. I understand the laws of the sea.'

'Yet you are no common sailor,' said the captain. He sucked in his gaunt lips, thinking. 'I will see you punished, but not by the lash.'

The crew, at first impressed by Nathan's determination to suffer as they would, now screamed out in disgust. Mercia stepped back, for something in their manner told her they were in the mood for blood.

'Quiet, you men!' shouted Morley. 'There are women on deck!' They fell silent, suppressed mutiny in their eyes, and he continued. 'Nathan Keyte, for the crime of beating insensible a fellow on my ship, by the authority given me by the Articles of War, I command you be keelhauled in sight of the crew, the punishment to be delivered immediately.'

The crew let out a massive roar, this time in firm approval. Nathan looked at the deck, clenching and unclenching his fists in anxiety, but he took a deep breath and readied himself for his ordeal, pulling off his doublet and shirt. Mercia looked at his strong back, then up at his long hair, and felt an unnatural anger.

'What have you done?' she hissed, storming towards him. She could not look him in the eye, so she looked at the scar running over his chest. 'Why cannot men get along? Why?' He reached out to touch her, but she flung his hand away. 'Look what you have done to yourself – half-naked, about to suffer the Lord knows what! By God's truth, Nathan! What has Nicholas done to you?' She curled up her hands. 'Are you jealous? Is that it?'

The anchor had now been dropped in readiness, and the crew was beginning to grow restless, banging their feet faster and faster on the deck. Nathan opened his mouth to speak, but nothing came out. Instead he allowed himself to be led to the ship's side. Exasperated, Mercia stood silent herself, her hands arched over her lips.

The captain walked up. 'I am sorry, Lady Mercia. I hope you understand. I have to keep discipline.'

'What is going to happen?' she asked. 'I do not even know.'

'Do you see that rope?' He pointed out a sturdy cable tied to the mainmast that led out over the ship's starboard side. 'Now do you see that fellow climbing back into the port side with the other end? He has just swum the rope under the ship, so that now it encircles it. We will undo the rope from the mast, then tie the two ends together and loop the middle tightly around Nathan's waist. He will jump into the sea, and we will pull on the rope to haul him under the keel, the bottom of the ship. He will come out the other side and we will bring him back up.'

Mercia nodded her understanding.

'What often happens is the man scrapes against the ship's underbelly, which is covered with sharp barnacles and the like. It can tear a man to pieces.' Her eyes widened. 'But,' the captain lowered his voice, 'I have made sure the rope is long, and he will pass under the keel unharmed. He just needs to hold his breath.'

'I understand,' said Mercia. ''Tis an acceptable punishment, then.'

The captain nodded. He walked back to Nathan, checking on the fastness of the rope now tied around his bare waist. 'Very well,' he said. 'Begin.'

One of the crew pushed Nathan forward. With a glance back at Mercia, he leapt into the sea. She ran to the side, watching as his head bobbed in the choppy waves, before he vanished underwater. Behind her, three sailors tugged hard on the other side of the rope. They heaved away, dragging Nathan's heavy body under the keel, the strong wind whipping into their eyes.

She rushed to the other side of the ship, waiting for a sign that Nathan was about to emerge. The sailors continued to haul, grunting at each pull. Around her the crew were singing some sort of chant, but she was too agitated to make out the words.

Nearly a minute passed. She realised she was holding her own breath as though she herself were beneath the rolling waves. She grasped the rail, unheeding its roughness, waiting, until a dark shape approached the surface and Nathan's head broke through. He took in huge gulps of air, but he had survived, and angry as she was she felt a surge of relief.

The three sailors kept up their task, dragging Nathan roughly up the ship's side. After more agonising seconds he was back on deck, breathing deeply and clutching his wet belly as he lay in a growing puddle of seawater. His bedraggled hair was sticking to his face, and his breeches were soaked through, but he managed to look up at Mercia and smile.

'Of course I am jealous,' he said. 'How could I not be?'

She refused to smile back. As the sailors stepped forward to untie him, she paced up and down, trying to decide how she should react. Then a growing murmur from the crew turned her attention to where the barber-surgeon had emerged from below. Nicholas was behind him, his cheek still stained with blood, but he seemed to be mostly unharmed. Taking in the unquiet around him he blinked in surprise. Instinctively she raised her hand and he stumbled across to where she stood. He stopped when he saw Nathan laid out on the deck, wet through.

'What's happened here?' Nicholas looked at the rope leading over the side, the cheering crew, Nathan's dripping torso. He stared at her. 'Don't tell me he's been—?'

'Keelhauled,' she confirmed. 'For beating you senseless.' She examined his cut lip. 'Are you much hurt? I found you myself.'

His face was ashen. 'He struck me, 'tis true, but he had reason. Mercia, I—' He could not finish.

She looked at him, then at Nathan on the deck. 'Nicholas, I am not a fool. This is no common dispute. What is going on?'

He nodded weakly before addressing the captain. 'You should not have done this,' he said. 'I deserved to be hit.' He glanced at Mercia and then quickly away. 'He was right to strike me. I have betrayed my lady's trust.'

He walked to the side of the ship. Nathan was urgently shaking his head, signalling him to keep silent, but Mercia went after him, puzzlement across her windswept face. Spray from the wild sea leapt into her eyes, but she scarcely noticed.

'What are you saying?' she said.

He took a deep breath, raising his head to look her in the eye. A lone tear was rolling down his red cheek, his bravado dazed by Nathan's assault. At that moment, the roar of the wind, the crash of the sea, the cacophony of the sailors' voices, everything faded, even Nathan, until all that was left was Mercia and Nicholas, isolated from all else.

'I have betrayed you,' he simply said. 'All this time, I have been in false trust.'

A coldness entered her body. 'I do not understand.'

He sniffed, and his lower lip twitched, but when he next spoke he was determined. 'You suspected someone of passing information to your enemy, someone who helped trace where you were.' He paused. 'Well it was me. I told them you would be at the Moor Fields. I helped them arrange yesterday so your cabin could be searched. I have repaid your kindnesses with betrayal. Nathan is not the one to be punished. It should be me.'

Mercia stared, a bitter heartbreak building in her soul. She looked at this man she had grown to like, to trust, a great sadness rising over her until she could no longer hold back. The pain burst out, and she struck at him without aim, he merely accepting the blows wherever they fell, until Nathan came over and pulled her shaking body away.

Chapter Twenty-Five

'I did not want you to know,' said Nathan, as they were sitting in the shade of the mainsail that afternoon. 'To be hurt. He asked to see me in private, took me to the hold where nobody else would be. He confessed it all.' He risked putting his hand on hers. 'I lost my temper. I am sorry for it, but I was so angry. I went to hide in the foretop for a while, to try to calm myself.'

She stared at the rough planks of the quarterdeck, all other concerns vanished from her mind. 'But why did he do it? I met him by chance. It cannot have been arranged beforehand.'

'I did not let him say much, in truth. He says he was approached after he met you, that he was offered a reward. He says he was told your life would not be endangered. I think when he saw Daniel in trouble in the rigging yesterday, his conscience finally objected. That was a diversion, as you thought.'

'So he did it for money, while I have been paying him as well.' Mercia scratched at the deck with her nails. 'Did trust die in the war too, Nat?'

'Not everywhere.' He squeezed her hand.

A skittish boy approached. 'Nicholas is asking for you,' he said. 'He's at the bow.'

She clenched her fist. 'Nicholas can—No. I do want to speak with him.' She silenced Nathan with a jerk of her hand. 'I want to understand how I could have been so deceived.'

He was sitting on the rail at the front of the forecastle, the wind blowing gently through the unfurled sail above. The crew must have given him privacy, for nobody else was near.

'Mercia,' he said. 'I'm glad you have come.'

She did not greet him. 'My son was in danger yesterday.'

He lowered his head. 'I know. I am truly sorry for it. I did not think he would try to fetch the toy himself.'

She folded her arms. 'He is a boy.'

Nicholas looked up. His right eye was bruised, but his cheek was now free of blood. 'I want you to know, I hardly told them anything at all.'

'And I believe that?'

'It is the truth.' He leapt from the rail, his boots thudding on the deck. 'When you dismissed me that time back in London, I felt aggrieved. I'd helped you with Michael, with Fell, and you just turned me adrift. Someone was watching your lodgings and saw me go in. He hired a linkboy to wait for me to leave and take me to him.'

Mercia's heart raced. 'To the nobleman?'

'No. I don't know who he is. This was his servant.'

'Of course.' She let out a bitter laugh.

'He's the one who got into your house that same night. He said he was called Jerrard, but I'm not sure that's his real name. He claimed to be an admirer of your father at first, that he wanted to ask whether you would receive him. I could tell it was a pretence, that he just wanted to find out what I knew about you. When he realised my true situation, he jumped on the chance. He offered me money to pass him information.' He looked at her with pained eyes. 'Please understand, I had no steady job. I'd lost my work as farrier to the Markstones. When someone offers me money, I have to take it. I was angry with you. I said yes.'

She closed her eyes. 'You went to see your friend Pikey to find something you could use to get back into my confidence.'

'I didn't know you then. I certainly didn't expect you to come looking for me, to open your heart about your brother. I began to feel guilty. When we found North's body I said I didn't want to help them any more, but Jerrard claimed you wouldn't be put in danger, that they only wanted to frighten you. I thought I could take his money and watch out for you at the same time, maybe find out who was behind this. But they were too careful.'

'I see.' Her voice dripped with scepticism. 'The bowman on Moor Fields was arranged this way?'

'Yes. But he deliberately missed.'

'And you deliberately let him escape. What of yesterday?'

'You were right to think whoever is behind this would follow you here. Jerrard has been on the *Martin* the whole time.'

She went still. 'With his master?'

The reply disappointed her. 'I don't know. He is with the fleet, but he could have come on any of the ships. I was just told to find some way of getting to the *Martin* when we reached America to meet Jerrard.'

She shook her head. 'That's why you offered to ferry the provisions.'

'Yes, but by then I'd decided I was finished with it. I wanted to trick him into telling me who his master was, but I couldn't get him to say.' He sighed. 'And then—'

'Then he opened his coin box, I suppose.'

His lips twitched. 'All he wanted was a diversion, something small to keep you busy. I knew nothing could put you off, so I thought why not? I dared one of the lads to take Daniel's toy to the foretop, knowing you would have to waste time getting it back.' He hung his head. 'The boy wasn't meant to get involved.'

'Fortunately for you he is unharmed.' She unfolded her arms, an idea striking her. 'This Jerrard. Can he write?'

'Hell, no. At least, I doubt it. Why?'

'Oh, no reason.' She put her hands on her hips. 'Is there anything else?'

'No. I swear it.' He looked up at her, the sun casting his shadow on the deck as the ship made a slight turn. 'You must think me a demon. I would do anything to win back your trust.'

'My trust?' The word made her angry. 'All this Jerrard need do is dangle coin in your face. You cannot tell me you need the money, not while you are earning from me. This is just about greed.'

'No,' he said. 'I do need the money.'

She scoffed, turning to leave. 'Did I not pay you enough to come with us?'

'For myself, yes. But 'tis not that simple.'

'Well?'

He hesitated. 'I don't want the money for me. I want it for my daughter.'

Mercia stared at him. 'Your daughter?'

'Yes. Her name is Eliza.'

'Daughter?' she repeated. 'Why have you never mentioned this before?'

'I don't tell anyone.' He rested his hands on the rail, looking out to sea. 'I'm not married, am I?'

'No, you are not.' She came closer. 'What happened?'

He shrugged. 'I fell in love. Foolish, I know. Then she left, no warning, no goodbye. Eight months later she came back, clutching a babe in her arms. She held the child out to me, telling me take back what is yours, I don't want it. So I did. I've never seen her again.'

Compassion trickled into Mercia's heart. 'But that is terrible. A woman who could do that.'

'I tried to find her afterwards. But she'd left London and no one would tell me where she'd gone.' He turned to face her, his green eyes betraying his sadness. 'That was three years ago. I've raised Eliza ever since, or rather my sister has. Eve tells everyone Eliza was a cousin's who died. I do all I can to pass her money, for my girl and for her own brood. The money you paid me before we set out – it all went straight to her.'

The trickle became a flood. Mercia looked directly into his eyes, and she found she wanted to believe him. She thought of how she would do anything for Daniel in his place. But she couldn't forgive him. Not yet.

'What happens to us now?' he said.

She tugged at a ringlet fallen loose in the breeze. 'I will not ask the captain to bring out his lash. I am . . . not indifferent to what you say. But you have been crossing me, whatever your motives. I would stay away from Nathan for a while.'

'Nathan wants to protect you.'

'He is a good man.' She sighed, a heavy wave of bitterness sweeping through her. 'But men all seem to abandon me in the end. My husband to war. My father to his beliefs. Now you. Perhaps it is in men's nature. Perhaps it is me.'

He shook his head. 'I have not abandoned you. If you'll let me help, I will do anything to make this up. And Nathan will never leave you, that is certain. Do not scare yourself from him.'

She began to walk away. 'His wife was my friend, my husband was his. Now we are friends for each other. There can be nothing more.'

'You believe him?' Nathan asked, staring out to sea. Mercia could tell he was thinking about his own daughter, lost to that terrible nursing accident two years before.

'He seemed sincere. And he confessed to you of his own free choice.'

'It does not excuse what he did.'

'I know. I am not about to trust him straightaway. Let us see how he behaves when we arrive in New Amsterdam. At least we have answers to some of our questions now.' She patted his shoulder. 'I am glad you are here, yet again, old friend.'

'I will always be here for you, Mercia.'

For a moment they looked at each other, longer than usual, before she glanced across at the mainsail to study the frays around its edges. 'Come, then. We know now our enemy has a man working for him on the *Martin*, but this Jerrard was not on the *Redemption* when the note was left, nor is it in my uncle's hand. What of Sir William and Sir Bernard?'

'I couldn't get into their cabins last night, it was too late. And this morning I was . . . occupied.'

'Indeed.' She smiled wryly. 'Well, when I was looking for you earlier, the captain told me he has invited them all to a dinner this afternoon, with Lady Calde and Lady Markstone.' She raised an eyebrow. 'He is anxious our nobility disembark with a better impression of this ship than yesterday may have given them.'

Nathan laughed. 'Did he not ask you?'

'He knows I would not want to. But while they are eating . . .'

He nodded. 'I will search their cabins. And – oh,' he clicked his fingers, 'speaking of Lady Calde, before we had our . . . disagreement . . . Nicholas said it was she who told him where to find the necklace. While you were in the rigging.'

'What?' She frowned. 'I did see them together, but it makes no sense. 'Tis her own necklace.'

Nathan shrugged. 'When did anything about this make sense?'

From her elevated position at the stern, Mercia watched the dinner guests come out onto the main deck to take the early evening air. Lady Calde emerged first, the puzzling necklace prominent against her pale skin and low-cut violet gown. She remained alone at the rail until Sir William, equally resplendent in his grand fur coat, came up to take her arm, but she thrust him aside. With a frustrated shake of his head he returned the way he had come. Lady Markstone ducked past him, patting her belly as she talked with Sir Bernard, seemingly haven forgiven him his insensitivities of the previous day. She excused herself to join Lady Calde at the rail; the two women talked for a while until Lady Calde dismissed her companion with an angry wave. Tugging at the necklace, she bustled up the steps to the quarterdeck, disappearing towards the fenced-off section where the women of the ship found their privacy.

As Lady Calde passed out of sight behind the mizzenmast, Nathan's head rose up from the planking at Mercia's feet. She turned to look as he climbed the ladder from the quarterdeck.

'Nathan,' she said. 'I didn't see you coming.'

He smiled. 'I was watching them all come out. By heaven, Lady Calde is in a foul mood.'

She waited for him to join her, a tingling nervousness in her stomach. Conspiratorially they turned to look out to sea. 'What did you find out?' she asked.

'They have more with them than I thought. Sir Bernard has even brought across his commission from the Duke of York.'

'To impress my uncle, no doubt.' She leant in closer, even though nobody could hear. 'Did you find samples of their writing?'

'I did.'

She held her breath. 'And?'

'And nothing. Neither matched the writing in the note.'

She stared. 'How is that possible?'

'I checked carefully. The writing was nothing like.'

'Then who in God's name did write it?' Confused, she took another look at her half of the note. 'There is still something about this that looks—'

A piercing scream resounded from the quarterdeck, followed by a mighty splash. Mercia jerked her head round, her subconscious registering a blurred image obscured by the cabins moving swiftly to the sections below.

'What was that?' She craned her neck to see round the mizzenmast. From somewhere she thought she could hear panicked screaming, but the quarterdeck was empty. She brought her hand to her open mouth. 'Oh no. No, no, no.'

'Mercia?' said Nathan, but she was already away, ignoring the friction burns on her palms as she slid down the ladder to the quarterdeck. She peered over the side to see a heavily clothed figure in the water, arms waving about in a futile attempt to gain purchase.

'Lord save us! Lady Calde is overboard!' She ran to the ship's bell, ringing it frantically to alert the sailors. 'Quick, stop the ship! We are leaving her behind!'

With Nathan following she hurried down the steps to the main deck to find help. Moments later Sir Bernard appeared, looking over the rail to where Lady Calde's head was swiftly vanishing under the water. 'Jesus, 'tis Harriet!' he muttered. He called behind him. 'Turn this ship about! Quickly men! And you,' he ordered Nathan, 'fetch Sir William!'

While Nathan did as commanded, Mercia scanned the deck for a rope to use when they came about. Her back turned, she heard heavy footsteps running towards her, then two dull thuds as two boots hit the deck and skidded into her vision. Looking up, she saw Nicholas clambering barefoot onto the rail, stripped of his shirt. With a nod at her he clasped his hands together and dived over the side. She looked over to see a ripple where he had entered the sea, before his head re-emerged and he began to swim towards Lady Calde.

Mercia watched him in anguish, but the ship was moving too quickly and the figures in the water were growing too small to see. Close by, another female scream was ringing out, evidently Lady Markstone, but she did not pay much attention, ensnared by the drama in the waves.

'Turn the ship!' she cried, frustrated they were still going forward. Behind her, Lady Markstone was pacing the deck, repeating over and again: 'This voyage is cursed! This voyage is cursed!' Dragging herself from the side, Mercia tried to calm her, but in vain.

'Millicent,' barked Sir Bernard. 'Be quiet!' But she continued to rave until he lost patience and slapped her cheek hard. The elderly woman crumpled into the corner of the deck, her face in her hands, her eyes wild above her white fingertips.

'How dare you,' began Mercia, but Sir Bernard had already moved away, shouting at the crew to turn the ship, the captain now at his side giving orders. Instead she stooped to help Lady Markstone stand, calling across the deck to Daniel to ask him to sit with her for a while, feeling a surge of pride when he took the shaking woman's hand without protest. As she watched him lead her away, Sir William appeared with Nathan.

'Is it true what he says,' said Sir William, 'that Harriet is overboard?' She nodded. 'By the Lord, I will have her head for this! She has gone too far this time.'

She broke from watching Daniel. 'What do you mean?'

'She has thrown herself over, 'tis obvious.'

Mercia was astonished. 'But – why?'

He waved his hand impatiently. 'You have seen how she is. She has been in a melancholy for a long while now. She looks to gain my attention.'

'Sir William, I do not think—'

'Think what you want,' he said, then he ran to the side, screaming the same order as everyone else. 'I want this ship brought about. Now!'

Sailors swarming in the masts above their heads furled and released sails as quickly as they could so that the ship gradually slowed. In the steerage room the pilot must have been leaning on the whipstaff, for the ship began to turn in a wide arc until it faced the way they had come. But they were now heading into the wind that had been propelling them along and it took much longer to sail back to the spot where Lady Calde had fallen overboard.

It seemed everyone was standing against the side of the ship, clinging onto the rail in their impatience to return. Finally Mercia spotted two tiny heads bobbing in the sea ahead of them. She squinted to see more clearly. Nicholas was holding Lady Calde afloat, her head lolling left and right above the water.

'He must be strong,' said Nathan. 'To support the weight of her clothing.'

'He is strong,' said Mercia, ignoring Nathan's sideways look. 'And brave to have jumped in.'

Using their years of skill, the crew steered the ship towards Nicholas and Lady Calde, lowering the anchor at just the right moment to come to a halt alongside them. Nicholas was in difficulty now, his face sinking below the water's surface as he struggled to hold on to Lady Calde, who was making no movement herself.

His head bobbed back above water. 'I cannot keep her up,' he shouted. Head under. Head up. 'I have to let her go.'

'We will throw you a rope!' cried Sir William.

'You do not understand,' shouted Nicholas, and he went underwater again, this time only re-emerging several seconds later, barely holding on to the violet dress.

'He will drown!' shouted Mercia. 'Nicholas, she is too heavy!' She turned around. 'Can you sailors not jump in and help him?'

As she spoke two sailors were already pulling off their shirts. They leapt into the water as Nicholas went under a fourth time. For a few terrible seconds he did not resurface, but then his head came up and he coughed out water, gasping in large gulps of air. He no longer had hold of Lady Calde. The sailors dived down in search of her.

'Harriet!' cried Sir William. A great quiet descended on the ship. Seconds passed.

More seconds.

Still more.

One of the sailors broke the surface a short distance from the ship. He clawed at the ocean with his left arm, his body toppling back, straining to bring his right side up. With a mighty tug he wrenched Lady Calde above the water, but the force of it caused his grip to loosen, and he scarcely clung on to her dress. His mate reappeared on her other side, trying to push her up, but the effort was immense. Her limbs were now utterly still.

In visible agony, the exhausted sailors were struggling to keep themselves afloat. Nicholas swam towards them, ignoring the rope that had finally been thrown him, but his strength too was spent and they were too far away. Barely now able to remain above the sea, the sailors looked at each other and shook their heads.

They let go. For an instant Lady Calde bobbed on top of the water, the necklace she had reclaimed glittering in the evening sunlight. Then her face slipped under the waves, and she was gone.

Chapter Twenty-Six

Sir William paced the deck, his face pale. Betraying no sign of feeling, Captain Morley took his fur-lined sleeve and led him towards his cabin.

'She had no chance,' said Nicholas, slumped against a barrel under Mercia's pained gaze. 'Her clothes were too heavy to pull her up fast enough. She must have started to breathe in water long before I got to her.'

Mercia closed her eyes. 'She's dead, Nathan. She was here, and now – she's not.' She walked to the rail, looking out to sea. The saltiness of the air seemed particularly strong. 'When she screamed, I'm certain I saw someone running away.'

'Running away?' Nathan fell in beside her. 'What are you saying?'

The waves seemed too usual, too uncaring for the prey they had taken. 'That maybe she was pushed.'

'Why?'

She shook her head. 'I'm not sure. Perhaps connected to my purpose, but I do not see—' Of a sudden she jerked up her head. 'No. It cannot be.' She fished her half of the note from her pocket and examined it. 'My God. That's why it seemed so strange.'

She ran off without explanation, leaving Nathan to his puzzled thoughts. Two minutes later she was back, her face grim. Looking around to make sure they were unobserved, she pulled Lady Calde's green-leathered journal from under her dress.

'You can't take that,' said Nathan.

'I'll put it back. But look at the writing.' She opened the journal at random and laid her half of the note on the page. 'It is the same.'

Nathan stared. 'You are right. But . . . I cannot believe it.'

'Then read what she wrote last night.' She flicked to the final entry, looking at the words as he read.

A remarkable day. I at last had occasion to act on my plan when the harlot (Bernard's word, but a good one) lost her irksome boy in the ropes. Her manservant fell for my ruse and I was able to confront William with my necklace in front of everyone as I hoped. Now they all know, he must surely be forced from the sl_t.

'Jesus,' said Nathan.

'Read the rest.'

Yet I become suspicious about the message I composed. The words I was told to write were exceeding violent, and the proposal of 'JN' in signature may not have been unconsidered. I will ask more tomorrow.

There was a moment of silence as Nathan took in what he had read, and then –

'By God's truth.' He banged his fist on the rail. 'She wrote that note. The coward preyed on her mistrust of you and talked her into writing it.'

'She hated me,' said Mercia. 'Everything she did was to drive me from her husband. She searched my cabin for evidence of an affair. She waited to embarrass him with the necklace she found. But with that message she was just being used. And then I think killed.' An angry tear fell down her cheek. 'Nathan, I will find this bastard and I will make sure he suffers for what he has done.'

A pair of chattering sailors walked by. 'Mercia,' said Nathan, when they had gone. 'Does this not exonerate Sir William? I understand how he could want to scare you from uncovering his past while pursuing an . . . interest . . . in you now. The two things are separate. But would not Lady Calde have thought it strange for her husband to demand she write such a note?'

She shook her head. 'I don't know. Nothing about this is simple. I don't think we can rule anybody out.' She returned to where Nicholas was staring into nothing, his eyes pale windows of sorrow. She took his hand and he looked up in surprise. 'Nicholas, tell me she had chance to speak before she died.'

His voice was a monotone, shirking emotion. 'She must have been in agony. She must have felt her life slipping away in that cold, cold sea.' He shivered, droplets of water still covering his bare skin. 'I could see the ship turning in the distance. I was holding onto her, no matter what. She tried to talk, but all she could manage was a hissing sound, hardly anything.'

'Like an S?' she pressed. 'Like a sir?'

'Maybe. I do not know.' He stared up at her. 'She died, Mercia. She died in my arms.'

His eyes watered. She pulled him towards her and held him close.

The sun set, and it rose again. Despite Lady Calde's animosity towards her, the revulsion Mercia felt at what had befallen the dead woman did not diminish. If anything her resolve had hardened. Finding the Oxford Section, unmasking the person responsible, it was not just about her house any more, or her family's reputation. It was to protect innocents, and to revenge, not Lady Calde perhaps, but the criminal's seeming disregard for life.

Nathan suggested they keep their suspicions quiet, and she was happy to feign a subdued profile with a killer likely on board, awaiting the chance to speak with the fleet commander when they arrived at New Amsterdam. It was a matter of days now. The aptly named Long Island was drifting by to their north, a blue-grey blur stretching on for miles, a useful means of navigation to their goal.

Coming onto the main deck, she was surprised to see Nicholas talking with Lady Markstone opposite the stowed longboat. To her recollection the two had barely spoken on the long voyage.

'I keep thinking I could have saved her,' he was saying, his eyes cast down, his elbows on the rail. 'But she was so heavy. When the ship came back, she was already dead.'

Lady Markstone looked out to sea. 'Do not be troubled with guilt. You risked yourself to try to save her. I will not forget that. We have known so much war, but when death becomes personal – for me at least, 'tis hard.' She glanced at him. 'Tell me, was it quick?'

He breathed out heavily, in echo of the wind in the sails above. 'She was thrashing in the water while I was swimming. But her head was under by the time I got there. I brought her above the waves, but her breathing stopped. I am sorry. I cannot say if it was quick.'

Mercia wrapped her hood about her as she joined them. Although it was summer, the sea wind meant the deck was often cool. She looked at Nicholas's back, uncertain how she should feel, anger at his betrayal and pride at his attempted rescue fighting each other for dominance.

Sensing her presence, Lady Markstone turned. 'Good morning, Mercia.'

'Good morning, Lady Markstone. How do you fare today?'

'Shaken still, but I will live.'

'And you, Nicholas?'

He flushed. 'I am well. I . . . think I'll go below awhile.' Smiling weakly he pushed himself from the rail and walked away.

'His mind is troubled,' said Lady Markstone, watching him go. 'He seems in a deep melancholy.'

'Lady Calde's death has affected him. But he is strong. He will recover.' She faced her chaperone. 'How fares Sir William?'

'He keeps close in his cabin. He never liked Harriet, ever since they were married, but I was saying to your manservant, 'tis hard to lose someone when you have known them a long time. Especially like – that.' Her expression turned sour. 'Sir Bernard and your uncle, they seem to care not one bit she is gone. Too wrapped up in the impending invasion, playing at soldiers and war like they were still boys in the nursery. But I suppose 'tis what men do.'

Mercia nodded in sorry agreement. 'They were married long?'

'Harriet and William?' Lady Markstone scratched at her cheek. 'Three years.'

'Only three?'

'She was his second wife. But surely you knew this?'

'I knew little enough when my father was in favour under Cromwell.' Mercia frowned. 'I thought Sir William had been married many years more than that?'

'Yes, to his first wife.' Lady Markstone leant in closer. 'Harriet was his second, the same as he was with her.' She sucked in her top lip. 'The rumour is he married her for the fortune she amassed with her first husband. That marriage was childless, you see. But they had known each other for years beforehand.'

Mercia sighed. 'It seems everyone is motivated by wealth.'

'Not everyone.' Lady Markstone took her hand. 'I have not said anything, but I think people are beginning to wonder about your true purpose here. We all saw what happened between you and Wildmoor. Perhaps it would be better to confess the truth and leave the work of finding the paintings to others. I have worried on it since you came to see me in the Tower.'

'You know I cannot give in.' She forced a smile. 'Besides, the King is expectant.'

'And why let a man take on what a woman can do better?' Lady Markstone winked; the action seemed quite bizarre. It made Mercia laugh, for the first time in days.

'Lady Markstone, I must thank you for your discretion these past weeks.'

'Part of me wishes you would set up a new life here with me, but I am just being selfish. I hope you do find the paintings. It always vexed Edward he could not. And thank you, Mercia, for your company. When this is over, and I am settled, you will visit me before you return?'

'I will, if I can. But I fear there is a way to go yet.'

It was a day fit for glory. The weather was fair, the crew ebullient. All four ships were back together, the swift-sailing *Guinea* having awaited the rest near a long, sandy promontory that jutted north into the sea. After a final council of war on board the flagship, the captains ordered their crews to ready the sails, and in formation the fleet moved off. In just a few hours they would arrive in New Amsterdam.

At the raised stern of the *Redemption* Mercia had her eye to a telescope, leaning back on the rail to watch the other ships ahead. With the lower sails furled everyone was staring forward, straining for an ever closer glimpse of the land fast approaching. The tension was tangible. Would the Dutch fire on them as they came within sight? Would the soldiers on the warships get the battle they were aching for? Mercia felt the thrill of what was about to come, but apprehension too, ready to snatch her son from danger if she needed.

Certainly Nicholas had regained his spirits, shifting left and right beside her to see. Taking the telescope to pass to Daniel, Nathan eyed him with mistrust. The noblemen with Lady Markstone stood ahead on the quarterdeck, Sir William amongst them. The tips of his brown hair flapped beneath his ostrich-plumed hat, his gaze fixed on the bay ahead.

The tip of Long Island was now close to the right, a spectacular golden sheen to its coast as the sunlight reflected off the weapons of the dozens of local militiamen Nicolls had managed to recruit. It was almost certain the combined forces of the British outnumbered those of the Dutch, but nobody knew how events would unfold, whether the upcoming days would herald the formation of a continuous sweep of British territory from Jamestown in the south to Boston in the north, or merely keep things as they were, the Dutch consolidating their wedge in between.

The land came to meet them on either side as they sailed further in, reducing the sea to a small gap that gave into the New Amsterdam harbour beyond. As the ship powered on, Nathan pointed about him, reading from one of the captain's charts. Mercia glanced over his shoulder, but the map was not a detailed one. Aside from the coastal areas much of the land mass was blank. Even their destination, the small island of Manhattan, was largely bare: New Amsterdam was highlighted at its southernmost tip, and a pinprick called Haarlem to the north.

'Look, Daniel,' said Nathan. 'Staten Island. See, to the left.'

'It does not look like an island,' said Daniel, and Mercia laughed, for no, it did not.

'Well that is what they call it. And there to the right is Gravesend. Mercia, do you recall Lady Moody? The captain says she founded that village.'

'From long ago. But I did not know she was living in Dutch lands.'

'Many English folk live that way. Some of them were not welcome in New England, I believe. I wonder what they will think, when they are forced back in the fold?'

Mercia smiled. For those on board it was not about if they were victorious, but when. As if to prove the point, the sailors on the *Elias* upfront released an impromptu cannonball towards a Dutch merchant ship operating in the bay. But the shot splashed into the sea, no others were fired, and the fleet continued on.

They were now moving through the middle of the narrow harbour entrance way, one ship behind the other as they came out into wider waters beyond. The wind was concentrated at this point, whipping through Mercia's hair and stinging everyone's eyes as they peered forward, waiting for their first glimpse of New Amsterdam itself. And there, as the ship tracked right, Mercia could just make out a settlement at the very tip of a hazy sliver of land. She reached for the telescope.

'Is that . . .?' she asked, holding the instrument to her eye. The town was still a way off, but she could make out a low fort, a windmill behind it, and a number of ships in the harbour in front. She passed the telescope to Nathan, who leant it against the rail, holding it steady. Daniel pulled at his breeches, eager to look for himself.

'I think so,' said Nathan. He threw the telescope to Daniel, who caught it deftly. 'I think so! New Amsterdam, Mercia. Right there in front of us. We have made it!'

The fleet edged further into the harbour. As they got closer, there was no warning gunfire from the fort she had seen. Some of the faster Dutch ships moved off as they saw the Union flags of the British approach, but otherwise all appeared tranquil. It was a radiant day, if humid.

'It is staggering,' said Mercia, enraptured by the ever-approaching view, individual red-brick houses now visible at the water's edge. 'That a town can be built in such a place as this, yes, but look beyond the town, just look, the forests going on and on, the intensity of the green, the deep blue of the rivers on either side, the flashes of sunlight on . . . what is that, over there?' She took back the telescope. 'A waterfall! And these islands across the harbour, like miniature versions of what lies beyond. It is as though they are sentinels, come to welcome us in.' She shook her head, feeling emotional. 'What a setting.'

'Beautiful,' agreed Nathan, smiling at her.

Between the little islands they sailed, deeper into the harbour that the captain called simply the Bay, until the *Guinea* up ahead dropped anchor just outside reach of the fort's guns, and the other ships lined up alongside it.

'Right,' said Mercia, as the *Redemption* took its place opposite the fort. 'Now we start the hard work.'

Part Four

Chapter Twenty-Seven

The maddening order came down from fleet commander Nicolls: movements on and off ship were to be strictly regulated. Sir Bernard returned to the *Elias*, Sir William and her uncle to the *Martin*, but Mercia was confined to the *Redemption*, prevented from interrogating Nicholas's contact Jerrard or from going ashore to locate the agent Pietersen. After three days of worrying he might flee, she lost patience. The cannons had not fired on the town, the troops had not invaded, and the Dutch were equally intransient. When Nicolls came on board to review the state of the ship, Sir William and Sir Bernard imparting their experience of the vessel in his wake, she seized on the chance to intercept. Nicolls agreed to talk – once he was finished with his task.

She observed him concluding his inspection from her station at the stern. Dressed to intimidate in gleaming helmet and breastplate, he peered into everything, running his hand over rails and ropes, asking brief questions of Captain Morley, nodding curtly with each response. Behind him followed Sir Bernard, in turn pursued by Sir William: the pecking order, comprised of strutting cocks. The inspection over, Nicolls dismissed them and strode directly towards her. She could see Sir Bernard following him with his eyes, irritated at being abandoned for a woman, and an impertinent one at that.

Colonel Richard Nicolls was a man with natural authority. What he told people to do they invariably did, not surprising from a man hand-picked by the Duke of York to be the first British Governor of the town across the bay. He marched in a perfectly straight line, deviating only to avoid an open hatch or a coiled rope, not moving for any man – they all gave way for him. Despite his armour he bounded up the ladder to the stern, where he removed his helmet and bowed. He stood straight and tall, his face expressionless, his demeanour demanding brevity and intelligence.

'You wished to speak with me, Mrs Blakewood.' He lowered his voice. 'And from what I have been told, I certainly want to speak with you. Sir William tells me his wife is dead, that your man tried to save her when she fell overboard.' He roved his eyes across her face. 'What happened?'

She held his gaze unblinking. 'It is of that tragedy that I wished to speak. But I am afraid it is worse than you fear. I think she was pushed.'

He frowned. 'Pushed?'

She persevered despite his evident doubt. 'We were right to suspect that the man who contrived to steal the Oxford Section would sail with the fleet. Someone on board persuaded Lady Calde to write a note designed to scare me from my purpose. But then it seems her suspicion of him deepened. I think he killed her to protect his identity.'

A brief shadow of disgust fled across Nicolls' face, but the inherent seriousness returned at once. 'You have proof of this?'

'Her journal.' She sighed. 'There is no mention of a name. But I am certain I saw someone running from her as she fell.' She let her hood, already loose, slip back in the breeze. 'Colonel, now we have arrived,

I must locate the agent Pietersen and discover the name of this man who has betrayed the King. I must ask your permission to go ashore.'

Nicolls clicked his tongue. 'A fiery sentiment. But even if you are right that this man is amongst us, all these here are in the Duke's trust. I cannot simply question them, nor will I risk your safety.' His left eye narrowed slightly; she could sense his mind working on a course of action. 'Yet I do not want to involve anyone else. That companion of yours – Keyte. He has been a soldier?'

'Yes.' She smiled, appealing to Nicolls' traditional views. 'Nathan provides the strength, and I the finesse. Which I think is called for in this affair.'

Nicolls stared at her. 'The King spoke true when he called you an impressive woman.' He gripped his helmet to his side. 'Very well, Mrs Blakewood. Although it is against my inclination, you and Keyte may pursue this matter, but after we have taken the town.'

'Colonel, I fear that may be too late. Could I not row to shore in secret?'

He shook his head. 'It is too dangerous.'

'But if Pietersen flees,' she persisted, 'or is killed during an attack?' She swept her hand out at the harbour. 'You have boats rowing between the ships and the soldiers on the Long Island shore. What if whoever is behind this takes the opportunity to sneak into the town to warn him? Colonel, if the Oxford Section has come to America, Pietersen brought it. If I do not go now, we may lose our best chance to save the paintings for the King.'

Nicolls drummed his fingers on the rail. 'By heaven, this is a distraction from the Duke's business, but you have kindled his brother's passion, Mrs Blakewood. You know one of those pictures is a portrait of his family, painted when he was just a boy?' His forehead wrinkled the tiniest amount. 'He seems to want that more than the town itself.'

It was hard not to know: *The Royal Family of Stuart* was encircled in deep black ink at the head of the King's list. She pushed a ringlet back into place. 'So I may take a boat?'

Finally Nicolls smiled. 'You are a brave one. Somewhat unnatural, but brave.' He ran his tongue round his upper lip, thinking. 'I have dispatched another demand of surrender to Governor Stuyvesant. The obstinate fool returned my first because I had neglected to sign it.' He looked out towards the fort. 'I am minded to send someone to discuss terms in person. Maybe Winthrop. He knows better than I how these butter-boxes think. Perhaps you can go with him.'

She raised an eyebrow. 'Butter-boxes?'

He waved a dismissive hand. ''Tis what the sailors on the *Guinea* have been calling the Dutchmen. Because they are spreading themselves all over the globe.'

She laughed. 'The crew here call them Froglanders.'

'After their wet homelands, I suppose. Very well. If Stuyvesant has not replied by tomorrow I may send for you. You are right, 'tis time for action.'

He marched back down the ship. Mercia watched him go, impressed.

Pleased with her conversation, Mercia returned to her cabin to find Nathan crouched on the floor playing Daniel at draughts. She looked at the board. Nathan had an obvious winning move, but he made a different play instead. She squeezed his shoulder.

'We may finally be getting off this ship. Colonel Nicolls might send me over tomorrow.'

Daniel looked up. 'To Mad Hatton? Can I come?'

'Manhattan, Daniel, and not just yet. The soldiers will make it safe and then you can go.'

He pulled a face, but Nathan tickled him in the stomach and

he laughed. 'Your move,' said Nathan, getting up. 'Think about it carefully while I speak with your mamma.' Taking Mercia to one side, he lowered his voice. 'Is he seriously sending you there before we've even invaded?'

She shrugged. 'He sees the sense of not waiting for Pietersen to flee. He wants you to come with me, clearly.'

'But how will we avoid the townsfolk wondering—'

Impatient, she interrupted his question. 'You said yourself there are plenty of English in these parts. We will claim to be fugitives who fled to America when the King returned to his throne. We are worried by his fleet's arrival and have come into town for news.'

'I see you have thought this through.'

'Of course.' She glanced at her son shuffling around the draughts board, pondering his move. 'Did you find out about Lady Markstone?'

'Yes. The captain finally got permission for her to leave the ship. But Danny won't like it.'

'He won't have a choice. I want him away with her as soon as possible, well behind those troops lined up on Long Island. 'Tis only for a few days, until this is over.' She smiled as Daniel made a happy cry, leaping several of Nathan's pieces in one move. 'He is getting good at that. Let us hope I am as effective in New Amsterdam.'

There was a knock on the door. They turned to see Nicholas on the threshold, his expression subdued.

'I'm sorry to come in,' he said, his eyes flitting downwards. 'But I wanted to tell you . . . I've agreed to join the soldiery for the invasion.' He fiddled with his sleeve. 'Or rather Sir William has just pressed me. I would have argued, as I did before, but I thought it might be best.'

'I understand,' said Mercia.

'If there is cause, I will fight.' He looked up, attempting a weak smile. 'And perhaps I can listen for anything that might reveal your enemy.'

Nathan folded his arms. 'Anything you don't already know.'

Nicholas looked at him. 'I know you don't trust me, but I swear on my daughter's life I know no more than I've said. If I get to the *Martin*, I'll try to get some answers.'

'That is a point,' Nathan acknowledged. 'Mercia, why didn't you tell Nicolls about this Jerrard?'

She sighed. 'Because, Nathan, if Nicolls arrested him and secured a confession, it would be he who uncovered the nobleman and the paintings and the King would be beholden to me for nothing. I have not come all this way merely for his benefit, have I?' She turned to Nicholas. 'Our enemy will not be pleased you have confessed your part in this. Be careful a rogue musket shot is not fired your way.'

'I'd best find a good helmet, then.' Nicholas arched his eyebrow, but although her lips twitched she refused to allow herself to react. Instead she inclined her head, and he left.

It did not take long for the summons to come. The following day a soldier arrived with a terse message: *Come with this man, you depart at noon.*

She watched as Nathan swung on a flimsy rope ladder, dropping into a small boat waiting alongside the ship. Placing one foot over the side to follow him, she stopped to look at the deck of the *Redemption*, her home for the past three months. More than anything she felt an intense excitement, but her eagerness was mingled with the nerves of anticipation. Still, it was with enthusiasm that she began to descend.

As she lowered herself down the ladder, Daniel appeared directly above, shouting farewell. She paused, her head level with his scuffed shoes.

'Goodbye again, Danny. I promise it won't be long.'

He bent to kiss the topknot of her hair, triggering a swell of love inside her – love, and a great responsibility. If she failed here, she could lose Halescott for her family for ever.

She resumed her clumsy descent, gripping on to each rung, spray splashing her face as she approached the bottom. Her brown woollen dress bunched up more with each step: she was no longer in her mourning clothes for fear they might attract attention. As she jumped the last foot into the boat, a gust of wind nearly toppled her into the water, but Nathan caught her, a suppressed smirk on his face.

'I hope he will be safe,' she said, waving at Daniel as they were rowed away. Beside him Lady Markstone was pointing out the boat, encouraging him to wave back.

'He will,' said Nathan. 'They will leave as soon as she is ready.'

'Good. There are snakes about.' As they glided across the harbour, she saw her uncle and Sir William on the *Martin*, watching them depart.

The short trip brought them directly to the *Guinea*, its nineteen formidable starboard cannons pointing straight to shore. The ship was massive, able to ferry five times the cargo of the *Redemption*. Hundreds of soldiers were awaiting the invasion order on board. But there was no time for a tour: not two minutes after Mercia had embarrassed herself clambering up another rope ladder to the huge main deck, Nicolls appeared in his military regalia. Next to him walked a grey-haired man of around sixty years of age, his clothing somewhat more restrained. In spite of the day's heat, he wore a dark frock coat over a buttoned waistcoat, a white cravat encircling his neck. A group of similarly dressed followers trailed a reverent distance behind.

'Governor Winthrop, this is Mercia Blakewood,' Nicolls introduced. 'As I explained, she is on the King's business and is to be allowed wide discretion. Mrs Blakewood, Governor Winthrop has joined us from the Connecticut colony.'

The governor bowed so low he revealed the worn top of his black hat. 'I have met you before, Mrs Blakewood.'

It was news to Mercia. 'Then I must apologise, for I do not recall it.'

Winthrop smiled. 'You will not. It was in the thirties, when you were merely a babe. I stopped at your father's manor house in – Halescott, is it? I had been at Broughton Castle to discuss the founding of the Saybrook colony with Lord Saye and Sele.'

'Indeed?' Mercia nodded. 'Broughton is not far from Halescott. I have been there myself.'

'I was told your father was a man of learning, interested in certain pursuits I too enjoy. He showed you off in a cradle crying away, very proud.' His smile faded. 'I am sorry for his death.' He glanced at her mourning ring. 'He was a quick-witted and understanding man.'

'Thank you, Governor. I am glad you were able to know him.'

Winthrop studied her from over his long nose. 'You yourself are a woman of some learning, I hear.'

The comment pleased her. 'I like understanding things. It gives meaning to God's world.'

'Then perhaps you would care to visit me in Hartford when your business here is done. I have some remarkable instruments I think you would admire that reveal the very heavens.'

Nicolls cleared his throat. 'This is a charming and unexpected reunion, but there are important matters at hand.' He held out a piece of paper to Winthrop. 'Here is the letter with my terms. Try to make him see reason.'

Winthrop grasped the paper. 'It will depend how the

townsfolk think. Stuyvesant is proud. He will not easily give in.'

'Then convince him.' Nicolls' eyes burnt into Winthrop's. 'The King is relying on you.'

A stiff silence fell as Winthrop held the colonel's gaze. Then he bowed. Turning away, he indicated to Mercia that she should descend again to the boat. She nodded to Nicolls and followed Nathan back down the precarious ladder, the small vessel rocking as she eased herself in. Nathan removed his hat to lie down alongside her, the two of them hiding beneath a pile of blankets thrown down from the ship. The boat moved off, the oars plying the choppy water, each stroke heightening the anticipation she felt.

'Hold up the white sheet,' she heard Winthrop say. A few minutes later the boat jolted to a halt, banging against a hard structure on their left. She rolled lightly against Nathan.

'We come to talk,' shouted Winthrop. 'Fetch the governor.'

For a time Mercia could only hear anxious breathing and the lapping of water, but soon she made out the rhythmic sound of men marching in jangling armour, the metallic noise growing louder until it ceased close to the boat. One of their number broke off from the rest, his footsteps alternately sounding a dull clunk and a peculiar thud.

'Governor Winthrop.' The man spoke English in a thick Dutch accent. 'I trust you have come to explain that these ships are merely resting in my harbour.'

'Governor Stuyvesant. It is a pleasure to see you again. May we talk?'

'I think we should.'

'I will leave one man here with the boat, if that is allowable.'

'It is.'

One by one Winthrop's group disembarked, shaking the boat, but Mercia stayed as still as she could, Nathan gripping the blankets tightly around them. With much muttering on both sides, the men on the shore walked off, their footsteps gradually fading away.

'Mrs Blakewood,' whispered a voice, evidently the man left behind. 'There are two guards nearby. I will distract them, then I suggest you move quickly into the town.'

The boat rocked again as the unseen man climbed out. 'Beautiful day,' he said a few seconds later, this time more distant. 'Is it always like this here?' A curt reply came in Dutch. 'I'm afraid I don't understand,' he said. 'Let me teach you some English.'

Mercia peered from under the blanket, squinting as bright sunlight assaulted her eyes. The boat was stationed at a pier, moored beside a three-runged ladder that led to a dusty waterfront. To her right, the man had his arms around the two guards, keeping them faced away from the boat. In the other direction a stone bridge led across a canal to a side street: if they moved quickly, they should be able to slip into town unnoticed. Signalling to Nathan, she wriggled out of the blankets and ascended the short ladder, alert for witnesses to their subterfuge, but the few people about did not seem to notice. They hurried over the bridge into the side street where she stopped, leaning against a brick wall.

'Nathan!' she exclaimed. 'We are on land! American land!'

'I know. I hardly dare believe it.' He balanced himself against the wall. 'But three months at sea. My legs are about to give way.'

She laughed before realising she felt unsteady herself. They spent the next few minutes reacquainting their legs with a ground that did not continuously sway. It was a strange feeling, and for a time she felt nauseous, but the sensation quickly passed.

'Shall we explore?' she said when they were ready.

'After you.' Nathan gestured in front with his hat. 'New Amsterdam awaits.'

* * *

Tall houses rose up on either side as they made their way down the shadowed street. The smell of freshly baked bread wafted from a doorway where a man in a broad-brimmed hat stood staring at them, but they put their heads down and walked on.

'I just thought,' whispered Nathan. 'Will anyone here speak English?'

'That is where this will help.' Mercia stopped, surreptitiously pulling the corner of a notebook from her pockets. 'I compiled a list of the Dutch words Captain Morley knows. There are not many, but it may help. I call it my phrase book.'

'Most ingenious.'

'I have my moments.'

They came into a large, open space dotted with scurrying townsfolk. The presence of the fleet was clearly having an impact. People were hurrying across the square, talking on its corners or else ducking down the adjoining streets to the safety of their homes. Some looked suspiciously at the two strangers in their midst, but for the moment nobody stopped them: New Amsterdam was a thriving trading post, with new arrivals all the time. Directly in front loomed the low-rise fort Mercia had seen from the ship. Several heavy British guns were currently trained on it: she was thankful Nicolls was not about to fire while Winthrop was trying to negotiate the town's surrender.

'Let us make a quick circuit,' she suggested. 'This town is so small we should be able to walk it in an hour.'

But it took even less time than that. Skirting right at the base of the fort, they immediately came to a very wide street that led up to a wooden palisade at the edge of the settlement, clearly designed to repel a land-based attack from the north, but, thought Mercia wryly, rather useless against a maritime invasion from the harbour. The wall stretched the breadth of the settlement, standing twice Nathan's height and oozing with soldiers, but they were not once challenged as they walked alongside it, the soldiers intent on their own chatter.

Reaching the end of the palisade they turned south, the broad east river between Manhattan and Long Island flowing by on their left. Passing houses and storefronts they walked purposefully in front of a large, guarded building before once more meeting the canal where they had come ashore. The man from their boat noticed them pass, but he pretended not to know them. They crossed the same stone bridge, this time keeping to the waterfront, before rounding a promontory to curve back north and so arrive beneath two windmills turning behind the fort. Back in the marketplace the church clock within the fort complex showed only three-quarters of an hour had passed.

'Well, if we cannot find Pietersen here, we will never be able to find him anywhere,' said Nathan. 'This place is barely larger than Halescott.'

'Do not forget there are other Dutch villages further upriver. He may yet flee.'

'So where do we start?'

'The best place to seek out information,' she smiled. 'The tavern, of course.'

Chapter Twenty-Eight

For a small town, New Amsterdam had an alarming number of taverns, although many were closed with the threat of invasion. The few whose doors swung open were mostly empty. It seemed the inhabitants were preferring to gather with family and friends at home, occasionally sending one of their number into the streets for the latest news. On every corner, small groups of people were talking hurriedly – men, women, Africans, Europeans. Most spoke Dutch, but Mercia recognised Spanish too, and there were a host of other languages she did not know, unsurprising in a trading hub such as this.

She was beginning to despair of finding anyone with whom they could have a meaningful conversation, her phrase book not being up to much more than asking where the inn was, or whether she should turn right or left, when outside a large warehouse they came across a pair of traders arguing in English over a pile of crates labelled Beverwijck. After some curt pleasantries she asked whether they knew Pietersen.

'Course we do,' one said, a thickset middle-aged man. 'You want to do serious business here, you have to deal with Pietersen at some point.' He glanced towards the harbour. 'At least you used to.'

Her breathing quickened. 'I need to speak with him. Is he in town?'

'No idea. But he's probably nearby, with all this going on.'

'I see.' She sucked at her lip, thinking. 'Then . . . do you know James North, by any chance? He was a carpenter here.'

'English, was he?' He shook his head. 'I never met him. But try Marta's tavern down Bridge Street. Davids should be there today.' He winked. 'He knows everyone.'

'What did I say?' said Mercia. 'The tavern.'

'Why did you ask about North?' said Nathan, as they were walking in the direction they had been shown.

'Why not? If he lived here, then people will know him, and they may know about his past. Such as, what happened to certain paintings.'

He nodded. 'Just – be careful. Presumably nobody here knows he is dead.'

'No, but—'

'Wait!' A shout rang out behind them, making them halt. They turned to see a man running up, jerking back with his thumb.

'Those two,' he said. 'They told me you were looking for Pietersen.'

His accent revealed him for English, although it was hard to discern his features. His head was enveloped in a large grey hood, darkening his face.

Nathan frowned. 'Who is asking?'

'I know where to find him, is all. If you want, I can take you.'

'That would be welcome. But why the hood? 'Tis very warm to cover your face.'

The man leant in. 'I don't want to be seen,' he murmured. 'Some of the Dutch are starting to take a dislike to anyone English with the fleet out in the bay. You might want to conclude your business and leave town yourself.'

Nathan glanced at Mercia. She considered a moment, sharing his suspicion. The man was wearing English clothing, for one thing, rather than the more local fashions they had observed. But he may just have brought them from back home, and they needed to find Pietersen.

'Thank you,' she said. 'We will go with you.'

The man shifted on his feet. 'As I said, I don't want to be seen. Perhaps you could compensate me for the trouble.'

She sighed. 'I am sorry. I have no local coin.'

'Not even a bit of wampum?'

She disguised her ignorance of what that was with a simple no.

The man tutted. 'Never mind. I'll take you anyway.'

They set off, soon halting outside a white door in a nearby street. A dusty sign painted with some sort of crest rattled above. Satisfied nobody was watching, the man knocked and beckoned them enter.

Inside it was dark and hot with a strong smell of hops. The gloom made it hard to make anything out, but a well-established fire was burning further in. The sound of bubbling liquid penetrated the darkness. As Mercia blinked, waiting for her eyes to adjust, the door slammed shut, a bolt hastily drawn. She heard a heavy object being scraped across the floor, and then the smashing of pottery. Beside her, Nathan crashed down with a surprised cry.

She whirled around. Now able to see, she could tell they were in a brewhouse, beer bubbling in a large copper pot above the fire, a mash tub full of soaking malt alongside. But she was more interested in their supposed guide, who was standing over Nathan with his hood drawn back. He fished inside his pockets before turning to face her.

He was a young man, dark-blonde hair flowing down to his eyes. The dagger in his right hand looked sharp.

'Who are you?' she stalled, almost certain she already knew.

'It does not matter.' His voice was confident now, all but mocking.

'Then let me guess. You work for whoever is pursuing me. Don't you – Jerrard?'

'Maybe.' The man smiled, his youthful cockiness spreading over his smug face. 'You will never know.' He brandished the dagger, taunting her with it, turning it deftly in his hand. His arrogance gave her the second she needed to dash behind the mash tub. She dared a quick glance at Nathan's prone body. Shards of a pot were scattered around him, but his chest was rising and falling rhythmically. The young man slid around the tub, forcing her towards a corner. His hand was steady on the dagger.

'You cannot do this,' she said. 'Colonel Nicolls knows I am in the town. Tell me who ordered you to attack us, and I will forget you were here.'

He scoffed. 'I will never betray my master, not like that bastard Wildmoor did. If he hadn't gone soft, you would've been scared away by now and this would not be needed. Believe me, my master does not want you dead. But he cannot allow you to find the paintings.'

She edged against the wall behind her. 'So they are here.'

'If you say so.' He took a deliberate step forward, grinning with provocative relish. 'You won't soon care, lying dead in the brewmaster's outhouse 'til I can throw you in the river.'

'Wait.' Amidst his threats, his voice seemed somehow familiar. Of a sudden she realised from where. 'It was you who attacked me in London.' She looked at his ungloved hands. 'But . . . your fingers?'

'Four and a thumb?' he jeered. ''Tis easy to pretend you are one finger short.' With his dagger-free hand, he lowered his index finger

314

and made a squeezing gesture. 'You were meant to think I was North. If only you had given up then.'

He moved closer. Fearful, she looked around. On a table beside her lay a hooked pole, some sort of beer-making instrument. With no other option she grabbed it and thrust out. The pole was much longer than his dagger, and she managed to twist the hooked point into his clothing, penetrating to his skin. With a sharp jerk she wrenched the pole right. He cried out as the hook ground into his belly, making him drop his knife.

While he doubled over she tried to dart past, but his wound was not severe. He recovered to grab at the folds of her dress, stopping her short in front of the copper pot. The heavy vessel was wavering on its chain, suspended off a point above the fire. Praying she would be agile enough she pushed forward on the pot as hard as she was able, and with an outraged howl dragged herself from Jerrard's grasp before it began its backwards swing. The pot disturbed the air as it flew past her arm, colliding with Jerrard's shocked face. Some of the boiling water splashed out, and he fell to the ground, screaming.

She rushed to Nathan, rubbing his cheeks in an attempt to rouse him. His eyes were flickering to life when she was hauled back by the shoulders, her assailant once more on the attack. This time he threw her against the mash tub and she fell to the floor with a cry. But the force of the copper pot had dazed him, and when he bent for his knife he stumbled, staggering into the side of the tub.

Out of the corner of her eye Mercia saw Nathan sit up, confused, but the sight of her in trouble must have given him strength, for he rose to his feet, lurching towards the tub as Jerrard scooped up his dagger. Nathan drew back his fist, punching Jerrard's face hard, while on the floor Mercia lashed out at his legs. He swung at her with the knife, but Nathan struck his wrist, sending the blade flying into the fire, and for a moment the two men were locked together, hands around each other's necks.

Jerrard's fingers clenched as he squeezed tight, but Nathan thrust up with his elbows, flinging his arms aside. Unrelenting, Jerrard returned to the attack. A fierce anger in his eyes, Nathan pushed down on his opponent with a powerful strength, forcing his head into the mash tub. Jerrard flapped his arms, making weak, muffled groans, but in his rage Nathan persisted, suffocating him in the viscous malt until his trembling abruptly ceased.

'Stop!' shouted Mercia. 'You will kill him!' She grabbed at Nathan's shoulder. 'Nathan, stop! We need him to tell us who he works for!'

Nathan looked at her, a horrified expression on his face. He pulled the limp man from the tub and dropped him to the floor. Mercia bent down to revive him, but it was already too late. His breathing had stopped. Jerrard was dead.

Nathan collapsed against the barrel, clutching his neck. 'Mercia, are you hurt?'

'No, but – are you?' She looked at their assailant in shock.

'I will be fine.' He gasped, taking in deep breaths. 'I should have pulled him out sooner, I know I should, but I could not let him harm you. By God's truth, Mercia, he wanted to kill us.'

She stood for a moment, calming herself. 'Whoever is behind this has moved on from trying to frighten. He knows now we are here we will not give up.' She glanced again at the dead man, feeling sick. 'He must have found this place empty and gambled the brewmaster would not soon return.' She paused. 'Unless . . .'

He looked up. 'Unless what?'

'Unless he chose this place beforehand. He spoke of an outhouse where he was going to . . . put us. He must already have known about it.'

'You think he arranged it, with the brewmaster?' Nathan sidled over to the body, checking Jerrard's chest. 'Definitely dead.' He swallowed, wincing in discomfort. 'What should we do with him? We cannot carry him into the street.'

'We will have to do to him what he planned to do with us. Hide him in the outhouse and presume nobody will look. If the brewmaster is involved he will hardly alert the guard that there is a dead Englishman in his yard. And if he is not, well . . .' She sighed. 'When all is over we can tell Nicolls what happened. If we explain now, he will say there is too much danger and order me to stop.' She picked up a nearby cloth and bent down.

'What are you doing?'

'Cleaning him.' She rubbed the cloth over Jerrard's face, tidying his smooth features of traces of malt. 'He was so young. So confident in himself.' She clenched the cloth hard. 'Come. The outhouse must be round the back. And once that is done, let us find this Davids and hope he can help us.'

Bridge Street, where they had been told to look for Davids, turned out to be the same street they had first walked down on coming ashore. That was just two hours ago, but it seemed like two days had passed. Mercia's mood was grim as she pushed open the door to Marta's tavern. She walked straight to the serving hatch and asked for Davids. But the woman behind spoke no English, and simply shook her head.

Unlike the taverns they had scoured earlier, Marta's was relatively bustling, if still only half-full. A large group was clustered around a table on the right, poring over a clutch of documents. Many were enjoying that quintessential American commodity, the tobacco weed; most were drinking ale, reminding her of the brewhouse, but she put the awful image from her mind.

As they approached, the buzz of the group's animated conversation ceased. Mercia put on a smile, but she received black looks in return.

'*Wie bent U?*' asked a balding man, setting down his tankard.

'Who are you,' she whispered to Nathan. 'I do not need the phrase book to translate that.'

'*Ik herken U of deze man niet. Wat doet U hier?*'

'And that?' said Nathan.

'Hmm.' She held up her hands in a supplicatory gesture, addressing the seated group. 'I apologise. I do not speak Dutch. I am English, from a village on Long Island. We have come on the ferry from Breuckelen.'

The man who had spoken folded his arms. 'I've spent time on Long Island,' he said, switching to English. 'Which village are you from?'

Mercia probed her memory, but under the stares of the townsfolk the only village she could remember offhand was Boswijck, and that was Dutch. She ignored the question.

'I am looking for a man named Davids,' she said. 'I was told I could find him here.' When nobody spoke she dared a different tack. 'It seems he might know an old acquaintance of mine. A carpenter named James North.'

An older man in the midst of the group jerked his head up sharply at the mention of North. Next to him a red-headed woman rose, brushing down her grimy apron.

'We know no James North,' she said. 'Nor do we know you. But we do know there is a strange fleet at our door.' She narrowed her eyes. 'You wouldn't be come to spy on us now?'

Her companion stood. He was of an age with Winthrop, his thinning hair grey above a proud face. 'I know who she means, Marta. She means Jamie Thorn.'

Mercia stood very still, making sure she did not react. Jamie Thorn was the exact pseudonym for North the customs clerk had spotted in London.

'But Jamie's not been seen for months,' said Marta. 'Greet's starting to think he's found another woman.' She turned to Mercia. 'Your friend, is he? Special friend, no doubt.' The group laughed, sharing some private joke.

Nathan's gaze did not stray from the grey-haired man. 'And you are?' he asked, more blunt than usual. 'Your words have a Kentish note.'

'Keenly observed, sir. But the question is rather, who are you?' The man's eyes roved Nathan up and down. 'English, certainly. About thirty, thirty-five years old. A soldier's past judging by your demeanour. Too young to have fought in the war, unless perhaps at Worcester?'

'My elder brother was at Worcester. When he died I joined the army in his place. You fought in the war yourself?'

He nodded. 'Who did you serve under?'

'William Packer.'

'Packer, by God.' He looked slyly at Nathan. 'You will recall that incident, then, at the Christmas feast?'

As he was talking, Mercia studied his face. There was something familiar about it, although she was sure she had never met him before. That said, until today she had not known she had ever met Winthrop.

'There was never any feast,' said Nathan. 'Packer wished Christmas abolished.'

'Of course.' The man smiled, deepening the creases surrounding his eyes. He turned to Marta. 'I think these two are trustworthy – to a point. But I will talk with them some more.'

'As you want.'

Marta resumed her seat, and the group their discussion. The proud-faced man led Mercia and Nathan to an empty table by the door. A sunbeam fell through the narrow window above, illuminating the dust in the air.

'So,' he said, once they had sat. 'I am Davids, as you may have guessed. I call Long Island my home for now, but you two, I think you do not, whatever you say. You will forgive my suspicion, but as Marta pointed out there is an English fleet in the harbour. Charles Towne, is that what this place will be called?' He leant in. 'If you are part of this, I will feed you to the dogs.' He looked at Mercia. 'But you are not a soldier. Why are you here?'

He spoke forcefully, but there was a frisson of worry behind his words. Mercia decided to adopt a strident tone herself.

'I have nothing to do with any designs the King might have on this town. But tell me more of yourself. You clearly have a past back home.'

'We all have a past, my dear.'

'Does yours involve James North? Your hearing pricked when I spoke his name.'

Davids stroked his chin. 'Nobody has called him North for years, at least not in these parts.' He ran his eyes down her face. 'Why are you so interested?'

'North has some . . . information I want. I had hoped to meet him to discuss it, or maybe talk with an acquaintance he had confided in.' She smiled at Davids, but he remained unmoved. 'But you are right. I am not from Long Island. I have travelled down from New

England, where he used to live.' It was a guess, but a likely one if North had sailed to Boston as the customs clerk had supposed. 'I did not want to alarm people who may be his friends into thinking I was pursuing him out of malice.'

'I see.' Davids sounded anything but convinced. He rested his elbows on the table, never shifting his gaze. 'And I wonder.' He peered at her still closer, staring at every inch of her face; she was about to turn away when he sat back, his lips creasing into a sudden smile. 'And you have nothing to do with the ships that have coincidentally arrived this week? Or with a clandestine entry into the town from an English longboat?'

Her eyes flicked to Nathan and back again. 'What boat?'

Davids laughed. 'In any case, North is not here any more. As I think you may well know, my English rose.'

It was obvious he had an advantage over her, but she could not think what. Uncertain how to react, she pressed on. 'If you will not speak of North, then you should be able to tell me about Joost Pietersen. He is important here, I understand. I need to know where he is.'

'Pietersen?' Davids frowned. 'Why ever would you . . . but very well. I should say he is with the rest of the council, waiting for Stuyvesant to return from his meeting with Winthrop.'

'Where is this council?' asked Nathan.

Davids turned to him. 'You have not said much since we sat, my friend. What is your role in this little game?' He smiled. 'But no matter. They will be in the *Stadt Huys*, the town hall to you and I, the tall building facing the water on the other side of the bridge.' He tilted his head. 'Perhaps you saw it when you circled the town? It is very close to the pier.'

Mercia pushed back her chair and stood. The conversation was making her uncomfortable. 'Thank you. We will go there at once.'

'Please do.' Davids gestured towards the door. 'I will see you again, no doubt.'

As she exited the tavern, Mercia looked back. Davids had his hands clasped together, his fingertips balancing his chin. His eyes were almost aflame with curiosity as he watched them retreat.

Chapter Twenty-Nine

'Well,' said Nathan as they crossed the bridge. 'There is a fellow who knows more than he says.'

She waited for a trio of shouting children to barge past. 'He was playing some sort of game, that is obvious. And his face, I don't know. I seemed to recognise it somehow. He was with the army, an officer perhaps – did he seem familiar?'

They rounded a corner to reach the waterfront. 'Lots of people were in the army, Mercia. How should I know who he is?'

She looked at him. 'I suppose not.'

He sighed. 'But he clearly knows of James North. When we have spoken with Pietersen, we should find him again.'

'I intend to. Ah, this must be it.'

She stopped in front of a five-storeyed brick building set slightly back from the waterfront. Its facade was pitted with symmetrical windows, its gabled roof bisected by a small, domed structure jutting up to the sky. A set of gallows stood nonchalant in the small courtyard in front, but nobody was swinging today.

Two guards at the entrance looked over. Giving them a quick

nod, Nathan walked Mercia towards an alley running down the building's right side.

'We cannot just stroll in,' he said. 'We will have to wait for Pietersen to come out. And I have just thought of a problem. We do not know what he looks like.'

'Hell's teeth.' She cursed herself. 'Why did neither of us think to ask Davids?'

'Too busy trying to work out what he was saying.'

'True. Well, we will find him out some other way.' She leant against the alley wall, gazing at the riverfront in silence.

Nathan bit his lip. 'Mercia, what happened in the brewhouse—'

She twisted her head to face him. 'It is disturbing you.'

'Yes.'

'It was as you said. He wanted to kill us.' She sighed. 'But no. I wish he could have lived.'

'I am sorry. I should have controlled myself, but—'

'It does not matter now.' She rested her hand on his arm. 'You were protecting me.'

'I know. 'Tis just that, I wish you did not have to see.'

'Do not think badly of yourself, Nat.' She tried a smile of reassurance. 'We are alive. Let's just stand here and wait.'

Twenty minutes later a commotion from along the canal made Mercia peek from their hiding place. A group of men were walking towards the *Stadt Huys*, Winthrop and his followers amongst a larger number of well-dressed townsfolk. In the midst of the Dutch contingent strode a sober man in a large feather-plumed hat, a wide orange sash decorating his breastplate of shining bronze. He was moving awkwardly, his gait off-centre, surrounded by his men.

'That must be Governor Stuyvesant,' she said. 'By the Lord, that is a huge nose. 'Tis bigger than Winthrop's.'

Nathan put his head round the corner but they hastily withdrew as the group approached. Once the men had passed and halted in front of the town hall, they looked again.

'We will leave you here,' Stuyvesant was saying. 'My council is assembled inside. I will talk with them, but I do not think much needs to be said.'

'Think before you act,' said Winthrop. 'You have our terms in writing. Let us know your answer by civilised means.' He bowed, leading his party towards the boat on which they had arrived.

'If they leave now,' whispered Nathan, 'how are we going to get back?'

'Hopefully they will delay.' Mercia was still looking at Stuyvesant's group. 'They will find some excuse – and if not—damn, will those soldiers not move?'

'Forget escaping. You just want to see his leg.'

'Of course.' She slipped as she stretched too far out, but she caught herself on the wall in time. 'Captain Morley mentioned it enough times on board ship. Ah, finally.'

Dismissing his soldiers Stuyvesant marched towards the town hall, his bearing as imposing as Nicolls', testament to a long history of command. Now he was fully visible, Mercia could see his long sword hanging down his right side, its tip sitting snug against a fine wooden leg that came up to his knee. The scuffed stump spoke to years of use.

'That must shape a man,' said Nathan. 'To survive an amputation – I have seen men lying on tables, their limbs shot through, choosing to die rather than face the surgeon's brutal cut.'

'He is impressive, I will say that.' She ducked her head back inside the alley. 'Now what do we do?'

'Wait here.' Nathan pulled his hat down low and disappeared round the corner. She peered out to see him walking at a brisk pace towards the nearby pier. He nodded at the boat where Winthrop and his men had now embarked before continuing on. Seconds later one of the men left the boat to follow him, but they soon passed out of her sight. Minutes later, when she was beginning to worry, she felt a hand tap her shoulder. She jumped.

'I'm sorry.' Nathan was standing behind her.

'Where have you come from?'

'All the way round this group of buildings. I thought the guards might notice if I was constantly walking in front of them.'

'Very sensible. What were you doing?'

'Finding a way to talk with one of Winthrop's men. I asked him to wait for us, but he's worried if they stay too long the Dutch will be suspicious. They will give us what time they can. Now follow me. I noticed the town hall extends right down here.'

He led her down the alley and leapt over a low wall into a large backyard, startling an old woman passing by. Mercia smiled at her, shrugging her shoulders, but the woman frowned and continued on her way.

'You should be more careful,' she said, joining Nathan on the other side of the wall. 'That woman kept looking back. I had to wait for her to turn the corner.' She looked around. They were in a dirty yard littered with the detritus of construction, a number of semi-mature trees doing their best to disguise the mess. 'Why are we here?'

'This is the back of the town hall.' Nathan pointed upwards. 'Winthrop's man said the council usually meets in the central room on the second floor. If Davids is right, Pietersen is there. We can look through the window to try to pick him out.'

She craned her neck. 'What, up there? 'Tis too high.'

'That shouldn't be a problem.' He shook the trunk of a leafy tree growing directly beneath. 'But it won't take my weight.'

He smiled at her.

'Oh no,' she said. 'In this dress?'

'Steady,' said Mercia, climbing near the top of the quivering tree. She edged along a thick branch that extended below the second-floor window. Nathan was holding the trunk, but the stability he provided was minimal. Gripping the sill above, she inched up her head to see into the meeting room, hiding her face as much as she could.

'What's going on?' asked Nathan.

She wobbled on the branch. 'They're in there, but 'tis hard to see. Stuyvesant is in the middle, surrounded by several others. They look unhappy. He is shaking his head, gesticulating.' She swayed a little, trying for a better position. 'Now he is waving a piece of paper at them. Probably the terms Winthrop gave him. It looks like they want him to hand it over, but he is keeping it close to his chest. No, they are definitely not happy. Oh!'

'What is it?'

'Stuyvesant has torn up the paper and thrust the pieces in his pocket.'

'Why?'

'Nicolls said he was obstinate. Maybe he wants to reject the terms. But now the others are really upset. One of them is screaming so loudly I can hear. Not that it helps, 'tis all in Dutch.'

'Any idea which one is Pietersen?'

'Not yet.' She risked a look down. 'Why don't you come up?'

'Too heavy.' A bird settled on the tree, shaking the smallest branches. 'Don't worry. I'll catch you if you fall.'

'Thank you so much.' She went back to looking through the window. 'This is better than the theatre. Stuyvesant is standing with his arms folded, refusing to listen.' She winced. 'That must hurt. Someone is shouting right in his ear. Now he is backing away. He is taking the scraps of paper from his pocket. He has handed them to one of the others. Who is coming towards a table by the window—Hell!'

She ducked down, making the tree shudder unnervingly, but after a few seconds she risked looking back up.

'I can see two men at the table. One is trying to put the pieces back in order. The other has turned to the rest. He is asking a question. Stuyvesant looks livid.' She waited. 'I think they are taking a vote. Yes, someone is shouting out names.' She listened closely, repeating the names as they were called. 'De Decker. Steenwick. Van Cortlandt. Pietersen.' She nearly fell from the tree. 'Nat, I know which is Pietersen.'

'Then come down.'

'No, I want to see how this ends.'

But the meeting did not last much longer. The vote was concluded, Stuyvesant clearly in the minority. He brooded in a corner, furious. The council began to file from the room. Mercia followed Pietersen with her eyes, registering his unassuming clothes, his dark hair, his hooked nose.

'Pietersen is leaving,' she hissed. 'We have to get to the front in case he comes out.'

She slid down the trunk, a jagged twig ripping a tear in her dress as she streaked her hands on the rough bark. Once on the ground she raced through the yard to hurdle the low wall. But then she pulled up short, colliding with Nathan as he halted in the alley, an unimpressed guard blocking their way.

The guard raised his long musket. When he spoke it was in English. 'Come with me.'

* * *

They were marched to the courtyard in front of the town hall. Mercia glanced at the adjacent pier where Winthrop was still holding off his departure. Remarking their predicament, he turned his head towards them before looking quickly away.

'How are we going to get out of this?' whispered Nathan. 'Winthrop will have to leave.'

'Quiet,' growled the guard, one of the two who had been stationed at the town hall entrance. The old woman from the alley was hovering nearby, talking with his colleague – or rather at him. The harassed man hurried over as soon as he saw his fellow return.

While the soldiers were talking, Mercia mumbled at Nathan from the corner of her mouth. 'Should we run to the boat?'

'The guards seem worried. I don't think they know what to do. They may panic and—'

'Nat,' she interrupted. 'That's Pietersen, leaving the building now.' She nodded to where a quartet of men were exiting the hall. 'The man with the ribbons on his waistcoat. Look.'

The man she recognised as Pietersen broke off from his group as he noticed what was happening in the courtyard. He peered at the two prisoners, taking a tentative step in their direction, staring at Mercia in particular. Then his eyes widened and he looked down, speeding away on his original course.

'*Meneer Pietersen!*' shouted one of the guards. '*He, Meneer Pietersen!*'

The sentry's voice rang out clear in the small space but Pietersen walked still faster, pretending not to hear. By the time he rounded the corner, his walk had become a jog. The guard went back to muttering with his companion.

'Did you see that?' whispered Mercia. 'He looked at me and ran off.'

Nathan nodded. 'Someone must have warned him about you.

Perhaps that Jerrard—' He fell silent as a musket was poked into his back.

'No talk!' said the guard who had brought them there. 'Now wait.'

He lowered his musket and entered the town hall. The remaining soldier stayed with them, holding his gun vertically, the barrel pointing up from the ground. Mercia looked at him more closely. He was wearing a breastplate and helmet, but would it be possible to overpower him? She glanced at his musket. His grip was firm – if she grabbed it and pulled, it might throw him off balance, allowing Nathan to attack. But before she could catch Nathan's eye to suggest they attempt it, one of Winthrop's party appeared from the boat. She smiled to herself. This would be some ruse of Winthrop's.

The approaching envoy nodded, addressing the guard. 'Before we return to our ship, Governor Winthrop wonders whether any answer is yet available from Governor Stuyvesant.'

'I do not understand,' said the guard. 'You want the governor?'

'No, I want to know if there is any message.'

The guard shook his head, unable to comprehend. He shouted a question towards the town hall entrance. From the shadows someone disappeared inside, re-emerging moments later with a freckled clerk.

'I speak English,' the clerk said to Winthrop's man. 'What do you want?'

'I want to know if there is any message from the governor.'

The Dutchman smirked. 'So you try to find out from me what is happening, now your friends here have been caught?' He jerked his head at Nathan. 'Spying on the council is not a good idea.'

The envoy blinked. 'I do not know what you mean.'

'They were looking through a window. They are English. We know you sent them.'

'Oh, come now. Do you think we would employ a woman to do a

330

soldier's work?' He glanced at Mercia and scoffed. 'Well then. I shall leave you to your duties.'

He walked back to the boat. Mercia watched him go in disbelief.

She was still reeling from Winthrop's abandonment when the sentry reappeared with a more grandly uniformed guardsman, evidently his superior. The time for a quick escape had gone. The guards debated energetically, gesticulating at the captured pair, looking at Winthrop's boat, staring back at the town hall. The officer in charge considered what to do, clearly as uncertain as his subordinates. Finally he barked out an order and returned inside.

The guards raised their muskets. 'Move,' said one, jabbing Mercia in the back. The other fell in behind Nathan, forcing him to walk alongside her towards the canal. As they passed the pier, she saw the boat had already cast off and was being rowed back to the fleet. She looked for Winthrop, but he was facing the other way.

At gunpoint they were marched along the New Amsterdam streets, over the stone bridge, past Marta's tavern, out into the large marketplace in front of the fort where the murmuring locals ceased their chatter to stare. One of the guards shouted a command, and the fort's hefty gate grumbled open, scattering a cloud of dust.

Another musket prod nudged Mercia through. She stumbled with Nathan into the Dutch stronghold, triangular bastions topped with fearsome cannons at each corner, ramparts manned by dozens of soldiers along each edge.

The gate clanged shut, trapping them inside.

Chapter Thirty

The fort was not large. They were thrown into the same windowless storeroom.

Nathan heaved his body against the locked door. 'No use. But we need not worry. If we cannot free ourselves, the invasion will.'

'Except our own guns are aimed directly at us. If Nicolls fires on the fort, we do not have much chance.' She looked at him. 'Can you believe Winthrop just left us here?'

Nathan was still fiddling with the door. 'It does not help to dwell on it. Let's think how to get out.'

She slumped against a crate of horseshoes. 'What, through the locked door, past all the guards and then storm that massive gate?'

He circled the musty room, feeling at intervals along the walls. 'There is a way out of every prison. The old King himself managed to escape from Hampton Court when Cromwell locked him away.' He pulled at a loose plank, but it held firm.

'Yes, but as I recall, the old King was promptly recaptured. And the next time he tried it at Carisbrooke, he got stuck in the bars of his cell.'

He came to crouch beside her. 'Do not be despondent. We will get out.'

She blew out her cheeks. 'I am just feeling sorry for myself. Besides, I have been in prison once this year already. I should be used to it.'

The door swung open. Lit up by the bright August day, a guard entered, placing a tray of food and drink on the straw-covered floor before reaching behind him to retrieve a pisspot. He smirked as he placed the earthenware bowl right next to the tray and then left, relocking the door.

'Thank the Lord,' said Mercia. 'I need that.'

'Go ahead. Eat. Eat it all if you want.'

'I was talking about the pisspot.' She stood up. 'Now please, look away. It takes a while in all these clothes.'

It was several hours more before the door next opened. The store was full of horse equipment, reminding her of her own grey Maggie, and they sat on the straw reminiscing about life back in England, about family and friends they had left behind. The talk was intended to distract her from their plight, but underneath she grew more and more concerned about Pietersen. Now he knew they were in the town, what would he do?

The answer surprised her. By now it was night, and the cloaked man who entered was brandishing a flaming torch. Balancing it in a wall sconce, he shut the door and upturned an empty crate. He sat astride the splintered box, the flickering torchlight exposing his angular face.

'Mercia Blakewood and Nathan Keyte.' He spoke in a broad Dutch accent. 'I was warned you would be coming, but I did not think we should meet in such an elegant room as this.' He rocked on the crate, pulling at the sleeves of his cloak. 'I would introduce myself, but I think you know who I am.'

Mercia drew up her own makeshift seat. '*Meneer* Pietersen. I am pleased to finally meet you. Although I am surprised you are here.'

Pietersen smiled. 'The governor wishes to know of his enemy's plan. I am here to interrogate you on his behalf.' He flicked a ruffled wrist. 'What is your commander's intent, how he hopes to achieve it. Those sorts of questions.' He removed his black hat, resting it in his lap; its brim was broader than any Mercia had seen.

'We know nothing of that,' said Nathan.

'And if I ask you the same of the Oxford Section?' Pietersen studied them, but neither reacted. 'I know why you are here. You have a strange delusion that you will find what was thought lost.' He let out a mock sigh. 'But it was lost. It burnt to nothing in your own fair land on its way to Cromwell's Great Sale. My clients were so . . . disappointed.'

'Then they must have been cheered indeed when the paintings came back out of thin air,' said Mercia. She leant forward. 'We know the Section still exists, *Meneer* Pietersen. Your one-eyed smuggler friend admitted as much.'

Pietersen stroked his trimmed moustache. 'What else do you know, Mrs Blakewood?' He smiled. 'Should I be . . . concerned?'

'I will find the paintings with or without you.' She felt a warmth on her face as the torch flared in a draught. 'We will not be locked in here for ever. If you help us now, Colonel Nicolls will not be displeased.'

Pietersen scoffed. 'You think to bribe me, Mrs Blakewood? Maybe threaten? But let us play this game the other way round, no?' He made a circular motion with a finger. 'Why should I not go to Stuyvesant right now to demand your execution?'

Behind her, Nathan made a sudden, unseen move. Pietersen jumped from his crate.

'I do not think so, Mr Keyte. There is a guard outside with orders to run in and shoot you if I so much as cry out. Yes, that is better.' He waited for Nathan to retake his position. 'Good. Now, Mrs Blakewood, you were about to tell me what you know.'

She toyed with a ringlet of her hair. 'You are very agitated, *Meneer* Pietersen. I assume this means we have been right all along, and the paintings are close?'

A brief flash of uncertainty flew over his face, but he quickly composed himself. 'You know nothing, do you?' He laughed, but his uneasiness was clear. 'Not who stole them, not who bought them, not where they are. Except there is no Oxford Section, Mrs Blakewood. It is nowhere.'

'You said yourself you were told we were coming. Someone has put considerable effort into warning me from a collection that does not exist.' Riled by his demeanour, she decided to test his response. 'Who did you buy the paintings from, all those years ago? Was it Bernard Dittering? William Calde?'

Pietersen turned to leave. 'Whoever you think you are after has clearly overrated you. And, Mrs Blakewood, a word of advice. I am valuable in this town. There are men in your fleet who would kill to retain my services. I know all the local trade routes, the value of the goods for sale, the principal Indian tribes. I have nothing to fear.' Replacing his hat, he reached for his torch. 'Goodnight, Mrs Blakewood. I trust you will sleep well.'

She stared at the back of his departing cloak. 'I will discover the truth, *Meneer* Pietersen. I have come too far to give in.'

He stopped with his hand on the door. 'Perhaps you should. Sometimes 'tis better to stay ignorant.'

Nobody else visited them that night. As the hours passed they tried to sleep, but the air became too close. Every time she dozed

Mercia woke within minutes. Nathan succeeded no better, so they sat and talked in the nocturnal heat, worrying what Pietersen would do, hoping the next time they spoke with him the odds would be more in their favour. Otherwise they just sat. Once, Nathan looked at her in a certain way, and she feared he might use this chance to confess what she knew he must feel, but he remained as silent as ever.

She looked at him as he tried to sleep. He was compassionate, loyal – and handsome. He owned lands. Her son loved him. So why was she afraid? Did she feel she would be betraying her husband by replacing him with his friend? Did she prefer their relationship the way it was, not wanting it to change? Did she worry he would want more children, putting her again through the pains of childbirth? Did she panic she would lose her independence, surrendering her freedom to a husband's will? Usually she chose to ignore such thoughts. But she was finding it harder to do so, much harder, than it had been just weeks before.

Striving to occupy her mind, she reviewed the contents of the store: bridles, horseshoes and the like. When Nathan next stirred, they briefly discussed using it to break down the door, but they gave up the idea, aware they would not get far. Maybe, she thought as she tried again to sleep, she could convince Stuyvesant it was in his interests to let them go. And what had Pietersen meant, when he had hinted she might be better off ignorant?

Tugging straw from her hair she wriggled into a more comfortable position, thinking now of Nicholas. She understood why he had acted against her, but it still saddened her, mostly because she just liked the man, and she did not allow herself to get too close to people as a rule. Thoughts of Nathan floated back. She shifted her head, looking at his silhouetted body. Yes, she liked their friendship the way it was. And yet . . .

She closed her eyes. This time she slept.

A grey light swam under the door as dawn broke over America. Waking, Mercia yawned as she stood to brush clean her crumpled dress. Her mouth felt dry, so she took a sip of ale from the jug on the tray the guard had left, but it tasted rancid. Banging and clattering from the fort drifted in, but like her, it had not slept much last night, too alert to the threat in the bay.

The light under the door grew steadily brighter. Soon the bolt was thrown back and the door flung open. Two guards walked in, shaking Nathan roughly awake. He sat dazed for a while, massaging his neck where a red mark had since appeared from his struggle in the brewhouse. Then the guards clicked their fingers, and out they marched into the golden morning sun.

They were taken up a crumbling staircase to one of the cannonaded bastions. As they climbed, the whole town was laid out before them: the broad street running from the square below, the gabled rooftops, the wooden palisade glinting with weaponry. Beyond that wall, settlers had begun to plough farmland and the beginnings of estates, but mostly the far view was an endless green, a whole nation of trees encircled by the rivers' embrace.

At the top a fine panorama of the bay opened up, the gleaming waters adorned by the three little islands under a vibrant blue sky. Closer to shore, Mercia noticed the fleet had moved much nearer, while across the rampart the governor himself stood gazing out at the ships, his patriotic orange sash taunting the British gunners even as the feather on his black hat seemed to dance in the wind. He stood for a while then turned to look over his town, resting his peg leg in the space between two bricks. Seeing the prisoners approaching, Stuyvesant pulled himself up straight, dismissing the guards with a curt nod.

'Look out there,' he said in English. 'Your fleet is ready to attack. But I will not allow it. I cannot.' He pointed at the flag flying over the fort, its orange, white and blue stripes, the insignia of the West India Company at its heart. 'This is Dutch land. Company land. It is my home.'

'We are not with the fleet,' began Mercia, but Stuyvesant held up a hand.

'Do not pretend with me, my lady. I know every person in this town, every person in Breuckelen, in Haarlem, in all the villages around. It is my business to know them. I am their governor. Do not try your falsehoods here.'

She nodded, respecting the intelligence of the man. 'You have worked for the Company a long time.'

'I have. I acquired this in its service.' He kicked his wooden leg lightly against the wall, looking again at the ships. 'It was a moment like this, two foes facing each other, only that time it was the Spanish I was fighting, and they controlled the fort. During the assault my leg was blown away. Yet I survived, and twenty years later am now governor here.' He turned to her. 'And your commander wishes me to give this up?'

'I fear,' she ventured quietly, 'that many more will suffer the same fate if you do not. Many of your own men.'

'Ha,' he exclaimed. 'You know nothing of battle, so do not speak of it.'

'But I do,' said Nathan. 'I have watched men die, seen our commanders make terrible decisions valuing pride over sense.' He came closer. 'You will not be betraying your men if you surrender this place. You will be saving your people.'

Stuyvesant stared. He gestured at them to follow him to one of the cannons, where a soldier stood waiting.

'If I give the order, this man will light the taper and touch it to the cannon. We will step back, watch as the ball flies across the water until it crashes into one of your ships. And then we will be at war.' He looked at Nathan. 'Why should I surrender? This place was a hovel when I arrived, a den of prostitutes and thieves. It was nothing. I have made it succeed.' He choked out a bitter laugh. 'There has been opposition, oh yes, and I have had to pretend the Company knew what it was doing when at times it did not. But I have made this place strong, a victory for my people. Do you see those colours?' He nodded again at the flag. 'I am proud to serve under them. I would sooner die than betray them.' He looked at the gunner. 'Just one word.'

'If you light that cannon,' said Nathan, 'all the guns on our ships will roar in response. They will destroy this town, all that you have built. Those men waiting on the Long Island shore, they will rush into the town, they will loot your wealth, they will defile your women. Everything you have accomplished will be lost. Our places were ravaged in our recent wars, castles destroyed, homes burnt, families and friends broken. And for what? The King is back, much the same men in charge now as before. If you fire that cannon all you will achieve is your own annihilation.'

Stuyvesant looked out to sea, at the fleet, at the soldiers and the guns. He sighed a sigh of the years of pain.

'I held you overnight so you would worry what I might do to you. I was going to threaten you, coerce you, anything to get you to talk of the strength of your forces, about your plan. I wanted something I could take to my council, to prove that we could prevail. But I know in my heart you cannot give me what I need.' He let out an anguished roar, striking the battlement with his fist. 'But I am not willing to give in yet.' He pulled a letter from his pocket, handing it to Nathan. 'Return to Nicolls and give him this.'

He stepped back from the cannon, motioning into the courtyard for a soldier to come up. 'One of my council,' he said after a pause, 'would have you both hanged atop these battlements for your commander to see.' He glanced at Mercia. 'Tell him to consider that before he stoops again to sending women to act as his spies.'

Pietersen, she thought, but before she could delve further the soldier appeared.

'Row them back under a flag of truce,' Stuyvesant ordered. 'And summon the council. There are matters still to discuss.'

The guard saluted, leaving Stuyvesant to return to staring out over the harbour. He led them down the steps and across the restless courtyard. As they approached the gate, Mercia halted before two priests standing in the doorway of the fort's church.

'Go speak with him,' she said, looking up at Stuyvesant. 'I do not know if you can understand me, but he needs your guidance today.'

The elder of the priests bowed. She resumed her course, the gate grinding open with a cacophonous thud, releasing them back into the streets. As they passed through, she looked back. The sun was shining fiercely now, illuminating the men of God as they climbed to the man of war.

The guard marched them across the marketplace, aiming for the river. He walked quickly, but as they approached the square's edge he staggered backwards, lurching right. A jagged rock dropped from his helmet to the ground. Startled, Mercia looked up to see a fast-approaching group of screaming townsfolk hurling stones and wood in their direction. She raised her hands to protect her head from the onslaught.

'Quickly, down here,' shouted Nathan, pushing her towards the nearest street. A larger rock missed her head by inches and she began to run, Nathan directly behind her. They made it into the side street, but behind them the guard fell to the floor, struck down by a flying piece of wood. He got up and ran for the fort, but another rock caused him to stumble, and the mob was upon him.

'We have to help him,' cried Mercia, watching the mass of people in horror.

'They will leave him. They will see he is Dutch. But they will pummel us!'

Another figure came into view, not part of the mob's raw fury, but individual, calculating, searching. His eyes swept down the side street and focused on Mercia. He raised his head and smiled.

'*Daar zijn ze!*' cried Pietersen. She did not need to understand Dutch to know what he meant. The next instant a horde of angry townspeople flooded towards her. She turned and ran.

Chapter Thirty-One

One look back at the angry mob forced her onwards. Behind her, Nathan overturned an empty cart as he passed, but to little avail – their pursuers merely leapt it. Left they turned, then left again, trying to run an untraceable path, but New Amsterdam was not a large town, and there was no doubt if they stayed in the streets the mob would catch them.

'Did you see him?' she shouted as she ran. 'Pietersen? This mob is meant for us.'

'Yes,' Nathan panted. 'But how did he know we would be released?'

'Perhaps one of the guards told him, or Stuyvesant. Does it matter? He has them all worked up.' She ran across a bridge, ducking left. 'Now where?'

They were running along the canal in the direction of the palisade, townspeople not involved in the hunt staring in surprise. Mercia briefly recognised the blurred face of the serving maid from Marta's tavern, but when the baying mob appeared, she vanished into the streets.

'I cannot run for much longer,' she gasped. 'These clothes are too heavy, and these boots.'

'Just a bit more,' said Nathan. 'I have an idea.'

Turning into the next street, he tried the nearest doorway. Unlocked, it pushed easily open; Mercia followed him into a comfortable family home, warm-coloured wall hangings and a fading tapestry of a hare coursing party decorating a well-kept sitting room. A little girl sitting cross-legged in the corner looked up at them. Mercia smiled, holding her finger to her lips. The girl giggled and copied her. Nobody else seemed to be at home.

A great commotion whirled past in the street. The barking of dogs had now joined the shouting, but after a few moments the noise faded away. Nathan peeked out the door.

'They've gone,' he said, indicating to Mercia to follow him out. She returned to the street, rolling her eyes at the girl, who laughed. 'They turned right at the end of this road. Let's get back to the fort. Strangely, I think it will be safer there.'

Mercia limped after him, her feet sore. For a moment all was quiet, but when they emerged into a wider road a loud shout betrayed the renewed presence of the mob. Dispirited, she prepared herself to run again, but an urgent voice caught her attention.

'Down here. Quickly!'

'Davids!' she hissed. She made a quick calculation of which was the greater risk. 'Come on, do as he says.'

Davids was waving at them from the corner of the street. They swerved in his direction, pursuing him into a nearby town house. He locked the door behind them barely in time. From a window Mercia watched a group of men hurtle past, brandishing sticks and rocks, still fired up by their chase.

'You are not very popular,' said Davids. Shedding his coat he sat down, bidding them do the same. The serving maid they had passed at the canal stood beside him.

343

'We have not had the kindest welcome,' Mercia agreed.

He looked at her intently. 'And why do you suppose that is?'

'A simple misunderstanding?' While Nathan stayed standing she squeezed herself into an uncomfortable wooden chair, fit more for a skinny child than a sweating woman in a dress.

Davids laughed, signalling to his companion to bring forward a plate of biscuits. 'Try one of Frida's *koekjes*. They are excellent.'

He pronounced the Dutch word 'coo-kees'. Mercia picked one and handed it to Nathan before choosing her own. She took a bite. It was delicious, crumbling in her mouth to leave the taste of quinces. '*Heel goed,*' she said. Very good. Frida smiled and set the plate on a high-backed wooden sideboard before retreating to the back of the house, leaving the three of them alone.

'Why are you helping us?' asked Mercia.

Davids tugged his doublet straight. 'Because you are not who you say you are.'

'Am I not?' She smiled in feigned nonchalance. 'Then who am I?'

'You are not from New England, that is certain. Rather, you are a woman who is prepared to endure a crossing of the ocean to achieve her aims.' He took a sip of beer from a bulbous *roemer*, waiting for her to reply, but she chose not to react. 'Well, then. At the least you are a woman with an interest in James North. Would it surprise you to learn I am an acquaintance of his?'

'Not especially. This is a small town.'

He set down the glass vessel. 'I knew of North long before he came to New Amsterdam. Back in England, before he went missing and reappeared here. Now, no more deceptions. You have the appearance of someone I once knew. Someone who has reason to investigate North. Someone with a daughter of about your years. Shall you tell me your name, or shall I guess?'

Mercia looked into his inquisitive eyes. He knows me, she thought, and I want to know how. She decided to take the chance. 'Very well. I am Mercia Blakewood. I am the daughter of Sir Rowland Goodridge.'

He leapt up. Nathan stiffened at her side, but Davids merely grinned. 'I suspected it when we talked at Marta's. You are so like him.' Overcoming his enthusiasm he retook his seat. 'We were both in Cromwell's government. We had different tasks, but our paths crossed from time to time. We shared views. We got on.'

Still cautious, Mercia studied him. 'If that is so, how have you come to be here, in New Amsterdam? Why all this ambiguity, if you knew my father?'

He supped at his drink. 'Come, you lived through the war. You know how families were riven by betrayal.' He raised a grey eyebrow. 'And you have arrived here with the King's own fleet.'

She shook her head. 'That is merely an expedient. I am not here as the King's spy, if that is what you fear.'

'I do not fear it. I think you are here because of a mystery.' He stared at her. 'The Oxford Section.'

She held his gaze, but his face was inscrutable. 'Why do you say that?'

He leant forward in his chair. 'I suppose you could say I set matters in trail. I am the one who wrote to your father.'

'You?' Mercia thought back to her father's letter, hidden inside her picture at Halescott Manor. Much had happened in the months since she had broken into her own home, but she had not forgotten his words. In the letter he had hinted at a source of information, someone who could be in danger if his identity was revealed. Could this be Davids, her father's alleged colleague who had also known North? But the glass of ale beside him recalled her experience in the brewhouse. For all she knew, this was another trap.

'Convince me,' she said. 'Tell me what you know.'

Davids laughed. 'You are certainly Rowland's daughter. I will tell you, and then you can say how the Section has led you back to me. I am madly curious.'

'That is reasonable.' She outstretched her palm, biding him continue.

He scratched the back of his head. 'I know the Oxford Section never burnt, for one. That your father was ordered to keep North's theft of it secret. He discussed it with me at the time. He thought the whole affair peculiar.'

She nodded. 'Go on.'

'He and Edward Markstone were never able to trace North. They always suspected someone had hired him, and then was hiding him. But Cromwell did not like to be made such a fool. In the end they had no choice but to drop their investigation.'

It fit with what she knew. 'Did my father ever say who he thought was responsible?'

'Oh, he had a grand list of everyone he felt could have been, with points in their favour and against ranged neatly alongside. But it did no good.'

'That sounds like him.' She bit her lip. 'Did his list include William Calde or Bernard Dittering?' She paused. 'Or Francis Simmonds?'

Davids frowned. 'He may have mentioned Sir William, in amongst a host of others. But Sir Francis is his brother-in-law, is he not, and Sir Bernard went into exile with the King straight after Worcester. Why? Do you suspect one of them to be behind the theft?'

His hand on the back of her chair, Nathan coughed. She

recognised it for what it was, a signal to be careful. 'You did not answer her earlier question, Mr Davids,' he said. 'How is it you are here, in New Amsterdam?'

Davids looked up. 'As you ask, my friend, it relates to this whole affair.' He reached to the sideboard for a cookie. 'When Cromwell's son was Lord Protector back in '59, there was a rumour, I don't remember from where, that North had been seen in New Netherland. Mercia's father remained keen to pursue it, but then war threatened anew, the King returned, and everything fell apart. I fled to Europe but my enemies were closing in.' He bit into the cookie. 'Then I remembered the rumour. I thought if someone like North could be safe in Dutch America, why could not I be too? And I admit, I thought if I could get him to tell me about the Oxford Section, I might glean some information I could use to bargain with the King.' He puffed out his cheeks. 'But then I realised, nothing could help me do that.'

'Nothing? Fled to Europe?' She frowned. 'Who are you?'

'I am James Davids. I am unimportant.'

She sighed. 'So you came to New Amsterdam and found the rumours were true, that North was here. Did you discuss the Oxford Section?'

Davids shrugged. 'I asked him about it once, when he was drunk as he often was, but he grew violent and had little to do with me afterwards. Bit by bit he lost all his money, what little he had left, to the sailors who came into port. His wife was always lashing him with her foul tongue for it, but one day he boasted to all and sundry that it mattered not, that he would return to England to get more from a worthy gentleman who had paid him a great deal in the past. He had to be talking of the Oxford Section.' Finishing his cookie, he took a sip of his drink. 'When it became clear he did mean to go back, I wrote to your father. I thought it might provide him with the chance denied me, that if he could discover the truth from North it might restore him to favour. I am glad to see the message must have arrived.' His story done, he leant back. 'Now tell me what you hope to accomplish sailing all the way here. Has Rowland sent you?' He grinned. 'The old dog could not face the journey himself?'

She rubbed her temples. He didn't know.

'What is the matter?' he asked. 'You seem pale.'

A sudden emotion prevented her from responding. Nathan answered in her stead.

'Sir Rowland is dead. He was executed in March.'

'Executed? Why?' Davids sounded genuinely horrified. For the first time Mercia felt she could truly believe him.

'They said he had dangerous ideas.' A sadness fell upon her. 'But they wouldn't let me see him. I spent a night in Newgate when I protested it too forcefully.' Nathan reached over to squeeze her shoulder. In the silence that followed, she thought she heard knocking from down the street.

'So many good men,' said Davids, staring forward. 'So many dead, in battle or revenge. On both sides.'

Mercia looked sharply up at him. 'North is dead too.'

'What?' He blinked. 'How?'

'He was murdered in London,' said Nathan. 'By his old paymaster, we presume.'

'My God. Poor Greet.' Outside the knocking grew louder, accompanied now by shouts.

'We are here because everything points here,' said Mercia. 'North lived here, as does the agent who smuggled the paintings out of England. Joost Pietersen.'

'So that is why you were asking about him.'

She nodded. 'We think he brought the paintings to America.'

'The paintings here?' Davids creased his forehead. 'I suppose if North, and Pietersen . . . but how? I have never heard anyone speak of them.'

Frida entered the room, looking worried. She leant down to whisper in Davids' ear. 'Are you sure?' he asked. When she nodded, he rose frowning from his chair.

'Frida tells me Stuyvesant's men are searching for you all over the town. It seems you have a letter he wants delivering to Nicolls. Tell me I have not made a mistake in trusting you.'

'We do have a letter,' said Nathan. 'But only because Stuyvesant finds it convenient to use us to deliver it.'

Davids scrutinised him. 'As you say.'

'It is the truth,' said Mercia.

Davids buttoned his doublet. 'Then I believe you. But we must part in any case. If Stuyvesant's men find me with you, he may decide I am some kind of spy, which is as far from the truth as you could possibly imagine.'

Mercia stood. 'Please, tell us who you are.'

'Let us just say I cannot be in town when Nicolls invades.' He picked up his coat. 'I will have to hide for a while. Perhaps for ever.' A loud banging reverberated through the walls. 'And now I really must go. You should wait for the guards.'

He held out his hand to take Mercia's, kissing her fingertips before clasping Nathan by the arm. 'Look after her, silent protector.'

'And you, look after yourself,' she said.

He smiled. 'I always do. It is second nature now.'

The front door shook. With a nod of farewell Davids vanished into the back. As he went, Mercia looked at this man who claimed to have known her father. A sense of her past swirled around her, so intensely she felt she could touch it. It was strange, she thought, that even here on the other side of the ocean she could feel its presence.

The townsfolk watched with quiet malevolence as Stuyvesant's soldiers marched Mercia and Nathan through the streets. A boat was waiting to ferry them back to the fleet. As they departed the pier they saw Pietersen himself, his arms folded, watching them leave.

Nathan directed the oarsman to the *Guinea*, closer indeed to shore than the previous day. Not quite reassured by the white flag of truce, four soldiers on deck raised their pistols at their approach, but Nathan dared to stand in the rocking boat to shout out who they were, and the soldiers lowered their guns. Once they were safely back on deck, the boat returned to the town.

Nicolls seemed unbothered by their night in the fort, firing questions at Nathan after perusing Stuyvesant's message. Mercia was more preoccupied with Winthrop, who had come out on deck to greet them, once more in his dark frock coat.

'Why did your man pretend not to know us?' she asked.

'I am sorry,' said Winthrop, his hat bobbing in the breeze. 'The situation was delicate. There was no possibility of rescuing you, so I thought if we disowned you it might confuse them as to why you were there. I relied on your ingenuity to keep you from harm.' He smiled. 'I see my faith was not ill placed.'

'In the event we were merely locked in the fort and run out of town.' She gave him a look, but it was benign. 'I see your reputation for cleverness is well deserved, Governor.'

He bowed. 'You flatter me. And please, forgive me.'

Taking her leave, Mercia crossed to Nicolls. 'No success then, Mrs Blakewood,' said the commander.

His attitude rankled. 'Success of a sort. Pietersen is there, but he is proving difficult. I am sure Nathan told you of the crowd he raised to chase us out.'

Nicolls pursed his lower lip. 'You think the Dutch may resist us?'

She glanced at Nathan. 'From what I could tell, most of them only want to get on with their lives. The people are not just Dutch, Colonel, they come from everywhere, even England. They enjoy their life and they want that to continue. Many of the council seem well disposed towards your terms of surrender. I am guessing they want to avoid bloodshed.'

'As do I, but this latest dispatch is no help.' Nicolls waved Stuyvesant's note. 'His pride holds steadfast, so my cannons stay trained on his fort, and his guns on my fleet. If he fires, I retaliate. If I give the order, so does he. And then hell breaks loose.' He sighed. 'Very well. I shall give his people a few days longer to convince him to concede. Otherwise hell it shall be.'

In the end hell was not called upon. Two days later, when Mercia had returned from braving the New Englanders' rowdy barricade to visit her son and Lady Markstone on Long Island, another boat approached under a white flag from the town. Within an hour the *Guinea*'s longboat cast off, carrying a party of delegates to the shore.

Rumour raced around the fleet, flying from ship to ship, bowsprit to mizzenmast, claiming the townsfolk had turned on their leader, renouncing his cause. And for once the bird of rumour spoke true, for news came back that Stuyvesant had yielded, surrendering his town. Looking at the ships' cannons trained on their fort, at the New England soldiers lined up across the bay, at the images of pillage and despair in their minds, his people had insisted on it.

At dawn the boats were made ready. New Amsterdam, so used to the waves of water rolling in from the bay, now witnessed waves of soldiers rowing across the harbour, hundreds of men, Nicholas amongst them, landing gleefully on the New Amsterdam shore. Mercia, Nathan and the nobility followed, wanting – no, needing – to be part of the triumphant moment. The energy was tangible, the very air resplendent, for the ships' boys who had won their captains' permission to go ashore, the most exciting day of their young lives.

So it was that an eager host of men from across the British Isles gathered in the dusty marketplace thousands of miles from home, ready for the gates of the American fort to open to allow them inside. But the moment was not yet arrived. Forming a path across the centre of the square, two ranks of Dutch troops lined up, to the last bearing themselves with stoic pride. Large flags of the United Dutch Provinces and the West India Company rippled at intervals along their line. All around the square, the townspeople stood by, looking on.

A drum sounded, then another, and a blast of horns. The guard of honour presented their muskets. The heavy wooden gates grumbled steadily open. Striding proudly, Governor Stuyvesant marched from the fort at the head of a procession of troops beating drums of their own. As the war hero passed along the line, the light breeze twisting at the strands of hair that fell from beneath his broad-brimmed hat, his soldiers saluted him, and he acknowledged them in return. An orange rosette decorated his immaculate single shoe, his long sword resting in its scabbard beside his renowned wooden leg.

Nearing the end of the line he drew his sword, turned back towards the fort, and held the blade high in tribute to his old home. Then he faced Colonel Nicolls, who was patiently waiting, surrounded by his own troops.

'The fort is yours,' said Stuyvesant. 'Take care of these people and this place. Any man who governs here has a special privilege. The land is fair, the people enterprising and diverse. I commend them to you.' He saluted. Nicolls returned the salute, and then Stuyvesant walked away, no longer Governor of New Amsterdam.

The lines of Dutch troops dispersed. At an order from a captain, British troops lined up to take their place. In reversal of the previous scene, Nicolls strode determinedly forward through the ranks of his men. He stopped just outside the entrance to the fort, nodding at a small party of soldiers to enter and take charge.

Nicolls turned to face the soldiers, the townsfolk, the hangers-on like Mercia, who were all rapt with awe at the remarkable changeover that was taking place before their eyes. Planting a pike firmly into the earth, he addressed the crowd in a strong and loud voice.

'I, Richard Nicolls, Colonel in the service of His most excellent Majesty King Charles the Second of England, Scotland, Ireland and France, do claim this place for His noble Majesty. In accordance with His Majesty's benevolent wishes that this town and surrounding province be invested on his Royal brother, His Royal Highness James, Duke of York, Duke of Albany, Earl of Ulster, I hereby rename them both to be known henceforth as New York, and this fort behind me, Fort James.'

And so New Amsterdam faded into the ragged folds of history, and New York was born. As the people watched, the Dutch flag was lowered on the pole above the fort, and the red, white and blue of the British was raised. A portentous wind rose up, powering through the flag, unfurling it over the town to a great cheer from the soldiers, which Mercia found herself proudly joining. The inhabitants of New York, of all backgrounds, nationalities and religions made less noise, but they were a hardy lot, and doubtless they would adapt.

Nicolls strode into the fort, accompanied by his men. The ceremony was over.

* * *

'So we are now in New York,' said Nathan, watching the crowd break up into smaller groups, all humming with a frenzy of talk. 'I wonder how life here will change.'

'Probably not much,' said Mercia. She readjusted her hat; once again in black, she had worn the best attire she had brought with her for the public ceremony. 'I looked over the articles of surrender. It seems the townsfolk will be able to carry on their business much as before. But forget that.'

He grinned. "Tis not just the excitement of the morning making your eyes so bright. Let's catch our rat.'

The town was bursting with people. It seemed everyone was out of doors on this momentous day, keen to experience the winds of change regardless of how they personally felt. Everyone but Pietersen. They looked all over the New York streets, but of him there was no trace. Emboldened by the morning's events, they even visited the offices of the West India Company, but there the mood was bleak, and nobody would speak with them, save to divulge the location of Pietersen's town house, and that only because Mercia threatened them with Colonel Nicolls' wrath.

But Pietersen was not at home either. A gossiping neighbour told them he had returned after the ceremony but then left. As the hours wore on, Mercia's excitement turned to despair. It was as she had feared. It seemed Pietersen had fled.

Chapter Thirty-Two

'Come,' said Nathan, rousing her. 'Let's go back to the fort. There may be some record of where he could be. He might own a warehouse, or a plot of farmland, perhaps. He can't have gone far if he was here earlier.'

She nodded. 'Very well.'

They trudged across the market square, the dusty space still throbbing with the chatter of a hundred people gathered to gawp at their incoming masters. Two guards at the side of the open gate stood aside to allow them into the fort, obviously briefed on who was welcome and who not.

Like the rest of the town, the fort now seemed a different place. Whereas before defensiveness and anxiety had reigned, now the courtyard was alive with action, teeming with soldiers glad to be on land after so many weeks at sea. The loudest sounds came from Stuyvesant's old quarters, a fine red-brick house where Nicolls was taking up residence as the first British Governor of New York.

Securing his permission to consult the Dutch archives, they climbed an external stairway to reach a dry, dark room full of impeccably ordered parchments and chests. A number of soldiers were rummaging around, poring over papers with the aid of fidgeting Dutch clerks.

Enlisting the help of a miserable young man who could have been no older than eighteen, Mercia quickly found the register of property. She scanned it for Pietersen's name.

'Here,' she said. 'Pietersen, next to . . . *Smee Straet*.' She looked at the teenage clerk. 'Did I pronounce that correctly?'

He shrugged. 'I'm sure you'll rename all the streets.'

'And *Smee Straet* is in the town, so that's his town house?'

'Yes.' The boy shuffled his feet. 'I was only posted here a month ago. I was looking forward to it.'

She looked up at him. 'I'm sorry.'

'Why?' he scoffed. 'You're English.'

She did feel sorry for him, but she returned to the document, tracing down its crispness with a finger. 'Here he is again. Could you tell me what this is, please?'

He leant over her shoulder. 'That's the list of properties outside the wall. That one you're looking at, that's Pietersen's bowery. He owns a few *morgen* of land on the way to the governor's farmhouse.' He slumped. 'The ex-governor's.'

She gave him a sympathetic smile. 'Is it far?'

'About a *mijl*. A Dutch mile, that is. About an hour's walk.'

She glanced at Nathan. 'Let's go.'

'You seem happier,' said Nathan as they came back into open air.

'We'll see. I just hope he is there.'

'I wager he will be.' He smiled. 'I assume you'll want my shoulder for any locked doors?'

'Of course.'

They began to descend the external stairway, but just four steps down she stopped, narrowing her eyes.

'I see that viper is here,' she bristled. She jerked her head towards where Sir Bernard was standing in the courtyard clenching his fists. He was staring at the gate; she followed his gaze and gasped, grasping Nathan's arm and making him wince.

'Nat, you lost your wager. Look over there. 'Tis Pietersen! Skulking with someone in the shadow of the gate.' She squinted to see better. 'By God's truth, 'tis my uncle!'

She ran down the staircase and across the courtyard, but the soldiers milling around impeded her path. Not paying attention, she bumped into a stocky man carrying in a barrel of food. He lost his balance, dropping his load. The deep thud caused Pietersen and Sir Francis to look up. Catching her eye, Pietersen bade a hasty farewell to her uncle and walked briskly through the gate. Nathan dodged past her and set off in pursuit.

Mercia swivelled on her feet. 'What were you talking about, Uncle?'

'What concern is it of yours?' he snapped. 'Do you not have a job to do for the King now we are here?'

He stormed off into the residence. Distracted by his words she delayed for a few seconds before going after Nathan, but she had only reached the gate before he reappeared.

'I lost him,' he said. 'There are too many people in the streets. He got on a horse, riding towards the wall. He must be heading to his farmhouse.'

She looked towards the governor's house. 'Nat, my uncle let slip he knows I am here on business for the King.'

Nathan followed her gaze. 'You don't mean . . . he knows your purpose?'

'It may just be Lady Markstone could not keep silent, after all.' She sighed. 'We can speculate all we like. Shall we try to find some evidence?'

He nodded. 'Let's get some horses of our own.'

They visited the fort stables, but all the remaining horses were allocated. It took twenty minutes of mounting anxiety and nerve-ridden pacing before a disinterested soldier deigned to tell them to go to the wall itself, where a number of shoed horses were standing ready beyond the town. All they needed to do was to convince the man in charge there to lend them some.

'And who is the man in charge?' demanded Mercia.

'Sir William.' The soldier yawned. 'Sir William Calde.'

She scowled. 'It would be.'

Pushing through the crowds in the marketplace, they hurried up the wide street to the wooden palisade built to protect the Dutch from the New Englanders, but which was now safeguarding the British. Its thick wooden stakes were imposing enough, but Nicolls had wasted no time in ordering Sir William to check its solidity. The nobleman was shouting orders from his position at the exit gate, for once out of his fur coat in the late summer's warmth. He was organising guardsmen along the seven lookout points that ran the length of the wall, two to her left, five to her right. Nicholas stood atop one of the nearest, leaning against a pike, looking bored.

In the headiness of the day she wondered whether now was the time to forgive. While they waited for Sir William she shouted across a greeting; Nicholas leapt erect but relaxed when he recognised her, waving his pike in reply. She nodded and turned away, pondering whether she should ask Sir William to release him from his brief service now the takeover had concluded without the need for arms. But then the nobleman himself appeared at her side.

'Mercia,' he said, 'do not talk with the soldiers. They need to stand guard.'

She looked at the wall. 'Against what?'

Ignoring Nathan, he put his arm around her shoulder and led her towards the gate. 'We may have taken New Amster—York, but the Dutch claim much territory far outside the palisade. We must be prepared.'

'I suppose we must.' She shifted her neck, feeling the weight of his arm. 'How are you faring now, Sir William?'

He sighed. 'Not badly. A widower now, it seems.' He looked at her. 'A condition we share in common.'

She resisted the urge to flinch at his insensitive remark. 'Sir William, I wonder if I might borrow two horses? I have not seen a green field since we left England.' She affected a smile. 'A woman's sentimentality, I know, but I do miss home.'

Frowning, he removed his arm. 'I am afraid I cannot allow it. Nicolls has ordered no one is to leave the town.'

'But the stable master said—' She deepened her fake smile. 'Sir William, surely that cannot apply to me? I would so appreciate it.'

'Mercia, I am sorry, but—'

'I could speak with the governor myself.' She played with the lace of her bodice. 'I am sure he would not mind.'

He hesitated. 'I suppose you can do no harm. But thirty minutes, no more.' He looked at Nathan. 'And Keyte?'

Her expression turned serious. 'You cannot expect a lady to ride out on her own.' Behind her, Nathan cleared his throat.

Oblivious to her facetiousness, Sir William merely nodded. He called to the guard at the gate.

'Give these two some horses.'

The guard wavered. 'But sir—'

'Is anything the matter?' Sir William snarled.

'Just the orders, sir, and we've already let—'

'Stay your insolence! You will do as I say.'

'Yes, sir.'

The guard saluted, letting them pass through the palisade under Sir William's inquisitive gaze.

The horses must have been taken from the Dutch, for none had made the long Atlantic crossing with the fleet. They were good steeds, although Mercia felt a trace of nostalgia as she thought of her own horse Maggie. They rode an obvious rain-parched path through well-tended meadows, strange low plants with tiny red berries lining the route to left and right. In the distance, a large stone cottage was pouring smoke from one of its two chimneys – no doubt Stuyvesant's retreat from the bustle of his official life, somebody cooking within. Mercia wondered if the former governor would be allowed to retain his fine bowery, or whether he would straightaway return to Europe.

After a couple of miles a side path branched off towards a smaller farmhouse showing no similar signs of life. According to the records, this must be Pietersen's. She spurred on her horse to canter down to it. Aside from the stone farmhouse itself, the bowery comprised a vegetable garden of considerable size, an orchard of newly planted trees, and a sturdy-looking barn surrounded by several outbuildings. Not bad, she thought. Being a corrupt art dealer had its benefits.

They dismounted, tying their horses to a large fence post where two others were already nuzzling grass. The town wall was not visible from here, nor did any sound travel the short distance across. It was idyllic, the trees rustling in the breeze, the birds chirping their happy music. A couple of wispy clouds crossed the sun-drenched sky. Chickens clucked. If they could have sat under a tree, dozing in the afternoon sun, watching Daniel chase the hens around the fields when they woke, Mercia would have been content.

But not today. Moving quietly, she approached the front of the farmhouse, motioning to Nathan to check the back. The large front door was locked, another horse tethered beside it. She looked up, but nobody was at the windows. A crunching of the dry grass behind her made her jump, but it was only Nathan returning.

'No luck,' he said. 'I could force the door, or we could try one of the windows.' He looked at the horse. 'He must be here. I think this is the one he—'

A loud gunshot rang out. They jerked their heads in the direction of the noise.

'My God,' she said, 'That came from the barn.'

She set off at a fast pace towards the wooden structure. Reaching it before Nathan, she heaved open the latticed doors. The musty smell of straw assaulted her nostrils. Cautiously, she advanced into the cool space. A smaller door was swinging open on the opposite side, while two wide beams of sunlight cascaded down through high window slats to illuminate the earthen floor.

'Oh hell,' she said.

In the middle of the barn a man in Dutch clothing lay sprawled on his back, his broad-brimmed hat askew across his face. Mercia hurried over the rushes and bent down to him. A deep red puddle was spreading from his side. He was coughing blood, groaning pitiful cries, his hand uselessly clutching his stomach. She lifted his hat, but she already knew who it must be.

'Who has done this?' She put her hand to her mouth, appalled.

Pietersen tried to raise his head, but the effort was too great. She rested her arm behind him as support. He stared up at her, a great fear in his darting eyes.

'God is coming,' he said. 'I can feel Him.' He clutched at her sleeve. 'After all I did . . . the bastard . . . shot me.' Although he was slipping away, his voice still managed to convey surprise.

Mercia looked at him, torn between compassion and urgency. His head tumbled to the side. Panicking she would lose this chance, urgency won. She shook him back to consciousness.

'Wake up!' she urged. '*Meneer* Pietersen, wake up! Let me help you get justice on the man who has done this. Tell me what you know about the paintings!'

'Jus . . . tice?' He breathed in whistling air.

'Tell me!'

He opened his fading eyes. 'You . . . were right,' he stuttered. 'Here . . . on the island.' His eyes closed, then opened again. 'Van . . . Arnhem.'

'Van Arnhem? Who is he? Does he have the Oxford Section?'

Pietersen shivered, gurgling blood. His voice was now scarcely audible. 'His . . . plantation. Near . . . Haarlem.'

'Who shot you?' She shook him, trying to keep him awake. 'Who?'

But Pietersen could say no more. He slumped to the floor, all his dealing done.

She lowered Pietersen's head, feeling numb. But there was no time for sympathy. A rush of air darted past her. She looked up to see Nathan running through the open back door.

'Be careful!' she called. 'Whoever did this may still be here!'

Dragging herself from Pietersen she followed, but outside nobody was in sight. Her senses on high alert, she ran left, the air warm on her face, the soil dry beneath her boots. She rounded the corner of the barn, but still she was alone.

Another shot rang out.

'Nathan!' she cried, running faster. She entered the orchard, searching wildly amongst the trees. It was humid, and her clothes were not light, but at that moment she cared for nothing save finding her friend.

'Be alive,' she repeated, over and over, running through the trees, her hat falling unnoticed from her head as she looked all around her. Near the orchard's edge she screamed as a hand landed on her shoulder. She whipped round.

'Nathan! Thank God! Did you hear the shot?'

'I thought he had got you. Mercia, do not do that to me ever again. I could not bear it.'

For an instant they looked into each other's eyes. Then the sound of metal on metal filled the air. Tearing themselves away they hurried from the orchard into an open field where an astonishing spectacle awaited them. Two men in sombre court attire were battling with swords on the edge of the meadow, the barrel of a smoking pistol protruding from the yellowing grass.

'By the Lord,' she said. 'It is my uncle and Sir Bernard.'

The two noblemen were engaged in a serious sword fight, attacking and parrying with equal fervour. Sir Francis forced Sir Bernard back, only for him to retaliate with a swift counterattack, putting his opponent on the defensive. The two were clearly skilled swordsmen. Despite their age, neither was out of breath.

'The pistol,' said Nathan. 'It must be one of theirs.'

'Yes! But which?'

The ringing of swords sounded loud across the open field, the elegant weapons clashing blow after blow, piercing the air with their resonant music. The men turned as they fought, moving right, forward, back, neither gaining much before the other retook the advantage. Mercia looked on amazed. She had no idea her uncle could fight like that.

Blocking another thrust, Sir Francis came in direct view of his niece. He lunged once more at Sir Bernard, causing him to fall back.

'Mercia, fetch help!' he yelled, not taking his eyes from his adversary. 'Sir Bernard has gone mad!'

''Tis not me who is mad, 'tis him!' roared Sir Bernard, parrying what should have been a successful attack. 'He has been deluding you all this time. Deluding me!'

With an angry shout he thrust forward one final time, his sword point penetrating Sir Francis's doublet. The wounded man staggered back, dropping his weapon. He looked up in shock as Sir Bernard pushed forward, ramming his sword into his side, and he toppled over, crashing to the ground.

Panting hard, Sir Bernard stepped back. Blood dripped from his quivering sword.

'Uncle!' Mercia cried, animated by familial sympathy despite the animosity she felt. Eyes burning fury, she rounded on Sir Bernard.

'Are you not content with my father's death that you must kill my uncle too?' She reached to pick up the fallen sword, swinging it at Sir Bernard. 'I will see you dead for this!'

Sir Bernard backed away. 'You do not understand. He shot that man in the barn. He shot at me!'

She hesitated, long enough for Nathan to wrench the sword from her grasp. 'Listen to what he is saying,' he said. Confused with rage, she held her arm in the same outstretched position, as though she were still grasping the hilt.

Sir Bernard swallowed. 'I saw them leaving the town. I admit, I did not trust him. I thought he might be working against me.'

She lowered her arm. 'What do you mean?'

Sir Bernard blinked at her, his eyes vacant, as though he scarcely noticed she was there. 'Pietersen – the man in the barn – I saw Francis talking with him in the fort. He knows everything about this town, this place. I suppose . . . I was furious. I thought Francis was trying to best me. I followed them. There was a gunshot. I confronted him. We drew swords.'

Somehow the air grew heavy. Mercia turned her head, looking on her uncle lying on the ground. 'No. It cannot be him. It cannot.' She stumbled into the field, not wanting to believe it, that this man who had usurped her house, who had strived to make her a mistress, this was the same man who had stolen the paintings, who had set a killer on her, who had murdered at whim to achieve his ends. Not her own uncle. Not her own blood.

But the dead man in the barn was not an illusion. Mercia looked to the sky and screamed an anguished howl.

Nathan came up behind her, but she waved him away.

'Why did it have to be him? I never realised before, I never wanted it to be him. I thought I hated him. I thought—God. I don't know what I thought.'

'I am sorry.' He inched closer. 'Please, let me help.'

She allowed herself to turn to him. Out of the corner of her eye she saw Sir Bernard reach down for the dropped pistol and feel inside his pocket for a pouch. Her fractured mind reassembled itself.

'Wait. Sir Bernard said he saw them leaving the town.'

'What of it?'

'Them, Nathan. He said them. But they cannot have left together.

Pietersen was heading for the wall while my uncle was still in the fort.'

'Maybe he just got it wrong.'

'Maybe. But why is he not curious about why we are here?'

'It must not have occurred to him. He is troubled by the fight.'

'Too troubled. He is not so impassioned as that.' She began to walk across. 'Sir Bernard, are you not—?' She stopped, her face grim. 'Of course.'

He was pointing the reloaded pistol directly at them.

'It was the other way round,' she said, furious with herself. 'You knew Pietersen was coming here and set off after him. My uncle saw you and followed. It was more like him to worry he might miss an opportunity.'

'You are too trusting,' said Sir Bernard, all pretence of shock gone. 'You and your swain.'

'You killed Pietersen.'

He signalled with the pistol for Nathan to move beside her. 'I suppose I did.'

'And Lady Calde? James North?'

He shrugged, saying nothing.

A powerful mixture of anger and sadness filled her. 'Do you care so little for life?'

Sir Bernard looked at her, bemused. 'We have lived through the greatest war our country will ever know. Do you know how many men died, Englishman against Englishman, so Cromwell could play at being King? They say one in every ten. So many friends cut down in front of me, a pistol ball tearing through their shredded flesh. So no, I do not feel much sorrow if a handful more join them.'

'That was a long time ago,' said Nathan. 'You cannot simply

explain these deaths. And Nicolls knows why we are here. If you kill us too, he will understand why.'

Sir Bernard looked at him as though he were a child. 'I do not think so. You are going to put me in an impossible position.' He waved the pistol at them. 'Walk back to the farmhouse. You will get on your horses and ride back to the town. You will stay in front of me. Any attempt by either of you to escape, I will shoot the other dead.'

Sir Bernard made Mercia mount first, then with surprising agility swung himself onto his own horse before Nathan could try an attack. Pointing his gun from behind, he ordered them to ride. Dusk was falling as they reached the palisade, its sentries greying in the fading light. One hand on his gun, the other on the reins, Sir Bernard called out to the guards.

'Fetch Sir William! I have caught these two discussing secrets with a Dutchman. They and Francis Simmonds are traitors to the King.'

Her back to him, Mercia laughed. 'You think Nicolls will believe that?'

'Indeed, he trusted you,' said Sir Bernard. 'He will be mightily angered to learn you invented your tale of lost paintings to gain passage across the ocean.'

'And why would I have done that?'

'To help your uncle pass secrets to Stuyvesant in revenge for your father's death, as Harriet Calde found out to her cost. What a shame the townsfolk were so lily-livered and refused to put up a fight. The information was useless. So you thought to ride north to the other Dutch villages.'

'You are mad,' said Nathan. 'He will see through that deception in an instant.'

Sir Bernard scoffed. 'I am Sir Bernard Dittering, close advisor to the Duke of York himself. I fought at the King's side throughout the war. Later I joined him in his exile. I have been nothing but loyal in his eyes. Why in heaven would Nicolls believe this traitor's daughter over me? And he will have no occasion to question you, Keyte, at all.' His horse pawed the ground as he shifted his position. 'Now, Keyte. Ride away from the wall, or I kill the woman. My pistol is aimed at her heart.'

She stared at Nathan in horror. 'Stay where you are. If you ride off he will shoot you. He will say you tried to flee.'

'Very clever, Mrs Blakewood. But I will certainly shoot you if he does not. Turn around, the both of you.' He waited for them to comply. 'I have observed you, Keyte, on the *Redemption*. I have seen you looking at her. This is your chance to save her life. If you ride off, I will kill you, but I promise I will not shoot her. Nobody will take her word over mine. She is but a woman. She will be safe.'

Nathan looked at Sir Bernard, at Mercia, at the fields in front of him. He gripped on his reins.

'Do nothing,' said Mercia. 'No one will believe his ridiculous tale.'

'They will when I have others to confirm it.' Sir Bernard smiled. 'Oh no, I am not alone in this enterprise.'

'What?' She glanced up at the wall where Sir William now stood, arms folded, looking down on the scene. 'My God.' She closed her eyes. 'There are two of you.' A wrenching despair twisted in her stomach.

Sir Bernard ignored her, addressing Nathan. 'I swear I will kill her if you do not ride away now. You have ten seconds.'

Nathan bit his lip. He looked again at Mercia. His face was set.

'Mercia,' he began. 'Mercia, I love you. You are a beautiful, amazing woman. I love you with all that I am.' He grasped his reins towards him. 'I have been too cowardly to admit it. Tell Daniel . . . I hope I have been as a father to him.'

A look of abject sorrow crossed Mercia's face. She looked imploringly at him, begging him not to go. But in vain.

Nathan kicked his horse's flanks and rode away from the wall.

Chapter Thirty-Three

In that instant Mercia was back beneath the table at Halescott Manor, a fourteen-year-old girl once more. She stared, paralysed with dread. Then an intense feeling of anger flooded her whole body, and she remembered her brother's face as he lay dying in her mother's arms, and how her fear and her frailty had made her useless. The memory gave her an immense strength, clawing her back into that dusky field beneath the palisade.

'Not this time!' she cried.

As Sir Bernard moved his aim away from her, she kicked hard into the sides of her horse to ride straight at him. At the last moment the horse swerved to avoid his, but their two flanks collided, knocking the nobleman off balance. He recovered to fire the pistol, but his aim was thrown; the ball missed Nathan by inches, ploughing instead into his horse's hind. Its back legs failed and it went down, taking Nathan with it.

Scared by the gunshot, Mercia's horse shied away, giving Sir Bernard time to reload the pistol with gunpowder and ball from his pocket. But she mastered her horse, and again she charged at Sir Bernard's mount, this time daring to seize the gun with her hands, tearing her dress as she swung to grip her horse tightly with her legs. The horses reared and tossed as if they were the waves of the storm-swept ocean, buffeting Mercia and Sir Bernard in their wake, but she did not fall. She pulled hard on the barrel of the gun, forcing it downwards. Her enemy resisted, but frightened by the tumult both horses flung back their heads and separated. She tugged with all her fury-driven might, and when the horses pulled apart, she was the one holding the gun. She pointed it at Sir Bernard.

'Keep back.'

He laughed. 'Really, this is even better. Now everyone will think you are crazed.'

She cocked the gun. 'They may be right.'

A number of soldiers brandishing pikes were pouring from the wall, six in total, half of them peeling off to encircle Nathan, who was rising from his fall apparently unharmed. The other three ran towards her.

'I will have your heads for this,' smirked Sir Bernard. 'As I had your father's. He should not have snooped into old business.' The arrogance on his face was absolute. 'I did not especially want him dead, but I had no choice. He was as inventive as his daughter has proved to be in his place.'

A deep chill descended on her. 'Are you saying you had him killed because he would have found you out? It was nothing to do with his beliefs?'

Sir Bernard laughed. 'Of course.'

The anger inside took over. She took aim. And this time, she fired.

It was a close-range shot. But deep down she wanted him alive to face trial, so that everyone could know the truth. Shooting blankly at his sides, the ball still skimmed the top of his left forearm. He let out a cry, clutching the wound with his right hand.

'Arrest her!' he growled at the soldiers now surrounding her. But preoccupied with his injury he failed to recognise the young, blonde man amongst them, who had been watching from his post and had run out to help.

Nodding at Mercia, Nicholas called out loudly, just one word, so Nathan could hear: 'Attack!' He swung his pike right and left, knocking his fellows to the ground before they could retaliate. At the same moment, Nathan ducked away from the three guards facing him, giving Nicholas time to snatch one of the fallen soldier's pikes and run over, dragging the ends of the long weapons across the ground.

'Go!' Nicholas cried to her. 'We will keep them busy. Whatever you must do, go now!'

He rolled the spare pike at Nathan's feet as the two floored guards staggered upright to join the affray. Together Nathan and Nicholas stood, finally comrades-in-arms against men who were not their real enemy. But the vipers had incited the soldiers, who were ready to do as they were ordered.

Mercia looked at Sir Bernard clutching his wrist, at Sir William standing hands on hips atop the palisade. The thought of abandoning her friends was abhorrent, but she knew there was only one thing she could do to sort out the turmoil that would follow. She needed proof. She needed the paintings. Praying they would endure, she turned her horse north.

By now the sun was below the horizon. Ahead of her the cultivated land ended and the untamed forest began. A single shot whistled past as she galloped away, intended to frighten her into turning back. But there was no chance of that. Allowing herself to be arrested so she could explain to Nicolls what had happened was not an option; for all his and the King's chivalry, she knew her family was still viewed with suspicion, while Sir Bernard was not. The surest way to convince them was clear.

Onwards she spurred her horse, out of range of the guns along the wall. She was heading for Haarlem, to van Arnhem's plantation, according to Pietersen where the paintings could be found. From Captain Morley's vague chart she knew Haarlem was somewhere towards the island's north, roughly by the eastern river. Wherever it was, the plantation had to lie in cleared land: once she made it through the trees, she would skirt the shore until she found it.

At the edge of the forest, she looked back. The scene at the wall was distant now, but she could just make out two men being led away, ultimately no match for the soldiers ranged against them. Nathan and Nicholas had fought to win her the chance to escape, Nathan who had admitted his love for her, Nicholas who had put himself at risk when he could have stayed apart. One she had known a long time, the other a matter of months. But she owed it to them both to accomplish her goal.

Steadying her horse, she plunged into the deep woods.

The tall trees of the Manhattan wilds enveloped her. If she rode at random she would easily become lost, but she was following a well-worn Indian trail along the east side of the island, used lately by the Dutch for accessing the island's north. Aside from the clipping of her horse, the only sounds she heard were of birdsong or of animal grunts, and once the trickle of water from a fast-flowing stream not far from the path. The warm evening air was still.

The light that penetrated the tightly packed trees began to

disappear. Pockets of the path became dark, shaded by the vast trunks and branches. She did not want to be out here at night, a lone woman with no torch, and she was worried about Daniel, but after weeks at sea she knew he would be safe on Long Island. She pressed on, encouraging her horse to go faster, climbing a hill, cantering over an open patch of grass, crossing a stream.

She had ridden for twenty minutes when a large animal stopped on the side of the trail ahead, examining the approaching horse. As she drew closer she recognised the black creature from its cousins in the gambling pits of Southwark. But this was no captured beast kept in cruel chains. It was a wild bear, free to roam the unspoiled island and hunt. She felt a frisson of fear as she passed by, but it made no attempt to attack, and when she looked back it had vanished into the woods.

She slowed the horse to listen for sounds of pursuit. A great chirping now filled the air, strange insects singing their crepuscular chorus, but she heard no horses' hooves, no soldiers shouting to each other as they rode. She was about to continue when she saw a human face peering from behind a tree. The semi-darkness made it impossible to make out features, but it was clearly watching her. Panicked, she hurried on. A few yards down, the light of a fire illuminated a black horse nuzzling the ground for fallen snacks. She rode past as quietly as she could, then sped on ever swifter into the fast-approaching night.

She had not gone much further when a slender figure stepped out from the undergrowth in front. There was nothing she could do to prevent herself from being seen, so she reined in the horse and trotted up, hoping she would be able to pass. But the figure, a dark-skinned woman wearing nothing but a skirt, seemed as startled as she was. A rustling in the bushes churned Mercia's stomach, but it was only two small children darting from the underbrush to join the woman on the path.

The bemused trio stared up at Mercia on her panting horse. Probably wondering what I must be doing here, she thought, equally fascinated by them and especially by the woman's immodesty. It was the first time she had seen one of the indigenous people. Although she knew they traded with the Dutch, none had been in New Amsterdam during the invasion, perhaps waiting to see how events would unfold.

The woman pointed north. 'Haarlem?'

'Yes,' replied Mercia in surprise, but the woman frowned, so she tried Dutch instead. '*Ja.*'

The woman smiled. '*Niet ver.*' Not far. To her amusement Mercia understood, thinking it extraordinary she could communicate with this woman, both using an unfamiliar tongue.

'*Dank U,*' she said, and she carried on her way.

Not five minutes later she came to a fork, the trail splitting either side of a smooth rocky outcrop. The wider road continued left into darkness, but a smaller path went right. Calculating how long and how fast she had ridden, she guessed she must have travelled around eight or ten miles, surely distance enough to Haarlem based on Morley's chart, and the Indian woman had said the village was close. The secondary path was also brighter, so she took it, hoping it would at least lead out of the forest to where she could better see where she was heading.

Very soon it appeared her choice was correct. The night now on her, the trees began to thin until at the forest's edge she came to a flat expanse of cleared land sloping to a broad watercourse on the right, undoubtedly the eastern river between Manhattan and Long Island. To the left, the forest stretched on for miles further. In the near distance, two black rows of houses were merging into the night, evidently the settlement of Haarlem, while closer to hand, pinpoints of light drew her gaze to a larger edifice. Her breathing quickened as she realised this must be the plantation house.

She stopped. Looking out between the trees, she could see two flickering lights continuously circuiting the house atop a defensive palisade, presumably torches carried by two guards. But Mercia herself was shrouded in darkness, and she was wearing black clothing. If she was stealthy there was a good possibility she would remain undetected. It was not much of a defence, but it was the best she had.

She dismounted, tying the horse to a tree somewhat away from the path. She still had Sir Bernard's pistol but without bullets it was useless, so she left it in the saddlebag, worried the guards might shoot if they spotted her wielding a gun. She patted the horse's head and set out on foot, keeping low and quick, marvelling that the plantation grounds could seem larger than the town of New York itself. There, hundreds of people had come together to forge a mercantile life at the mouth of Hudson's River, while here, the wealth of one man had carved an exclusive territory on the island's northern shores.

She crouched as she approached, watching the guards, assessing their routine. There was a blind spot lasting roughly four seconds when the entrance gate through the palisade was out of view of either, and it appeared to be open. She stole as close as she dared, waited for her chance, then ran.

She made it to the gate and paused a few moments, hardly daring to breathe. Under cover of a small grove of trees that must have been left in place when the forest was cleared, she edged towards the house. A final open stretch, her heart pounding wildly, and she was there. She sidled along the wall until she came to a door, but it was locked. She moved on, pressing her body as tightly as she could against the bushes surrounding the residence, searching for another. She caught her breath as she found she could pull the next one open.

Very slowly, she tugged the door just wide enough to peer through. The room was lit, but nobody was inside. She eased the door open and stepped over the threshold, leaving it slightly ajar in case she needed to make her escape. This was the second house she had broken into this year, but unlike Halescott Manor, which she knew inside out, the Haarlem plantation house was totally unfamiliar.

She was standing in a large back room. Candles were burning in wall sconces and a fireplace was blazing, the flames casting a sedate glow over a fine chair drawn up to its warmth. An embroidery pattern was lying discarded on an adjacent table, needle and thread alongside. Whoever had been using the room was absent for now, but they could return at any minute.

The room's only internal door sat half-open. It was dark beyond, so she rummaged in various drawers until she found a selection of candles, lighting one at the fire and wedging it into a holder. She squeezed through the gap, her dress rustling against the door jamb, but the passage beyond was empty of people, and she could hear no sounds from elsewhere in the house. She tiptoed down the corridor, encircled by the candle's light. Otherwise the darkness was complete. At each step she battled her overwhelming instinct to turn around and leave.

She reached the foot of a large, twisting staircase opposite the main front door. The hall seemed vast, its dark recesses hiding unknown threats. Gripping the candle holder, she waved the light around the space. Something on the landing above caught her eye. Thinking to ascend, she had one foot on the staircase when a dog sprang out. She stared in terror as it advanced, but it merely licked her hands. She breathed out. Fortunately, this was no guard dog.

She began to climb the stairs. Each tiny creak raised the tension running through her body, but if anyone heard they must have thought she was a legitimate resident, not some foreign interloper determined to uncover dangerous secrets. She reached the top, releasing the bannister she had been clinging onto hard.

A series of rooms gave off the landing, but she stopped up short as she beheld the magnificent sight that had grabbed her attention. It was positioned perfectly so that anyone who climbed the stairs could not fail to be impressed. It was a painting, and it was huge, a gargantuan scene of the canals of Amsterdam. The signature in the corner testified to its creator: the great Dutch master Rembrandt. The painting was not part of the Oxford Section, but seeing its splendour gave her hope.

She listened at one of the doors. Hearing nothing, she released the iron latch and pushed. The light from the candle illuminated an opulent room dominated by a grand four-poster bed, the wooden panels on the headboard and base teeming with beautiful carvings of native wildlife – beavers, cranes, bears. On the wall beside the bed, the candlelight fell on another painting, this one a still life of a bowl of fruit, but again, this was not from the Oxford Section. She ran the light across the walls to find two more paintings, but they were two more disappointments.

She crept next door, another bedroom that was as empty of sleepers as it was of the Titians and Van Dycks of the King's lost collection. The next room, the night air fluttering the thin elegance of half-drawn curtains at an open window, a delicate writing desk strewn with perfumed stationery beneath, exactly the same. Her uneasiness growing, she descended to the hall, the candlelight reflecting off two huge porphyry vases and the magnificent mosaic pattern of a beautiful marble tabletop. Yet on the wall beside the staircase, where she would expect a man of van Arnhem's status to show off the greatest part of his wealth, slumped an uninspiring Flemish tapestry.

She progressed from the hallway to a hexagonal salon. The six walls were covered with paintings; for a moment excitement bloomed, but as she roved the candlelight across them, all she revealed was a succession of individual portraits. From the list the King had compiled, she knew the only such pictures in the Oxford Section were a pair of his father, Charles I, and his mother, Henrietta Maria, but neither were represented here.

Mercia stood dejected in the middle of the room. Had she come all this way for nothing? The Oxford Section was supposed to be in the plantation house. Pietersen had admitted it. But it did not seem to be here at all.

A popping from behind a door in the corner rallied her from her gloom. It was slightly ajar, a quivering orange light playing through the gaps around the frame. She shuffled towards it, holding her breath. The wood felt warm. There must be a lit fire within, the second she had come across. So where were all the people?

Very carefully, she leant on the door, taking a full thirty seconds to ease it half-open. She peered through to see a red-walled study that was overflowing with leather-bound volumes and rolled-up charts, all crammed into mahogany shelves. But for once these were insignificant to her as she looked amazed on the grandest object in the room, a canvas above the fireplace that dominated all else.

It was a painting of a family, a man and his wife with their six children, the eldest around ten years of age, the youngest a newborn in his mother's arms. The man stood proudly around his brood, who were looking at the viewer with an innocence that belied their status. For this was no ordinary family. It was the family of Charles I, the proud father, and of Charles II, the ten-year-old boy. With a leap of her heart Mercia realised this was the very painting from the Oxford Section the King coveted above all.

Relief surged through her as all her hope returned. Forgetting the lit fire she stepped through into the study, eager to look more closely on her prize. After all she had suffered, here it was, right before her. For some reason it was out of its frame. Then a crinkling sound, as of clothing being smoothed, forced her attention to a fireside armchair. Facing the other way, a head of grey hair was resting on its embroidered back. She began to retreat, but then a voice from the armchair spoke.

'Stay, Mercia. There are matters we need to discuss.'

She stopped. She knew the voice. She knew it well. She had known it since she was a girl, had grieved with it in the Tower, had listened to it across the ocean all this way. In the end she was not surprised, for little could surprise her now.

The woman stood up and turned to face her.

It was Lady Markstone.

Chapter Thirty-Four

'Such a beautiful family.' Lady Markstone swept her gloved hand over the royal painting. 'The old King looks so happy there. But then this was done before the war, and now four of those sorry children are dead, struck down by sickness or else melancholy.' She looked keenly at Mercia. 'Dread reckoning, perhaps, for the innocents he sent to die for his base cause.'

Mercia closed her eyes. 'Like Robert.'

'Like Robert. My eldest son. He would have been nearly forty now, had that man not stolen him from me in his futile conflicts.' She thrust her finger at the depiction of Charles I. 'Instead he died when he was just eighteen. The King took him from me, so I took something of his back.'

Mercia scanned the room, suddenly panicked. 'What of my son? I sent Daniel to Long Island with you. Where is he?'

'Do not worry, your darling child is safe. I took him back to the ship. Captain Morley is teaching him knots.'

She breathed out. 'Then you still have some compassion, at least. I cannot say the same for Sir Bernard.'

Lady Markstone stared at the flames, shadows dancing in the folds of her green silk dress. 'So you know.'

'I must admit, I am surprised. I did not think you could stand each other.'

'It was my husband and I to begin with.' Lady Markstone's eyes lit up in a furious passion. 'When Robert died at Marston Moor, I went mad with grief. I spent years trying to understand why God had taken him from me, why He had allowed him to die on that terrible field of war. Then He spoke to me, told me my fortitude would be rewarded, if I would only wait.'

Mercia glanced at the painting. 'You sold these for profit, Lady Markstone. There is not much of heaven in that.'

The elder woman pivoted her head, looking at Mercia as though surprised she was there. 'For Edward it was about profit. For me, it was a divine revenge. God kept the paintings at Oxford until the moment was right, then He used Cromwell to deliver them to us. Edward devised the plan to acquire them, knowing he would be charged with investigating their loss. The money we made selling them we used to support our other son. Leonard became a wealthy and respected man. Robert's death was no longer in vain.'

'And the other deaths, Lady Markstone?' Mercia sidled away, brushing against the study's grand desk. 'The guards escorting the paintings to London? All that has happened since?'

Lady Markstone blinked. 'It was on North's conscience how he obtained the paintings. That had naught to do with Edward or me. It all happened according to God's intent.' She looked up. 'Surely you see that? It was His recompense to me for losing my boy.'

'I lost family in the war.' Mercia's voice was expressionless. 'I coped.'

'But your mother did not. She gave in, even as we strove to survive, you and I.' Lady Markstone stepped closer, holding out her hands. 'Robert's death had a purpose, to help Leonard, as your brother's had a purpose, to help you. It has made you the determined woman you are.' She smiled. 'I admire you, Mercia. You have come so far, just to find me out.'

The presumptive words angered her. 'And now I have, will you let Sir Bernard have his murderous way?' Images of her uncle and Pietersen flashed into her mind, of Nathan riding from the wall. 'He is a monster.'

'No, child. Merely scarred by the war, as are we all.' Unconsciously, Lady Markstone scratched at her forearm. 'You see Bernard has simply been protecting me. When he returned from his exile, we formed a . . . friendship. His wife had died of a wasting illness, and my husband, well, I have told you how he was abusive. Bernard and I became close.'

'Oh, very good.' Mercia realised the truth. 'You were lovers.'

Lady Markstone inclined her head. 'We wanted to marry, but Edward still lived, and you know a divorce is impossible. So Bernard poisoned him, and when the arsenic was found, as we knew it would be, I took the blame, protesting he had died of a disease of the bowel. Nobody could prove the charge of murder. Bernard was able to use his influence to obtain the sentence I indeed longed for. We hoped to sail to New England to live out our lives and be married there, far from the prying eyes of home.'

'Ingenious.' Mercia set her fingertips on the gnarled desk. 'But while you were plotting your future, James North returned.'

Lady Markstone sighed. 'North was always difficult. When he beat that boy before the battle at Worcester, your father should have had him hanged. But with the Oxford Section about to be sent to London, Edward realised he could use him instead. He visited him while he was in chains and offered him an alternative. He could help us acquire the paintings and leave the country with a fine reward, or he could die.'

'What a choice.'

'An easy one. Edward persuaded Rowland to assign North to the escort that was to accompany the Section. Afterwards he passed him off as one of the Scottish prisoners who were captured at Worcester and he was deported with the rest to New England. We sold the paintings to van Arnhem; then, years later, when he moved here to set up this little fiefdom, he needed a local man to help his agent smuggle in the paintings. He sent Pietersen ahead to hire North, as we ourselves suggested.' She smiled. 'Everything had to be a secret with van Arnhem. He never did want anyone to know he had the Section. But then neither did we.'

'And when North was done with his task, he stayed here,' mused Mercia.

Lady Markstone scoffed. 'Hardly surprising. No doubt the piety of the New England folk was too restrictive for him. This town would have been much better suited to his coarse tastes.'

'Until he came back to England.' Mercia frowned. 'Were you not in the Tower by then?'

'Yes.' Lady Markstone was bitter. 'And Edward was dead, so he found out Leonard instead. North threatened to go to the King if he did not give him money.' A sadness descended on her face. 'Leonard visited me in the Tower, in a panic. He never knew where his money had come from until then. You must see, Mercia, there was no other solution. At first Leonard refused, but then he did it.' She looked at her as if beseeching her forgiveness. 'He has not spoken to me since.'

'You got your son to kill North?' Mercia screwed up her face, disgusted.

'It weighed heavily on him. The price I pay is he will never forgive me. But it is an acceptable price, if his reputation remains intact.'

'And my father's death?' Mercia stepped forward, gripping the back of the armchair. 'Was that an acceptable price? Do not deny it, Lady Markstone. Sir Bernard has admitted why he had him killed.'

Lady Markstone closed her eyes. 'Rowland was intelligent. He may have uncovered the truth with Edward not alive to delude him. I was forced to confide in Bernard. In spite of appearances, he has no love for the King. He promised to keep me safe.'

Her palm grew hot. 'At such cost?'

'I do . . . regret it. But Bernard said it was necessary.'

Mercia stayed her mounting anger. 'And so he influenced the King to condemn my father, and to prevent anyone from seeing him to pass on what he knew. But you did not count on how clever father really was. He left me a clue in his own execution speech.' A great pride surged through her. 'He was a remarkable man.'

'Oh, he was.' Lady Markstone took a sip of red wine from a half-full goblet. 'Then you took his place. A pity you gave yourself away by visiting me in the Tower. We tried to warn you off, but you persisted. When we found out you were joining the fleet, of course we realised why. But the Duke always knew Bernard wished to come to America. Securing his commission was not hard. It chimed well with our designs.'

Mercia wrenched her hand from the chair. 'To think I begged the King for you to come with me.'

'That helped, although Bernard would have convinced him in any case. The King was keen to . . . dispense with me. Letting slip you had met Wildmoor, that was your mistake. It was easy to bribe him.' She stroked the goblet's base. 'Money is a powerful persuader when one has a bastard child to raise.'

Mercia narrowed her eyes. 'I only wonder you did not dispose of him after he confessed his part.'

'What would have been the purpose? He never knew who we were and you shunned him after that.'

'And Lady Calde?' Involuntarily, Mercia clenched her fingers into a fist. 'I know it was she who wrote the message left in my cabin. Did Sir Bernard feel any remorse when he threw her into the sea?'

Lady Markstone stared into space. 'That was not Bernard. I killed Harriet.'

'You?' Mercia felt sick. 'My God.'

'She detested you. It was easy to convince her to write the note. I wanted to scare you off, don't you see? But she became suspicious. I followed her behind the fencing and pretended there was something to see in the waves. It was easy to fool people afterwards, raving on the deck, a poor, senile old woman. Bernard hit me a little hard, but it was a nice touch.' She studied her hands. 'It was remarkably easy pushing her over. I suppose God gave me the strength to carry it out.'

'You are as mad as your lover.' Mercia's anger with the woman who had claimed to be her friend was now acute. She snatched a china cup from the desk beside her, thinking to throw it, but she checked herself. Instead she smashed it down, drawing blood. 'I trusted you. I trusted you with my son. I am going to tell Colonel Nicolls everything. But you can tell me where the rest of the paintings are first.'

'The paintings will never be found,' came a voice from the doorway.

Mercia whipped round. Sir Bernard stood on the threshold, his left arm bandaged where she had shot it. He strode into the study, a rope loosely coiled around his right.

'And neither, Mrs Blakewood, will you.'

'Quite the conversation,' said Sir Bernard. 'I have been standing at the door for the past several minutes. As soon as Sir William took your lover and your monkey away, I bandaged my arm and followed you here. It has been amusing listening to your prattle.'

'The murdering sweethearts reunite,' mocked Mercia. 'See, Lady Markstone, you are well matched. He has murdered my uncle as you murdered Lady Calde.' She held her gaze on Sir Bernard, but he did not flinch.

'You have killed Sir Francis?' Lady Markstone's face fell. 'Why?'

Sir Bernard removed his hat and sword, resting them on a side table. 'I did as we agreed. I met Pietersen at his farmhouse. The preening fool thought to threaten you so I would help him keep his position. I had to shoot him, but Simmonds had followed me. He saw what happened.'

'But Bernard—'

As they continued to debate, Mercia glanced around the study. Sir Bernard was blocking her path to the door, but a window was close by to her right. If she could escape and elude pursuit, she might be able to return for the paintings, or at least get out with her life. She began to inch towards the window, but Sir Bernard looked across and she stopped.

'Are you not worried Nathan will reveal the truth?' she stalled.

'Not especially. He and Wildmoor will be in a cell by now. Sir William will make sure nobody listens to them.' He smiled. 'I know certain things about him he would prefer to keep quiet.'

'Naturally.'

'It is my business to know them. It has been maddening not to have a single thing to use to silence you.' He started towards her. 'But now I have this rope.'

'Where is everyone?' Backing towards the window, she blurted out the first thing that came to mind. 'The house is deserted.'

He paused his approach. 'A fair question.'

'Van Arnhem got Jerrard's message when the fleet arrived,' said Lady Markstone. 'He has sent his family upriver to Fort Aurania. But he himself – 'tis as you feared. He thinks he can hold onto the paintings.'

'The obtuse fool. Where are they now?'

'Locked in the strongroom he built to house them.' She held up a key. 'As is he.'

Sir Bernard laughed. He nodded at the portrait of the King's family. 'What of this one?'

'Bait.' She turned to Mercia. 'You see, neither of us could come here before today. I was trapped behind the troops on Long Island, and it would have been suspicious for Bernard to leave the fleet for so long until the invasion was complete. But I knew you would sneak around the town as soon as you could, asking questions. Even without Pietersen, it would not have been long before you learnt of van Arnhem and his love of art.' She reached for the painting, setting it on the desk. 'I arrived this afternoon. I fooled van Arnhem into ordering his guards to let you through the gate if you did come, as I thought you would. I even left the side door open.' She began to roll the painting. 'As long as you were in the house, I wanted you with me. I knew the firelight from this room would attract you, and with the painting here, I at least had the chance to keep you talking until Bernard could arrive.'

'I should have taken it and run,' said Mercia, now alongside the window. Pretending to scratch her back, she rested her arm on the sill, wondering about the strongroom Lady Markstone had mentioned. 'So what now?'

'Is your mind so dull?' rasped Sir Bernard. 'Why do you think we are here? The Oxford Section must finally be destroyed. We will take the pictures and burn them.'

'Burn them?' Mercia stared at him, appalled. 'But that is barbarous!'

'I am afraid there is little choice.'

'Van Arnhem will resist,' said Lady Markstone, not looking up.

'Then I will make sure he understands.'

'What will it be this time?' Mercia felt her anger rising again. 'A carving knife? A blow to the head with a kitchen pot? A faked accident, like you prepared for Colonel Fell?'

Sir Bernard frowned. 'That fool gunsmith who shot himself? That was not me.'

'Of course not.'

'Believe what you will. And you are not one to talk of murder, after what happened to my man in van Arnhem's brewhouse.'

'That was his brewhouse?' She shook her head. 'So it was arranged.'

Lady Markstone's face twitched. 'What are you talking about?'

'Did you not know?' Mercia nodded towards Sir Bernard, feeling behind her for the window clasp. 'He sent his man to kill us. Unlike him, I feel a great guilt about what we did.'

'Bernard?' She stared at him. 'I never knew of this.'

Putting down the rope, Sir Bernard went to take her hands in his. The partly rolled canvas unwound slowly on the desk. Mercia paused on the clasp, her eyes flitting between the painting and the now accessible door. It was tantalisingly close. Could she?

'I promised to protect you, Millicent,' said Sir Bernard. 'I agreed with your plan to scare her off. I sent Jerrard after her in London, blackmailed that sodomite archer of the Queen's to shoot at her, paid that son of a dog Wildmoor to help us. But she would not give up. There was only one thing left to do.' He released her hands. 'She is here of her own meddling will. If you want to stay safe, it has to be done.'

As fast as she could, Mercia sprang to the desk. She grabbed the painting and ran for the open door. But swift as she was, Sir Bernard was faster. Roaring in annoyance, he thrust aside chairs and tore straight after her. He grabbed the folds of her dress before she was even out of the room, the large canvas too restricting an encumbrance. Reeling her back in with an agonised cry, he flung her carelessly in front of the fireplace.

'Enough,' he snapped, rubbing his injured arm. 'We have to do this now. Millicent, take the painting and wait outside. I will fetch the rest once I have finished here.' He reached for the rope.

Lady Markstone picked up the painting, a sadness in her eyes. She looked at Mercia crumpled on the floor. 'You promise it will be quick?'

'If I can find a pistol.' He held up his injured arm. 'She took mine in the town. Otherwise I have my sword, but I need to tie her first.'

With one last look, Lady Markstone left the room. Sir Bernard unravelled the rope, then forcing Mercia onto her front he pinioned her to the ground with his legs. He twisted her wrists together, holding them firm; she winced as his fingers ground into the soft flesh.

Desperate, she kicked at the fire. At first she missed, but then her heavy boot connected with the blazing pile of wood, tumbling burning logs onto Sir Bernard's thigh. He leapt up in irritation, brushing hot embers from his breeches. Her wrists still free, Mercia rolled to snatch up the log basket beside the fire, staggering to her feet and bringing it down hard on his wounded arm. He screamed out in pain. She seized this new chance and ran.

She fled into the hallway, across the back room, out the side door, heading for the gap in the palisade. As she neared it the front door smashed open behind her. She looked back to see Sir Bernard brandishing his sword in pursuit, shouting in rage.

She ran on, but her dress was heavy, hindering her escape. Atop the palisade she could see the guards hurrying towards the gate, alerted by Sir Bernard's cries. With nowhere to go but out, she put her head down and sped through.

'Leave her to me!' shouted Sir Bernard from behind.

Stirring herself onwards, she dared another look back. The guards seemed to have understood, for they were standing above the gate, not making any move to follow. Sir Bernard himself was gaining, but if she reached the forest it would be pitch dark. She might be able to elude him in the trees.

She nearly made it. At the edge of the plantation grounds, within feet of the forest, he slammed into her. She tumbled to the ground with a cry, her head bouncing off the springy earth. With his good hand he struck her face hard. She recoiled, stunned, the trees blurring. He yanked her to her feet. In a daze, she felt the sharpness of his sword against her side.

'I will not allow a woman to best me,' he growled. He pushed the sword through her dress, scratching at her skin. 'Now move. Your time in America is over.'

Chapter Thirty-Five

It had been a calm evening, but the wind was strengthening, the tops of the forest trees rattling in its sway. Mercia herself felt anything but calm, tied to a solitary elm in the field beyond the plantation house palisade. Fighting her rising panic, she watched as Sir Bernard and Lady Markstone drew painting after priceless painting from the saddlebag of a horse, setting them in amongst a pile of logs and straw laid all around her: the Oxford Section finally in reach, and yet never so far away. A pistol from the house lay at Sir Bernard's feet. It had already been used to encourage the guards to wait patiently in the strongroom with van Arnhem.

'Please,' she said, her voice shaking. 'People will ask questions if I die.'

'So they may,' said Sir Bernard, holding a burning torch. 'But they may also believe you lost your head and fled into the forest, perhaps to be devoured by a bear, or to live amongst the Indians. I am told it has happened before.'

She squirmed in the ropes that held her. 'How will you explain my corpse?'

'No one is coming, Mrs Blakewood. I shoot you, I light the pyre, the flames devour your body, and your precious Oxford Section is gone. By the time one hour is over, maybe two, the fire will be extinguished. It will not be hard to dispose of your blackened body in the forest.'

'Lady Markstone!' Mercia's words quivered with fright. 'Please! I have a son!'

Lady Markstone bowed her head, but in the wavering torchlight Mercia could see her biting her lip. Her nervousness was infecting the horse. It was unable to keep still, agitated by the flickering of the torch.

'You should have thought of that before you left England,' said Sir Bernard, setting down a vivid depiction of the Venetian canals, astonishing in its detail. He looked on grimly. 'Now I imagine he will become a ward of court.'

'I did this for him, Lady Markstone! Like you did this for your son.'

Lady Markstone hesitated as she placed the final painting on the pile, an allegorical work of goddesses and satyrs, overwhelmingly green and of flesh. ''Tis true, Bernard. Young sons need their mothers. Perhaps his life could be the price of her silence.'

'Millicent, she knows everything. Do not let your woman's sentiments delude you now. Think of Robert. He would want you to be safe.'

'Robert would want you to admit the truth,' said Mercia, and she knew she had overstepped a line, for Lady Markstone's face set.

'How dare you tell me what Robert would want! Your precocious son is nothing compared to him!' She took the horse's bridle in her hand. 'Do as you like, Bernard. The paintings are in place.' She walked briskly away, leading the horse back inside the palisade.

'Farewell then, Mrs Blakewood,' taunted Sir Bernard. 'America was not so kind to you after all.'

'You will not succeed,' she trembled. 'I will not allow it. Nathan will not allow it!' She struggled violently against the ropes. They loosened slightly, but did not give her up.

'Keyte will hang for treason. And you can hardly protest, tied to this tree.' He flexed his left hand. 'I had thought to be merciful. I told Millicent I would shoot you before burning your lifeless corpse.' He leant in closer. 'But you have caused me such trouble, Mercia Blakewood. The truth is, I do not intend to shoot you at all.'

'No!' she cried, a great fear piercing her heart. 'You cannot!'

'Burnt alive. A fitting punishment for a witch.' He spat out the word. 'And amongst all the paintings you thought to bring you hope.' He smiled. 'Mrs Blakewood, there is no hope.'

He threw the flaming torch on the straw.

The speed with which the flame took hold was astonishing. Much of the dry straw burst into fire within the first awful minute, the edges of the paintings setting alight where they rested on the burning mass. Mercia watched horrified as irreplaceable masterpieces by the greatest artists the world had known began to crackle and blacken at her feet. The fire spread quickly across the pile, consuming its expensive prey with hungry relish.

For a moment Sir Bernard stood transfixed by the flames until he turned to walk away. 'Coward!' she cried through her terror. 'Stay to look on what you do!' But in the noise of the fire he could not hear, or chose not to, and bathed in orange light he disappeared behind the palisade.

The logs atop the straw began to sizzle, whistling and popping as moisture was spirited away. Mercia could already feel the air being polluted with asphyxiating fumes. She worked frantically at the rope, rubbing her wrists together, pulling at the knots with all the strength her confined arms could muster. The rope came a little looser, but still she could not pull free. With a mighty effort, she kicked at the pile around her with her unbound legs, trying to keep the encroaching fire at bay. There a pastoral landscape, there the portrait of Charles I himself, there all the other paintings that had been thought lost, fulfilling their destiny by burning to ashes in this far-off land.

The wind whipped up, blowing the smoke and flames outward, giving her a few seconds' respite. She rubbed and tugged some more, never giving up. The rope slipped slightly, and now she could reach the knots with the tips of her long fingers. She worked as quickly as she could, scrabbling at the knots, scratching at the rope, cutting into her skin with her nails. It seemed an age, the fire burning, always burning, but finally the loop around her left wrist fell loose enough for her other hand to grasp. Crying with pain she tore her wrist through the loop, stripping away sore layers of skin, but her hand was free.

By now the fire was singeing her boots where the straw had been piled closest. The smell of burning leather began to permeate the air. Quickly she freed her other hand and bent towards the heat, wrists bleeding, clawing at the rope around her waist. But there Sir Bernard's rope work was firmer; coughing in smoke, she shifted left and right to agitate the bindings against the rough bark, but with little result, and as the flames grew ever hotter, the hems of her dress caught alight.

Deeply scared, she looked into the eyes of Charles I, whose image was now blackening around his neck in a perverse parody of his beheading. In turn he stared out at her, calm, composed, facing his fate as the real King had done fifteen years before. In that instant, Mercia was infused with the spirit of her father's struggle to throw down tyranny, and an image of her son filled her mind, motherless and afraid.

'I will not . . . let them . . . win!' With an agonised cry she pulled at the rope round her waist, pulled hard and true, drawing on all her father's strength, her mother's pain, her brother's courage, her son's love. The rope began to give; she pulled harder, still harder, until a weak strand frayed and with an almighty effort she was able to wrench herself free.

She began to climb, the bottom of her dress still burning. Only when she reached the safety of a higher branch did she stop, ripping off leaves to rub the fire from her hems. She was safe, for the moment, but the flames would soon follow, and she was sad, so desperately sad, that the paintings she had dreamt she would bring home in triumph were shrivelling to nothing beneath her, and even sadder to know the truth of who had stolen them.

The logs amidst the straw below were now firmly caught, smoke rising ever thicker and greyer. Inhaling the noxious fumes, she was beginning to gasp for breath when she thought she heard shouts from the forest. She stared through the smoke, straining to listen over the crackling of the fire, until through gaps in the haze she saw three dark horses racing towards the house. A small light appeared from behind the palisade, bobbing in the air, a torch held by a man's black silhouette. The horses encircled him, walking round and round before one broke clear of the rest, tearing the short distance to the burning tree. Reining in, its rider leapt from the saddle.

'Mercia!' Nathan cried. 'Dear God! Mercia!'

'I am here!' she yelled. 'High in the tree!'

He looked up. 'I can see you!' He came nearer, recoiling against the wall of heat, but he forced himself to bear its intensity. 'Jump!' he shouted. 'I will catch you!'

She hesitated. The smoke was making it impossible to see the ground, and she was beginning to feel light-headed.

'I will catch you,' he repeated. 'I promise.'

She needed no more encouragement. She inched towards the end of the branch, coming as low as she dared. Then she leapt out into space. She fell, feeling the rush of the night air against her face, until Nathan caught her firmly in his arms.

He pulled her away from the burning tree, holding her close. For a few seconds she stayed still, gulping in the sweetest air she had ever breathed, before a violent coughing took control. She staggered backwards, bending over until the fit subsided.

'The paintings!' She looked up in desperation. 'Nat, they have burnt them!'

He looked at the pile, now a blackened mess roaring out of control. The heat was penetrating the branches just above, and as they watched, the first leaves and twigs burst into flame. He turned to Mercia, taking in her bruised wrists, her singed dress, her dirty face.

'To hell with the damned paintings. How are you?'

She gasped in air. 'He was going to kill me, Nat. Burn me alive.' For a moment she stood there, shocked, uncertain whether to be angry or to cry. Then she turned towards the house, where the silhouetted figure trapped against the palisade had coalesced into the hated features of Sir Bernard, and she knew. She stormed towards him, the fury inside her raging as surely as the fire now devouring the elm tree behind.

She struck him in the face, as hard as she was able. 'I will see you hang for this,' she hissed. 'You are the worst kind of man.' But the anger in her words rekindled her cough, and she bent to the ground, retching. Nathan put his arm around her, holding her upright.

One of the two other horsemen looked down, his face rugged

under matted blonde hair. 'Hello, Mercia,' he said, holding a pistol at Sir Bernard. 'We seem to have caught your rat.'

'Nicholas!' Tears welled in her eyes. 'You came for me too.' She looked between him and Nathan. 'But I saw you being captured. How did you escape?'

Nicholas nodded at the third man, still enshrouded in darkness. 'We had help.'

The man came into the light. 'I know I said you were unpopular,' he said. 'But this is in the extreme.'

'I thought you had ridden north!' She looked on James Davids in wonder. 'Mr Davids, once again you have helped me.'

From the corner of her eye she saw Sir Bernard leaning forward, examining Davids' face. Nicholas jangled his pistol, but Sir Bernard ignored him. His mouth fell open in surprise.

'Dixwell!' he exclaimed. 'By the Lord, you are still alive!' He looked at Nathan. 'Do you know who this man is?'

'He is Davids,' frowned Nathan.

'Oh, he is not.' Sir Bernard's eyes roved back to Davids. 'So, Dixwell. You will hang now we have you.'

'I think it more likely you will hang, Sir Bernard,' said Davids, spitting out the 'Sir'. He moved his horse around the prisoner, keeping him close against the palisade.

'But this is John Dixwell,' Sir Bernard persisted. 'Think, Keyte! He is wanted as one of the late King's murderers. Anyone found helping him is committing treason.'

Mercia thought back to the London customs house where the likenesses of the men who had signed the old King's death warrant, the so-called regicides, had been laid out. Was that where she had seen his face before, why it seemed so familiar? She looked at Davids. 'Is this true?'

His face glowed in the firelight. 'It is. But believe me, I am no demon. I did what I thought was right.' He turned to Sir Bernard. 'They are not helping me. I am helping them. I do this gladly for the daughter of Rowland Goodridge.' He produced a pistol of his own. 'Now be silent.'

Sir Bernard smirked, his head defiantly erect. Behind her Mercia realised she could feel a growing heat. She looked round to see the entire elm tree now madly ablaze. The wind was carrying burning leaves and twigs over the palisade, as far as the house itself. Some floated in through the open bedroom window, settling on the contents within.

She stepped further from the tree, out of range of the expanding smoke that was swirling in all directions with the changing mood of the wind. Then another five horsemen burst from the forest. They cantered towards the burning tree, wielding pistols of their own. Their leader urged his horse forward, ordering his men to surround the rest. Mercia closed her eyes in resignation.

'By the heavens,' Sir William cried. 'This is a strange affair. Why is that tree burning so?'

Mercia looked around her. Nicholas had his gun still on Sir Bernard, while Davids was steadying his pawing horse, eyes on Sir William. Over Nathan's head she could see an orange glow had sprung up through the open window.

'Arrest this ring of murderers and spies,' Sir Bernard shouted. 'Especially him.' He pointed at Davids. 'Take a good look at his face, William. 'Tis John Dixwell.'

Sir William nodded. 'I know who he is.'

'Then order your men to seize him.'

Mercia waited. Beside her Nathan laid his hand on her shoulder. Sir William rode slowly round the group, taking time to look at each of them, his expression unreadable. Finally he turned to Sir Bernard. 'Oh, my old friend. I think not.'

Sir Bernard frowned. 'I do not understand.'

'Do you not? Then let me make it clear.' Sir William sat up in his saddle. 'Sir Bernard Dittering, under the orders of Governor Nicolls, I am commanded to arrest you on charges of murder and treason.' He signalled to his men. 'Take him. Use force if you must.'

Mercia stared as Sir William's men moved in on the fallen man, a heady relief coursing through her body. Briefly Sir Bernard struggled, but a hefty soldier subdued him with a well-timed punch.

Sir William moved his attention to Davids. 'You have been of use this night, helping us catch this murderer. So I have decided you were never here. I presume these others will act likewise.'

'I thought I would have to fight my way out.' Davids smiled. 'Sir William, we have had our differences, but thank you.'

Sir Bernard seethed in the guard's grasp. 'You cannot do this, Calde. I will tell Nicolls what you did after the war, how you passed information to Cromwell while claiming to support the King.'

'While you yourself were pure, I suppose.' Sir William laughed. 'Bernard, you stand accused of trying to thwart the King himself. You would say anything for clemency.' He turned back to Davids. 'And you, Dixwell. Should I be asked, I will say the man who helped tonight was named Davids. But if you are found again, you will be taken yourself. Is that clear?'

Davids nodded, taking up his reins. 'Goodbye, Mrs Blakewood.' He bowed to her from his saddle. 'I hope we meet again.'

Then he rode towards the forest, heading for who knew what new shores.

* * *

A bang shook the air across the palisade. Everyone turned to the house. Above the gate, Mercia saw flames licking around the upstairs window. She gasped, putting her hand over her mouth.

'Lady Markstone! She may still be inside!'

'Millicent?' said Sir William. 'Why should she be here?'

'She is involved in this. I have not seen her leave. Come!'

Ignoring her breathlessness she ran through the gate. A shadowed figure was lurking behind the palisade: Lady Markstone, facing the gate to watch events unfold. Seeing Mercia approach she retreated rapidly to the house. Dimly aware of pursuing footsteps, Mercia followed her into the hall where the top of the staircase was filling with smoke, enveloping the canvas of Rembrandt's Amsterdam. Unsure where Lady Markstone had fled, Mercia dodged one of the porphyry vases to run through the salon to the study, but it was empty, a gaping space above the fireplace, the portrait of the King's family gone.

She returned to the hall, colliding with Nicholas as Nathan skidded to a halt beside them. She led them to the sitting room where she had first entered the house. On the threshold of the outside door, Lady Markstone was panting, out of breath, a rolled package against her side. She looked up, the tiredness of years sapping her pained face. Then she surprised them, darting outside and slamming shut the door. A low thump signalled she had blocked it.

Nicholas ran to bang his shoulder against the door, but it did not give. He tried again; it moved slightly, but remained closed. 'Together,' said Nathan, and the two of them launched into the wood, crashing it open, sending the pole that was securing the door flying into the night. They rushed through, Mercia just behind.

The brief delay had given Lady Markstone time to mount her horse, but it could sense her nervous panic. As she struggled to fit her package into the saddlebag, Nicholas leapt at the reins, but the horse swung its powerful neck at him and he fell back. Leaning forward, Lady Markstone caught Mercia's gaze, a transitory plea in her old eyes for – what was that? Forgiveness? She urged the horse on, but it was fearful of the elm burning over the palisade, and the fire now taking possession of the upstairs of the house. It whinnied and writhed, scared by the noise and the light, careering in random directions, not knowing where to go.

A loud crash from inside the house startled it. It reared up on its hind legs, the action too much for Lady Markstone, struggling with the saddlebag, to control. She was flung from the horse, hitting the ground with an awful thud. Terrified, the horse sped away, but finding its path obstructed by the grove of trees, it swept around, looking for a means of escape. It saw the open gate into the field beyond, illuminated by the flames, and with no other option raced towards it. But the prone body of Lady Markstone lay directly in its path. Mercia turned away, horrified, as the horse rode over the unseen woman, trampling her with its shod hooves. It fled through the gate, its loose saddlebag tumbling to the ground.

Mercia ran to kneel where Lady Markstone lay still. The horse had forced her breath from her body, her ribcage completely crushed. But then her fading eyes flickered, and she looked up to the sky, a spark of life catching for a last, brief moment. Slowly, she raised her arm to a tiny white light that was shining through the haze. When she spoke her voice was almost nothing, just a flutter of air.

'Robert,' she shivered. 'Robert, is that you? Oh my precious boy. I am coming now. Your mamma is here.'

Then her eyes closed, her arm fell, and she went to the stars to walk with her son.

Mercia stood up, brushing away a tear. As she looked towards

Nathan and Nicholas, deeply upset, she caught sight of the package Lady Markstone had been struggling so hard to take, a creased canvas tube now fallen on the ground. Bending to pick it up, she carried it to the gate where there was sufficient light to see.

She beckoned to Nathan to help her. But even as they unrolled it, she knew what she would find. The one thing that could be used as a bargaining tool, should a deal with the King ever be needed. The one painting from the Oxford Section he coveted above all the rest, above the town of New York itself. Mercia glanced at Lady Markstone's body, admiring her ingenuity and her guile, before she looked down to see a man, his wife, and their six children, gazing serenely out.

Chapter Thirty-Six

The sun rose on New York for the first time that morning, but Mercia did not see it, asleep in a welcome bed in Colonel Nicolls' residence, exhausted from the night's events. She had returned late, her strange group riding into Fort James behind Sir William Calde: herself, Nathan, Nicholas; Sir Bernard Dittering at gunpoint, disgraced; Claes van Arnhem and his men, freed from his strongroom where his dog had been pawing at the door, yowling for his master's release. The plantation house itself was beyond saving, the whole edifice beginning to collapse as they forced the Dutch *patroon* screaming from his burning home.

All through the great Manhattan forest she was silent, glancing now and then at the painting of the King's family rolled up beside her, but more often at the horse two in front, Lady Markstone's body stretched out across its back. Inside the fort she dismounted, sliding down the wall of a storehouse to sag despondent on the ground, struggling to take in what her chaperone – her friend – had done. But when the governor appeared, and she roused herself to present him with her prize, he scarcely seemed bothered that the rest of the paintings were lost, and that rekindled her hope. For as Nicolls said, when the King spoke of the Oxford Section it was this that he meant, the only portrait ever made of those six sorry children together, and for the woman who could deliver him that, he must surely be in her debt.

Sir Bernard was thrown into a well-guarded cell, where he would await transport to England to face trial. Most likely he would be executed, yet Mercia felt no satisfaction that the man who had manipulated her father's end would suffer the same fate. The realisation that Lady Markstone had been behind the theft cut her deep. But as the dead woman's body was carried to lie in the fort's church, she prayed for her all the same.

She woke to find Daniel on her bed, fetched from the *Redemption* by Nathan. Seeing her son cheered her, and she followed him out to join Nathan and Nicholas on the New York shore, watching him play with a local boy beside Hudson's mighty river. The flagpole over the fort thrummed its British colours in the breeze, the softly turning sails of the windmill behind them a pleasing accompaniment.

'How are you faring?' said Nathan as she sat on the grassy bank. Beside him Nicholas looked up at her, clearly worried. She had cleaned the grime from her hair and face, hidden her bruised wrists beneath gloves, but her appearance must still have been haggard.

'Fine,' she said. 'A little rested.'

Nathan bit his lip. 'I have news for you. I think it is good.' He looked at her askance. 'Your uncle is yet alive.'

She turned her head. 'Alive?'

'Sir William sent men to Pietersen's farmhouse. They found Sir Francis in the field, still breathing. He had staunched the sword wound with his doublet. The surgeon is not certain, but he thinks he will live.'

She looked at the river flowing calmly by. 'I hope so. In spite of what he has done, there has been too much death of late.' She paused. 'I know you are thinking of Halescott. But even if he were . . . gone . . . his son would step into his place. 'Tis the King's patronage I need.' She sighed. 'Should he be willing to give it.'

'You have found his painting, the one he yearns for. The others may be lost, but if he is as gallant as he claims he is bound to you. I hope he will be generous.'

'As do I.' Weary, she changed the subject. 'How did you escape from the town? When I rode off, the guards were leading you away.'

'We tried to fight them,' said Nicholas. 'But we didn't have much chance. They marched us back towards the fort, down that broad way. But Dixwell – Davids – whatever his name was, he'd told some people about the two of you, and they put themselves in our path, pretending to protest the invasion. In the confusion they brought us horses and we came back through the gate. Sir William sent his men right after us.'

'They nearly caught us by Stuyvesant's farmhouse,' said Nathan. 'But Nicholas rode into plain view, led them round and round and lost them in the darkness. It was impressive riding.' He nodded at Nicholas, who smiled. 'We assumed you had gone into the forest, and carried on.'

'And Davids?' said Mercia. 'Dixwell?'

'Dixwell was camped in the forest, hiding while he decided what to do after the invasion. It seems you rode right past him, but he couldn't make out who you were. He worried you might have been a soldier come north, so he was watching the path closely by the time we came past. He says he followed us, although we never heard him. We stopped at the turning to discuss which way to go. He recognised my voice and came up. And then the soldiers found us.'

'They pulled pistols on us,' said Nicholas. 'We were readying for a fight when Sir William arrived, his horse heaving like a mad beast. He'd ridden hard to follow his men fast. He'd spoken with Colonel Nicolls, you see, set everything out.'

Nathan leant back on the grass. 'Nicolls put it all together. He dispatched him immediately with orders for Sir Bernard's arrest. It was quite something to see Sir William's expression when he saw Dixwell in the forest.' He shook his head. 'An actual regicide. I wonder what went through his mind when he signed the paper that would condemn the King.'

'Maybe he was principled,' said Mercia, in no mood for a political debate. 'Or maybe just naïve. I am surprised Sir William let him go.'

'They knew each other from the war, I think. What was said about him only pretending to be on the King's side might be true.' He glanced at Nicholas and then quickly away, but Nicholas had seen.

'Mercia,' he said, looking down. 'I am truly sorry for what I did.' He turned to her, his face troubled. 'I hope you can forgive me one day.'

She tugged at a ringlet of her hair. 'I know you did it for your daughter's sake. I would be lying if I said I was ready to trust you completely.' She held his gaze for a few moments. 'But I would love to see Eliza someday.'

'I would like that. Believe me, if I'd known you better, or if you'd—' He checked himself. 'I'm sorry. That's not fair.'

'If I had not been so dismissive at the beginning, you mean.' She held up a hand. 'No, you are right. I am sorry too.'

There was a momentary silence. Nathan shifted on the hard ground.

'Nicolls wants to return the painting to England as soon as he can,' he said. 'Now the town is British, he has threatened van Arnhem with imprisonment for possessing the King's personal property.' He smirked. 'That scared him. He confessed he bought the Section with embezzled West India Company funds.'

Mercia let out a bitter laugh. 'Why does that not surprise me?'

''Tis why he went to such trouble smuggling it here, sending Pietersen to arrange things with North, and then sending him again with the paintings under lock and key. He fears if his former colleagues find out, he will be in worse trouble with them than he is with Nicolls.'

'Will we go back on the same ship, do you think?' said Nicholas. 'That could be an uncomfortable journey, if Sir Bernard goes too.'

'I have been thinking about that,' said Mercia. 'We have come so far and at such cost. Yes, we found the painting that the King badly wants. But the deaths.' She swallowed. 'So many. And Lady Markstone. I liked her. I respected her.' She rubbed her tired eyes. 'Winthrop invited me to Connecticut. Perhaps I will take up his offer before we return.'

She looked at Nathan, expecting him to give her a reason why she should not. But in truth she was exhausted. After three months at sea she wanted at least some respite before she braved another long journey. And she was curious about this new world, this America. While she was here, she wanted to see more.

He surprised her. 'If you can, why not? I am sure Daniel would enjoy it.' He reached over to squeeze her hand.

'Well.' Nicholas stood up. 'I will leave you two alone.'

Mercia craned her neck. 'Do not forget Nicolls is treating us all to dinner. Apparently Stuyvesant's cooks are rather good.'

'They're staying on?'

'I don't know. I suppose Stuyvesant will be recalled to Amsterdam.'

'Looking for a new job,' he said. 'As it seems must I.'

She watched him walk away. 'Perhaps not,' she called.

Nicholas turned and smiled, his green eyes dancing in the New York light, before he vanished into the town's embrace.

When he had gone, Nathan sidled closer.

'Congratulations. You have done it.'

'We have done it. But I am tired, Nat, and not a little sad. I hope it is all worth it.'

'If it were not for you, that painting would still be lost. And perhaps when the King learns your father was a victim of Sir Bernard's treachery, it will worry his conscience.'

'Perhaps.' She watched Daniel looking for his new friend in a game of hide-and-seek. The Dutch boy was the other side of the windmill; Daniel would find him quickly enough. 'Do you really think he would enjoy a trip to New England?'

'I do. And perhaps . . .' he hesitated, 'I might come too?'

She looked at him. 'Do you not have to return to your land? Once the first ships go back, it could be a while until others leave.'

'My land can wait. My brother is proficient. I would rather . . . stay with you.'

She edged up to him. 'I nearly lost you yesterday. When you rode from the wall, I thought Sir Bernard was going to shoot you.'

'I have no doubt he was. But I would do anything to make sure you are safe.'

'I know.' She grasped his hand. 'Thank you for looking out for me this whole time.'

'Well, you saved me, remember?' He laughed. 'You rode your horse right at him. And then shot his arm off.'

'Not quite off,' she said, joining in his laughter.

'Come, then. We should tell Nicolls of your plan. Depending

how long we are gone, by the time we return you may have received a message from the King.'

'Let us hope the answer is good. I want Halescott back.' She nodded towards Daniel. 'Not for me especially, but for him. I want him to have the future he deserves. And I hope' – she paused, looking at the sky – 'I hope my father is proud of me.'

'He is,' said Nathan, drawing her towards him. 'He definitely is.'

She rested her head on his shoulder and smiled. Together, they looked across the river, the sails of the windmill turning gently up above.

Historical Note

The seventeenth century was a period of intense drama in shared British and American history. It was in 1664 that New York was founded by the British, not by settling a new town but by taking charge of the existing – and thriving – Dutch settlement of New Amsterdam at the southernmost tip of the forest-covered island of Manhattan. At the time, the Dutch and the British were at irregular war, and the conquest of New Amsterdam, if it can be called a conquest in the absence of a fight, was part of a much larger design of expansion and consolidation, a policy that also witnessed an exertion of royal authority on the New England colonies. Much has changed since Richard Nicolls replaced Pieter Stuyvesant to become the first British Governor of New York, but the majesty of Manhattan remains, albeit with soaring man-made structures replacing the former verdant beauty, then as now surely the most breathtaking introduction to the American continent any ocean-crossing traveller could have envisaged.

At the time *Birthright* is set, Britain was a country finding its greatness. Ravaged by the civil wars of the previous decades, the restoration of Charles II was viewed by many as a welcome return to peace and harmony. Others were less keen – men such as John Dixwell, one of the real-life regicides who had signed the former King's death warrant, and who like many of his fellows was forced to flee the country else die. Still others who had supported Oliver Cromwell in the Parliamentarian cause kept their profile subdued, relying on the King's amnesty to permit them to live out their lives in relative obscurity. Amongst them, the fictional Sir Rowland Goodridge was not so fortunate.

As an original work of fiction, *Birthright* is dominated by such imagined characters. Mercia Blakewood, Nathan Keyte and Nicholas Wildmoor are all my creation, as are Lady Markstone, Sir William and Lady Calde, Sir Francis Simmonds and Sir Bernard Dittering; so too are One-Eye Wilkins and James North, Joost Pietersen and van Arnhem, but I hope they reflect plausible lives and attitudes of their time. Certainly, it has been a joy to create them and get to know them. The book is nonetheless strewn with real-life people drawn from the richness of the times. So it is that the characters of Charles II, the Duke of York, Richard Nicolls and Pieter Stuyvesant are all real, as are Captain Morley of the *Redemption*, Governor John Winthrop of Connecticut, and James Davids aka John Dixwell, who did indeed disappear for a time before resurfacing in New England in the mid 1660s, and so why not first in New Amsterdam?

Throughout the novel, I have endeavoured to keep the story as true to life as possible, weaving the action around actual events, but there are naturally instances where I have taken a modicum of liberty with the past. In such cases I hope the knowledgeable reader will indulge me somewhat, and understand that first and foremost I have attempted to create a believable, lively fiction, drawing on history as my support. So, for example, the London customs office is entirely my invention, but a scene where Mercia could learn more about

James North while happening on the portraits of the regicides was helpful to the plot. Again, and more specifically, as a representative of the West India Company, Stuyvesant's title would have been Director-General rather than Governor, but I have chosen the more political designation to set him on an obvious par with Nicolls and Winthrop. There will be other deliberate inaccuracies of this sort; any accidental errors are, of course, my own.

The village of Halescott will not be found on any map, present day or historical. The Oxford Section too is my fabrication, but it fits the facts. Charles I did move his court to the university town during the civil war, and he did of course amass a huge – and expensive – collection of art throughout his reign, lusted after by the competing collectors of Europe. Cromwell's Great Sale of these works likewise did take place, and if that part of the collection I have termed the Oxford Section ended by being stolen and sold on to a rich businessman before being destroyed at his vast American estate, then so much the more intriguing for Mercia and her friends. As for the painting Mercia did recover, the family portrait the King coveted above even New York, were it real it would have been painted in 1640, the only time when those particular eight members of the royal family would have been alive concurrently (the King's youngest sister Henrietta was some years from being born). Henry, Duke of Gloucester would have been but a few weeks old, his infant sister Anne sadly about to die: indeed by 1664, as Lady Markstone says, four of the six children and of course the father were all dead. A poignant and irreplaceable reminder of lost family: surely, the King would have rejoiced in its return.

If the Oxford Section is a construct, then the historical references in the story are genuine – the King's celebrated regular walks in his newly restored royal park, for example, or the menagerie Mercia comes across at the entrance to the Tower of London. The backdrop to the second half of the story – the invasion fleet and the takeover of New Amsterdam – is firmly historical fact, save that I may have toyed with the precise sequencing of events. As in *Birthright* the real fleet constituted four ships, three of them named as I have them here: the *Guinea, Elias* and *Martin*, although I have amended the fourth from the *William and Nicholas* to the *Redemption*. The surrender of the town happened much as I have described it, and several of the scenes in Part Four – in the town hall where Stuyvesant rips up the terms of surrender, for instance, or on the battlements as he looks out to sea – are reported by a number of historians. The several available primary sources make for wonderful reading, amongst them the fascinating letters exchanged between Nicolls and Stuyvesant. A search of the internet will locate these quickly enough: such a marvellous research tool for the writer.

The vestiges of New Amsterdam are apparent in New York to this day, if nothing of the physical settlement survives. The famous Wall Street, for example, is named after the wall or palisade at the northern edge of the town through which Mercia passes on her way to Pietersen's farmhouse. The even more celebrated Broadway runs along much the same route today as it did when it was a dirty, wide track that led from the gate of Fort Amsterdam and up through the island beyond. Stuyvesant himself is remembered in several ways in Manhattan, including in the name of another street. Quite touchingly, after he was recalled to Amsterdam to explain the loss of his colony, he returned to New York despite its new masters to live out the rest of his life there. He is buried in the grounds of an East Village church near the *bouwerij*, or farmland, where he lived – the modern Bowery being yet another reminder of the Dutch presence, as are the place names Harlem (Haarlem), Brooklyn (Breuckelen) and so on. Van Arnhem's plantation house is my invention; Stuyvesant's peg leg is not.

Whether Mercer Street in Lower Manhattan is named for Mercia Blakewood is open to debate.